The Distraction

Titles by Sierra Kincade

The Body Work Trilogy

THE MASSEUSE

THE DISTRACTION

The Distraction

SIERRA KINCADE

HEAT | NEW YORK

THE BERKLEY PUBLISHING GROUP
Published by the Penguin Group
Penguin Group (USA) LLC
375 Hudson Street, New York, New York 10014

USA • Canada • UK • Ireland • Australia • New Zealand • India • South Africa • China

penguin.com

A Penguin Random House Company

This book is an original publication of The Berkley Publishing Group.

Library of Congress Cataloging-in-Publication Data

Kincade, Sierra.
The distraction / Sierra Kincade. — Heat trade paperback edition.
p. ; cm.—(The body work trilogy ; 2)
ISBN 978-0-425-27800-0
I. Title.
PS3611.I564D57 2015
813'.6—dc23
2014031313

PUBLISHING HISTORY
Heat trade paperback edition / February 2015

PRINTED IN THE UNITED STATES OF AMERICA

10 9 8 7 6 5 4 3 2 1

For Jason, always

ACKNOWLEDGMENTS

A huge thank-you to my agents Joanna MacKenzie, Danielle Egan Miller, and Abby Saul. I am doing what I love because of you and I am so proud to have you standing by my side. I am ever grateful for the kindness and support of Leis Pederson, editor extraordinaire, and Jessica Brock, my super-cool publicist. Go Team Masseuse! Cupcakes all around!

A special thank-you to my most excellent beta readers: Deanna, who nicely lets me know when she trips in plot holes so that I can fix them; Courtney, who gives Alec the best legal advice; and Katie, who is the master of backing up a "this doesn't work" with a "but this does!" I love you guys.

And always, thank you to my husband, who knows me better than anyone and likes me anyway. I love you.

One

closed my eyes, swaying my hips to the hard hit of the bass. The music flowed through me, a stimulant, urging my heart to keep time. My hips swung right, paused, and I reached down one sweat-slicked leg to drag my fingers seductively up my calf. Arching my back, my pelvis made one slow, tempting circle that defied the fast rhythm, and I placed both open hands on my stomach. I was already drenched, and the thin fabric dragged across my skin as I pulled it up.

"Slower," commanded Jayne. Her voice was raspy, like a moan. Everything about that woman oozed sex. I did as she said because I wanted her approval. I wanted to *be* her.

My hips made a figure eight as I inched my shirt up to my bra line. My stomach was hard and flat, conditioned by weeks of workouts, but my legs were already trembling.

"Good," she said. "One hand on the pole. Easy. Grab it like a cock."

I bit my lower lip to stifle the giggle, but the way she said *cock* made my groin ache. It had been too long since I'd had what I wanted, what I needed. The hard, insistent pressure pushing into me, filling me, bringing me to the edge of my sanity with powerful thrusts.

I'd had to find another way to keep my desire under control.

Slowly, without opening my eyes, I felt for the erect pole and gripped it with just enough pressure, just as she'd taught me. It was slick, too wide for me to close my fingers around.

"Show me what you're going to do to me," Jayne said. She was farther away now, behind me, evaluating my every move.

I spread my legs wide and bent my knees. Holding on with only one hand, I dropped nearly to the floor, the pole sliding through my grasp. I rose then, feeling the cool metal brush high on my inside thighs.

"Make me want you," said Jayne. "Make me so hot I can't keep my hands off you."

Dark eyes appeared behind my closed lids. A flash of broad, muscular shoulders. A drop of perspiration sliding down the ridges of hard, washboard abs. Desire pooled deep inside me, lapping against the surface of my womb with each swivel of my hips.

"*Anna,*" he whispered. "*Come for me.*" I could still hear his voice.

I hooked one knee around the pole, feeling a wave of self-consciousness as I pushed off with my opposite foot, spinning in a slow circle to my knees.

"There are some hot bitches in this room tonight!" shouted Jayne, suddenly enthusiastic.

Cheers erupted around me. I opened my eyes, a huge grin spreading across my face as Jayne shut down the stereo. Beside me, a woman in her forties with some brand-new silicone laughed hysterically as her friend, easily twice her weight, tried to pull herself out of the splits. Near the front, two college girls pulled their tank tops back on over their sports bras. A woman who was easily sixty was still dancing around one of the ten poles that had been evenly spaced around the room.

Strip-aerobics had become my new Missing Alec Management Plan. It didn't make me feel half as sexy as he could, but it worked to take some of the edge off.

I stood, and jolted upright as someone slapped my ass.

"Girl, you should seriously consider a dancing career." Jayne planted her fist on one cocked hip and grinned. She looked like a stripper: fake eyelashes, heels that could have been murder weapons, and boobs the size of my head. It was impossible to tell how old she was under all that makeup. She was wearing a purple pleather bodysuit tonight, one of her many exciting wardrobe choices for the pole dancing class she taught twice a week at the gym.

My face lit up. I twisted my rib-length black hair into a wet knot at the back of my head with a band from around my wrist.

"You think?"

"Totally," she said. "I can get you an audition if you're interested." Her brows wiggled.

I laughed. "Thanks, but that's okay. I'm not sure my boyfriend would love the idea of other men watching me take off my clothes."

My smile faltered. I still called Alec my boyfriend, but I hadn't seen him in almost three months. Eleven weeks and four days to be exact. I'd written to him, but he hadn't written back. He hadn't called either. My dad's friend on the Tampa Police Force had said this was because he couldn't, that the FBI had locked down his communications with the outside until they could build a case against Maxim Stein. I hoped this was true. All that I had to hold on to was a promise I'd made the night before his arrest. That I'd wait for him, no matter what.

"*Boyfriends.*" Jayne rolled her eyes. "Dance with me, and you'd have a new lover every night."

I giggled as she hiked a leg up my thigh and attempted to treat me like the pole I'd spent the last hour grinding against.

"Fine," she pouted. "If you change your mind . . ."

"I know where to find you," I said. "Thanks for the class, Jayne."

A couple of ladies gave me high fives on our way out the door.

I loved this class, one of the many perks the gym owner had offered me after I'd started offering massages here six weeks ago. I'd signed up after trying to burn off my sexual frustration on the elliptical trainer, and I hadn't been sorry. Now I was toned, hot, and had moves. I hoped they were appreciated when Alec got out of jail.

"I still don't see why they black out the windows."

I smirked and turned toward the frustrated voice originating behind me. Trevor Marshall may have worked in advertising, but he was built like a runner, which is exactly what he'd spent the last hour doing in the main equipment room of the gym. He was tall and lean, with long pronounced muscles that I had the privilege of digging my thumbs into every other Wednesday, in the massage room at the gym. He ran a towel over his sweaty face, revealing a light smattering of freckles across his nose, and scrubbed at his blond hair that had turned dark with sweat. He was handsome, there was no denying it, and the attraction stirred inside of me as it always did when I saw him.

Attraction, but not lust.

"Because freaks like you would fall off their treadmills trying to watch," I told him. "It's a liability issue."

"Seems more like a killer marketing strategy." He smiled, and his gleaming green eyes dipped, just for a flash, to check out the damp tank top and shorts that clung to my curves. "And as an aside, I'm not sure you're allowed to call paying customers *freaks*."

"On the job," I specified. "We're not in session, so I'm allowed to call you whatever I want."

His gaze narrowed. One of his hands slid down his sweat-soaked T-shirt, making it stick to his chest. It wasn't all together a terrible sight.

"My mind is literally racing with possibilities," he said.

I pushed him back with a snort. "Freak."

We began walking toward the locker rooms on the gym's lower level. The bottom floor was lined with weight machines, and the pop music piped in over the speakers was accented with the clank of metal. At the top of the staircase was a cart with a stack of towels, and he passed one to me.

"I had to move my session up to eleven this Wednesday," he said. "If you've got a break after, we should grab lunch."

Trevor had started signing up for massages here about a month after Alec had gone to jail for his association with Maxim Stein's white-collar crimes—crimes he had tried to make right by reporting to the FBI. We'd hit it off immediately. He'd come right when I needed a friend, someone who didn't know that Maxim Stein's nephew Bobby had tried to kill me, or about Charlotte MacAfee's death, or about how hard it was without Alec, the only person who I could really talk to about any of it. Trevor was fun and interesting, and a perfectly good distraction from the chaos that had become my life.

"Can't," I said. "I'm busy Wednesday." The nerves jolted to life in my belly, and I grabbed the handrail so I didn't accidently backflip down the stairs.

"Oh," said Trevor knowingly. "Loverboy comes home this week, I forgot."

I hadn't. I *couldn't*. The countdown to Alec's return had been permanently seared in my memory. I practically had a clock ticking down the seconds transposed over my vision. A month ago the Department of Corrections had sent a letter to Alec's father informing him of his son's release date. Alec hadn't confirmed his arrival, but I was going to be prepared nonetheless.

"Three days," I said, my throat suddenly dry. "Two, if you consider that today is practically over. Well, the workday anyway. If you work a nine-to-five . . ." I trailed off.

Trevor refrained from rolling his eyes, but I could tell this was difficult.

"Where was he again?" he asked, scratching his chin to hide the frown. "Seattle?"

My eyes flicked to the floor. "Yeah. Seattle."

"He left you alone a long time." He threw his towel into a laundry basket. "I guess you gotta go where the work is."

"Right," I agreed. It wasn't that I was embarrassed Alec was in jail, but it really wasn't anyone's business.

"What's he do again?"

"Security," I said, quickly changing the subject. "I'd love to stay and chat, but I've got some stuff to get ready before he comes home."

"Sure," said Trevor, looking a little dejected. "I'll see you Wednesday."

I smiled, and made my way to the locker room. After changing, I saw that I'd missed a call from Amy. The gym was downtown, just a few blocks away from Alec's high-rise apartment, and after stepping into the warm June evening, I called her back.

"I am giving up men," Amy announced. "For real this time. It's all women, all the time."

"That sounds great," I said.

"It is. It's awesome. You know why? Because women aren't dicks."

"I feel like there's a joke somewhere in there . . ."

"A fruit arrangement, Anna," Amy said. "I told David about Paisley and he sent me a we're-not-working-out note on a fruit arrangement. One of those stupid fucking cantaloupe and strawberry flower things."

I cringed, inside and out. Amy was constantly dating men that rejected her, and there had been a string of them lately that had checked out when she'd told them she had a daughter who'd just turned six. Because of that, she stopped introducing Paisley to anyone who hadn't passed the three-date mark.

No one had passed the three-date mark in two years.

"Did you eat the flowers?" I asked tentatively, waiting until the pedestrian sign lit up so I could look both ways and cross the street.

"Of course I did, but that's not the point. Who breaks up with someone with a fruit arrangement? It's like the tackiest thing in the world."

"Agreed," I said. "I'm so sorry. You'll find someone better, I promise."

She groaned. Then sighed. "I'm ruining your birthday."

I paused outside the French bakery that stood between the gym and Alec's place. Pink and white cakes were showcased in the neatly framed window, and they pulled me closer like they were made of magnets. Damn this place for still being open. It was clearly out to sabotage my life.

I went inside. Instantly, my mouth was watering. Croissants, French bread, and cupcakes. Enough cupcakes to fill an Olympic-sized swimming pool. Or at least a moderately sized hot tub.

My gaze honed in on the red velvet with cream cheese frosting. It was the sexiest of all the cupcakes. And it was calling to me in its little cupcake voice.

"You're not ruining anything," I told Amy. "I had a fabulous weekend with you, Dad, and Paisley. Today's just another day."

It wasn't really. It was the day before the day before Alec came home. I'd spent most of the weekend with my father, assuring him that everything was going great and downplaying how nervous I was for Alec's return. I'd taken him to the airport this morning before going in to the salon, and since then, I'd been all jitters.

Thank goodness for pole dancing.

"Well, if Pais and I didn't have this stargazing thing for her school tonight, we'd totally subject you to more cake."

"Don't worry," I said, pointing out the cupcake to the skinny emo kid behind the counter. "I've got it covered."

After another rendition of the Birthday song, I hung up with Amy and, fancy cupcake box in hand, made the trek across the street to Alec's place. I kept a small apartment on the south side of town now—that was where I stayed when my father was visiting—but I spent a lot more time here. It made me feel closer to Alec, even when we couldn't talk.

As I entered the main foyer, impressive with its gray-green marble floors and black leather couches, an athletic man wearing a white dress shirt and slacks greeted me with a smile. His skin was the color of milk chocolate, and his eyes were bright amber—gorgeous, and impossible not to notice.

"Hey sweet girl," he said. "How many days we got left?"

"Two and a half," I answered. "How are you, Mike?"

"Better now," he said, reaching to pull me into a suffocating embrace. "Tell Alec to stay where he is so I can keep you for myself."

I laughed. Mike and Alec had been friends in high school. When Maxim Stein bought the building, Alec had hired Mike as the head of security. A blush crept up my neck as I considered some of the things Mike may have seen on the building's security cameras.

"I'll tell him, but I don't know if he's going to go for it." I hoped he couldn't see how thin my confidence was.

"He will when he sees these," Mike quipped, rolling up his sleeve to reveal a massive flexing biceps.

I fanned myself, moving toward the elevator. "Is it hot in here or is it just me?"

Mike laughed as I stepped into an open car, and pressed the button for the thirty-fifth floor. When I was hidden I sighed, and rubbed the heel of my hand over my eyebrows. Things were going to be fine with Alec. What we had was real, unbreakable. A few months apart couldn't change that.

When I'd reached his floor, I made my way down to his apartment and used the key to get inside. Familiar sights greeted me; a few pictures on the wall of the beach, a cherry dining room set up ahead, a hook where I hung my keys. Things I'd put out over the last couple of months—things Alec wouldn't recognize because he'd been gone. He'd asked me to make the place a little homier. I hoped I hadn't gone too far when I bought a spice rack and a toilet seat cover.

This place was only temporary anyway, I reminded myself. Once Maxim went to jail for the rest of eternity—something I hoped would happen once Alec testified—the building would be sold, and Alec would probably have to find another place. One that was unfortunately not quite so rent-free.

I turned into the kitchen, and put down my bag and cupcake box on the counter beside the knife block. I toed off my shoes and left them on the beige tile, then opened the refrigerator. It had the basics now, but I definitely needed to restock before Alec got home. There wasn't anything good to eat for dinner, and the freezer was too packed with ice cream to fit any frozen meals.

"Pizza it is," I said aloud, then made the call for delivery to a place in South Tampa famous for their thin crust. It probably would have been a good idea to pick something up while I'd been out, but I'd been too focused on my beautiful red velvet friend.

I opened the lid of the box and removed the pretty cupcake, feeling a surge of loneliness. I'd only known Alec a few weeks before he'd gone to jail, but sometimes I missed him so badly it hurt.

"Happy Birthday to me," I said quietly, peeling back the dainty wrapper and taking a bite. Twenty-eight years old, and in a serious, committed relationship with a man I hadn't spoken to in eleven weeks and four days. Living in an apartment still owned by an imprisoned billionaire mogul who'd sent his nephew to kill me. And spending my birthday alone. The cream cheese icing only took a little of the sting away.

I still had an hour before the pizza was delivered, so I hauled my bag into the bedroom, now adorned with a nightstand lamp and a drawer full of my clothes, and left the cupcake on the dresser so I could shower. When I was clean, I towel-dried my long, wet hair, and laid out two outfits side by side on the bed.

One was a black teddy with thigh-highs. The other a red lace bra and panty set with a frilly little skirt. Just looking at them gave me a little thrill. For Alec's first night back I wanted to wear something special. And then I wanted to make him act out every fantasy my overactive imagination had come up with in his absence.

"Red or black?" I took another bite of the cupcake. He'd liked me in red. He'd liked me in black, too. I giggled a little. He wasn't really all that hard to please.

At least, he hadn't been.

I put the outfits back into the bag and stuffed it into the drawer. The big decisions could come later. I still had to clean and figure out what I needed to pick up at the supermarket tomorrow.

Because the next day Alec would be home.

I closed my eyes, and rubbed one hand over my breasts, remembering the way he caressed them. The way his fingers felt dipping beneath my panties. How my body became charged and ready, just from a look.

The memories were enough to make my blood heat.

If he didn't want me anymore, I didn't know what I was going to do.

I ate another bite of the cupcake.

A moment later, a knock came at the door. I checked the time, surprised to see that the pizza guy was still twenty minutes early. Throwing on some pink pajama pants and one of Alec's T-shirts, I hurried back toward the kitchen to get my purse.

"Just a second," I called. "I'll be right there."

Wallet in hand, I glanced at the baseball bat I left leaning against the wall—a safety precaution I'd added since Bobby had abducted me—and opened the front door. I looked up, and then up higher, into the stormy blue eyes of the man who stood in the hallway.

My heart stopped in my chest.

"Hey." Alec's gaze lowered slowly down my body. "Nice shirt."

Two

For a second I thought I was dreaming. Before me was Alec, at least, a man who looked like Alec. The careless waves I'd run my fingers through were gone, his hair cut short. His chest seemed broader, and his arms hung loosely at his sides—arms defined by hard muscle that stretched the sleeves of his white T-shirt. But that was where the differences ceased. His eyes, piercing and blue as the deepest part of the bay, locked me in place as his trademark smirk lifted the corners of his mouth.

He was hot enough to melt the polar ice caps. Even more gorgeous than I remembered, which seemed impossible. He had a mouth made for kissing and a body made for fucking, and as he sized me up I was battered by images of both. The space between us turned electric. I could practically hear it hiss like a drop of water on a live wire. My purse fell from my hand and I grabbed the door handle just to keep my legs from buckling.

"Wh-what are you doing here?" I managed.

He was early. Two and a half days early. I hadn't cleaned up; my stuff was everywhere. There wasn't any food. I wasn't wearing any makeup, my hair wasn't combed, and my underwear wasn't even remotely sexy. This wasn't what was supposed to happen. I was supposed to pick him up at the police station. We were supposed to have sex in the car twice. Maybe three times. Then we'd come back here so I could make him a huge homecoming dinner wearing dirty lingerie, only to have to warm it up later because he'd been unable to keep his hands off of me.

I couldn't move.

His head tilted to the side. "I live here. At least I used to."

I pulled the shirt away from my chest, hiding my body's immediate reaction to him. Was it weird that I was wearing his clothes? I hoped it didn't freak him out.

He still stood in the hallway, as if waiting for me to invite him in. It hit me all in a rush how rude I was being, and I quickly stepped back and pulled open the door.

"Sorry, I . . . Hi." I stepped forward and rose on my tiptoes to give him a hug. "Welcome home."

Touching him was like brushing against open flames. Scalding, terrifying, but also fiercely addicting. His arms surrounded me, drew me closer, until my feet were barely touching the ground. My breasts, bare beneath the soft cotton, grew tender and heavy, and my fingers grasped his broad shoulders too tightly. I inhaled, dizzy from that familiar masculine scent that I'd missed so much these last few months, and then shuddered, like I hadn't really breathed since he'd left. He had to feel my heart pounding against his hard chest.

His head turned, and his mouth found my neck. He whispered something against it that I couldn't hear, and my whole body quivered as his breath warmed my skin. The desire was still there, stronger than before. The intensity of it frightened me; I was almost afraid to set it loose. We would burn each other to the ground.

Then he was pulling back slightly, his mouth seeking mine.

And for some absolutely insane reason, I turned away.

"Chocolate," I said, too loudly. He set me down, his hands lingering on my waist. "I just ate a cupcake, I have chocolate breath."

No, I did not just say that.

He didn't move for a moment, as if waiting for me to tell him this was a joke. Then he scowled, and withdrew his hands from my sides. One thumb tapped his lower lip. "All right."

"It's my birthday, that's why I had the cupcake." *Shut. Up. Anna.*

He froze, gave me a look that bordered on horrified.

"I didn't . . ."

"Oh, I know." I waved my hand as if I wasn't disappointed. "I don't even know why I said that."

He didn't know it was my birthday. I knew he didn't, but it still struck me how little time we'd actually been together.

He was frowning.

"It doesn't matter," I said. "Really."

I had clearly lost my mind. Or my nerve. Or both. Whatever the case, my sex drive was running full steam, but my brain was running interference. This wasn't supposed to be awkward, but since I'd acted so strangely, he was pulling back as well. It was as if there were a barrier between us, a wall of glass that neither of us could break.

Now inside, he took a slow look around, gaze lingering on the bat for a moment before I hurried around him to close the door. The bolt sliding home clicked loudly enough it might as well have been a prison cell.

He stepped into the kitchen, getting his bearings. Goddammit. The plates were one thing, but I'd totally overdone it with the spice rack. I knew it.

He picked up a mug beside the sink, then ran his index finger over the lipstick mark I'd left there. I bit my bottom lip, wishing he'd touch my mouth in the same way.

And now I was jealous of a ceramic cup.

"If it's too much, I can get rid of some of this stuff," I said.

Please say something, I willed him. The silence was unnerving. I tried to keep all my fears at bay, but they were pushing hard at the forefront of my mind. Things had changed. We had changed. I didn't belong here. I'd made myself too at home in his absence.

He had continued on to the dining room, and in the narrow computer nook between the two rooms he paused, brows lifting. While he'd been gone, I'd gotten his college degree certificate from his father, framed it, and put it up. At the time it had seemed like a nice thing to do, but as I watched his hand slide down his throat, I wasn't so sure.

"Look," I said quietly, unable to stand it any longer. "You probably want some time to relax. I should go home. You can call me later if you feel up to it." I didn't even know if he had the same phone number that he did before he left.

His head snapped toward me.

"You still live in the studio?"

I shook my head. "No. Didn't seem like the safest place after the whole stalker/abduction thing, you know?" I tried to laugh, but there wasn't much breath behind it. "I got a little apartment in South Tampa. I didn't want to suffocate you."

He pushed his hands into the pockets of his jeans and leaned against the wall, looking disappointed. Hope lifted my spirits, but they crashed again as the seconds wound on.

"There's a little food in the refrigerator," I said. "I meant to stock up before you came home, but I thought you would still be a couple days." I wiped my damp palms on my sweatpants. "I did get you ice cream."

I turned to the freezer and opened the slender silver door. Inside were eight different cardboard cartons—exactly seven too many, I realized now. I closed my eyes, waiting for the cold air to cool me off.

"That's a lot of ice cream," he said, a trace of humor in his voice.

I winced. "You told me once you liked vanilla. I didn't know which kind—French vanilla, or vanilla bean, or plain—so I got them all."

Stupid. Stupid. Stupid.

"I don't want you to leave, Anna." The quiet way he said my name made my heart hurt, and I turned around to face him. His back was against the counter, hands still fisted in his pockets. His arms were definitely bigger than before. Both of my hands together wouldn't fit around his biceps, and that realization gave me another thrill. I couldn't help but wonder what he looked like without his shirt on. If his pecs, his abs, that thin, sexy line of hair that disappeared beneath his waistband, were still the same.

"Anna," he said again, and I shook my head, refocusing on his face. "What are you thinking?"

"Why didn't you call?" I sagged back against the cool doors of the refrigerator. There was only five feet at most between us, but it might as well have been five hundred.

He looked down at the floor, where I'd left my shoes earlier. "I wanted to. The FBI kept me pretty tied up." He hesitated. "I got your letters."

The air left my lungs in a whoosh. Terry Benitez had told me he wouldn't be able to talk to me, but I'd needed to hear Alec say it.

Alec reached in his back pocket and pulled out an envelope. It was a little wrinkled, but otherwise in good shape. Carefully, he opened it, revealing a stack of notes I'd sent him. As he flipped through them I could see that the paper was worn, the creases nearly torn. He'd read them. A lot. Another shimmer of hope made me stand a little taller.

"How'd you get out early?"

He gave me a small smile. "Good behavior."

"That doesn't sound like you."

His smile widened. "I'm a changed man, Anna."

"I hope not too changed."

He hesitated, and his gaze fell to my neck. The exposed skin around my collar heated. It took several heartbeats for him to find my eyes again.

"Happy Birthday."

I shrugged. "It's not that big of a deal."

"I'm sorry I didn't get you something."

You. I wanted to say. *You're here. That's all I want.* It made me sad that he would even consider I needed more.

"What?" I said. "You couldn't stamp me out a license plate or something?"

His hand twitched, and my mouth went dry. I pictured that hand coming down on my bare ass, the sting smoothed by his tongue.

"Ouch," he said, eyes gleaming.

"Too soon for jail jokes?"

He looked like he wanted to say something, but was holding back.

"I should take a shower," he said. There was an unspoken question at the end, but since he didn't say the words out loud, I didn't answer.

"Okay. It's just . . ." I groaned. "Sorry. It's your place, you know where the shower is."

He pushed off the counter and entered the dining room. "It doesn't look like my place."

I cringed. "Is it too much? Be honest."

Without looking back at me, he said, "I didn't say I didn't like it."

I grinned.

He made his way toward the bedroom where I had spent the majority of nights over the last three months. The door was left open, but I wasn't sure if this was an invitation to follow him or not. A second later the water turned on in the bathroom. He'd probably seen that I had left all my toiletries strewn across the counter by now. Maybe he didn't mind a spice rack or a dining room table, but most men would flip when they saw the amount of products that went into maintaining my wild hair.

"Come on, Anna," I said quietly. "Time to pull your shit to-gether."

Things were going to be okay between us. So they weren't as

comfortable as they'd been when we'd parted, but that didn't mean they couldn't be again. I just needed to relax, help him readjust.

I meant to go back to the kitchen and clean up, but before I could stop myself I'd taken one step, then another toward the bedroom. Each time I moved forward, the butterflies in my belly seemed to multiply, until I had to keep both hands on my stomach just to contain them.

Soon I was standing on the threshold of the bedroom, my bare toes digging into the carpet. Thirty minutes ago I'd been walking around this place like it belonged to me, now I felt like a stranger surrounded by my own things. I peeked inside, and found his clothes strewn over the plush comforter I'd brought. His jeans were crumpled, his shirt thrown across them.

I closed my eyes, imagining him naked in the shower. His soapy hands sliding over his perfect body. The water running through his short hair down his face. I wondered if he was hard, if he had touched himself and thought of me while we were apart. If he was doing it right now.

Heat crept over my skin, and soon just the thought of him, accompanied by the steady spray of the shower, had me breathing hard. My breasts were aching, the apex of my thighs becoming sensitive and damp. I pictured his hand moving up and down his thick cock. His eyes drifting closed. His head falling back. I wanted to hear him groan. I wanted my name to be on his lips as he came.

I hadn't realized I had closed my eyes until the water shut off. It took a few seconds for my brain to catch up, and when it did, I looked up and caught his reflection in the bathroom mirror. It froze me in place and I gasped, startled.

He stared at me unflinchingly, a dark, possessive look in his eyes. Lust tightened his features, drew his mouth into a tight line, made his jaw flex. The counter hid everything below the waist, but his chest was in full view.

He looked incredible. Just one glance at his wet, firm body and my sex contracted. My lips parted. I could almost feel how smooth his skin would be as I spread my fingers over his chest.

My shoulders were rising and falling with each breath. God, I wanted him. Around me, over me, inside me. Now.

A knock at the door rose over the static in my ears.

I blinked, unable to tear my gaze away from his until he disappeared from view behind the door and came out of the bathroom, a towel wrapped around his waist.

I stared at his collarbone, the hard line disappearing beneath the swell of muscles at his shoulders. He was like a walking fantasy; he felt untouchable, too good to be true. My hands started to tremble.

"Are you expecting someone?" he asked.

It was like he was speaking a different language.

"Anna," he said more insistently. "Someone's at the door. Do you want me to get it?"

"I . . ." I looked up, then back, shaking my head. My face must have turned candy apple red as the hypnotic effect he had on me wore off.

"It's nothing," I said, fumbling for the words. "I'll take care of it."

I retreated before he could respond, and had already begun to search the kitchen before I remembered that I'd dropped my purse when he'd arrived. I scrambled to the entryway, finding my wallet where I'd left it, and cracked the door, releasing the chain when I saw the square cardboard box.

I paid the kid more than double what I should have and told him to keep the change. With that I shut the door and carried the pizza into the kitchen, only to find Alec already there, considerably more dressed in his jeans and a fresh button-up shirt from his closet. The collar was damp and open, and beads of water still clung to the ends of his hair—hair I'd once dreamed of running my hands through. Now all I could think was how it would feel brushing against the insides of my thighs.

"You ordered pizza," he said, and the surprise in his voice caught me off guard.

I set it down, not hungry. Not in that way, at least.

"Who did you think was coming over?" I asked. It was so quiet you could hear the consistent buzz of the overhead light.

His gaze flicked to the side.

"There's been no one but you." I tried to sound confident, but I was hurt that he'd doubted me.

He nodded slowly. "I thought . . ." His Adam's apple bobbed. "I had too much time to think. I didn't know if you'd be here when I came home."

"I promised you I'd wait."

"You did." He crossed his arms over his chest, as if he didn't know what to do with them. I could think of a million things he could do with them in that moment, but I didn't know how to bridge the distance between us either.

"Your hair's longer." I was pretty sure this wasn't what he'd wanted to say.

"Yours is shorter."

He scratched a hand over his skull. "Yeah. They make you keep it short."

"Did you wear an orange jumpsuit?" I asked.

He snorted. "It was gray, actually."

"Did you miss me?" My chest ached, just to ask. His eyes found mine, and the room around him fell out of focus. The man could level me with just a look. If he touched me, I'd be putty in his hands.

"Every fucking second." He stared at me as if trying to figure something out, then took a step closer.

"There's a bat by the door, and another under the bed," he said. I swallowed as he came within arm's reach. "And there's five kinds of sleeping pills in the medicine cabinet in the bathroom."

I combed my fingers through my hair. This was exactly why I'd wanted to clean up before he came back. He didn't need to know that I woke up almost every night dreaming that he hadn't reached the bridge in time, that Bobby was beating me or throwing me into the water. That every sound got me out of bed at night, and that some days I was sure that Maxim Stein had broken out of his barricaded estate on Davis Island where he was under house arrest and was following me around. Alec had enough to worry about.

"I can't sleep sometimes." I didn't tell him that none of the pills worked. Maybe they knocked me out, but if I woke up there was no going back.

I didn't have to explain anymore; it was clear by the look on his face that he knew what had been happening.

"I should have been here," he said.

I shook my head, hating the tenderness in his voice because it made me feel weak. "Yeah, well. You have a pretty good excuse."

He took another step closer, and I bumped into the wall behind me. I hadn't realized I was moving backward. Now that he was closer, I had to look up to see him. I was overwhelmed by just how big he was.

"No one's going to hurt you again," he said, the promise clear in his voice. His words struck me deeply; it felt as though my lungs were trembling. My pulse began to kick faster. Faster, as his gaze lowered to my mouth. My tongue wet my dry lips.

"I was fine by myself," I said. It wasn't like I was too petrified to get out of bed every morning. I didn't want him to think it was *that* bad.

He smirked, moving closer again until his arms rose, and pressed against the wall behind me, boxing me in. His body was inches away from mine, but I could feel the heat coming off of him, and smell the soap from the shower mingling with his dark, masculine scent.

"I believe you," he said. "I saw the vibrator in the nightstand drawer."

I closed my eyes, scrunching up my nose. I placed my hand on his chest, intending to push him away but finding I couldn't. Instead, my hand gripped his shirt in a tight fist. "You shouldn't snoop around."

"It's still technically my place."

His head lowered, cheek nuzzling my temple, nose sliding up one side of mine, then down the other. I kept my eyes closed, savoring the feel of him. God, I'd missed him. Talking to him, being close to him. The way he felt, and the way I felt when he was near. The need inside of me increased until my back arched, and my hips jerked against his. He didn't move his hands, but his body responded, rocking back against me. His hard length pressed against my belly while his knee slid between my legs, opening me for him. Excitement jolted through my body as I felt the physical demonstration of his desire.

"Look at me," he whispered.

I couldn't. My head was swimming, my pulse pounding in my eardrums, my chest, my sex. With his knee rubbing against my damp center, the sensations were rising, the heat taking me over. I was getting close, and if I opened my eyes I was afraid he would disappear, and this would have all been some dark, torturous fantasy.

"Anna, I have to see your eyes."

They fluttered open. He stared straight into my soul, asking questions without words. My palm lifted to cradle his cheek, and he leaned into my hand.

"Christ," he murmured. "You've been haunting me."

He rocked against me again and I fought to keep my eyes open. That familiar tension was coiling tighter, threatening to snap, but now it was stronger and more acute because it had been trapped inside me for three long months. My blood felt like it was humming. Only he could make me feel this way. Only he could be my undoing.

"Alec." My breath was coming in little gasps.

"It hasn't changed," he said, giving voice to my fears, and

banishing them at the same time. His forehead pressed against mine.

He wanted me. Needed me. And there was love in his eyes, I was sure I'd seen it. I'd missed him so much there were times I could barely breathe.

There was still a chance to do this the way I'd wanted.

"Wait," I said, louder than I'd intended.

He pushed back, breathing hard. "Wait?"

"You need to leave," I said.

His brows rose. He fell back another step as if I'd punched him.

"Just for a little while. I have to do something." I was already pulling him to the door.

"What's going on?"

"You'll see." I unlatched the bolt and pushed him into the hallway. "Knock in five minutes. Don't go anywhere." I stared at him expectantly until he gave a confused nod.

Then I shut the door in his face.

Three

Never in my life have I stripped so fast. The T-shirt went over my head and landed on the floor somewhere. I nearly tripped on my pajama pants on my way through the bedroom door. Bursting into the master bathroom, I rifled through my makeup, found the compacts and brushes I needed and went to work. It wasn't as careful a job as I would have liked, but I got the basics: mascara, smoky eye shadow, and my new favorite lipstick that was appropriately called *Orgasm*.

I brushed my teeth while I combed my hair, teasing it a little. It was still mostly wet, but I didn't have time to dry it—not while Alec and his enormous erection were waiting in the hallway wondering what the hell was going on. I giggled, picturing the baffled look on his face as I'd shut the door. He'd understand soon enough.

I pulled the pretty velvet bag from the drawer, hoping Alec hadn't thought to explore there, too, and after a quick deliberation went for the black lingerie. The satin was soft and tight against my skin, and instantly bolstered my self-confidence. He wasn't going to know what hit him.

Thanking the universe that the esthetician had had a cancellation yesterday and been able to bump up my waxing appointment, I pulled on thigh-highs and found my best pair of patent leather fuck-me pumps.

One last run through to turn off a few lamps and light some scented candles, and I took my place on the couch, draping my body over the cushions. I should have thought about poses—legs open or closed?—and ended up readjusting myself half a dozen times while waiting.

He didn't knock.

"Come on," I muttered. I was so hot for him I was starting to get uncomfortable.

Nothing.

With a groan, I rose, and walked to the door. I cracked it, and caught sight of his back as he paced by.

"Knock already!" I whisper-shouted.

He turned toward me, but I was mostly hidden. Quickly, I shut the door, now unable to stop the nervous laughter that bubbled up. Making a last-minute decision to stay there, I cocked my hip out and waited.

He knocked twice.

"Come in," I called.

The door pushed inward, and he stood, gaping at me like he'd lost the power of speech. I bit my bottom lip seductively and tried to hide the smile. Now *this* was more like it.

"Fuck me," he muttered finally.

"That's the idea." I trailed one finger between my breasts, which were practically chin level thanks to some well-placed padding. The cups barely hid my nipples, and as his gaze became stuck there, I could tell he was thinking the same thing.

"This is what I wanted to do before," I said.

He took a step forward and slammed the door behind him.

"This is what *I* wanted to do before," he said, voice rough.

He was on me before I could take another breath. His hands flew over my body, sliding down the smooth satin, gripping my backside with a firm, demanding pressure. His mouth claimed mine; his lips were hard and wet, and when his tongue plunged into my mouth, he swallowed my hoarse cry. We battled for leverage, each fighting for dominance, but as his tongue slid over my teeth beneath my upper lip, I gasped with pleasure. He'd never kissed me like that before.

He pulled me against his pelvis, grinding his hard length against my sex while I frantically pulled his shirt up over his stomach. His abdominals flexed as my hands skimmed over them, driving me crazy. I reached for his belt, unhooked it, jerked open his fly.

Wet, frantic kisses trailed down my neck, hitting all the spots that made me wild. Finally, I got his T-shirt over his head and as he shrugged out of it I scraped my nails down his hard pecs.

"*Fuck*, that feels good." His eyes were dilated, his breath ragged. I loved knowing I had this effect on him. That I could make him as crazy as he made me. I wanted to watch him lose control, to see him fall apart, but as one hand swept between my thighs, I lost the ability to think.

"You're so hot," he said. "So wet." He circled the heel of his hand over my clit, the fabric between us now soaked.

"Inside," I gasped. "Inside. I need you."

He pressed harder and I shouted weakly.

"I thought about this every day. You squeezing my cock. Clenching around my fingers. I thought I was losing my mind."

His dirty words stoked the fire, and as his hand pushed aside the thin strip of fabric and his finger made a wide arc around my entrance, my knees buckled. He supported me with one arm around my lower back and pressed inside.

"Yes," he hissed as I groaned. "I heard those sounds you make in my head. They made me so hard." He added a second finger. It was a tight fit while I was standing, and the satin pulled taut against my swollen lips, bringing new sensitivity. I gripped his shoulders.

He lifted me, and the air huffed from my lungs as my back slammed against the wall. A framed beachscape fell to the floor with a crash. He leaned into me, his cock still sheathed by the jeans I hadn't managed to get off. Positioned higher, he had more access to my body and his tongue traced a searing line over the swell of my breast. One hand reached to pull the cup open, but the shoulder strap held tight.

"Rip it," I said.

He stared at me, mouth a tight grimace. Then he wrapped the thin strap around his finger and yanked, forearm flexing. The fabric scored my skin, and he eased the sting with his tongue as my breasts spilled free, licking a trail down to one hard nipple. He circled the tight peak, lapped at it, and finally drew it into his mouth, making me writhe in place still pinned between his hard body and the wall.

"Alec," I said. And then I shouted his name. "Oh God, oh God, oh God."

I was so close. So close and then weightless. He turned around, taking three quick strides to the dining room table and setting me down on it. His mouth never left my breast, and when his teeth raked over the sensitive skin I shuddered, and arched back.

I was coming, my center clenching and empty for a full second before he swore, and the smooth, hard head of his cock surged through my swollen folds.

The feel of him inside me lit my desire like gasoline. Spasms raced through my body. Every muscle flexed, pulling him deeper, hungry for us to be joined in the most intimate way. My nails dug into his shoulders and he groaned, and the sound stroked my sex again. It had been too long since we'd been together, and the desperation made the intensity of my orgasm nearly un-bearable.

"I couldn't wait," he said tightly. "I had to feel it. That way you grip my dick when you come. I needed it."

I whimpered as the tremors faded, aware that the other places our bodies connected—my hands around the back of his neck, his palm on my thigh—were now slick with perspiration. I hastily shoved the hair out of my face, closing my eyes to concentrate on the feel of his thick shaft inside me.

"You're so tight," he said. "Lie back, baby. I'm going to push all the way in."

I didn't understand what he meant until I looked down, and saw that he was firmly gripping the base of his cock in his fist. He'd stopped himself from plowing all the way in while I'd been coming, but now intended to fill me completely. For some reason this touched me; in the midst of his own lust he still put my comfort first.

"Oh," I said, and then "*Oh*" again as his fingers brushed the slick skin around my entrance. He unhooked the bottom of the teddy to give himself more room, and pushed the black, wet satin up my belly so that he could see my bareness. I lay back on the table, my hair fanning out around me, and he lifted my knees, latching his arms beneath my thighs.

"God, you're beautiful," he said. But he was the one that was beautiful. With the candlelight flickering off his skin, and the thin sheen of sweat accentuating the cuts of muscle, I could barely breathe. It seemed impossible that this sexy man had chosen me.

His head fell forward, breaking our stare. He was huge, rock solid and soft as velvet, and as he impaled me I felt our souls meld together with a searing pleasure.

"Breathe, Anna," he said tightly. "Relax."

I inhaled in a hard rush, then forced my clenching muscles to be still. It was difficult; my sex was a greedy bitch, and once she'd gotten what she wanted there was no stopping her from taking more.

I gripped his forearms, feeling them tremble. I could tell he wanted to drive into me, fuck me hard, but he was taking this first entry slow so as not to hurt me. He felt larger than before, and just as I wasn't sure how much more I could take, he pushed deeper.

"Alec, oh God."

He pushed until his big cock was buried inside me and his balls brushed against my ass.

"Wait," I said, wishing that I could do the same but finding it impossible. I was unable to hold still, but even so my body acclimated to him. Remembered.

"God, Anna," he said between his teeth. "You feel so good."

I rose onto my elbows, and he grimaced and squeezed my thighs harder. I was distracted by his flexing pecs momentarily before looking at his face, at his dark brows drawn together in concentration, and the thin band of scar tissue at the bridge of his nose. His high, solid cheekbones and square jaw, and those perfect, bitable lips.

His eyes, dark as thunderheads, stared into mine, and his cock twitched inside of me. The tiny move nearly made me combust I was so tightly wound.

"Now," I panted. "Now. Please."

He slid out, then back in slowly.

"More," I said. "Faster."

"I can't," he said, diverting his gaze to the side. "I won't last."

"*Please.*"

He groaned. "When you beg like that . . ."

He pushed into me hard. Withdrew. Buried himself again. "I can't say no to you."

"Yes," I said as he found a faster rhythm. My cries began keeping time with his thrusts. Soon, I felt it. The spark, deep inside of me, that would launch me into bliss once ignited. It had been three months since I'd felt that deep friction. Only Alec could reach it.

"Come with me," he said, already getting close. "*Now,* Anna."

I was suddenly desperate for the feel of his chest against my breasts and sat up. He locked me against his body just as my world erupted. Had I been able to think, I would have been glad for his hold on me then, because otherwise I would have bucked myself right off the table. His grip tightened—one arm slung around the back of my neck, the other hand digging into my hip. The pleasure wasn't gentle. It was hard and powerful and unrelenting. It consumed me completely. His drives became fast and punishing, and with a sharp curse, he slammed deep into me and held, head thrown back in victory.

I felt him coming, felt the warmth of his love and the strength of his passion. *Finally,* I thought. Finally, he was home.

Cock still pulsing, he lowered his forehead to mine.

"Again," he said.

Four

We lay on the floor on our sides, a tangle of arms and legs and shredded satin, slick with sweat and our own desire. He kissed me gently, but though his lips were soft, there was a passion behind it that made my heart thunder against my ribs. His fingers trailed over my cheek, down the nape of my neck, over each individual vertebrae of my spine, as if relearning the contours of my body.

"Black was a good choice," I said quietly as he began kissing each one of my fingers. How many orgasms had I just had? Six? I'd lost count after he'd pulled me onto his lap in the chair—now overturned beside us—and helped me ride him until my legs no longer worked.

He gave a little wince as he glanced at the teddy, now hanging by just a few small clasps around my waist. One thigh-high was gone completely. The other torn and pooling around my calf. He'd made certain to put my shoes back on.

"I may have gotten a little carried away," he said, reaching behind me to remove the rest of the tattered garment. He paused. "Wait. What do you mean, choice? Was there a second option?"

His cock stirred against my thigh, making me laugh.

"Yes. The super sexy pajama pants and T-shirt combo." I didn't need to tell him about the red bra and panty set yet—some things were better left as a surprise.

He pulled the bodice free and tossed it behind me, then kissed the tip of my nose. I didn't remember him being so sweet after we'd been intimate. I sort of loved it.

"I liked the pajama pants," he said. "Stretchy. Easy access." His hand lowered down my stomach and I wiggled away as he grazed over the ticklish spot on the front of my pelvis.

He pulled himself up on one shoulder and looked down at me. There was a calmness in his eyes now, the storm had passed. It was comforting, considering the anguish I'd seen there before he'd gone to jail.

"I did like it," he said, more serious now. "You in my shirt, making yourself at home. That wet hair." He growled a little, and I smiled.

I love you, I thought. But I didn't say it. And even though his lips parted again, and his eyes filled with emotion, he didn't say it either.

"I thought things might be different," I confessed. "All that time apart."

"Who says they're not?" He nuzzled my neck, nibbling my earlobe. "They're worse. Three months without a fix nearly killed me."

His words reminded me of something I needed to say, but had hoped for a better time.

"Alec . . . there's something I need to tell you."

He stiffened, pulled back. I wished I could erase the doubt from his mind, but only time could do that. He would have to learn to trust me again.

"Have you seen your dad?" I asked. The man's image immediately came to mind—dark hair, a flirty smile, his trusty Seeing Eye dog Askem at his side. Early macular generation had left him mostly blind before Alec was born, but that wasn't the issue he struggled with now.

His brows flattened. "I came straight here."

I took his hand and flattened it against my heart, circling his knuckles with my fingertips.

"He fell off the wagon." I searched his face for any kind of response, but there was barely a flicker of surprise. "I've been visiting him some. I hope you don't mind."

Now he had a response. His eyes pinched at the corners, and his mouth pulled into a frown.

"He called you? He's a real pain in the ass when he's been drinking."

"He was still sober the first time I saw him," I said, glancing away. "You didn't tell him you were going to jail."

Alec lay back on the floor, staring up at the underside of the dining room table. I rose on my side, my throat tightening.

"You told him," Alec said.

"He'd been trying to reach you," I said. "He was worried."

Alec made a noise of disbelief. According to him they got along all right now, but they hadn't always. His father's addiction had left them homeless, and driven Alec to sell drugs for money.

I bit my lip, hard. "I didn't know he'd start drinking again."

Alec laughed dryly. "Yeah. Well. That's what he does."

I pulled back, remembering one particularly notable visit with Thomas last month. He'd been too thin, substituting booze for real food, and I'd made him an omelet, which he'd promptly thrown up on my shoes.

I tried not to blame myself—it wasn't like I'd handed him a bottle—but I still felt terrible for triggering his relapse. My own birth mother had been an addict, and more than once she'd blamed her inability to quit on the stress I caused her.

I sat up and pulled my knees to my chest. I was small enough that my head still cleared the underside of the table. Right now I couldn't even remember how we'd gotten under here.

"I'm so sorry," I said. "Maybe I should have stayed out of

your business. It just . . ." I squeezed my knees tighter. "It just made me feel like you weren't so far away."

His head lifted, eyes round with surprise. When he sat he had to duck because he wasn't nearly as compact as I was. Giving up on getting comfortable, he scooted out from under the table.

"It's not your fault," he said. "I'll call his sponsor tomorrow."

"I already did." I winced. "Too far?"

Alec's brows arched. He shook his head slowly.

"Thanks," he said, looking a bit perplexed.

I nodded.

"I have to work in the morning," I said, looking for a change of subject. "But maybe we could meet for lunch."

He nodded. "I have to meet my lawyer. Then my parole officer."

I stiffened at the mention of parole. Sometimes it all felt too real. Alec had served time in prison. His life would be different now. Mine, too.

"What?" he asked, like he expected me to bolt.

"Nothing," I said, not wanting to dampen the mood further. "You're about to become a very good boy."

He smirked. "They gave me the rules with my discharge paperwork. No drugs, no fighting, no weapons." One of his fingers slid down my breast and circled the hard point. "No running away to Mexico."

"How will you ever manage?"

"I'll figure out something."

His gaze was turning hungry again, removing any uncertainty from our previous conversation. He began to lay me back on the floor, mouth making a straight line down the center of my body.

He had a talent for making me feel desired. The exploration of his tongue over my ribs was almost enough for me to forget the slipperiness between my thighs.

"I should clean up," I said, wiggling as he pinned my hips to the ground.

"Later," he murmured against my belly, causing my skin to pepper with goose bumps. "I'm not done with you."

I gave a little gasp as he blew on the damp skin he'd just kissed.

"And here I was worried that you wouldn't want me anymore."

He paused. Looked up. "You thought that?"

I took the opportunity to twist away. "Maybe."

"That's not possible," he said. "The things I've dreamed of doing to you . . ." His hand lifted to my breast, cupped it gently, and then in contrast plucked at my sensitive nipple. My spine arched, and his arms snaked beneath my back to pull my breast into his mouth. He licked at it leisurely with the back of his tongue, a rough friction against such a sensitive bud, and I clenched my knees together because the pleasure was building again.

"Not many people are fortunate enough to fantasize about the person they're with," he said.

"I fantasize about you, too," I admitted, giving a short moan as he switched to my other breast.

His fingers slid up the inside of my calf, easing my knees apart. "What kinds of things?"

"Dirty things."

"Tell me," he demanded.

I bit my lip. "I'll show you."

His face lifted, desire bright in his eyes. I wiggled out from underneath him and stood, pulling him by the hand behind me to the master bathroom, where I turned on the shower. When it was warm, I stepped inside, and lathered soap on the washcloth. Quickly, I cleaned myself off, and then moved behind him.

Something caught my eye that I hadn't seen before. A thin scar below his ribs on his left side. Slightly raised, it couldn't have been more than a couple of months old. It had certainly not been there the last time we'd been together—I would have remembered. I couldn't believe I hadn't felt it earlier.

"Alec, what happened here?" My fingers traced the line, at least four inches long. He twisted to face me, an anger I didn't understand flashing over his features before he settled me in his arms and smiled.

"Metalwork," he said. "That was my assignment in prison. Making parts for boats and cars. Lost control of one of the pieces."

I frowned. "The cut's on your back."

He kept smiling. "It's a risky job. That's why they pay big money."

"Big money, huh?" I had a bad feeling about this, but Alec had promised never to lie to me again, and I wanted to believe him.

"Sure," he said. "Eighty cents an hour. You impressed yet?"

I couldn't help but grin. "Not as impressed as you're going to be."

I turned him back to face the spray, then reached around his body to slide my soapy hands over his stomach. He tensed, jerking a little as I reached his cock. He was already hard; he'd been that way for most of the night. It pleased me immensely that he was so insatiable, that I was the object of his lust. It made me feel powerful, feminine. Wanted.

He grew thicker in my hands, heavy and impossibly smooth. My breasts slid against his back and he uttered a sharp curse.

"Come here," he said, his intent clear. If I let him have his way, I'd be halfway to my next orgasm right now.

"No," I told him. "Not this time."

I stroked him with both hands until his back muscles began to clench, then I reached lower and cupped his balls. They tightened immediately, giving me room to rub the smooth skin behind them with my middle finger. All the while my other hand squeezed his shaft, drove to the head, and then returned to the base.

"I fantasize that you touch yourself like this and think of me," I said, my cheek pressed against his back. "That you can't wait between the times that you're buried in my pussy." The word made me blush, but a harsh breath came from his throat as I said it, making me realize how much he wanted my naughty words.

"Do you like it when I say that?" I whispered. "Pussy?"

"Fuck yes."

"What about *cunt*? I want your big cock in my cunt."

I stumbled over the word, but the shudder that raked through him told me he didn't notice. I returned both hands to his shaft.

"But right now I want something else," I said.

I slipped around his body, never letting go of him. He was radiating pure energy, but it was captured, and only I could set it free. His piercing stare, flexing muscles in his neck, even his knuckles, white from his fingers gripping his thighs, sent a potent thrill through me. In that moment, he was mine.

"Do you want to come?" I asked.

"Yes," he hissed, flashing his teeth when I squeezed hard.

"You're going to when I say," I said, a little worried that I was being too bold. "And I'm going to watch you."

His eyes narrowed. "You want to watch me."

My cheeks flamed. I glanced over his shoulder, then forced myself to look at him. "I want to see what I do to you. That's my fantasy. Well, one of them."

He chuckled softly. "Do your worst."

I stroked him twice more, then let the water wash away the soap. Pushing him back a little, I lowered to my knees and began to tease the underside of his cock with my fingertips. A bead of precum formed on the tip of his head immediately.

"You're going to kill me," he said tightly. "Look at my dick. Look how hard I am."

I bit my lip, trying to maintain some illusion of innocence. I drew one of his balls into my mouth and slowly began to swirl my tongue around it.

"Fuck." He gripped my hair. I closed my eyes, lapping his scrotum as I moved to the other side. Above, his abs flexed, and he began to breathe roughly.

Yes.

I wanted more. I wanted to see him lose control.

I sucked him harder, all the while stroking his shaft. A stunted groan came from his throat as I circled the engorged head, and my sounds echoed his as I drew him into my mouth, because I knew just how it felt pushing past the threshold into my cunt.

"You like that," he rasped. "You want me to fuck your mouth."

"Yes," I said, briefly wondering if that was wrong. Was I supposed to like it this much? Did it make me dirty? Too far gone, I pulled him deeper. I stroked him all the while, my fingers rising to my lips and pushing back down. My other hand slid beneath his balls, massaging gently. I pulled my knees closer together, desperate to still some of the need coiling inside of me.

He kept watching, lips parted.

I took him as far as I could go, sucking hard as I backed to the head. He seemed to like that; his whole body tensed each time. I reached around him, feeling his firm, perfect ass as I went faster. Faster. He fell back a step, the tile wall supporting his weight as his hips gave small, uncontrolled thrusts into my mouth. I nearly gagged but kept going, sealing my lips so hard around his shaft they tingled. His head tilted back as he siphoned in a hard breath. Then he looked down again, a wild need in his eyes, and I knew I had him.

"Anna," he said. "Enough."

Not enough. Not yet. I clenched my thighs together. My heavy breasts were bouncing with my exertions.

You want me to fuck your mouth.

I moaned around his dick. I could practically feel him inside my cunt, pulsing the way he was now with each stroke of my tongue.

"Anna . . . fuck. *Fuck.*"

I scraped my teeth down his shaft, and his grip on my hair tightened. He gave a hoarse shout, and I felt the first blast of come coat the insides of my cheeks. I pulled back, hot liquid spurting onto my lips and chin. But I was looking up at his face, at the carnal look in his eyes, stunned and impossibly turned on by the single moment he'd stopped caring about anything but finishing. The sound of my name on his lips staggered me. How could I possibly have thought I had control of him? He owned me.

I rose, rinsing off in the spray. He said nothing, and for a moment we stood a foot apart, both watching each other. His chest rose and fell, and then gradually steadied. His cock stayed semihard.

"Was that what you wanted?" he asked.

A sudden dose of shame heated my veins, followed by uncertainty. Strange, uncomfortable feelings that had been placed on hold after I'd told him I'd helped his father. We clearly connected on a sexual level—there was no denying that. But what about the rest? It had seemed so second nature to decorate his house and check in on his family, but he'd barely said a word about it. Was there more to that, or simply the shock that I'd done more than what was asked?

Time had changed him. There was a harder, more severe look about him than before. Of course there was; he'd been through so much over the past months. It softened when we were intimate, but now it was undeniable.

"What do *you* want?" I asked quietly. I'd been so focused on him coming home that I hadn't bothered to consider where we might go from there. We were in uncharted territory, and not exactly working with a fairy-tale scenario.

He stayed against the wall, his brows pulling inward. "What do you mean?"

"When's your birthday?" I asked.

His frown deepened. He reached around me to turn off the shower.

"November third," he said.

"What's your middle name?"

He sighed.

"I don't have one," I said. "Or if I did, I don't remember my birth mother ever saying it."

"What are you doing?"

The awkwardness was back, the space between us filled with all the things we didn't know about each other but should have, considering the strength of our feelings.

"I don't know," I said.

I reached for a towel, but he stopped me with one hand on my lower back. I froze in place, a shiver racing up my spine. Heat seemed to pulse through his hand into my tensed muscles, giving me the calm I craved.

"You smell like sandalwood," he said. "You bite your lip when you're nervous." His fingers moved slowly to my hip. "You think you're afraid of being left because your mom fucked you up, but really you're afraid of being the one who leaves."

I turned, holding the towel between us. My teeth pressed together. I didn't want to talk about that stuff. Especially not when I was already feeling vulnerable.

"I know the sounds you make when I'm inside of you," he said, stepping closer, and moving the towel out from between us. "And I know it tears me up when you cry."

I felt like I might cry right now. He was unraveling me, the way he did when we made love, only now it wasn't with my body, but my heart.

"I don't know everything about you, Anna. But if you give me time, I will."

I could barely breathe. What he was proposing scared the hell out of me—the prospect of being known, really, truly known, and knowing someone in return. It was exactly what I wanted from him, but it came with a price. He could hurt me, worse than Bobby or Maxim Stein could hurt me. He could rip me apart, and I would be helpless to stop him.

I tilted forward, until my forehead came to rest on his chest. He wrapped the towel around my shoulders, and pulled me against him. Gently, he kissed the top of my head.

"Stay with me," he said, as I'd once told him.

And we stayed just like that, for a long time.

Five

At nine a.m. I parked my totally-used-but-new-to-me electric blue Ford Fiesta on the street in front of the courthouse downtown. The Kia had sadly succumbed to its injuries after I'd run it into a concrete pylon to escape Bobby three months ago, and when insurance had sprung for a new car, I'd gone with something that stuck out in a crowd. Not because I liked being in the spotlight, but because I wanted to be easily recognizable in case someone tried to, I don't know, abduct me again. So what if it was a little paranoid. No one in their right mind was jacking a neon blue car.

It was a double-shot espresso morning, and even that couldn't break through my sex hangover. After the shower, Alec had ordered Chinese food—the pizza having become a little questionable after spending so many hours on the kitchen counter. There was post-Chinese food sex. Then middle of the night sex. Then Good Morning sex, and of course, an after breakfast quickie on the back of the couch.

The man clearly intended to kill me.

I grinned into the plastic lid of my paper cup, thinking death by orgasm might be an all right way to go.

We'd agreed to meet near the salon for a late lunch between my clients. He had some things he needed to do—checking in with his parole officer and father being the most pressing. He didn't talk about it, but I knew returning to the real world after three months in prison couldn't have been easy. His situation had changed considerably. Before, Alec's work as Maxim Stein's bodyman had consumed most of his life. Now he didn't even have a job.

But he had me. And I wasn't going anywhere.

It felt strangely liberating to think that way. Before, I'd believed wholeheartedly in keeping things light, simple, not getting too attached to anyone or anything. My feelings for Alec were anything but light and simple—they were deep, confusing, sometimes absolutely crazy-making—but they felt more real than anything I'd ever known.

A woman outside screaming at her two teenagers snapped me out of my thoughts. A defensive edge rose up within me, but before I had gotten out of my car they were already inside. Despite the balmy temperatures I shivered, standing before Lady Justice with her sagging blindfold, and hoping the blind truth she saw wasn't my fear, but my strength. I smoothed out my black pencil skirt and white ruffled tank, and adjusted a little sweater over my shoulders. My long hair was wrapped in a loose knot at the back of my neck. I'd been shooting for conservative, but all Alec had seen was naughty librarian.

"Anna?" A familiar voice behind me had me turning toward the side of the street where the police officers parked.

"Hey, Terry." I smiled warmly as my dad's friend, Terry Benitez, approached, wearing a beige suit that didn't quite fit right around the middle. Terry and my dad had worked together in Cincinnati before they'd both become detectives. He'd been the first cop on the scene when Bobby had abducted me, and a crucial part of the team supplying evidence to the prosecution.

He gave me a hug, patting my back in a friendly way. "Did you hear the news?"

"What's that?"

As if trying to temper a smirk, he stroked one hand over his short, graying beard. "Robert Calloway pled guilty. The prosecution is settling."

Automatically, my jaw locked, and I had to concentrate to work it back open. The memories were still right there under the surface. Bobby, cornering me in the empty restaurant while I waited for Alec. The feel of his hand striking my face. The friction of the bindings around my wrists and ankles as he drove me toward the bridge.

"He did?" I took a deep breath. "I didn't see that coming."

Bobby was Maxim Stein's nephew and therefore had access to Maxim Stein's bazillion dollar attorneys. He'd skirted around the law more than once before; I just assumed they'd fight to do the same now.

A sympathetic look passed over Terry's face. "I didn't either. Came across my desk early this morning. My best guess? Stein's people figured out he was a sinking ship and decided to cut him loose before the big trial."

The big trial. Maxim Stein's trial. Where Alec would testify that he'd stolen Green Fusion's clean fuel plane engine design, and conspired to kill the president of the company, Charlotte MacAfee.

The coffee suddenly tasted like rusty nails.

"So what does that mean for us?"

Terry edged me into the shade under the statue.

"It means you're off the hook," he said. "Robert Calloway will be sentenced for your abduction and Charlotte MacAfee's murder and sent to prison. I take it the other part of *us* is Alec Flynn?"

I nodded, my throat too thick to speak.

"Isn't he still locked up?"

I shook my head. "He got out early on good behavior."

To Terry's credit, he didn't look surprised.

"Keep him off Davis Island."

I was 99 percent sure Alec wouldn't try to confront Maxim Stein, especially where he lived. Maybe 98 percent sure. That would have been bad for everyone.

But that didn't mean Maxim wouldn't try to contact Alec.

My frown etched deeper. That would be just as crazy. It would totally jeopardize the upcoming trial. But Maxim had been desperate enough to protect himself that he'd allowed Bobby to kill someone to prevent his secrets from getting out. I didn't put it past him to try something.

"Nothing's changed for Alec," Terry continued. "He'll still be the key witness. The only witness, unless Calloway has a change of heart and flips in prison, which I doubt will happen."

"Why?" I asked. Bobby didn't exactly seem like martyr material.

He stuck his thumbs into the front of his belt. "I'm sure there's some deal in the works where he gets a cushy cell and a weekly conjugal so long as he keeps his trap shut. Stein would have made sure to take care of him in exchange for his silence."

So Alec was still going to have to testify, but I was safe. I didn't feel safe. I felt like I needed to find the nearest storm shelter and curl up into a tiny ball.

"Maxim Stein had a secretary," I said. "Ms. Rowe. Surely she would know something." She might be able to help corroborate Alec's story, take some of the pressure off of him.

"Missing," said Terry. "Disappeared the night of MacAfee's murder. I think the FBI put a search out for her."

I pictured the shapely brunette with her flawless appearance and icy demeanor. She's been cool under pressure and well organized, and I had a hard time believing she'd split without a specific plan in place.

Before I could stop myself, I imagined Bobby running her off the bridge, the same way he'd done to Charlotte.

"Cheer up," Terry said. "This is good news. Once the trial's over, you can put this all behind you."

"The date hasn't even been set yet." It was out there looming before us, this vague, ambiguous thing that was supposed to fix everything. I wanted to believe it would, but I couldn't help but feel doubtful.

Because Terry was starting to look a little worried, I forced a smile, but it probably looked a little scary.

"So if you're not here for that, what brings you to the court-house today?" he asked.

"I'm volunteering." My voice sounded small. Terry was right, Bobby's confession was good news. I should have been doing cartwheels down the middle of Florida Avenue.

I cleared my throat. "I'm volunteering," I said more clearly. "For CASA."

"Court-appointed Special Advocates?" he asked. "Hard work. You ever done that kind of thing before?"

"A while ago," I said, referring to a previous career in social work and a burned-out stint in child welfare.

When Terry said the work was hard, he didn't mean the hours or that it was particularly complicated. He meant that it came with an emotional burden, the kind that was hard not to take home at the end of the day. I knew this, which was why I had de-cided to start out slow, take one case at a time. If I did well, I'd look into re-upping my social work license. If not, I could finish out my one client—the one I was meeting for the first time today—and move on.

"Well good for you," said Terry. "Your dad's proud, I'm sure."

I'm sure he would have been, if I'd told him. The truth was, I hadn't told anyone, not even Alec or Amy. I wanted to make sure I could hack it first.

Terry held the door open for me as we stepped through the

glass doors into the busy main lobby. Signs for different special-ties pointed right and left, just beyond the metal detector manned by two security guards. My eyes immediately fell to Juvenile Court, where I had been told to go this morning.

"Thanks Terry," I said before we parted ways. "For all of it."

"Sure," he said. "Glad I could help. And really, call me if you need anything, all right? I'll check in from time to time."

Under no prompting from my dad, I was sure.

"Thanks," I said.

After I had stripped all the metal from my body and gotten a stern reprimanding from the security guard about not bringing my keychain Mace into a courthouse, I headed down the hallway toward the family wing. I didn't go into a courtroom, but a small office filled with crying children and mothers who looked be-yond overwhelmed.

"I'll be back to get you," one woman was telling a boy, who looked to be about five. His eyes were red with tears, and by the quivering of his lower lip I could tell he didn't believe her.

How many times had my birth mother told me that when she'd left me somewhere? She'd said it the last time, too, when she'd taken me to that fast-food playland and overdosed in the parking lot.

"Can I help you?" called the clerk over the crying.

I was still standing in the doorway. I hadn't even let go of the metal handle. My grip tightened. What was I doing here? I'd wanted to make a difference in a child's life, help someone like Alec when he'd been young and lost, but now I wasn't sure that I could.

"Ma'am?" called the woman.

"Don't be a baby," said one little girl to her sibling.

"Yeah," I said under my breath. "Don't be a baby, Anna."

I put on my best smile and walked to the counter.

"I'm Anna Rossi," I said, showing the ID they'd given me in the training course I'd taken two weeks ago. "I'm working with CASA."

A hard-nosed woman with tortoiseshell glasses and a million flyaway hairs looked down at a list on her desk.

"I'll buzz you through," she said, nodding to a door to my right.

I stepped over the wooden puzzle pieces and dented plastic stacking rings strewn across the floor, and pushed through the door into another hallway. The woman was already there, and without a word she led me to a closet-sized office crammed tightly with two chairs. I sat and waited, and waited, and waited, my anxiety growing by the second, until a man in his forties with a buzzed head popped in.

"Anna?"

I jolted up. Smiled brighter than a five-hundred-watt lamp. "That's me."

"This is Jacob. And I'm Wayne."

I shook Wayne's hand, but didn't see Jacob until I stuck my head out into the hallway. There, a boy about ten or eleven was leaning against the wall with his hands in the pockets of his dirty jeans. His T-shirt was two sizes too big, and his skin was the color of cinnamon.

"Hey Jacob," I said. He didn't answer.

Wayne handed me a file that had been tucked under his arm. "I'm Jacob's caseworker, and he just got done in court. Looks like the judge approved foster care, so I'm going to go look at getting him a placement for tonight. Would you mind taking him for an hour or so? You can go for a walk or something."

And so begins the child welfare shuffle.

"No problem," I said. A few years ago, I would have been the person finding Jacob a home. It was a little jarring to be in a different role.

"You can get what you need out of the file. Let me know if you catch any special circumstances I need to know about. Allergies to dogs or whatever."

Jacob was twisting the heel of his worn-out shoe into the buffed linoleum.

Clearly Wayne had a packed schedule, so I moved around him to Jacob's side.

"I think we've got it from here."

Still nothing from the kid. This could be interesting. But already I could feel myself rising to the challenge. I'd worked with tough kids before. Hell, I'd been a tough kid before. Parents were the hard part, but kids I could manage.

Wayne nodded gratefully and left us in the hallway.

"I'm Anna," I said.

Nothing.

"Tough morning in court?"

Nada.

"How old are you? Ten?"

Zilch. The kid's lips were sealed tighter than a waterproof safe.

"I feel like tacos," I said. "Want to get out of here for a while?"

He glanced up at me to see if I was bluffing, then looked away, but not before I saw the anger in his pretty brown eyes.

"It's not even lunchtime," he mumbled.

I scoffed. "Wait," I said. "Wait. Are you telling me you've never had tacos for breakfast?"

"Nobody makes tacos for breakfast."

"Huh," I said. "I guess we'll just have to see if they're open."

I walked past him toward the entrance, as slowly as I could without looking like I was waiting for him to follow. A few seconds passed, and when he pushed off the wall and came plodding after me, I grinned.

"Why don't they just call it pork if it's pork?" he asked.

"*Carnitas is* pork." I laughed. "That's the word for it in Spanish."

I sat across from him in the wooden booth at the Taco Bus across from the police station, picking at my black beans and rice while he polished off his third taco. Clearly the kid hadn't eaten in a while. That, or he didn't know when he'd eat next. I made a mental note to place a to-go order before we left. His hungry days were in the past, as far as I was concerned.

After a while, he glanced up at me, reluctant to stare too long.

"So are you my new social worker or something?"

I shook my head, thinking back on the suspicious-eyed kids that had asked me that over the years. "I'm just a friend."

"You got another job?"

"I give massages."

"Oh," he said. "Like a hooker."

I choked on the soda I'd been drinking. "Not like a hooker. Nothing like a hooker."

"My dad went to get massages at the Asian spa sometimes. My mom said it was 'cuz the girls there were hookers."

Well. He had me there.

"I can tell you that I am *definitely* not a hooker," I said. I was relieved that it didn't appear he knew what a hooker actually did.

"Tell me about your dad," I said.

Jacob's little mouth pulled into a tight frown. He crossed his arms over his chest.

"Anything," I said. "I'll start. My dad likes to work on cars."

He wrapped the straw from his drink around his finger.

"My dad's an asshole."

I tilted my head, thinking about the file I'd glanced through before handing it back to the receptionist at the front desk in the courthouse. It was so similar to countless files I'd seen before. Abusive father. Drug-addicted mother. Parents were given three strikes before custody was lost. What stuck out was that Jacob had been flagged for a psych eval due to violent outbursts. The kid didn't look violent to me, but there was definitely a lot going on under the surface.

"Want to talk about it?"

"Nope."

"How about your mom?"

He flinched. "She's sick a lot."

I nodded, remembering my own birth mother passed out on the bedroom floor, shirt soaked with her own vomit. Moving in that slow-motion way and slurring her words, and then gradually ramping up faster and faster until she was scratching at her skin and so agitated you couldn't even look at her without her thinking she was getting sassed.

"My mom was sick like that, too," I said.

He looked up at me, again for confirmation. *Can I trust you?* that look seemed to say. *Or are you full of shit just like everyone else?*

"Sammy's staying with me," he said assertively. "I don't care what you or anybody else says." He shoved his empty plate away.

"Who's Sammy?" I asked.

"Sammy," he said. "My sissy."

The word made him sound so much younger than the tough expression on his face suggested.

"I didn't know you had a sister."

"She's six," he said.

"Where is she now?"

He shrugged, then began kicking the leg of the table.

Was this what Alec had been like years ago? A kid who'd been hardened by life, staying loyal to the people he loved because they were all he had?

"Why does your file say you're violent?" I asked. It was a big question for a kid so young, but he seemed old enough to handle it. I wondered if Sammy had been taken away because he'd hurt her in some way.

"I didn't hit her," he said. "I told them that. He hit her. I hit him."

"Who hit her?"

"My dad," he said. "So I hit him back with a plate."

"A plate."

"Yeah," he said, as if challenging me to defy him. "A plate, all right?"

"You were defending your sister?"

He shoved out of the seat and stood, but didn't go anywhere. "She's staying with me, all right? I take care of her."

"Jacob," I said clearly. "I want to help you. But I need you to sit down and tell me everything."

He waited one beat. Two. I thought he was going to run. I thought I was going to have to chase him. In those seconds I even contemplated slipping off my heels, just in case we were going to have to go tackle football style out in front of the Taco Bus.

He sat down.

An hour later we stood side by side in Wayne's office. Jacob had agreed to let me explain what had happened, and he listened with interest.

"Jacob never hit his sister. He needs to be placed with her," I said.

Wayne gave me an exasperated look. "I know he didn't," he said. "But we can't keep them in the same house. There aren't a lot of openings for two kids, much less a boy and girl. Most places take one or the other."

Jacob stormed into the hallway, but there was nowhere to go. I kept my eye on him as he paced to the end and kicked the wall.

"I know it's tight, but you have to make it work," I said quietly. "Or he's going to run, I promise you."

Wayne scratched his hands over his head. "You'll go to the judge with that?"

I nodded.

"All right," he said. "I'll see what I can do."

Six

I was still thinking about Jacob as I pulled into an open spot on the street in front of Rave salon. There was a small lot in the back, but after everything that had happened I wasn't comfortable walking even short distances where someone couldn't see or hear me if I was in trouble.

Derrick, Rave's fabulous owner, was working the front desk, and as I walked in my eyes drew to his mouth, and the shimmery silver lip balm that matched his eye shadow. The man wore makeup better than any woman I knew.

"Good morning," he said with a wave, and picked up the tablet where he kept our schedules. "You have three back-to-backs starting at eleven. Swedish, Swedish—maternity, second trimester, and hot stone." He checked to make sure he had the massage types listed correctly. "Your first client is with Amy now, she'll bring her back when she's done."

"Thanks." The salon was split into two main areas—the spa, where all clients entered, branched into a quiet, dimly lit corridor with several rooms for massage, facials, and waxing. The other side was the salon, a bright eruption of silver and black, where hair clips and jars of dye clattered against metal carts, and stylists talked loudly over the whirring of the blow-dryers.

I caught Amy's eye and waved. She raised her scissors in response, and I smirked at how absolutely adorable, and still somehow sexy, she looked in pigtails. I wondered if Paisley had anything to do with today's look.

When she raised her brows at me, I ducked away. Amy had an uncanny ability to read people's moods. Even across a crowded salon she could see that something was up. She'd press me later I was sure, but I wasn't ready to talk about Jacob, or how when I'd given him my number he'd asked if I was really coming back, and as terrible as it was, part of me had wanted to say no. For the first time in my life I'd sympathized with my birth mother. Maybe Alec had been right when he'd said that I wasn't scared of getting left, but of being the one who leaves.

I dropped my things in the cubby in the back, spending no more time in the break room than necessary. Though Derrick had outfitted all the rooms with panic buttons after Melvin Herman—my very persistent stalker—had locked me inside, it still wasn't somewhere I could kick my heels up and relax.

Amy dropped off our shared client—a divorcée who was revamping her life, starting with plastic surgery and ending with a trip to the spa—and while she was getting undressed, I followed Amy into the laundry room.

"So . . ." she started.

"Alec's back," I said before she could pry. "He came home last night."

"Early," she said. She'd known I'd been practically counting the minutes until his arrival.

"And I ran into Terry Benitez this morning," I said, hurrying because I only had two minutes before I needed to begin the massage. "Bobby pled guilty. For my abduction and for Charlotte's murder. He's going to prison."

And for some reason I was suddenly crying.

"Oh, Anna." Amy had an incredibly strong hugging grip for someone who weighed a hundred and fifteen pounds soaking wet. "He's gone now. You don't have to worry about him anymore."

"I know," I sniffled. "I don't know why I'm crying." I gave a watery chuckle and pulled back to blot the smeared mascara under my eyes.

"Because you're safe," she said, still holding my elbows. "You get so used to looking over your shoulder it feels wrong not to."

Sometimes Amy just got it. It was like she'd been walking in my footsteps this past month.

"Come here." She licked her thumb and wiped away some smeared eyeliner on my cheek.

"*Eww,*" I said.

"Shut up." She stuck her tongue out at me. "When you're a mom, you'll do it, too."

When I'm a mom. I'd never deeply considered the possibility. I didn't think I had the right genes for it. Even if I wanted kids, I wasn't sure I deserved them after the thoughts I'd had when I'd left Jacob at the courthouse this morning.

"Go," she said, "you're going to be late." But before I could turn, she grabbed my elbow. "Things are okay with Alec, right?"

I nodded. "Things are great."

She smiled, but I was pretty sure she didn't believe me.

After I'd finished the hot stone massage, I crossed the street and made my way to the deli at the corner. The sun was shining, and the tourists were in full invasion mode thanks to the cruise ship in port, but I had a prickly sensation on the back of my neck like someone was watching me.

"Bobby and Maxim Stein are locked up," I said to myself. Even Melvin Herman was locked up in a psych ward. The people that had tried to hurt me couldn't hurt me anymore.

Still, I kept looking over my shoulder and carried my keys in my hand. I didn't relax until I was safely inside the restaurant, and had a seat with my back against the wall.

When the server, a perky thing in her early twenties, came around to my table, I ordered a sweet tea and a Cuban sandwich. Alec had sent a text saying he was running a little behind but would be here soon. I trusted he would show; he knew better than to stand me up.

"It doesn't seem right for a beautiful woman to sit alone."

I turned in my seat, surprised to find not Alec, but Trevor Marshall before me. He sat down before I could stand up, and grinned in a way that I was sure made his advertising clients believe every word he said. He was wearing a suit, blue pinstripes, no tie. I'd never seen him dressed for work before. I hardly recognized him.

"Wow," I said. "You clean up nice."

"I should say the same to you," he said.

I tore my eyes away from his to stare at the menu, remembering too late that I'd already ordered when the waitress brought my tea.

"Since we're both here," he said. "Why don't you let me buy you lunch for your birthday?"

I eyed him suspiciously. "How'd you know it was my birthday?"

"I'm psychic," he said. "And after you left the gym the girl at the front desk said you forgot to get your Happy Birthday smoothie."

"Ah," I said. She'd told me that when I'd arrived, and honestly I had forgotten. Not that I was sorry. A wheatgrass shot and a banana didn't exactly compare to a red velvet cupcake.

"That's sweet, Trevor, but I'm actually meeting someone."

His brows shot up, and he brushed back his curtain of golden hair.

"Alec," I explained. "He came home a few days early."

"Lucky you," he said quietly. "Or should I say, lucky him." There was a probing look in his eyes that made me fidget in my seat.

"Thanks," I said.

He leaned back in his chair. "You know, some people say I'm a good listener."

"They do, huh?" Did I have it stamped across my forehead that I was in personal turmoil or something? Jesus.

"Things a little rocky in paradise?"

It annoyed me that he, like Amy, had assumed I was upset about Alec.

"Things are great," I said flatly.

Trevor's look darkened. "Look, if he hurt you . . ."

"No." I shook my head emphatically. He'd misunderstood my tone. "*No*. Why would you say that? Alec would never hurt a woman."

He stared at me, a sharp, uncomfortable strain fraying between us. I'd never felt that before with Trevor, and when I blinked it was gone.

I sighed. "I'm doing this volunteer thing," I said, focusing on my silverware. "Trying to help this boy who's had it pretty rough."

"Rough how?"

I glanced as someone came through the door. Not Alec.

"His parents just lost custody. Mom's on drugs. Dad hit his sister so he hit his dad." I couldn't divulge too many details without breaking confidentiality.

"Good for him."

I tapped my fork on the table. "He's ten. Half my size. He could have been really hurt." Still, I couldn't help agree with Trevor's sentiment. As ugly as the situation was, I was proud of Jacob.

"If someone hurt my sister, I'd kill them."

He said this like a fact, as if he'd just said that the sky was blue, or birds could fly. And I shivered, because I had no doubt he meant it.

It kind of made me wish I'd had a brother when I was little.

"I didn't know you had a sister," I said, trying to change the subject.

Trevor leaned forward, green eyes more intense than ever.

"What happened to the dad?"

I frowned. "Not sure. Probably a little jail time and some mandatory parenting classes."

And then he could petition for custody, and Jacob would go home. Just like I went home every time my mom screwed up.

"There's not enough eye for an eye in the justice system," he said. "Someone hurts a child, they deserve to be hurt. Someone beats a woman, they get beaten. Or castrated." His gaze flicked to the side. "That woman on the news that was driven off the bridge? Someone should make the guy who's responsible jump."

I had frozen in my seat. Did Trevor know of my involvement with the Maxim Stein case? Did he know Bobby had intended the same death for me as for Charlotte? Or was he just making conversation? We'd never talked about it before, and the times the story had played on the news at the gym I'd always been careful to avoid discussion.

Trevor waved his hand. "Sorry. Stuff like that just gets under my skin."

"Me, too," I said.

"Anna."

I jolted in my seat at Alec's voice. He was standing beside me, but with the café's music and all the voices I hadn't heard him approach.

For a moment, I could only stare at him, my heart in my throat. In jeans and a plain white T-shirt, he was dressed like half the men in here. But he didn't look like any of them. He was on a different level, the type of man other men envied, and every woman wanted. The kind you looked at from beneath your eyelashes and dreamt about later because there was no possible way he'd noticed you. But Alec Flynn *had* noticed me, and here he was, danger, intrigue, and red-hot heat all rolled into one mouthwatering package.

And he was glaring at Trevor.

"Alec," I said quickly. "This is Trevor. A friend of mine. From the gym." *In case you needed that clarification.* I had nothing to hide, but it suddenly felt very wrong for these two to be in the same room together.

Trevor rose quickly; his thighs banged against the table and rattled the silverware. Alec had lifted his arm to shake hands, but Trevor stared awkwardly at it for a moment before taking it.

"Alec Flynn." He rolled his shoulders back, appearing more relaxed in response to Trevor's discomfort, which was becoming more obvious by the second.

I hadn't known Trevor long, but he seemed like the kind of guy who wasn't easily rattled. He worked in advertising, and had told me several times about high-pressure presentations he'd had to make. He ran to manage the stress.

Right now it looked like he could use a marathon.

"Have we met?" asked Alec. "You look familiar."

"I don't think so," said Trevor, regaining his composure. I didn't blame him for being intimidated. Half the time *I* was intimidated by the man, though perhaps in a different way.

"One Cuban sandwich!" said the waitress cheerily. "Can I get you anything, babe?" She put one hand on Alec's biceps, and I fought the urge to slap it away.

"Maybe in a minute," said Alec.

Trevor's body was visibly tense, and I stood to try to ease some of the pressure between them.

"Anna mentioned you'd come back from Seattle early," said Trevor. "Sounds like you were busy. Bet it's good to be home."

Oh no.

I didn't have to look at Alec's face to see the damage. I could feel it. The white lie on Alec's behalf had been the wrong choice.

"It is," said Alec cryptically. I reached for his hand, gave it a tight squeeze.

He didn't squeeze back.

Instantly, I could feel the pressure mounting in my chest. *Breathe, Anna.*

"I'm sure she's been dying to show you those dance moves."

I turned to stare at Trevor. What the holy fuck was he doing? I wasn't violent by nature, but I was about three seconds away from punching him in the teeth just to get him to shut up.

"What dance moves would those be?" Alec continued to stare at Trevor, who seemed to have found his balls and was now staring straight back. Neither acknowledged me in the slightest.

"I'm taking ballet," I blurted. "It's a class at the gym down the street from the apartment." I still wanted to surprise Alec with what I'd learned but Trevor was threatening to ruin it.

"Ballet," said Trevor, still not looking my direction. "She's a hell of a *ballerina*."

"Like you would know," I snapped. "Okay, clearly both of you have huge dicks and everyone is really impressed, but my sandwich is getting cold."

Trevor glanced at me for the first time since Alec had arrived. "My fault. Enjoy your lunch. We'll go out to celebrate your birthday some other time."

And then, right in front of Alec, he bent down and kissed me on the cheek.

I might have stepped back if I'd had seen it coming, but I was too in shock that he would even attempt something so bold in front of a clearly territorial man who had at least thirty pounds of pure muscle on him.

Trevor took a step away, then turned. When he looked back at me, there was a familiar kindness in his eyes. It was as if the last few minutes hadn't happened at all.

"Good luck with the volunteer gig," he said. "That kid's lucky to have you."

I stared at him, wondering if that friendly little remark was exactly what the last nail in the coffin sounded like.

Seven

When Trevor left the deli, my lungs deflated. I offered Alec an apologetic smile, and stood on my tiptoes to kiss him. I wasn't shooting for porno tongue, but I'd seen more emotion between sixth-graders playing spin the bottle.

"Hi," I said.

He sat across from me in the seat Trevor had just occupied, tapping his thumbs on his thighs. His expression may have been a perfect, blank mask, but he was pissed. I could feel it coming off of him in waves.

"Bobby's pleading guilty," I blurted. "To all the charges. Terry thinks he made a deal with Maxim, but I don't know." Once again I felt a surge of terror, as Bobby's incarceration was somehow bad news.

"Good to know," he said.

The waitress dropped a plate. I jumped in my seat as it shattered on the floor. Alec didn't even flinch.

"And Maxim Stein's on house arrest. You shouldn't go anywhere near him. Not that he can leave anyway. I saw his house on the news. Media choppers overhead. Reporters and police outside. It's a circus."

Alec's eye twitched.

"I'm not sure what's happening right now," I said tentatively. The pressed sandwich was growing cold on my plate.

"Apparently I just got back from Seattle." His eyes flickered with fire. He meant to punish me, and though the thought baffled me, I wanted him to. There was something definitively sexual about his anger; it was so pure and hot, I had to concentrate to stop myself from stoking the fire.

"I didn't think it was anyone's business where you were."

"So you told him I was . . ."

"Working," I said, glancing at my hands woven tightly in my lap. "In security."

"Now that I know, I'll try to do a better job covering." He tilted back in his chair, hands clasped behind his head. His biceps flexed, and my stomach tightened, betraying my convictions to stay strong.

"You won't have to," I said. "Amy and my dad are the only ones that knew where you were. I didn't tell anyone else anything." The truth was, I'd thought Trevor had been hitting on me the first time he'd approached me at the gym, and I'd used Alec as an excuse to get out of a potentially awkward situation. Later that week he'd scheduled a session, and we'd been friends ever since.

At least, we *were* friends. When he came in for his scheduled session next week I was going to do some serious deep muscle work. The kind that involved elbows and knees and maybe a sharp wooden stick.

"It's fine," said Alec, and for a second I glimpsed the hurt in his eyes before he carefully tucked it away. It just about ripped my heart out.

"I'm sorry," I said.

He shook his head, dropped his arms to his thighs again. "I was gone a long time. I didn't expect you to put your life on hold."

My chin pulled in. "What's that supposed to mean?"

Alec looked as nonchalant as ever. "Exactly what it sounds like. You had to keep going. Take ballet. Volunteer with kids. Make *friends*."

I didn't want to fight. I wanted to talk to him about what Terry Benitez had said about Bobby—about anything related to what had happened three months ago. I'd gone so long holding it in, it felt like it would burst out of me at any second, but I couldn't share it with just anyone. It had to be Alec. He'd been there. He knew what it was like. But he was stonewalling me.

"If you have something to say, just say it." My insides were turning to water.

He looked straight into my eyes, straight through me, as if I was made of glass.

"Are you ashamed of me, Anna?"

It felt like the world was crashing down around us. He'd changed me in so many ways, opened my eyes and my heart, saved my *life*.

"How can you say that?" I said, my voice breaking. I wanted to throw my water cup at him and fall to my knees all at the same time. I wanted to punch him and kiss him and shake the stupid insecurities out of him. Instead, I did the one thing I was good at.

I got up and left.

I made it out the door and onto the sidewalk before I heard the waitress calling for me.

"Ma'am! You didn't pay for your sandwich!"

"Goddammit," I muttered. I flung open my purse and searched blindly inside for my wallet. The tears were already stinging my eyes but I wasn't about to break down on the sidewalk and make even more of a scene.

"I've got it," Alec told the waitress. When I heard his voice, I took off toward the crosswalk. Maybe my client was early. If so, they were about to get a hell of a massage. I had some tension of my own to work out.

"Anna, stop."

It was like he'd thrown an invisible roadblock up right in front of me. My feet slammed on the brakes, leaving me gripping the side of the cigar factory for balance.

Alec's hand on my arm spun me around.

"Don't run away."

I hated it when he said that. I hated more that I gave him a reason to say it.

His grip loosened, and then he shoved his hands into his pockets as if to keep himself from touching me. We parted the people walking by like two stones in a river, but he didn't seem to notice. His dark eyes were set on mine, and he was waiting.

"I told Trevor you were in Seattle because I didn't know what else to say," I confessed. "I couldn't talk to anyone about what happened. My dad was already freaked out, and if Amy knew the full extent of it she'd never let me out of her sight again." I looked up, blinking rapidly to hold back the tears. "I took a job at the gym because I needed the cash, they needed someone who did sports massages, and I couldn't do home visits anymore because . . ." *of Maxim Stein.* "Because I couldn't. I took dance classes to keep busy because I missed you so much I was losing my mind, and I started volunteering as a court-appointed advocate because those kids remind me of you, but they remind me of me, too, and so I'm not sure I can actually go through with it because it's bringing up all this *stuff.*"

My hands were making frantic circles, and he grabbed them and pressed them against his chest. I was breathing so hard I thought I might hyperventilate. Welcome to the worst day of my life. Okay, maybe not the worst, but certainly not the best.

"Everything in my life comes back to you," I said. "And if you think I give a damn about what anyone else thinks, you're wrong."

His eyes, which had been carefully trained on mine, filled with pain. He pulled me close, held me so tightly I could barely breathe.

"I'm sorry," he whispered. "Jesus, Anna. I didn't know."

I reached for his face and kissed him, needing more than just his words, but the confirmation from his body that we were okay. His lips answered with crushing force, taking my forgiveness and striking a match that sent flames licking through my veins. A slight tilt of his head, and his tongue forged into my mouth. I groaned, gripping the back of his neck as his hands tightened around my waist.

"Close your eyes, kids," said a woman nearby, jolting me from the haze.

"Gross," replied a young boy.

Alec stepped back, but the desire was still burning inside of him. I could feel it echoing in my racing heartbeat, my tingling skin, the warmth racing down my limbs.

We were in public. In the middle of the street. It took a second for that to sink in.

He took my hand and led me back to the corner, around the outside of the deli to a metal door. He pushed inside to a stairwell, and the sign that faced us said that the bar upstairs opened at five.

As soon as the door shut, he pushed me back against it and kissed me again. With more privacy, I let go of my inhibitions, scratching my nails through his scalp, moaning as his hungry mouth lowered down my neck. I hiked my knee up his side, and he slid his hand up the inside of my skirt, searing my skin with his touch.

"You were killing me out there," he murmured, releasing my hair from the band so that he could weave his fingers through it. "I don't deserve you."

My own hands rose beneath his shirt, sliding up his hard muscles and traveling around to his back. I felt the puckered scar he'd gotten in the metal shop in prison, and pressed my fingers just inside the winged tips of his shoulder blades. He held his stress there, and at my touch he kissed me again, faster, harder, biting my lower lip with just enough pressure to bring a staggering flash of heat between my legs.

He took my right breast in his hand, over the shirt, rubbing his thumb over my nipple until it strained against the thin white satin of my bra. He lowered his head and nipped at it, and somehow, even through my clothes, the sensation was enough to make me tremble.

I needed his touch. I couldn't wait for it. The door was cold and dirty against my back. I had no doubts it was marking up my white shirt, but I didn't care. Feeling him was more important than breathing.

I grabbed his hand, guided it between my legs. With a tight groan, he cupped my mound, hiking up the rest of my skirt with his other hand. As his fingers traced my slit, I bucked against him. He swallowed my cry, and then hurriedly pushed aside my wet panties so that two fingers could plunge inside. One rub against that deep, hidden place and I lost control of my legs. He pressed me harder against the door, and I gripped the back of his neck for support. I could hear the sounds of him working his fingers inside of me. I could smell my desire heavy in the air. He looked into my eyes, watching. Always watching.

"Put it in," I said. "Hurry."

He undid his pants and his huge cock sprang free. I braced myself against his shoulders, waiting for him to lift me, but he didn't yet. His hand left my body, and he stroked himself with my juices, leaving a thin sheen of my arousal on his skin.

"Oh God," I said. "Why is that so hot?"

"Is this okay?" he asked.

Was he kidding?

"Yes," I said quickly.

He moved closer, pressed aside my panties again and positioned the broad head of his penis at my entrance.

He didn't push in.

"Last night in the shower, you were so fucking beautiful."

I looked up at him, lost in the emotions swirling deep in his eyes.

"I didn't mean to make you feel dirty." He gritted his teeth. His thumb began to circle my clit. But still he didn't give me what I needed.

"Alec . . ."

"You're perfect to me."

My heart clenched, just as the springs deep in my belly coiled tighter.

"I saw it when you touched me. How much you needed to. It was . . . overwhelming."

He slid in an inch and my back arched, my body trying to take more of him.

"It's how I feel every time I'm with you."

Another inch.

"It's how I feel right now."

I began to pant.

"You're never wrong when we're together. You're perfect. Fucking perfect."

He bent his knees and then, in one hard thrust, we were joined. I didn't have time to catch my breath. He hoisted me up, and my legs wrapped around his hips, but only for a second before I climaxed. He rode it out, shafting me slowly, and as deeply as I could take. Then, when he couldn't stand to wait anymore, he let go. He fucked me in an urgent, primal way, spreading me wide for his rigid cock and bouncing me on his hips as he used the door as leverage.

I squeezed my inner muscles and his knees nearly gave way.

"Do it again," he commanded, breathing harshly.

I did, and he groaned, going at me with everything he had. And as the block of hurt I'd been dragging around all day cracked into a thousand pieces, he shuddered hard and started to come, ramming into me over and over until he was finally spent.

Eight

Lucky for me, I had extra clothes in my car. Since I no longer lived down the street, I'd started bringing my gym bag on the nights I went to exercise right after work. After a quick, heads-down dash to the car, I put up the sun visor and changed in the passenger seat. Alec folded himself behind the wheel while I shimmied into a tank top and a little wrap sweater. It didn't exactly go with the pencil skirt; it was a good thing I worked in dim lighting.

"What kind of ballet class is this?" he asked, pulling the spandex yoga shorts out of my gym bag. They didn't leave much to the imagination.

I snatched them away with a smile, and threw them into the backseat.

"It's heavy on the cardio," I said. And when he gave me a suspicious look, I added, "The windows are blacked out so naughty boys like you can't watch."

Unconvinced, no doubt thanks to Trevor, he sifted through the extra pepper spray, pens, and scissors I kept in my center console. Maybe it was a little excessive, but I wasn't about to be caught without something to defend myself with in case I got in trouble again. Without commenting on what he'd found, he asked for my keys.

"You need a car wash. I'll bring it back before your shift's up." He scoffed at my confused look, and tried for the third time to roll the seat back another notch to accommodate his long legs. "Believe me, I'm not taking it for any longer than I have to."

"Don't you have more important things to do than get my car washed?"

"Nothing in the world is more important to me than the cleanliness of your car," he said seriously. "It's all I could think about while I was locked up."

I handed over my keys with a snort. "Well I wouldn't want to disappoint you."

"You couldn't if you tried."

Cue butterflies. They fluttered around my stomach like I'd just chugged a gallon of coffee.

"I get off at eight," I said, suddenly not sure how this went. "If you want me to stop by . . ."

He brought my hand to his lips, and scraped his teeth along my knuckles in a way that made me really contemplate calling in sick for the rest of the day.

"Try something for me."

"What's that?"

"Say, 'I'll be home after eight.'"

He might as well have asked me to the senior prom. My smile stretched a mile wide.

"I'll be home after eight," I said.

The planets were all aligning in my favor it seemed. My after-lunch client was stuck in traffic and twenty minutes late, and Derrick had taken off early for personal business. Everything lagged a little behind, but I hardly minded. My day had done a one-eighty thanks to Alec, and I was looking forward to ripping his clothes off as a thank-you as soon as I got home.

Home. Because that was where we lived. Together. Not his place where I stayed, but our place. Maybe I was overthinking it, maybe— well, probably—we were moving too fast, but I couldn't shake the feeling that for the first time in three months I felt really good.

But that didn't mean I was ready to get rid of my apartment. The most amazing things could end in an instant. The day I'd turned eight years old my birth mother woke up and announced that we were going swimming. I'd never been to a pool before, so she got me a suit, took me to the YMCA, and taught me every-thing from floating to how to do a cannonball off the diving board. She'd called me a "natural" and signed me up for weekly lessons. It was the best birthday I'd ever had.

The next day she OD'd in the parking lot of a fast-food res-taurant.

I wanted things to work out with Alec, but that didn't mean I shouldn't be careful.

While I was cleaning up after my last client, Amy appeared in the doorway of the massage room. She held my key ring on one finger, a wary look in her eyes.

"Alec brought these by for you."

I took them and tucked them in my cleavage so I could keep folding laundry.

"Thanks."

"He's looking . . . fit."

I couldn't help but smirk, despite her concerned tone. Best friends didn't forget things like your boyfriend's affiliation with white-collar criminals and attempted murderers, despite how much you tried to convince them he was a good guy.

"Hot, you mean."

She waved her hand. "If you like that whole action-movie-star-slash-male-model thing."

"Which you don't," I inferred.

She made a noncommittal noise and jumped up to sit on the counter beside the oils while I finished.

"You're here late," I said, changing the subject. "Who's got Paisley?"

"Miss Iris," she said, referring to the elderly black woman in the apartment upstairs. "She has her granddaughter on Thursday nights. Paisley's BFF."

It warmed me to hear Paisley was doing normal kid things. She'd been so quiet after Amy's ex-husband had left.

"What are you guys doing tonight?" Amy examined her nails.

I put down the laundry and leaned beside her on the counter.

"Probably just working out the details for our next bank heist."

"Ha," she said. "You're *so* funny."

I turned to face her and put my hand on her knees. "He's okay, Amy. I'm okay. All that trouble from before is over."

Amy crossed her arms over her flat chest. "He's on parole. He's about to testify in one of the biggest trials in the country. What makes you think your trouble isn't just getting started?"

I took a step back, feeling sharp defensive edges rise up inside of me.

"Thanks for the support."

She tilted her head back and sighed. "I'm not trying to be a bitch. He's crazy about you, you can see it all over his perfect, high-cheekboned, sexy-mouthed face."

"He does have a sexy mouth," I said.

"Some people just can't shake their demons," she continued. "No matter how fast they run. I know, trust me."

"You don't know," I argued. "If you'd just spend some time with him, you'd see."

"Well forgive me if I'm not jumping at the opportunity," she snapped. "I don't need to get hit by a bus to know it hurts."

"What the hell does that mean?"

"It means open your eyes!" She slid to the floor, her anger

buzzing like a live wire. "In the month that you were together, you were lied to, beaten up, kidnapped, and nearly killed. He was only seeing you in the first place because his boss told him to!"

Her words hit me like a punch to the gut. I wanted to laugh at how crazy she sounded, but I couldn't, because everything she was saying was true. All those things had happened. And nothing I could counter with would convince her they wouldn't happen again.

"You don't know him," I said quietly.

"But I know scared when I see it. And I've seen it all over you since he came into the picture."

I turned, and hastily gathered the laundry in my arms.

"That glowy feeling you have right now? They call it the honeymoon phase for a reason," she said as I stalked out of the room. "Don't wait until it's too late to leave."

I wished I had something nasty to toss back at her, but I was so mad I couldn't think straight. Amy had a point—in my short time with Alec I *had* experienced some crazy things—but those weren't all his fault. She was completely missing the other side of it. She didn't know how good he was, or how much he cared about me. She hadn't been there when he pulled Bobby from the car after he'd followed us for miles, wondering if I'd been hurt. She didn't know the way he took care of his father, or how he held me when I woke from a nightmare, or the way he looked at me when we made love. All the reasons I stayed with Alec outweighed what had happened since I met him, but she was too damn shortsighted to see it.

I left the salon feeling like my blood was made of lead. Amy and I had fought before, but this seemed so much worse. I wanted her to be happy for me. I wanted her to like Alec. But I had a feeling neither was going to happen.

My car was parked on the street in front of the salon, not particularly hard to recognize even in the dark due to the bright blue color. It didn't look any cleaner than before; maybe Alec had been busier than he'd anticipated.

Amy had already been gone by the time I'd finished the laundry. Part of me wanted to call her, even if I had nothing to say. Even if all I *could* say was hurtful. Yelling at each other was a hundred times better than silence.

But she'd never been this wrong about something before.

I opened the car door and slumped into the passenger seat. I tossed my purse onto the passenger seat but paused before starting the engine when my eye caught a glint of metal on the center console.

A small license plate—one of the little aluminum souvenirs they sold at gift shops. It said ANNA in turquoise letters. Stuck to the back was a note that said "Happy Birthday," in Alec's handwriting.

And suddenly I was laughing so hard I couldn't breathe.

I called him immediately, sliding my thumb over the flimsy metal.

"Hey," he answered, a smile in his voice.

"You're ridiculous. You know that, right?"

He chuckled. "I've been called worse."

"I love it." *I love you.* "It's just what I always wanted."

"Only the best for you, baby."

He was teasing me, but I liked the tenderness in his voice.

"This almost guarantees that you're going to get laid tonight," I told him.

"Damn," he said. "If I'd known that, I would've stopped there."

I felt my brows pull inward and automatically looked down to the center console where I'd picked up the license plate. I hadn't noticed beneath it was another sticky note. This one said, "Open Me."

I squeezed the plastic handle behind the cupholders and the armrest between the two seats popped open. Where my collection of pens, scissors, and pepper spray had been was a sealed metal box about the size of a bag of an ice cream sandwich. On one side was a green button, currently lit. On the other was a dim red button.

"Alec?" I said. "Why does it look like there's a bomb in my car?"

He adjusted the phone against his cheek. It sounded like he was walking into another room.

"It's a kill switch," he said.

"That doesn't sound much better."

"Start your car."

I turned the key in the ignition and the engine hummed to life. It didn't sound much different than it normally did—like a high-powered sewing machine.

"Now reach below the cupholder. There's a switch, do you feel it?"

I tucked the phone on my shoulder and inched my fingers along the rigid plastic, finally finding the small raised metal knob, hidden to anyone who wasn't looking for it. Curiosity took ahold of me. Sometimes I forgot that Alec had a degree in engineering.

"Yes."

"Hit it."

I did what he said, and the internal lights died, right along with the engine. In the center console, the green light switched to red.

"The car shut off," I told him.

"It stops the flow of electricity to the battery," he said. "If you leave the switch in the off position, you can't turn on the car. If you're already in motion, you can shut it down."

I closed my eyes, leaned forward until my forehead pressed against the steering wheel. If this had been in place before when I'd been taken, things would have turned out differently. It might not have stopped Bobby, but it would have slowed him down, given Alec and the cops a chance to get to me faster.

He cleared his throat. "There's a way to wire it to automatically dial the police but I'll need to order those parts."

Amy had been wrong. This was no honeymoon phase. This was a good man protecting a woman he cared about.

"Anna?"

"Yeah," I said, voice thick. "I'm here."

"My middle name's Thomas," he said. "After my dad."

I took a deep breath.

"Thank you," I said.

"Don't mention it."

He adjusted the phone again, and I longed to touch my fingers to his jaw, and to see the look in his eyes right now.

"I'm at my dad's," he said. "I might be a while longer."

"Okay."

We sat on the phone a minute longer, not saying anything, just being together. There was no way I could tell him how much his work on my car meant to me, but I think he knew. I could hear it in his voice when he finally said good-bye.

Nine

Mike had Thursday nights off, something I'd forgotten until I walked into the lobby juggling two armfuls of groceries and squeezed by his half-asleep backup, a middle-aged Irishman who mostly worked the graveyard shift. I missed Mike immediately—in Alec's absence I'd always felt safer with him standing by the front door. I'd wanted to ask him to join us for dinner sometime. If he was single he would have been a great date for Amy.

Not that *that* was going to happen anytime soon.

I focused my thoughts away from my best friend and onto Alec. I hoped things were going well with his father. Part of me wondered if I should have volunteered to stop by and help. Thomas and I had formed kind of a friendship while Alec had been away—mostly centered around how much we missed him. But I didn't want to intrude if Alec and he were working things out.

When the elevator doors opened, I stepped out into the hallway, searching for my keys in my purse. There were only four apartments on this floor, and as I passed the first two, I saw a woman standing in front of Alec's door.

Her suit was the first thing to catch my eye—it was cream colored, with a knee-length skirt and matching pumps. Not many people could pull off a suit like that, but she had a kick-ass body—the kind that came with good genes not a gym membership. Her dirty blond hair that was swept back in a twist and her makeup was impeccable. She was probably a few years older than me, and looked a hell of a lot more professional than I did in my workout top and dirty skirt ensemble.

"Can I help you?" I asked.

Her head snapped in my direction as if I'd startled her, and the color rose in her cheeks.

"No, thanks," she said. "Sorry. Wrong floor."

With that, she adjusted her purse strap over her shoulder, and hurried past me toward the elevator.

I stared after her, perplexed, and watched her jab the lobby button repeatedly, as if that would somehow get her out of here faster. As the doors closed, our eyes met, and I was gripped by a hot, prickling jealousy. Strange, unwelcome images rose in my mind of her body and Alec's, tangling in the dark. Her slim legs wrapped around his hips. Her nails dragging down his chest. Her blond hair splayed across his pillow.

It seemed entirely likely that this wasn't the wrong floor at all. She'd come here purposefully, and had changed her mind when she'd seen me.

She'd come here to see Alec.

I unlocked the apartment door, shaking off the wave of insecurity. I was just being paranoid. He'd told me before he'd never brought another girl to his home and I believed him. In all my time staying here, no strange women had randomly shown up looking for him.

I locked the dead bolt behind me, set down the grocery bags in the kitchen, and kicked off my shoes, remembering afterward that I wasn't here alone anymore and should probably line them up neatly against the wall. Tossing my purse on the dining room table, I made for the bedroom to change into more comfortable clothes but was stopped by a knock at the front door.

Had the woman changed her mind and come back?

I returned to the entryway and cracked the door, just enough that the chain on the second lock I'd installed caught.

A man wearing a black leather jacket and dark slacks stood in the hallway. He had a perfectly trimmed goatee and short raven-colored hair, clipped so close to the skull that you could see the white scalp peeking through. His eyes were hidden from view by designer sunglasses, and I bit off a sigh of annoyance because only assholes and blind people wore shades indoors. This guy clearly was not blind.

"Can I help you?" I asked for the second time that night.

"I'm looking for Alec Flynn."

"And you are?"

He reached into his back pocket and withdrew his wallet. Inside was an ID badge with his picture that stated he worked for the state in corrections.

"Reznik," he pronounced clearly. "Jack Reznik. Parole officer."

I'd thought that Alec had an appointment to see his parole officer earlier today. It surprised me that he had come to the house, but of course that wasn't unreasonable. When I'd worked in social services, parole and probation officers had dropped in unannounced all the time on my clients' parents to see if they were ditching work or using drugs.

I unhooked the chain and opened the door a little farther, checking the baseball bat out of habit. It was still against the wall, handle side up.

"He's not in right now," I said. "If you leave your number, I'll have him call you."

He removed his sunglasses, and the puckered scar that ran over his right eyelid gave me a little start. On second thought, the shades were a good call.

"You're his girlfriend?" he asked. He squinted a little as his eyes trailed down my body. I shivered and crossed my arms over my chest.

"I am."

He took out a notepad. "Name?"

"Is that necessary?"

He smiled.

"Mind if I take a look around?" It wasn't a question. "Need to see his living space."

He stepped through the threshold, bumping into me as he walked by.

"I do mind, actually," I said, my pulse rising.

He stuck his head into the kitchen, then walked to the dining room. When he replaced the notepad in his back pocket I caught a glimpse of the gun in the back of his waistband. This didn't sit right; he should have had a holster, like a police officer.

Unless he had a concealed carry permit. But why would he need that if he worked for the department of corrections? He wouldn't be undercover.

"Nice place," he commented.

"He's not here, I told you." Subtly, I reached for my keys on the dining room table, and held the Mace tight in my fist.

Reznik turned toward me, brows lifted. "You're uncomfortable."

"You're goddamn right, I'm uncomfortable."

He smiled, a smooth twist of his mouth that made me take a step back.

"That was not my intent," he said.

He retreated to the door.

"You'll tell him I stopped by?"

"Do you have a card?"

Reznik gave me the once-over one more time, then reached into his pocket and removed his wallet. I took the card he handed over without looking at it. I wasn't willing to take my eyes off of him for a second.

With that he stalked toward the elevators, leaving me staring at his back. He was definitely the creepiest parole officer I'd ever met, but that didn't mean he wasn't legit. For the last three months I'd admittedly been more suspicious than before. Trusting, which had always come hard for me, was proving even more difficult, something that I hoped would settle down in time.

Only then did I look down at the business card. It wasn't a parole officer's card; there was no state seal or professional emblem. It gave the information for a sushi restaurant called Raw that was north of the 275. I knew the place—I'd passed it on my way to Alec's father's apartment, but had never stopped there because it looked so shady.

It could have been a mistake, but I doubted it. Something about him was off, given Alec's past history, I wasn't sure my suspicions were entirely out of the question.

Back in the dining room, my cell phone buzzed. Still rattled and now decently annoyed, I went to find it, searching through my purse until I found the glowing screen. The caller ID said THIS IS YOUR FATHER—PICK UP, something he'd proudly programmed in himself a few visits ago.

"Hi Dad," I said, catching him on the last buzz.

"Answer faster," he said. "I was just getting ready to catch the next flight to Tampa."

He was only kind of kidding. Always protective, he'd become a flat-out worrywart since the whole kidnapping thing. I supposed that was his right, seeing as I was his only daughter.

"Geez," I said. "Give me at least seven seconds to answer next time."

"Don't push it," he said. "I'll give you what I give you."

I smirked, dropped the card in the basket I'd brought for mail, and went to change into my comfy clothes.

"What's up?" I asked, trying to even my voice so as not to concern him any more than he already was.

"I don't know, you tell me." Those words, in that tone, were enough to send me back to age sixteen, when Amy and I were two hours late for curfew, reeking of booze and the orange tic tacs we'd binged on to try to cover it up.

"Should I sit down?" I asked. "This sounds serious."

"I got a call this afternoon," he said. "From Alec Flynn."

My chest clenched at the way he chewed on Alec's name. "Oh yeah?"

"Oh yeah," he said, and I could practically see him giving me that withering detective look.

"What did he say?"

"What you should have," he said with a huff. "That he's back in town, and he's . . ." He trailed off.

"And he's what, Dad?" My heart leapt, and before I could catch myself, I had a glimpse of white dresses and rings. My knees buckled and I sat down hard on the bed. The image vacated a moment later, and in its place was uncertainty. When I was little I'd dreamed about getting married, but then I'd grown up, and dated people, and realized how totally dysfunctional I was when it came to relationships. Marriage wasn't exactly in the cards for people like me.

"He's going to take care of you," my dad said a little too articulately. "He apologized for what happened and said I shouldn't worry because he's not going to let you get hurt again."

My whole body warmed. That was more like it. Why would Alec have called my dad for any other reason? Me and my crazy imagination.

"That's . . . nice," I said, choosing my words carefully. "And yet something tells me it didn't go over too well."

"Anna," he sighed. "Your mom and me only ever wanted you happy."

It hurt to hear him say that like she was still alive. Like she hadn't been ripped from him—from both of us—when the cancer had taken her.

"Alec makes me happy," I said.

"Alec Flynn almost got you killed."

I groaned. "Did Amy call you, too? Because I just got the same speech from her about an hour ago."

"She didn't, but you should listen to her. I always liked Amy. She's a smart one."

"Because she agrees with you."

"Well, you know what they say about great minds."

I slumped. "I'm tired of defending him to the people who should be happy for me."

"There's a reason you're defending him," he said sternly. "It's because he did something wrong. It's because he just got out of prison. It's because his friend busted your face up . . ."

"Not his friend," I said. "Bobby was *not* his friend." The anger was just under the surface, ready to rip through. "We've gone over this a hundred times since it happened. Every time you've come down to visit."

"And I'm still waiting for it to sink in."

"You know, I realize you and Mom did everything perfectly, but it's not that way for everyone."

"Anna . . ."

"I have to go," I said, hating that I was now fighting with two of the most important people in my life. I hung up the phone and shoved it across the table. It slid to the end, and then hit the floor with a clunk.

I wasn't being stupid. Being with Alec was the most important thing I'd ever done. This was my life, and my choice, and if my dad and Amy really loved me, they'd support me.

I just had to keep telling myself that until I believed it.

Ten

I dreamed of water. A slow drip in the darkness that turned to a trickle, and then, like a pipe under pressure, a more persistent spray. My eyes adjusted slowly to the gray-green haze, then to the car's dashboard in front of me. The passenger-side window cracked, and my panic broke loose. I fought, but to no avail; I was bound to the seat, unable to break free. The car was underwater, and sinking fast. The light was fading again. I looked left, but the woman in the driver seat—the woman with red hair—stared at me with dead eyes.

I jolted awake, the scream caught in my throat. Sitting up, I gasped for air, shoving off the bindings on my arms and legs that still lingered in my imagination. My hearing was sharp, my eyes already focused. I was lying on the couch in the living room— the leather stuck to my damp skin as I moved.

I wasn't alone.

Someone was moving through the hallway toward the living room, deliberately taking soft steps to keep quiet. I gripped the wooden spoon I'd fallen asleep holding. Not the ideal weapon for defense, but I was too far away from the door to grab the bat.

It's Alec, I told myself.

But Alec would have turned on the lights. This was his home.

Fingers tightening around the wooden handle, I rose as quietly as I could, keeping to the shadows. My heart was pounding, memories of Bobby too close to the surface.

He was closer than I'd anticipated, and when my arm rose automatically to strike, he took a quick step back.

"Whoa," said Alec. "I surrender."

I dropped my arm as he maneuvered the large cardboard box he'd been holding to one arm and flipped on the living room light. My eyes blinked as they adjusted to the sudden brightness. He was still wearing the same jeans and white T-shirt I'd seen him in earlier, but he looked exhausted.

"What is that? A spoon?" he asked.

"Why are you sneaking around?" I snapped.

Stupid question. He lived here. He could army crawl from room to room if he wanted.

He tilted his head slightly. "I didn't want to wake you."

My breath came out in a hard huff. He carried the box into the living room and set it on the dining room table. I glanced at the clock on the wall behind him. It was after ten. Whatever he'd been doing, it had taken a long time.

"Sorry. Weird dream." I tried to walk past him to return the spoon to the kitchen, too jittery to hold still, especially when he was looking at me like I still might hit him. He reached for my forearm, squeezing tighter when I paused.

"Anna, you're shaking." His voice had lowered, and his shoulders tensed, like he was prepared to kill whoever had scared me. The power inside of him was as moving as it was frightening.

I took a steadying breath, giving in to the heat that traveled up my arm from his touch. He eased me closer, until his arms were around me, and I shuddered as the last bit of the nightmare was chased away. I rested my cheek against his chest and listened to his heart, strong and steady as it pulled me back to calm.

"What was your dream about?" he asked.

I tensed, struggling to find the words.

"Something I need to get over." My fears were irrelevant. Bobby was in jail for a long time, and I was no longer in danger. Now I just needed my subconscious to figure that out.

His arms tightened so quickly I gasped. He seemed as surprised at this as I was, and released his hold.

It occurred to me that we were both avoiding the herd of elephants in the room. Bobby. Maxim Stein. My abduction. The trial. How did you start to talk about things so big, so necessary, when so much time had already passed?

I took a step back, putting more space between us.

"It was just a dream," I said, before he could ask any more. It was late, and we were together after three months apart. We should have been enjoying the time we had, not focusing on what had nearly killed us.

But even telling myself that felt like a lie. We'd have to talk about things at some point, I just didn't want to do it right now.

He nodded reluctantly. "All right."

I thought of what Amy had said about the honeymoon phase— the glowy feeling. Was reality already tarnishing it? Because I felt the strain now between us, just as I'd felt it when we'd been with Trevor at the restaurant earlier. The attraction between Alec and I was undeniable, but there had to be more to make a relationship work. Even I knew that. But I didn't know how to fill the gaps.

And if I couldn't fill in the gaps, he was going to slip right through them.

"You cooked?" He looked at my shirt, and then over my shoulder into the kitchen, where two pots and a glass dish were covered on the stove. After the call with my dad, I'd been on a tear. Homemade red sauce, meatballs, sautéed spinach, and garlic bread.

Alec's expression was caught somewhere between desperation and awe. I thought he might fall to his knees and worship me.

"It certainly looks that way."

His brows drew together.

"Why?"

I tucked my hair behind my ears. "I like to eat when I'm hungry. I assumed we were similar in that way."

He stared at me. "You made me dinner."

I didn't know why this seemed to baffle him so much.

"You're not listening," I said. "I made *me* dinner. You can join me if you want."

I hadn't done the noodles yet, and as I went to turn on the stovetop to boil water, I noticed that my shirt was streaked with tomato paste and splattered with oil. I wasn't exactly a sexy cooker. Take away the kitchen and I easily could have been arrested as a murder suspect.

"I was with my dad," he said. "It took longer than I thought. I'm sorry. I should have called. This . . ." He motioned to the kitchen. "I didn't expect this."

I snorted. "I think I'd have to slap you if you did."

He shook his head, smiling in a sweet, embarrassed kind of way. Obviously he wasn't used to someone taking care of him— not that I was particularly used to taking care of someone either. Still, I would have been lying if I said I didn't like how thrown off he was by the gesture.

I wondered what kind of state Alec's father had been in. They certainly had a lot to talk about, and none of it would go very well if Thomas wasn't sober.

Alec peeked into a foil-covered glass pan of meatballs. Inhaling slowly, he closed his eyes in bliss.

"How did you do all this?"

"Magic." I couldn't help but smirk. "Surprise. I'm a witch."

"That explains a lot."

I went to smack him with a dishrag, but he swept me up in his arms and gave me a dizzying kiss. The kind that erased nightmares, and made everything okay again.

"Hi," he said.

I rubbed the tip of my nose against his. "Hi. How's your dad?"

He leaned back, and I was sorry to be the cause of the lines that formed between his brows.

"Fine. Hungover. He asked about you. A lot."

"He misses me," I said, trying to lighten the mood. "I don't blame him."

He opened one cabinet. Then another. I pointed to the opposite side, above the dishwasher, where I'd moved the plates. It felt strange knowing more about his home than he did. He didn't seem to be annoyed, but I wondered if that bothered him.

"He kept asking if I'd scared you off yet."

Alec was facing the other way, but his voice had hardened a little. I wrapped my arms around his waist, noting the way he still flexed for just a fraction of a moment before he could relax, as if the gesture was a surprise.

"Looks like I'm still here."

He didn't respond.

We finished preparing dinner together. There was something comforting in the way we moved around each other. He didn't ask me what he could do, he just did. I didn't tell him what would help, I just handed him a spoon and he began to serve. He touched me often—his hand on my lower back as he passed by, his shoulder brushing against mine as we stood beside each other. He tucked my hair behind my ear when it got in my eyes and rolled up my sleeve when I reached across him. In those moments it was so easy being around him, I couldn't believe we hadn't known each other our whole lives.

We moved to the table, and he set the cardboard box he'd brought in earlier on the floor. On the outside, *Alec Flynn— Storage* was scratched in permanent marker.

I nibbled the garlic bread, worrying about both of our fathers and the impact they had on our lives.

"I know you called my dad today," I said. "You didn't have to do that."

He paused mid-bite.

"Actually I did," he said, avoiding my gaze.

"What did he say to you?"

A sad smile pulled at his mouth. "Nothing I didn't already know."

I twisted my spaghetti around my fork. Untwisted it. I could only imagine what words my father had chosen. *You're not good enough. Be a man and walk away.*

"I'm sorry."

Alec leaned back in his seat and sighed. "Does it bother you that your family doesn't like me?"

He was including Amy in with my father, a fact that both showed how much he knew me, and depressed me at the same time.

"They just don't understand," I said. "They will."

"And if they don't?" His gaze locked on mine, and I could feel the hurt inside of him. It made me want to take on the world in his defense, something no one ever did and that he never asked for. Things were supposed to be easier now that we were together, not harder, but here I was, torn in half by my love for him and the people who had known me longest.

"It doesn't matter," I said.

"It should."

The garlic bread was in ten pieces on my plate. He was right, of course, but that didn't fix anything.

"Hey," he said, reaching for my hand. "Tell me about these kids you volunteer with."

Some of the pressure in the room diffused with the change in topic.

"Just one kid," I said, and as he traced my knuckles with his thumb I told him about Jacob, and how hard it would be to face him again if I couldn't get him the placement with his sister.

"You're not letting him down," said Alec after I'd finished. "You listened to him. That's probably more than anyone else has done."

"But listening doesn't change anything," I said.

He shook his head. "It changes everything." He looked over

my shoulder, his thoughts drifting. "I fucked up for years before someone saw some potential in me. Just knowing he did was enough to straighten me out."

I squeezed his hand, touched, but saddened, too, because that person who had believed in Alec—Maxim Stein—hadn't really seen potential. He'd seen the opportunity for a scapegoat.

"Even if you walk away now, you changed that kid's life," Alec said.

I flushed with pride

"I'm not walking away." I made up my mind right then that I wouldn't. I was going to do everything I could to make sure Jacob had a fair shot in this world. It was what my father had done for me, what Max had only pretended to do for Alec.

Alec smiled. "I got a job, by the way."

"What?" I dropped his hand. "Why didn't you lead with that?"

I hopped onto his lap, and the chair rocked back. He caught it before we tumbled to the floor, his grin widening. Closer, I traced my fingers along the contours of his face, feeling the roughness on his jaw contrast with his smooth lips.

"What is it?" I asked. "How did you get something so quickly?"

"Don't get too excited," he warned. "I know a guy who set me up unloading freight at one of the shipping yards. It's nothing big, but it's work."

It wasn't nothing. Alec had a record that now included a stint in prison and an association with white-collar crime. Since he was a teenager, his work had consisted of things he couldn't mention on a resume. Getting a job—any job—was a big deal.

"Well I'm excited," I said. "We should celebrate."

I wiggled my hips suggestively on his lap, and his fingers tightened around my waist. Instantly, I could feel him start to grow hard against my thigh. I bit my lip, and ran my fingers through his hair.

He kissed me slowly, fingers rising up my back beneath my shirt. I arched into him, ever responsive to even the smallest touch. He slowed before things got too heated, and held my face in his hands. There were questions in his eyes. I didn't know what they were, but I wasn't sure I wanted to answer them all the same.

I focused over his shoulder.

"What's in the box?" I asked, reading the words again: *Alec Flynn—Storage.*

This distracted him. He followed my gaze, then turned back to me.

"Handcuffs." His lips, feather-soft, trailed down the side of my neck.

"Is that right?" A shimmer of excitement raced through me. With the exception of the vibrator, something I'd only ever used solo, I'd never played with any sexy toys before.

"They're real handcuffs," he said, chuckling. "They don't have fur lining or anything. But if you were interested, I might be able to get some . . ."

I scooted off his lap and moved around his chair, lifting the box onto the table. At his nod of consent, I pulled back the flaps. He was right, there were handcuffs on top of worn steel-toed boots, a few file folders, a black utility belt, and a pair of work gloves.

"Is this for your new job?" I asked.

"Some of it. Some of it I used working for Max," he said, a note of regret in his voice.

I pulled out the handcuffs. They were cold, heavy, and didn't look particularly comfortable, but beneath them was a coil of nylon rope. I held it up by one finger, erotic images of being tied to the bedposts flashing through my mind.

He cocked a brow, leaning his hip against the counter.

"Want to play, baby?" he asked in a low voice that felt like a velvet finger stroking over my sex.

I did want to play. This was exactly what we needed—we connected physically in a way that was stronger than words, and right now I was done thinking about family, and work, and all the things outside of this apartment.

I tossed him the rope and walked slowly from the room.

Eleven

In the hallway I removed my shirt and let it fall to the floor.

As I passed the couch I shimmied out of my shorts and kicked them up on the armrest.

I could hear the floor creak behind me as I crossed the threshold into the bedroom, feel the heat rise to my skin as his gaze roamed over my back and down my bare legs. I was wearing cotton panties and a matching bra with a little cherry pattern on the white fabric. I hoped he liked cherries.

I didn't turn on the light as I crawled on the bed. I took my time, glancing over my shoulder at him standing in the doorway. The expression on his face was enough to scramble my senses. It was so raw, so filled with need. It made my breath hitch, my chest constrict. I could hear my heart pounding in my eardrums, a slow, primal beat that began to quicken, and echo deep in my core.

Even then I felt it. We were walking a line, driving too close to the darkness I'd banished to the back of my mind. My very soul was quaking, unsure as he approached with the rope in his hand, but the desire was impossible to retract. I needed him to take me to the edge, wherever that was. I needed him to go there with me.

He didn't take off his clothes, but even fully dressed he was breathtaking. With the moonlight coming through the window I could see the flexing muscles of his forearms. He never hid his desire from me, it was there straining against the fly of his jeans as his free hand slid over it. The urge to claim him rose up fast; I needed to touch him, take him inside me. Make him mine.

He moved closer, like a hunter stalking his prey. I turned, sliding down onto my back, and he leaned over me, one finger drawing a line up the inside of my calf to my inner thigh, and then higher. My legs fell open for him, as if modesty was a completely foreign concept.

I gasped as he pushed aside the fabric, and dipped into my wet cleft.

"Is this what you want?" he murmured.

Eyes closed tightly, I nodded, unable to process anything but the slow, easy way his finger fucked me. I tried to hold still, but my hips began to thrust up against his hand.

"I've wanted you like this," he said. "Laid out for me. Unable to make the pleasure stop."

His words intensified his touch, until I was fisting the comforter to prevent myself from pulling him down over me. The anticipation of what he might do sent a dark thrill quaking through my core.

His finger pulled out slowly, and I pinched my thighs together, hating the emptiness he'd left.

When I opened my eyes he was unraveling the rope. He looped it around the bed frame, then reached for my right wrist. His touch was gentle, but a sudden bolt of nerves made my stomach clench.

"I'm going to make you feel good, Anna," he promised. "For a long time. And when you think it's over, I'm going to start again. Are you all right with that?"

I turned my head to the side, the fire already raging inside of me. I feared this exquisite torture as much as I longed for it. I knew what he could do to me without tools—more pleasure seemed impossible. And yet knowing he wanted this, that he'd fantasized about this, made me all the more eager. I wanted to please him. I wanted to rock his fucking world.

"I need the word, baby."

"Yes," I said.

The rope wound around my right wrist, not too tightly, but with enough pressure that I wouldn't be able to shake free. My anxiety rose another notch. He rounded the bed and reached for my left hand. He was good at this. Practiced.

"Have you done this before?" I asked.

He smiled. "I've thought a lot about it."

The rope fastened around my left wrist.

My heart began to pound harder.

"Don't we need a safe word or something?"

He paused, then sat beside me on the bed.

"Sure," he said. "How about 'no'?" He ran his fingers down my cheek.

I bent my knees, twisted my hips to lie on my side, but my bound arm prevented me from rolling all the way.

"Safe words are for heavy stuff," he said, leaning down over me. "We're just going to play. And if you ever want to stop, just say so. We don't need a special word for that."

I nodded. "Okay."

He kissed my lips gently, sweetly, and soon I forgot all about the rope. I gasped as his hands slipped down my sides, and then as his mouth lowered to my collarbone, making a hot, wet line down my cleavage.

One hand slipped between my legs and I jumped at the contact, instantly reminded of the bindings. I wanted to reach for him, run my hands through his hair and over his shoulders, but I couldn't.

I couldn't move.

I pulled harder at the ropes and they tightened.

The cords dug into my flesh. My hands began to tingle. The panic that had begun as a slow drip now flooded through me. It made my head pound, my heart hammer.

I was in the car—my old car—and my wrists were bound together by bungee cords.

I was on the bed, Alec's tongue tracing my ribs.

Bobby was here, driving fast, talking fast. He was going to kill me. I needed to get away. I needed to fight.

I jerked hard against the ropes.

"Anna?"

I strained against them.

"Anna, stop," Alec's voice filtered through the darkness, through the buzzing in my eardrums. My blood pumped hard through my body. *Fight,* it said. *Get away.*

I kicked out, the comforter gathering under my back.

I was at home, with Alec. Safe. But I didn't feel safe.

"I can't," I said, with barely enough breath to form the words. "Get it off. Get it *off*!"

"I'm trying," he said between his teeth. "You need to stop struggling. You're pulling the knots too tight."

"Let me go!" The tears burned my eyes. I dug my heels into the mattress, arching back. I heard him, his words made sense, but I couldn't comply. My body was taking different orders, fueled by adrenaline.

"Please," I begged him, yanking my arms down, trying desperately to free myself. My shoulder popped, shooting pain through my chest. "No. I'm saying *no*. That's what you said."

"Goddammit!" Alec's knee was suddenly across my body. His weight crushed me, bringing the panic to a head. "Anna, listen to me. I'm untying the rope, but I can't get your hands free unless you relax your arms."

The fear was ripe in his voice and scared me even more.

"Can you count with me, sweetheart?" he asked. "Count to ten. One, two, three . . ."

I blinked, staring up at the white ceiling. How many nights had I stared up at it while I'd lain in this bed alone, counting the days until he came back?

"F-four," I stammered. "Five."

My right arm was free but he still didn't move. My wrist throbbed, the hot blood rushing back into my fingers. There wasn't enough air in the room. My lungs were crushed under his knee anyway.

He counted with me. "Six. Seven. Eight. Nine."

My left hand was free. He rolled to the side.

I didn't look at him. I jolted off the bed, ran into the bathroom, and slammed the door. I locked it immediately, sliding down the wood. I squeezed my knees against my chest.

Oh God, what have I done?

I'd lost it. I was crazy. I'd ruined things with the one person who I needed to get me through this.

I grabbed the towel hanging from the rack overhead, and pulled it over my face. I screamed silently, trying to rid myself of the terror, of my shame, of the fear I'd heard in Alec's voice. My body shivered like I would never be warm again. I cried until the tears were gone.

He knocked and said my name over and over. He apologized ten different ways. After a while he stopped. Then it was quiet, and I knew he'd left.

Twelve

Time passed slowly, and with it, my strength returned.
My pride did not.

I rose from the floor, and examined myself in the mirror. One bra strap had loosened in my struggle and hung off my shoulder. My wrists were bright red, like they'd been after Bobby had taken me. My chest hurt like someone had punched a hole through it.

My birth mother used to say I made her crazy. I left a mess, I made her crazy. I broke a glass, I made her crazy. I looked at her the wrong way, and I made her crazy. For years I walked around thinking I was cursed. That something was wrong with me. I drove good people straight to the bottle. Or the pills, or the needle, or whatever else she could get her hands on.

She'd had it wrong. She'd made *me* crazy. Bobby had just brought it all out.

I gathered all my hair products and makeup and put them in the toiletries bag I kept under the sink. I wrapped the cord of the blow-dryer around the handle and stuck it on top of the rest. Knowing I couldn't hide in the bathroom forever, I unlocked the door and poked my head into the bedroom. The lights were still off, and the comforter was rumpled, but the rope that had been slung from the bed frame was gone.

As was Alec.

I walked to the dresser, to my drawer filled with clothes and put on baggy sweatpants and a tank top. I tied my hair back into a ponytail, and then gathered some of my things in my gym bag. It was time I went back to my apartment.

Alec was in the living room. He surprised me; he'd been so quiet I thought he'd left.

For a moment we just stared at each other. He looked like he'd just taken a beating, and yet still had enough fight to be mad about it. Though his body showed no wounds, his pain was clear in his hunched posture and the tight lines around his eyes. He rubbed at his heart absently, and I mirrored the expression with my free hand.

"You're leaving," he said.

I nodded.

He shook his head, turned to face the window, as if all the answers lied somewhere in the Bay.

When he turned back, the regret in his gaze made my throat grow tight.

"I'm sorry," he said. "I wasn't thinking."

"Don't apologize," I told him, gripping the bag's handles. Why couldn't I move? We needed space. What had happened was too big, and it was obvious that neither of us knew what to do about it.

"I'm sorry I didn't ask you what happened," he continued. "I should have before I went away. I should have a dozen different times since I got back. Every time I thought about him putting his hands on you I hated myself more for not killing him."

I set my bag down, but only so I could wipe away the tears that were burning my eyes. The weight of his words made me tremble. He would have done anything to protect me.

"It's not your fault," I said.

"Leaving you to handle it alone, that's my fault," he said.

I shook my head. Forced myself to take a deep breath.

"Can you tell me now?" he asked. But his fists were flexing, and his jaw was working back and forth, and I knew as much as it would relieve me, it would kill him to hear the details of what Bobby had done.

"No," I said.

His chin rose, and he moved a step closer. It wasn't until then that I realized he'd pushed back the couch, leaving a large space open in the living room.

"Can you show me?"

"What . . ." I swallowed. "What do you mean?"

"Show me how you fought him."

I tried to laugh, but he wasn't laughing. This wasn't a joke to him in the slightest.

"Fight you, you mean?" I asked. This was twisted. Alec was not Bobby. I did not want to imagine their roles being reversed.

"Yes."

"No," I said. But the set look on his face as he drew closer made me wonder if he needed his hearing checked. I forced myself not to back away as he came within arm's reach. If he touched me now, I would crumble.

"He hit you. I remember the mark on your face." When he raised the back of his hand to skim lightly over my cheek, I jerked away.

The fury came on with shocking force, too fast to rein in.

"So you're going to hit me?" I pushed him back hard. "Try it. See what happens to you."

He exhaled with a shudder, then brought his right arm back. I couldn't believe it. Alec wouldn't hit me. He'd rather die.

He flinched, and in that instant instinct took over and I smacked his arm down, stepping around him to avoid the blow—not that there was actually any power behind it.

"Is this some kind of sick joke?" I asked, as he raised his hand again. This time he didn't just flinch, he followed through, adding a little more muscle. I pushed him away easily.

"What's wrong with you?" I could feel the tears sliding down my face and I hurriedly brushed them away with the back of my hand.

"Say *stop*," he said, eyes cold as steel. "Tell me to stop."

Tell him? Or tell Bobby? I didn't know who he was pretending to be, but I didn't like it.

We'd moved to the center of the room, rotating in a slow, watchful circle. My eyes darted from his hands to his face, looking for any sign of attack. This time when he lifted his arm to strike, I sidestepped and blocked him hard. Momentum carried him past. Any chance for him to grab me was eliminated.

"Was that supposed to be fast?" He rocked back and his open hand shot out so quickly I nearly missed the block. My breath came out in one hard whoosh as I dodged to the side and again let his weight carry him past me.

It pissed me off that he'd gotten so close, and when he came at me again, I pushed him down hard. He fell to one knee and I shoved him with both arms. He didn't fall; instead he swiped my ankles and I fell back hard on my butt.

My blood pumped like it was liquid fire. I'd never been so enraged.

He rose, and offered me his hand.

"Get up."

I slapped it out of the way and stood on my own. This time when he went to hit me he paused, grabbed my hand, and forced it into a fist.

"Like a hammer," he said.

I jerked away. "I know. I took six years of self-defense."

My dad had made me start after he'd adopted me. But Alec was right. I hadn't been using the proper technique. It made me even madder that I'd forgotten in the heat of the moment.

He matched my hard gaze. "You want to stop, say so."

I didn't say anything.

He swung his open hand toward my face and I sliced down hard with a hammer fist, this time hearing him grunt as I connected with his forearm. I shoved him through the motion, as I'd done before, and his knee hit the carpet with a thud.

Victory surged through me. I glared at him, breathing hard.

"Got you that time."

He looked up at me, forehead damp with perspiration. I was sweating, too. I hadn't even realized it. The neck of my tank top was stained dark gray from the exertion.

He rose, nearly a foot taller than me and brutally strong, and I was reminded why the first rule of self-defense was to run.

But I didn't run, because as angry as I was, as much as I hated him in that moment, Alec Flynn didn't scare me.

We did it twice more, and the last I hit him so hard, he hissed in a breath and gripped his elbow. I didn't ask if he was all right. Adrenaline was blending with something else, something darker. I wanted to inflict pain, and he wasn't just letting me, he was welcoming it.

"How'd he get you in the car?" he asked, shaking it off.

I hesitated.

"You remember," he said. "Show me."

I looked away, dug my chin into my shoulder. Of course I remembered. I could still feel it every time I closed my eyes.

"Knocked me out. Choke hold from behind."

He spun me around, and locked his forearm around my throat before I could take another breath. Again, I reacted, pulling my chin down, scratching at his wrist.

Just like I'd done with Bobby.

And just like with Bobby, I failed.

Alec placed no pressure on my neck, and when he saw me struggle he instructed me to use a heel strike to the knee. I followed his orders, but I couldn't balance enough to put any power into it. He was so tall, and every inch he lifted brought me higher on my toes.

"Use your weight," he said.

I struggled. Because of my size, this position was always the hardest for me to break free from.

"I can't."

"You can," he growled.

In one fluid motion, I dropped my hips back and slammed my heel into his shin. His grip loosened for only a second, and in it, I tucked my chin under his arm, giving myself enough room to breathe. He dropped his arm.

"You let me go," I said.

He narrowed his eyes, hands on his hips. I backed into him, ready for him to take me again. Somehow this twisted game had changed. I wanted to beat him. I needed to beat him.

I needed to do what I hadn't been able to do with Bobby.

Alec's arm slipped around my throat.

"Grab my elbow," he said.

"I know."

"Then do it." His tone was harsh, and I responded with an elbow to his ribs. He swore through clenched teeth.

I grabbed his elbow, tucked my chin, and dropped my weight. This forced him to lean forward, and when he did, I twisted my body, placing my leg behind his. I turned my head, slipped through his hold.

"Knee strike," he said.

In all my training, I'd never heard that.

"Where?"

He tapped the back of his knee. "Take me down and I can't follow you."

I did as he said and he fell forward.

"Good."

He rose, breathing hard. His shirt was stretched from our fighting. He crossed his arms and pulled it over his head, revealing a perfect, bronzed six-pack that made my body burn in an entirely different way.

He moved behind me, and I could feel the heat from his chest more acutely. His damp skin was slippery against my shoulder blades, hot as it rubbed the strip of my back exposed by the tank top that rode up my ribs. His cock, heavy, and growing thick, rested against the top of my ass. His warm breath in my hair had me pressing back against him. I could almost feel him bending me forward, sliding down my sweatpants, and burying every inch of his enormous length inside of me.

I craved that relief.

But I couldn't submit. Not yet.

He inhaled slowly. His arm loosened slightly. And in that moment I ripped through his hold and shoved him down on all fours.

"Jesus," he muttered.

We did it twice more all out, and on the last time I crouched, and then collapsed against the sofa. My lungs burned like I'd just sprinted a mile. My shirt stuck to my skin with sweat. A tangled mess of hair spilled from my ponytail.

"Enough," I gasped.

He sank to the floor, wiping the sweat from his brow on the back of his wrist. With each breath his muscles flexed, making me more aware of my own body, and how my lungs expanded with each gulp of air. I didn't understand how things had changed so quickly—fear, then fury, now something deeper and more powerful. He left me off balance, and yet somehow grounded at the same time.

"Why?" I asked.

His gaze held mine, though his shoulders bowed with guilt.

"Because you needed to win," he said. "Christ, I don't know. Because I needed to see you win."

I *had* won. I'd done everything I had with Bobby, but this time I'd changed the outcome. Maybe it was just in Alec's living room, and maybe I wasn't really in danger, but I felt stronger than I had in months.

"You're tough as fucking nails," he said.

My breathing slowly evened out, but my heart pounded harder. We were a foot away, too far to accidently touch, too close to not be aware of each other's every move.

"How did you know all that?" I asked.

He bent his knees, resting his elbows on them. His bare feet stuck out from beneath the bottom of his jeans.

"Mike teaches women's self-defense at the YMCA on Thursday nights. He's probably still there." He glanced over my shoulder at the clock in the kitchen. "I used to help him out sometimes."

I felt a surge of affection for Mike. I hadn't known he did that. It made me like him even more.

Alec bit into the pad of his thumb, watching me carefully. I pictured him standing in a gym, surrounded by women. Pictured him taking hit after hit in the name of empowerment. How could I not have fallen in love with him?

I inched closer. "I meant, how did you know that would work?"

"I didn't." He hesitated. "Some people talk with words. Some people don't. Sometimes you don't. It was a risk I probably shouldn't have taken."

He was right; sometimes I couldn't talk. Sometimes I needed to run, or fuck, or fight. It felt strangely comforting to have someone know me better than I knew myself.

"I'm glad you did," I said.

"I never would have really hit you."

"I know."

I crawled across the space between us, slowly, tentatively drawing closer until I was kneeling between his legs and our lips were a breath away. He'd grown as still as a statue, the only sign of unsteadiness in his eyes.

"I'm not scared of you," I said.

I kissed him lightly and he barely moved. Again, and this time he seemed to melt, just a tiny give. His fingers curled into the carpet. A small noise came from the back of his throat as his eyes drifted closed. My hands found his jaw, and my touch was gentle. No more fists, no more fighting.

He whispered my name like a prayer.

Then he let go.

He was on his knees, dragging me against his hard body. His arms were so tight around my ribs I couldn't inhale. His fingers dug into my back like a strong wind was trying to pull me away. And he kissed me.

He kissed me like it was the last time he ever would.

Like it was the last time any man would ever kiss a woman.

He poured such passion into that kiss that I wept, so moved by his physical declaration that I couldn't imagine another person feeling more necessary than I did right then. Desperate to feel his skin on mine, I tore my tank top over my head, taking my bra with it, and shuddered as he pulled me close again. My heart was swelling, pounding against his chest, and his responded, strong and true.

"I want to try again," I murmured.

He drew back, swallowed. Stared into my eyes for confirmation. Then he stood, and picked me up in his arms and carried me into the bedroom.

Thirteen

Alec laid me on the bed, kissing me in a long, tender way that pulled at my heart.

"Don't move," he whispered. He disappeared into the shadows and I rose to my elbows, brows creased in concern when I realized he'd gone into the closet. Surely he wasn't there to get the rope. When I'd said I wanted to try again I'd meant I needed him, not that I was ready to be tied up so soon.

He returned with two silk neckties—things I'd seen him wear when we first met. A lump formed in my throat as he sat on the edge of the bed, holding them in his fist.

"Alec, I don't want to ruin any more of your fantasies tonight."

His thumb whispered across my cheekbone.

"You didn't ruin anything," he said. "I don't have a fantasy where you're afraid."

His words eased my mind but not my body; I still shivered when the tip of one of the neckties tickled my belly.

"Stay with me a little longer," he said. "I swear, I won't hurt you."

I nodded, knowing that he didn't mean physically, but mentally. Still anxious, I laid back down.

"I did this wrong before." His voice was soft and low, and wrapped around me like a warm blanket. "Let me try to fix it. If it's too intense, just say the word."

I considered this. "Okay."

The silk slid up my shoulders and neck.

"I should have asked for your trust first," he said.

My nipples pebbled as the tie passed lightly over them. They became so tight they were almost painful.

"You have it," I said.

He trailed the material up the side of my cheek, and then slowly covered my eyes. As he reached behind my head to tie it, his lips found mine, and he kissed me for a long time, until the nerves scattered, and left in their place was something more demanding.

He drew back.

"I should have told you that I'll bring you back from any-where I take you. I won't leave you, and I won't let you go."

I gasped as he lifted my left wrist. He massaged the tender skin at the base of my palm, then kissed it. His tongue flicked over the red marks and I jerked, hypersensitive to his caress.

Let me try to fix this, he'd said. It hurt my heart that he felt he needed to, but what had happened between us in the living room had changed me, and I would have been lying if I said I didn't want to replace what had initiated it.

I concentrated on my breath, but was unable to feel Bobby's restraints binding me as the tie slipped around my forearm. I waited for him to lift my wrist over my head to fasten it to the bed frame, but he did not. As I felt through the darkness, I found that he'd tied the other side to his own arm, the knot loose enough to turn or slip free if necessary.

His fingers wove through mine, feeling their way over the pads of my fingers. When our hands clasped, I shuddered, feeling somehow more joined to him than I did with him inside me.

"Alec," I whispered. My senses were more acute with the wrap around my eyes. I could hear every compression in the mattress as he moved, feel the heat of his body as he adjusted his position to sit beside me. Desire throbbed low in my belly. I became desperate to know where he would touch me next.

"I should have told you I love you, Anna," he murmured. "Because I do. I love you so much it fucking hurts."

I stilled.

"I can feel you inside me." He moved our clasped hands over his heart, squeezing tightly. "When you're in pain, I can't breathe. And when you're scared, I want to kill the man who did it, even if that's me."

What he said slayed me. I wanted to take off the blindfold, see his eyes, but I didn't need to. The truth was right there in his touch.

"Forgive me," he said.

I couldn't speak, my throat was so tight. Instead I nodded, and he rested his forehead on my shoulder. He kissed my chest, right above my heart. And then my shoulder, and then higher— at the base of my neck.

I siphoned in a quick breath. The softest touch there was enough to ignite my senses.

"Is this okay?" he whispered.

"Yes."

He lightly pressed his lips just behind my ear and it felt like lightning zapping straight into my core. My back bowed, and my free hand squeezed the comforter.

He shifted positions, and his tongue swirled just below my collarbone, then drew a straight, wet line between my breasts. The peaks were tight, aching, and I turned my shoulders, trying to urge him to kiss there next.

He chuckled softly.

"Right here?" He blew on one nipple, and I arched, desperate for more contact. The cool air did nothing to ease the heat rising inside of me. I began to pant, turning feverish as he held back what I needed.

Feather-soft, his closed lips brushed a tightened tip, a brief whisper only. I quaked beneath him. My back dropped down hard enough to make the mattress bounce.

"What are you doing?" I asked.

He moved our joined hands, twisting his wrist so that my palm rested against the back of his hand. With our fingers overlapped, he drew a slow circle around my other breast. I pressed down, urging him to touch me more firmly, but he withheld.

"Watching you," he said.

My cheeks flushed. "Do you like that?"

He guided our hands lower, and switched positions again, so that his hand was behind mine. When we reached his jeans, he pressed my hand over his erection and my pulse quickened. I wanted to touch his bareness, wrap my fingers around his thick length. I wanted to stroke him until he couldn't take any more, and then guide him inside me so I could feel him lose control.

He groaned as I reached for the button at the top of his fly.

"Not yet," he said tightly. "Just let me touch you for a while."

What happened next was like nothing I'd ever experienced. He felt me, every inch of me. With his lips. His tongue. His fingertips, and sometimes mine. Each kiss took me higher, drew me tighter. Time ceased to exist. All thoughts vanished. There was only my body, trembling from the inside out, throbbing with a need so powerful tears soaked the blindfold to my temples.

He knew my body better than I did, and his attention to it was as reverent as it was meticulous. His tongue made a slow arc from my ribs to the rise of my pelvis. His teeth scraped the tender skin beneath my belly button. He eased my sweatpants and panties down over my thighs, blowing lightly over the top of my slit. Just when I thought he'd go lower, he turned me carefully, pulling our joined hands across my body, so that I was laying facedown with my forehead resting against my elbow.

The fingers of his free hand traced a line down the nape of my neck, between my shoulder blades. His thumb brushed over the small of my back, and then to the seam of my ass. He reached lower, and as I squeezed my thighs together I was sure he could hear the desire pooling there. A shattered groan broke free and I turned my face into the pillow.

"Don't hide from me," he said firmly, and when his fingertips traced the bottom of my buttocks, I cried out hoarsely. I was too sensitive there. His touch shocked my entire body. My hands fisted, my toes curled. When his fingers drew close to the center he pulled away and turned me on my side.

I lost control of myself then. I struggled, trying to touch him, kiss him. I reached for his pants, angry that they were still on. I couldn't do this anymore. I needed him to take me.

He pinned my free hand over my head. The other was locked in his grasp.

"I have to feel you inside," he said, breathing roughly.

My consent was a staggered moan. I'd been cresting the wave for too long. The hunger was consuming, greedy, and I was unable to keep it contained.

He lay close beside me, and lowered our bound hands down the center of my body. He'd switched our positioning again, so that my hand was beneath his, and when we reached between my thighs, the moisture made us both slippery.

"Feel what I do to you," he said, pressing my fingers into my folds. "How much you need to come."

My arm stretched as he pushed one of my fingers, with one of his, inside of me. It was different than when I touched myself. A million times more erotic. Our fingers twisted around each other as I followed his rhythm, in and out, twisting, *feeling*, as he'd said. I was soft and slick and hot, and I understood, for the first time, why he loved to put his cock inside me.

Then he shifted the pressure on my wrist against my clit, and I came hard.

I gasped for breath as the waves pelted me over and over again. Bolts of pleasure raging through my spasming muscles, across my belly, straight to my nipples and back again.

Somehow he'd twisted our hands, and I gripped his wrist while he gripped mine. He tossed one of my legs over his shoulder, dragging his tongue over the back of my knee while I bucked my hips. The teasing stopped there. With a growl of pleasure, he buried his mouth in my pussy and ate me. His tongue grazed over my swollen lips, then dove inside, a shallow, mind-blowing fucking that had me arching off the bed.

I shouted his name. He held me down with his other arm, pinning my thighs open wide. When his shoulders were wedged between, his mouth rose to my clit, swirled around the sensitive bud, and then lashed at it over and over again.

I was still coming.

His fingers plunged inside of me, spearing deep, ramming hard. His wrist rotated. Wet with my juices, his thumb reached lower, rimming that last unclaimed piece of me, and though my heels dug into the mattress and I pushed away, he kept at it. It was too much. Too good. He slowly pushed inside. Deeper, as I shuddered with a dark, forbidden pleasure. And then his fingers were fucking my cunt as his thumb fucked my ass.

I couldn't stop coming.

He withdrew all at once, leaving me empty for as long as it took to shove off my blindfold, rip open his fly, and shove his pants over his hips.

"Look what you do to me," he muttered. His eyes were dilated, his face a pained grimace. Every muscle in his body was straining. A sheen of sweat covered his brow and chest, as if we'd already been fucking for hours. He didn't enter me; he rubbed his huge cock over my cleft. He thrust again and again, the underside of his engorged head grazing my clit. Then he pinned my hands over my head and, with a shout of ecstasy, exploded, spurting jets of hot semen over my belly.

I screamed one last time, and then fell limp on the bed, our hands so tightly locked my fingers were numb.

Fourteen

Alec was gone when I woke up, but there was a baby blue silk
necktie on the pillow next to mine, and that made me smile.
I wrapped it around my wrist while I got ready, a constant reminder of what had happened last night. When it was time to
leave, I decided to go retro and tied it in a casual knot over my
white, button-up blouse. That way it would be like he was touching me all day long.

Though I should have shown up earlier to prepare for my 10:00
a.m. appointment, I breezed in at the last minute, telling myself it
was because of traffic, not because I was avoiding my best friend.

Amy didn't care one way or the other. She was lying in wait in
the laundry room, where I needed to get the supplies for my first
massage. When I rushed in, she shoved the door closed behind
me and blocked the way with her tiny, furious pixie stance. Amy
was always a model for edgy fashion, and her choice for today
was an outrageous black fur vest with a leather skirt. Knee-high
zebra patterned socks offset her red patent flats.

"So that's why PETA was picketing outside the salon," I said,
grabbing clean sheets for the massage table.

She tugged down the bottom of the vest, and though I didn't look directly at her, I could feel her glare.

"It's faux."

"I thought that was a Vietnamese soup." I reached for the towels, and shoved them in the warmer. Every client was given a warm towel for the back of their neck while I did the foot scrub. It helped them relax.

"That's *pho*," she said. "And since we're going there, the nineties called. They want their tie back."

I snorted despite myself, and after one silent, strained moment, she reached for the tie and loosened the knot, fixing it in a way that was no longer retro, but like I'd just stolen it from a hot man I'd left behind in bed.

Realizing there was no way out but through her, I sighed, and faced the music.

And then wished I could beat myself over the head with a broom because she was crying. Actual, honest-to-God tears. My chest seized up. I hadn't seen her cry since we were in high school and her brother had died overseas.

"Stop being mad at me *right now*," she demanded. "I hate it. I ate a half gallon of ice cream last night all by myself and then fell asleep in the middle of *Magic Mike*, which I'm pretty sure is illegal in like, nineteen countries."

I bit my lip to keep from laughing, and threw my arms around her.

"Was it good ice cream at least?" I asked.

"It was both delicious and expensive," she said. "And I wasted it on you when it was dedicated to a really lousy future boyfriend."

I let her go, and leaned against the door beside her. I didn't care if I was a little late. Things weren't right in the universe while Amy and I were out of sorts.

"I'm sorry for being a total bitch about your sex-god convict," she said, resting her head on my shoulder. "I pick the wrong guys, and so I like to forget the right guys are out there."

"Stop," I said. "First of all, he's an *ex*-con."

She hiccupped a laugh.

"Second, you weren't a *total* bitch. I'm lucky to have someone who worries about me. I'm sorry, too."

I reached for her hand and gave it a squeeze. Now I just had to clean things up with my dad and life would be back to normal.

"The right guy is out there." I hesitated, thinking about what she'd just said. "You don't pick the wrong guys on purpose do you?"

"Of course not." She frowned. "Maybe. Why?"

I was reluctant to bring it up, especially since we'd just gotten over a fight, but the way she was chewing her thumbnail pushed me to go there.

"You haven't had more than three dates with anyone since Danny."

She crossed herself at the mention of her ex-husband.

"Bad luck," she said.

"You sure you don't look for relationships that fail?"

"Why the hell would I do that?" She said it in a way that made my heart hurt, like it was a question she'd already tried to figure out. Not for the first time, I wondered if Danny had really messed her up when he'd abandoned her with Paisley. She'd never shed tears over him, but sometimes the deepest wounds were the ones you locked away.

"Because you're afraid of getting hurt," I offered. "Or so you don't have to break Paisley's heart if she gets attached." I rubbed the silk tie between my fingers. "Maybe because you don't think you deserve something good."

"Well that's not true," she scoffed. "I ate a half gallon of twelve dollar, peanut butter potato chip ice cream last night."

"Geeze," I said. "You sure you're not pregnant?"

"It has a chocolate base," she said, as if this explained everything. Which it sort of did.

She shrugged. "I actually did meet a guy yesterday."

"You did?"

"Yeah. He was checking out apartments at my complex. He's cute. And he seems . . . different."

"Uh-oh," I said. The warmer dinged, and I opened the microwave-sized door to fan out the towels. "Different how?"

"Nice," she said. "Into me. Not all aloof and meatheady."

"Well that's a good place to start."

"We're going out for lunch tomorrow. If things go well I might even spring for a babysitter next time." She returned to chewing her thumbnail. "I was thinking you and Alec should come over this weekend for a barbeque. We could all . . . talk."

Her doubt was obvious, but nevertheless I appreciated the gesture. I wanted her to get to know Alec better. She wouldn't be able to keep herself from liking him once they spent five minutes together.

"I'd love that," I said.

"Maybe I'll invite Jonathan, too. That way it'll be completely awkward, instead of just sort of awkward."

I smirked as she laughed at herself. It wasn't true of course; she'd never bring home a guy she barely knew to meet her daughter.

"I've got to go play masseuse." I used my most soothing, bordering-on-porno-mistress voice.

"What are you doing for lunch? We should get sushi."

"Shit."

Her words triggered my memory. I don't know how I'd completely forgotten to tell Alec about the visit from his "parole officer"—the jerk who'd barged in and left a card for a sushi restaurant.

"What is it?" Amy asked.

I rushed out of the room. "Nothing. Just remembered something. Got to go get my ten o'clock."

I raced into the break room, grabbed my phone, and texted Alec: Parole officer looking for you. Hoping that he'd get to the bottom of this, I relaxed my shoulders, summoned my calm, and went out to retrieve my client.

Amy was only scheduled for the morning, and since I had made myself late, I ended up snatching only a few pieces of take-out sushi from the break room before my two o'clock. Alec hadn't texted me back. I assumed this was because he was working his new job at the shipping yard, but it still made me nervous. Before picking up my client, I texted him again, in hopes that this would somehow help him get the message.

My cell phone buzzed moments later, but it wasn't Alec, it was a voice mail from Wayne, Jacob's caseworker. He must have called while I was grabbing my lunch.

"Hi there, Ms. Rossi, it's Wayne from the department of family services. Listen, I know it's last-minute, but I got you a slot with Jacob's judge today at four forty-five. You've only got ten minutes of her time, but it's our best shot at getting Jacob placed with his sister. Hope to see you then."

I tapped the phone against my chin. My last client was at 3:30 p.m. Even if I rushed, there was no way I was going to make that window. I had to see if someone would cover for me—after talking with Alec last night, I was even more resolved to find Jacob and his sister a good, stable home.

I checked my client list, but several of them had flip-flopped earlier during the day due to cancellations and rescheduling. Derrick was off, and the girl who worked the front desk had gone home for the day, so I didn't even know who my last client was.

It was a total cluster fuck.

I saw my one o'clock, and then my two fifteen, and had still not found a suitable replacement. I was just about to bite the bullet and leave "sick" when I caught sight of my three thirty in the waiting room.

Trevor was holding a men's magazine, but his eyes were set on the salon side of the building as I approached. In tailored gray pants and an oxford shirt he should have looked more relaxed, but his heel was beating a fast rhythm against the floor.

Memories of our last encounter in the deli came on fast as I approached. I bit the inside of my cheek, remembering the way he'd tried to treat Alec like a third wheel, and then kissed me on the cheek before leaving.

"What are you doing here?" I asked, hearing the edge in my own voice. He knew I worked here—we'd talked about it on more than one occasion—but I'd only ever seen Trevor for sessions at the gym, and either way his appointment wasn't supposed to be until tomorrow. My hand went automatically to the tie, and the smooth feel sent a spike of heat through my center. Immediately, I released it. That was a response I saved for Alec, no one else.

He looked up, as if surprised that I was standing there.

"Anna, hey." He stood, and set the magazine down. "Since you can't do lunch tomorrow anyway, I thought I'd grab an earlier session this afternoon. Your receptionist said you had a cancellation."

There he was, being all nice and friendly. No sign of the testosterone that had reared its ugly head yesterday with Alec.

"Well actually, I was going to try to reschedule this hour," I told him.

He looked like a sad puppy dog. That I'd just kicked.

"Because of what happened at the restaurant," he surmised. "That was out of line. I can explain."

He glanced again at the salon side, where four stylists were working their magic.

"Do you need a haircut or something?" I asked bluntly, crossing my arms over my chest.

"No." He looked back at me. "Sorry, thought I recognized someone. What was I saying?"

My brows lifted. "You were explaining."

"Right." He raked his fingers through his neat, blond hair. "I like you. And I don't want you to get hurt. And I guess I was still thinking that maybe he'd upset you and that's what was wrong . . . I don't know. I get defensive over people I care about."

My arms fell. The mad melted in a puddle at my feet. But I still didn't want him thinking he could just bat his long, dark eyelashes and get his way.

"That doesn't mean you can be an ass to my boyfriend."

He held up his arms in surrender. "I know. I told you it was out of line."

"And I told you, I was upset about my volunteering gig, which actually is the reason I was hoping to cancel this appointment." I pulled him off to the side, and quietly explained that I had a chance to meet the judge and make a case for Jacob's placement.

"Sounds like you better go," Trevor said when I was finished.

I gave him a careful once-over. His jaw was perfectly smooth, as if he'd just shaved before he'd come, and his blond hair was perfectly styled. If Alec hadn't been in my life, I might have seriously considered rolling in the sheets with him.

"You're a good friend, you know that?" I said.

He waved me off.

"*Please*," he said. "You're making me blush."

He was kidding, and I laughed, but there was a twitch in the muscles around his eyes that made me wonder if there wasn't more than friendliness to his "I like you" comment.

He said he'd call the gym to reschedule, and after watching him walk out the front door I went to the break room to get my things, and then hurried across town to the courthouse.

Less than two hours later I was running through the hallway of the courthouse after a very pissed-off ten-year-old boy. I dodged in and out of the people contesting speeding tickets and traffic fines, but still wasn't quick enough to catch him. Before he passed the elevators, a security guard blocked his way, and the chase ended abruptly.

"Thanks," I told the officer.

"This is bullshit!" Jacob spun to face me. His black hair was recently trimmed, and he'd been given new hand-me-down clothes and shoes. The foster-care special.

"You think I don't know that?" I asked.

I motioned him off to the side and reluctantly he followed.

"You said Sammy could come stay with me."

I waited until he threw himself down on the wooden bench before I sat beside him. I massaged one throbbing temple with my thumb.

"I said I would talk to the judge about it."

He swung his legs angrily. "And she said I can go to another house if I run away."

I groaned. I could have strangled that judge. She hadn't told him to run away. She'd told me, in front of him, that he didn't show evidence of being a flight risk, as I'd claimed, and that if he *was* she would consider another placement. For the meantime, both Jacob and his sister were safe, fed, and had a roof over their heads. There was no need to make special accommodations when so many other children were in more critical situations.

Translation: The state doesn't have the money to move kids to a private home, one that accepts boys with explosive tempers, and girls who've been abused.

Translation to a ten-year-old: Run away and you can live with your sister.

"Don't run away," I said. A chill crept down my spine. My own mother had used those same words the day she'd died. "If you feel like you need to, call me. You still have my number, right?"

He didn't answer. I hoped that meant yes.

"What the judge meant is that if you run away, they'll move you to a place where you can't run away again, do you get what I'm saying?"

He kicked his skinny legs harder.

"Jacob?" I prompted.

"Jail, you mean," he said. "With my dad." The way he paled at the mention of his father made me want to bring the kid home with me.

"Not jail," I said. "Just a different kind of home."

"Bullshit," he said again.

"You like that word, don't you?"

"It's *jail*," he insisted. "I'm not stupid, you know."

I tried to focus on the positive, for his sake.

"Hey, it's not all bad," I said. "You get to see Sammy more often. Every day after school. You get to eat dinner with her if you want. You just have to sleep at different houses."

He stared at the floor. "She needs me."

What he wasn't saying was just as clear as if he'd spoken the words out loud. If someone hurt his sister as their father had, Jacob wouldn't be there to protect her.

"Let me try to fix this," I said, strengthened by Alec's words from last night. If he could do it, maybe I could, too. "I'm not giving up."

"Whatever."

"Until then," I continued, "you've got to be strong, all right? Sammy's going to be scared if she sees you scared." I'd seen her in the courtroom—six years old and eyes as round as saucers. They had the same heart-shaped face and skinny build, but her skin was a couple of shades lighter than Jacob's. It made it easier to see the bruises on her arms and neck that hadn't yet faded.

"Can you do that?" I asked. "She's waiting to see you now in the kids' room."

It took a while, but he finally pushed off the bench and plodded down the hall the way we'd come. He didn't say another word to me, not even good-bye.

Fifteen

Dusk was just turning to dark as I stormed into the lobby of our apartment building. I didn't have to look far for Alec; he was at the security desk with Mike. They were laughing about something, and the low, happy sound of his voice chipped away some of the ice left from my time at the courthouse.

When Alec saw me, he stilled. The laughter died on his lips as his gaze roamed lower, to the tie that hung loosely around my neck. The warmth in his dark eyes was immediately replaced by hunger, and for a few beats of my heart I could do nothing but concentrate on my own breathing.

His work pants showed both the swell of muscles in his thighs and the long length of his legs, and the gray thermal, scrunched up to the elbows and perfectly fitted over his tight abdomen, made him look more like a male model than someone doing manual labor. My gaze fixed on his collar, and I had the sudden urge to pull down the neck of his shirt, and lick that sexy little V at the base of his throat.

"Anna!" Mike closed the distance between us, an obvious attempt to reach me before Alec. Not that Alec was making any move to approach. He was only staring, and waiting, like a lion preparing to pounce.

"Hey Mike," I said, mouth dry as my fingertips ran absently down the length of the tie to where it ended, just below my belly button. Alec's gaze followed my hand, and my pulse sped up another notch as his thumb began to tap against his thigh.

I would have him. Soon. How I had survived without him for three months seemed impossible. He was as crucial as water and I was getting thirstier by the second.

Mike reached for my hand, bringing it to his lips.

"I wouldn't," Alec warned him in a low voice that made my stomach quiver.

His friend paused, the back of my hand just inches away from the broad smile that broke across his handsome face. He had perfect teeth, I noticed. Bright white and straight, like he could have been in a commercial for toothpaste.

In one smooth motion, Mike turned to face Alec, who was looking dangerously possessive, and tucked my hand in the crook of his elbow. Clearly, he wasn't intimidated.

"So you didn't tell him." With a sigh, Mike's gaze rose to Alec's. "Look, man, you were gone a long time. A woman like this has needs."

I elbowed him in the ribs. "What's that supposed to mean, *a woman like this*?"

Mike gave me a suggestive look that traveled down to my toes and back up. For one second, one flash of a moment, I wondered what it would feel like to be pressed between these two beautiful men. Alec facing me, his tongue in my mouth and his cock in my cunt, while Mike fondled my breasts from behind. I could almost feel the heat from his flawless dark skin as he rocked against my ass.

Maybe it was longer than a second.

"I'm well aware of her needs," Alec said, stalking closer.

I choked, and tried to hide it in a cough.

"Then you should know that someone had to keep her satis-fied," Mike said.

"I kept myself plenty satisfied just thinking about Alec," I told him.

Mike's mouth fell slack. I smirked. Alec chuckled softly.

"You did?" Mike asked weakly.

I cupped one hand around my mouth and whispered, "It's be-cause he's got such a huge co—"

"Bye, Mike," Alec said, pulling me toward him. His fingers wove through mine as he led me toward the elevator.

"Sure," Mike called after us. "No problem. I'll just sit down here all by my sexy self. Think about ice-cold showers. And celery. And those nasty eyes on old potatoes."

"Poor guy," I said as we entered the elevator.

"How big are we talking?" yelled Mike as the doors closed.

As soon as we were alone, Alec lowered his face to mine and kissed me. His lips were strong and demanding and I yielded, allowing him to take the lead. Hand wrapping around the tie, he pulled me closer, but before we could get too carried away, his mouth softened, and slowed, leaving me off balance while my heart raced onward.

"You have to take this off," he said gruffly. He pulled the tie over my head and stuffed it into his pocket.

My cheeks began to glow. "You don't like it?"

"*Fuck,*" he muttered. "All I can think about is you riding my cock wearing nothing else."

I smiled, and walked my fingers up his chest.

"Is that a problem?"

He glanced at the red glowing numbers above the door. We'd only just passed the twentieth floor, and he lived on the thirty-fifth.

"Something's wrong," he said. "I saw it on your face when you walked in."

Deflated, I slouched against the railing, feeling guilty for letting Jacob slide from my focus so quickly. Not that there was anything I could do about it right now.

"Let's talk about it later," I said. "I'd much rather ride your cock wearing nothing but that tie first."

He grimaced. "You're making this difficult."

"What?"

"I . . ." The elevator dinged and we stepped into the empty hallway. "I want you to tell me things. However you can."

I felt a little embarrassed then, because I knew he was referring to last night, which was wonderful in the end, but only after some really ugly moments—moments that were a result of us avoiding certain conversations.

"That's fair," I said.

As we entered the apartment and got settled, I explained to him what had happened with the judge—how I felt Jacob's risk of running was increasing the longer I couldn't secure a placement with his sister.

Alec listened closely, a scowl fixed on his face. It made me feel a little bit better that he was genuinely upset on my behalf.

"And there's nothing you can do?" he asked.

"Not until a new placement opens up," I said. "I asked his caseworker to move him to a high priority list, but I doubt anything will come of it. The system continues to thrive on its brokenness."

We were in the kitchen, and he lifted me by the waist and set me on the countertop. His fingertips drew circles on the backs of my calves, distracting me from everything but the heat shooting up my legs.

"Good to hear that not much has changed," Alec said cynically. "Things could be worse, you know."

Jacob could still be in his father's care. Or he could be strapped with the prospect of losing his home and being forced to sell drugs, like Alec had.

"I know." I kicked my heel against the cabinet below, but

stopped myself when I realized Jacob had been doing the same the last time I'd seen him.

At least foster care was temporary. Soon we would know if Jacob's parents had lost custody, and if so, we would look at pre-adoptive homes. It would be hard to place two children instead of one, but I would make sure the adoptive families took my concerns into consideration. Jacob and his sister deserved a second chance, just as I had been given.

"I need to call my dad real quick," I said.

Alec's brows lifted. "Sure."

He pushed off my knees and left the kitchen, giving me privacy. Quickly, I pulled my cell phone from my purse, and hit the second speed dial number. My dad picked up on the first ring.

"Anna? You all right?" The worry in his tone made my insides twist.

"I'm fine, Dad." I took a deep breath. "I love you. I just wanted to tell you that."

He sighed.

"I love you, too, honey. Anna . . ." He hesitated. "Things with me and your mom, they weren't perfect."

I rubbed my thumb between my eyebrows. I wished I could take back the last thing I'd told him on the phone. Even if it was true, I'd said it out of spite.

"You always seemed so happy," I said.

"Things were tough in the beginning." There was a clicking noise on his end, like he was tapping something against a table. "Someday maybe I'll tell you about it."

This surprised me; my dad had always been an open book. When I'd come to him, I'd been so full of secrets, I didn't know what I could say and what I couldn't. He'd made it easy: anything and everything was open for discussion. But now I wondered if there was something he'd been hiding.

He didn't ask about Alec, and I didn't offer anything. But as the seconds ticked by I could sense we were both thinking about him.

"I'm volunteering for CASA," I blurted. My dad knew the program—he'd worked with them when he'd been a detective. "I've got this kid who's in bad shape, and I'm trying to petition for a new placement but the judge has tied my hands."

Another hesitation.

"Well, you could always do what I did," he said.

I laughed, feeling the tension in my chest ease some. "What? Adopt him?"

"It worked out all right for me."

I smiled. "I've got to go."

"Sure. Mug and I want to get back to our movie anyway." The mention of his Great Dane—the biggest lapdog in the world—made me feel both better and worse. I loved that he wasn't alone, but I wished he had someone who would talk back to him.

"I'm proud of you, Anna."

"Thanks, Dad."

Alec returned to the kitchen as I hung up. He'd taken off the thermal and was wearing a tight undershirt that gave a full view of his muscular shoulders. Hard lines defined his triceps, which flexed as he reached for a glass in one of the high cabinets. My mouth instantly began to water.

"Do you want kids?" he asked. Casual. Calm. Not even looking at me. He must have overheard my conversation with my father.

"*Now?*"

He smirked. "How's your dad?"

"Do *you* want kids?" I asked as he filled his glass with water from the sink.

"Sure," he said. "Some of my own. Some adopted, maybe. We'll see."

"You want to adopt."

His face became serious. "Only the ones who had it really rough."

"Well, that's all of them," I said quietly. Adoption wasn't something most people were comfortable with. They wanted to look down and see their own reflection, and I didn't blame them. But that left a lot of us all alone.

His face cracked into a smile again. "Then we'll have to get a bigger place."

"How many are we talking, here?"

He took a sip. "Twelve. Thirteen. What sounds good to you?"

I sputtered a laugh. He was kidding. He didn't really want twelve kids. But the thought of having any kid with Alec, especially one who was adopted like me, brought on a warm and fuzzy kind of panic. I never talked about things so far in the future, not even with Amy.

"You know what you need?" Alec said, looking amused.

"What's that?"

He turned to the refrigerator and opened the freezer door, where eight different variations of vanilla ice cream beckoned to me from the shelves.

"Sex," he said.

"That looks like ice cream."

He grinned over his shoulder at me. "It looks like foreplay."

I giggled. "*That's* why it's shelved next to the condoms. It's all making sense now."

He removed a carton of French vanilla. "Spoon?"

I spread my legs and pointed down. He set the ice cream beside me on the counter and gently set my legs even wider, rubbing his thumbs over the insides of my knees. There was no hiding my response to his touch; even if I'd tried to play coy he would have felt my body tense.

He reached between and opened the drawer.

Removing one silver spoon, he slid the drawer closed and eased between my thighs. I reached for his shirt, knuckles against his rigid abs.

He opened the ice cream, scooped out a spoonful, and fed it to me, letting the frosty metal linger on my lips. I closed my eyes. The cold contrasted with the heat of his body between my thighs.

It occurred to me somewhere in the back of my mind that my day had been filled with polarity, and that he was somehow tying it all together.

His lips pressed against mine softly. His tongue prodded my mouth open, and soon I tasted Alec and vanilla. Fire and ice. I groaned, my senses coming alive as his fingertips wove through my hair.

With one hand lowering down my back he took his first bite, and then with the cold cream in his mouth kissed my neck. His lips were still scalding, but his tongue was cool enough to make me shiver. My arms snaked around his shoulders, just as my ankles latched around his hips, and I inched closer, forgetting everything but the way he made me feel.

He took another bite, then pulled my shirt over my head.

"You taste so good," he murmured, sliding my bra strap off my shoulder. "Sweet and spicy."

He pushed down the cups of my bra, my breasts spilling free into his warm hands. His mouth made a slow line down, and the cold on his tongue made me gasp as he swirled it around one hard nipple. I would end up a sticky mess, but I didn't care. I grabbed his short hair in my fists, holding him close while he moved to the other side. He knew just how to touch me—just the right pressure to drive me insane.

"Put the tie back on," he murmured, pushing me back onto my elbows. My stomach flexed as he retrieved the blue silk from his pocket, and kissed the sensitive place just over my rib cage that made it hard to focus.

I placed it over my head while he reached beneath my pencil skirt and inched my panties down my legs. Everywhere his fingertips touched burned, but the silk felt heavy and cool. He watched me carefully, gaze lingering over my breasts. My nipples ached, skin alighting with goose bumps under his scrutiny. The clarity in his eyes, the raw need, infused me with excitement.

He was going to take me right here on the countertop.

Carefully, he rotated his wrists, winding the sides of my pant-ies around his fingers. I heard a seam pop. Then another. The taut fabric tightened around my thighs. Knowing he could rip them excited me. Knowing he was taking his time made me crazy.

Another seam popped. Growing impatient, I reached for his belt, but he leaned just out of reach, still holding my legs in place by the twisted fabric.

"That's not fair," I said.

"Who said it was going to be fair?"

I tilted my head back, groaning as the fabric started to rip. A long, strained sound of relief that made my thighs quiver in an-ticipation. I tried again to reach for him, but was denied. He was going to make me suffer.

"You're breaking the rules," I said. "What you're doing to me isn't even legal."

"So take it up with my parole officer."

His words reached through my cloudy brain, grasping a memory from the previous night.

"W-wait," I stammered.

He froze.

I debated telling him to forget it, but this was important, and chances were in an hour I wouldn't be able to remember my own name.

"Did you get my message?"

He blinked. Twice.

"About your parole officer," I prompted. The heat began to dissipate between us, despite the still-obvious bulge in his pants.

"Oh," he said, frowning. "Yeah. I got it. He said there must have been a misunderstanding. He didn't call you." He returned to kissing my neck.

I sat up.

"Goddammit. I *knew* it," I said.

He straightened, lines forming between his brows. "Knew what?"

"This guy came by last night while you were out. I got distracted and forgot to tell you."

Last night had been filled with distractions.

Alec's brows flattened. "My parole officer came by this apartment."

"No. I mean, maybe." I was starting to feel the air-conditioning now. I covered my breasts with my hands. "He didn't seem very parole officer-ish. Barged right in, looked around. I had to tell him to leave."

Alec considered this with a scowl, his fingers still hooked on the sides of my panties. My unease grew, and I felt a strong urge to fill the silence.

"He had an ID. Jack something . . ." I smoothed down my skirt. "Jack Reznik, that's it. I asked him to leave his number, but he left some card to a sushi place."

Alec had turned as still as a statue. His bronze skin paled, and a possessive fury settled on his features.

"Pack a bag," he said. "We're leaving."

Sixteen

Ten minutes later I was back in the lobby of the apartment building, a duffle bag with all my clothes and whatever toiletries I could fit sitting on the floor at my feet. Alec wouldn't tell me what was going on, but from the urgency in his movements, I could tell it was serious.

He was talking to Mike in low tones, and I inched closer to hear what they were saying.

"Who let him through?" Alec demanded.

"Last night . . ." Mike shuffled through the book. "Rich Murphy was working the desk. He had the log book . . ." Mike reached for a heavy journal with a list of names. Guests had to sign in when they came here. The high security was one of the perks of living in such a swanky place.

"Damn." Mike's head fell forward.

I glanced over the desk and saw that the page he'd opened to was completely blank.

"I'll talk to him," said Mike.

"I want to see the security footage," said Alec. The edge in his voice made my spine zip straight.

"Easy." Mike raised his hands. "You're not the boss anymore. I've got to get clearance for that kind of thing."

Alec had once managed some of Maxim Stein's properties, but since the trial, and Alec's incarceration, the duties had been handed over to a law firm.

"What's going on?" I asked, nerves making my voice higher than normal. "Who was that guy?"

Alec flinched, but didn't respond.

"Tell me," I demanded.

He turned, and the energy coursing through him was enough to make me step back. He watched my response, and inhaled slowly.

"I want to see the security footage," he said again.

Mike stood, and though he was built, he was still several inches shorter than Alec. His gaze was sharp as daggers though, and I was suddenly grateful for the desk between them. It seemed hard to believe that just an hour ago we were all laughing together in this same spot.

"Don't pull that crap with me," spat Mike. "In case you forgot, I'm one of the few people left who've still got your back."

Alec returned his glare.

"He was alone in my apartment with her," he said.

Mike swore and turned away. I put a tentative hand on Alec's back, feeling the anger running hot enough to burn my hand.

"Alec," I said, unable to hide the worry in my voice.

He took a slow breath, then threw the bag over his shoulder.

"Come on."

Ten minutes later we were in his Jeep, plotting a course toward the west side of town. I'd relayed the entire conversation with Reznik to Alec, and though he seemed relieved that I hadn't given the man who'd called himself a parole officer my name, he still insisted that we rent a hotel room, just to be safe.

He stared straight forward into the night, fingers thrumming against the steering wheel.

"Are you going to tell me what's going on, or do I get to guess?" I finally asked, and when he didn't answer, I added, "You promised no more lies."

He inhaled slowly.

"Remember when I told you I did things for Max that I'm not proud of?"

I sat a little straighter, fearing where this was heading more than I had just seconds before.

"I remember."

"There were men Max would call to do things even I wouldn't do. Things I didn't always know about."

I let these words sink in, remembering the scar on Reznik's eye, and the way I'd felt like I needed to take a shower after he'd left. He had a Bobby creep factor, minus the Neanderthal vibe. If Bobby was a hammer, Reznik was a Colt .45.

"He's a hit man," I said with a shudder.

"He's bad fucking news," Alec answered. "He and his boys hang out at the sushi place. He wants me to go there."

Cold dread squeezed around my chest.

"You're not going there."

Alec shook his head. "No."

"What does he want?"

"Fuck if I know."

But as he adjusted his position in his seat, I felt like he did have some idea, he just didn't want to tell me. I picked at my fingernails, fearful that if what Alec was saying was true, I might be on Reznik's radar now, as well. He could have hurt me when he'd come to the apartment last night. He could have killed me if he'd been so inclined.

"How did Maxim get to him? Aren't his phones tapped?" His whole house was surrounded by police and reporters.

"I guess he found a way." The sarcasm didn't escape me.

"We should call the police."

"No," Alec said adamantly. "He's not someone you want to play with, understand?"

"Who says I'm playing?" I said. "He impersonated an officer, that's a crime."

"One he'll get out of in five minutes flat but remember a long time after you think he forgot."

I didn't like his tone. It was like he thought he was talking to a child. The Alec who'd been kissing me senseless in the kitchen, talking to me about kids, was gone. This man was hard and cold, and without his compassion, my nerves began to twist and fray.

"Then tell the FBI."

"I will," he said, like it was the end of the conversation.

I shoved back in my seat, crossing my arms over my chest. I hated the out of control feeling that seemed to invade my life since I'd met Alec. It made me worry that Amy and my dad might be at least partially right about him. For every perfect piece I loved, there was one equally as destructive.

He turned into the valet drive of a big, lavish hotel on the beach, where a doorman in tails and a top hat pushed a luggage cart toward our car.

"This doesn't exactly scream low profile," I said.

"Max used to stay here when he wanted to get away from his wife." Alec turned off the ignition. "They're used to big clients—the security's as tight as it gets."

Which meant it was expensive.

He seemed to read my mind. "Contrary to what Mike says, I still have a few favors left."

The "favor" he was cashing in turned out to be a size-two brunette who worked at the concierge desk. Her name was Mandy, and from the way her lips lingered on his cheek when she kissed him hello, it was obvious they'd been intimate.

When Alec introduced me as Laura—an alias I assumed he was using for my protection—she looked like she wanted to laugh, and I stifled the urge to kick her in the kneecaps.

"Can I get a key to the suite?" Alec asked, reducing her to a puddle with that sexy smirk I thought he reserved just for me. She seemed to know what he was talking about, which led me to believe that Max kept an ongoing room here.

"You know I can't say no to you," she said, a little pout on her shiny red lips. "It's a pity you have company tonight."

"Behave, Mandy." Alec's advice blew right over her head.

"Now you of all people know that's impossible." She giggled, and the sound was like nails down a chalkboard. It seemed I was the only one to notice.

Visions of her naked body wrapped around Alec's flooded my mind. Her legs were nicer than mine, her skin lighter, her hair tamer. We were as opposite as we could be, and I hated Alec for making me care. All the anxiety from talking about Reznik transformed into one hard knot of jealousy. I didn't want to be here, watching Alec work this woman. I didn't want to be indebted to her for anything.

"I want to go somewhere else," I said.

Mandy raised her brows at me. "Is something wrong?"

"You, to start with."

"Anna," Alec grabbed my forearm, but I shook him free. His gaze was filled with warning, and I shot one right back.

"Maybe you'd like to find other accommodations," she said. "Alec, why don't I show you upstairs?"

She slid her hand down his shoulder, lingering over the strong muscles of his upper arm, and stared a challenge right at me.

"Why don't you show me outside instead," I offered.

I'd gotten in a catfight a few years after my dad had adopted me. A big, mean girl who liked to call me Orphan Anna and throw sawdust in my hair. It had been years since I'd sharpened my nails, but now seemed as good a time as any.

"We can find the room just fine on our own," Alec told Mandy, glaring at me. "One key would be great."

With a pouty nod, she went around the counter and had a key card made. When she was done, she handed it directly to Alec, and I made certain to smile at her as we walked away.

We rode the elevator to the eighteenth floor with an older woman who either had a very young lover or a very inappropriate bodyguard. I didn't say a word until we were in the room—which was, of course, amazing, with a huge four-poster bed and a separate living room with furniture nicer than anything I'd ever owned.

"Why would you bring me here?" I demanded, blood boiling.

"I told you," he said, avoiding my gaze. "Security is the best in the city."

Was he dense? Did I have to spell it out for him?

"You brought me to a place where you fucked another woman," I said.

He threw the duffle bag on the bed.

"It was a long time ago."

"Not to her," I snapped. "Seems like she still thinks you're on the market. I noticed you weren't in a big hurry to correct her, either."

"I needed the room."

"So you pretend I'm just another fuckbuddy?" I asked, stomach cramping with insecurities. "Was this where you two used to meet? How many women did you bring here?" I looked away from the bed I normally would have been excited to break in. "Jesus, Alec. Why would you shove this in my face?"

"It was nothing serious."

"Like that makes it better. How would you like it if our places were reversed?" Did he really think this wouldn't hurt me?

"I wouldn't."

"Really? That's strange. Because I'm having the time of my life right now."

"Anna, don't." He scratched his fingers over his scalp.

"Don't *what*?"

He turned and stared at me, shoulders rising an inch.

"Don't fucking doubt me," he said. "Not you. Anyone else, but not you."

I wavered. The energy coming off of him had changed from anger to desperation, and there was nothing that broke me down faster than his vulnerability.

He looked away. "I have to work tonight. I took the grave-yard shift at the shipping yard. It's too late to call in."

"You're going to leave me here?" *With Mandy downstairs?*

He grabbed the duffle bag off the bed and ripped the zipper open.

"You'll be safe."

"And what about you?"

"The place is covered with surveillance cameras and security to prevent theft. Reznik would be stupid to show up there."

I laughed dryly. "That makes me feel *so* much better."

"If I blow off this shift, I'm done. It's not like employers are lining up to take me, Anna."

There was that condescending tone again, like I was a clueless bimbo.

"How about you stop talking to me like I'm stupid?" I said.

He paused, then jerked the thermal shirt he'd been wearing earlier from the bag.

"Okay, how about this? I need a job. The last one I had, I fucking loved. I believed in that company. Private jets, new, cutting-edge engines. I even bought shares in it knowing full well Max would never give me any voting power."

"I . . . I didn't know that." My voice faltered, but his was rising, growing sharper.

"Here's something else you probably didn't know. It's only a matter of time before the people overseeing Max's properties realize I've been staying in my apartment rent-free. Legal fees are killing my savings. We haven't even gone to trial and I'm already on my third lawyer because everyone's scared shitless of Max." He gave the shirt he'd been squeezing in his fists one hard shake to spread it out. "I'm a couple months short of living in a cardboard box."

Remorse hit me hard, and I forced myself to keep standing tall. I'd never seen him so tortured. With all of this just below the surface, it seemed impossible that he could have had even one genuinely happy moment with me since he'd been released from prison.

He tore off the T-shirt he'd been wearing, and shrugged into the thermal.

"We have my place," I said. "We have my job."

"And I'm supposed to let you take care of me, is that it?"

Ouch. That one hurt.

"We could take care of each other." I moved toward him slowly, tentatively, but he stepped away.

"For how long?" With a burst of fury, he knocked the bag off the bed, spilling my clothes across the floor. "Until you get hurt again? Until you realize I'm the trash your dad told you I am?" He stepped closer, bending down to look me in the eye. "Until some guy comes along with a steady paycheck, and a clean record, and convinces you you're too goddamn beautiful to be hauling around dead weight?"

I slapped him.

I'd never slapped anyone in my life, not even in my one and only catfight.

"Who's doubting who?" The tears ran down my cheeks.

He huffed out a breath. And as our gazes met, I silently begged him to take it back, to hold me so we could forget all of this and focus on the real problems at hand.

But he didn't. He took one step back, then another. And then he turned and left.

Seventeen

In our hurry to leave the apartment, Alec had thrown everything from the bathroom cabinet in the bag, including my sleeping pills.

I took two. And even then I didn't crash.

The bed was big and plush and looked like it would have swallowed me whole, but I couldn't make myself sleep in it. Not when Alec had touched another woman there. Instead, I pulled on a sweatshirt, laid on the couch, and fantasized about what Alec would do when he came back and realized I'd taken a cab to my apartment.

I never went to my apartment, though. As much as I wanted to punish him, I didn't want to do something stupid. If Alec trusted the security here, I believed him.

But that didn't mean I was comfortable.

I tossed and turned, thinking about Mandy in all of Alec's favorite sexual positions. I knew he'd been with other women, but I'd never had to put a face on any of them until now. When my imagination was exhausted, I replayed his words, over and over. He was going broke. He needed a job. He'd loved Force, and even if he hated flying, he'd loved working with jets. I wondered how he'd bought shares in the company; articles I'd read even recently made it clear that Maxim Stein had never opened the company up publicly. It must have been privately negotiated. Another chance to strengthen the illusion that Maxim was like a father to Alec. The whole thing was so unfair.

It hurt that Alec doubted me after everything we'd been through. After I'd waited *three months* for him and would have waited a lot longer if I'd had to. I hated that he was lost and I *hated* that he was too proud to let me help him.

When I finally fell asleep, I dreamed that he was missing, and though I looked everywhere, he was simply gone.

I woke to the sun shining through a crack in the drapes. My head was muddled with a sleeping pill/crying jag hangover, and my eyes throbbed straight through to my skull. For a few minutes, I snuggled deeper into the blanket, nuzzling my face against the soft feather pillow.

And then I realized I hadn't brought a pillow, or a blanket, to the couch.

I was in the bed—the one I very deliberately had avoided—and Alec was lying beside me on top of the covers in nothing but a pair of sweatpants. On his side, he faced the opposite wall, and for a moment I stared at the muscles in his back, at the tension that didn't ease even when he was asleep.

I didn't remember him coming in or bringing me here. I certainly didn't remember him undressing me. But all I was wearing was a pair of panties, and my sweatshirt was nowhere to be seen.

For the first time ever, the sleeping pills had actually worked.

My fingers itched to touch him, spoon up behind him with my knees tucked behind his and my arm over his chest. I could smell him—dark and musky—and my bare breasts began to tingle. I could have lowered my hands down his chest, and woken him with my hand sliding up and down his big cock.

But Mandy had probably already done that here.

Silently, I slipped from the bed and made my way to the bathroom. On the way I picked up the customary morning paper that the staff had left under the door and scanned the front page. The Sunshine Skyway Bridge was going to be closed in two weeks for painting and renovations. I wished they'd just knock the damn thing down after what happened there three months ago. The next story was about a manatee exhibit at the Lowry Park Zoo.

The article at the bottom caught my eye. It was an update on the Maxim Stein trial, with side-by-side photos of his grim face and an aerial view of his barricaded estate on Davis Island. There was mention of Robert Calloway—or Bobby, as I knew him—pleading guilty to vehicular homicide and abduction. I was glad the reporters hadn't attempted to contact me about either—they had more than once after his arrest—but it surprised me that the lawyers were holding back. Maybe they had enough evidence to hang him without me.

Near the end was a quote from William MacAfee, Charlotte MacAfee's brother, a man Alec had only briefly mentioned to me once.

"Yes, I'm glad that Calloway is behind bars, but he didn't act alone. I won't rest until all those involved with my sister's murder are brought to justice."

I shivered, wondering if he knew that Alec had been unintentionally tied to Charlotte's death. If so, I doubted he would be pleased to learn of Alec's release from prison, even if it was for the greater good.

I quickly got ready for my shift at Rave, and after a short text exchange with Amy, came back to the bedroom, unable to leave without looking at him one more time.

My chest ached as I watched him. He shouldn't have brought me here, shouldn't have flirted with Mandy right in front of my face. He shouldn't have assumed that I wasn't strong enough to love him. As much as I understood his motives I hated his actions.

He was still facing the other way, and as I gazed down his back my eyes focused on the thin scar that ran across his lower back. He'd told me it was an accident in the metal shop at the jail. For some reason it hurt me to look at it, like I'd been the one cut, and I reached out gently to cover it with my hand.

The next second found me flat on my back, staring up at him.

"What . . ." He blinked his eyes, then released my shoulders he'd been holding like they were red-hot. I swallowed a trembling breath, hoping my heart would slide back down my throat.

"Are you okay?"

There were dark circles under his eyes, and scruff on his jaw. Maybe he was the one who needed the sleeping pills.

"Are *you* okay?" I asked.

He looked me over, and I couldn't tell if he was disappointed I had clothes on, or still mad about last night. Either way he didn't answer.

"I didn't mean to wake you," I said.

He squinted at the clock on the nightstand, which said it was close to nine a.m. "I need to wake up anyway. I'm scheduled for a double."

He moved away as if he hadn't just nearly tackled me. I sat up slowly. He was more on edge than I thought—an observation that worried me greatly.

"You've barely slept," I said.

He rubbed his eyes, elbows on his knees. Slowly, my pulse settled.

"You could call in," he answered. "Stay here."

"No thank you," I said, ready to get away from this place. "I'm going to work."

He nodded slowly, glancing away. "I'll take you."

"Amy's going to pick me up."

For a while neither of us spoke, but the air was so thin between us I thought it might shatter.

"Anna . . ."

"I'll be fine. I won't be alone. I'll go to the gym after work and then . . . I don't know."

I didn't really want to come back here.

He turned to face me, still seated on the bed. I didn't want to play the poor injured girlfriend, and if we stuck around here much longer, I was going to.

"Yeah, all right," he said finally. "I'll walk you downstairs."

I didn't fight him, and twenty minutes later, when Amy pulled up in her mom-mobile, I kissed him on the cheek and made my escape. There were no apologies between us. No *I love you*s. It was worse than a good-bye after a one-night stand. I was just glad Mandy wasn't in the lobby to witness it.

"Fancy place." Amy wiggled her eyebrows at me as I slid into the passenger seat. She looked pretty in her short, green A-line dress, and I was reminded of her day date today with the non-meathead she'd met at her apartment complex. "I brought coffee. I figured you'd probably need it after your all-night sexcapade."

I didn't disagree with her, and instead took the coffee in both hands, hoping the warmth from the cup would stop the growing chill inside of me.

Alec was still standing outside, waiting for us to leave. Amy rolled down the window and leaned over me.

"Hey," she said.

He offered a polite smile, but his eyes stayed wary.

"Lunch at my place Saturday. You can bring hamburger buns and prepare a speech about why I shouldn't kick your ass."

"Amy . . ." I sank in my seat, staring at my coffee, and willed her to press the gas pedal.

"It's already prepared," Alec said. "I rehearsed it every night in prison."

Amy took a moment to gauge if he was joking, and then snickered.

"It better be good then."

He smirked. "See you Saturday."

As Amy pulled out of the drive, I watched Alec in the side mirror. The coffee didn't warm the cold as I hoped it would; it just made me more aware of it. I couldn't shake the feeling that something bad was going to happen, and as the day continued, it just got worse.

My car magically appeared parked on the street right outside of Rave by the time my shift was up. My keys had been left at the front desk. I'd hoped for a note on the dashboard, anything to say that he'd missed me, but I was out of luck. Even the little aluminum license plate with my name on it was sitting in the coin tray, right where I'd left it. He felt further away now than he had when he'd been gone.

I went to the gym straight from work and knocked out two sports massages before taking advantage of my own stress reduction. I wasn't particularly in the mood for pole dancing, but I needed a mood fixer and Jayne had never let me down before. I was immediately glad I'd come; as I entered the room she was wearing a full police uniform, complete with a black cap and glitzy gold badge.

The poles had been cleared to the back of the room, and judging from the looks on the other girls' faces, I wasn't the only one surprised by this.

"Get inside before I lock you out!" Jayne yelled into the hallway as the last ladies hustled in. I set my gym bag on the floor by the door as she shut the door behind them.

"Tonight, my little bitches, we're going to learn something new."

"But I just nailed the upside-down pole splits," said a woman who jovially complained about menopause and had clearly not done anything of the sort. We all laughed.

"Can it, sweet cheeks," ordered Jayne. "Or I'm going to spank you." She removed a leather riding crop from the holster on her utility belt that should have held a nightstick and cracked it down on her own thigh.

"Ooh!" The woman clapped her hands. Her friends giggled.

"Lap dancing is an art," said Jayne. "And before you start to boohoo about it, let me tell you how this is going to go. You're all going to strip, and you're all going to like it."

A few of the college girls cheered.

"Okay," said Jayne, stepping out of character for a moment. She picked at one of her overly long false eyelashes. "You don't actually have to strip. The gym says I can't make you and I don't want to lose my gig here, blah blah blah."

She slapped the crop against her leg again, hardcore once again.

"What's the point of a striptease?" She pointed the crop at me. "Anna."

"Taking off your clothes?" I guessed.

"Wasted potential." She clicked her tongue as she shook her head. "It's about control. The stripper has it. The stripee does not. The second you lose control the dance is over, and believe me, as much as they think they want to dive into the main course, they don't. They want to be tortured. So what is your job?"

"To torture?" I said.

"Now she's got it," rasped Jayne. "Music!" she snapped. "Lights! Chair!"

A couple of girls ran to do her bidding.

For the next five minutes, Jayne danced in front of us, removing one article of clothing at a time until she was down to her sequined blue thong and tassels, riding a wooden chair like it was a bucking bronco. It was, quite frankly, one of the most inspiring moments of my life.

For the rest of the hour we followed her lead, duplicating many of the same pole dancing moves on our designated chairs while we pretended to remove our clothes. Jayne passed by, occasionally shouting helpful hints like: "Eye contact: make him break first," and "You touch him, he doesn't touch you," and my favorite, "A little humping goes a long way."

I worked that chair like it was Alec, and punished him accordingly. In my mind I made him pay for ever touching another woman. I made him forget all other women existed. By the end I was damp with sweat, chest heaving with each breath. My thighs burned from every bump and grind and I was horny as hell.

"Some poor schmuck's in trouble tonight," said Jayne as she walked by. She'd replaced her blue zip-up police pants and white blouse, but it was still completely unbuttoned, giving a glimpse of her tassels every time she turned too quickly.

The woman had incredible boobs. I could see why men paid her hundreds of dollars for lap dances, as she'd boasted earlier.

"Yes," I said. "He is."

"*Boyfriends.*" She rolled her eyes. "If you're not stroking their cock, you're stroking their ego."

I smirked as she sauntered away.

"She's not all wrong." I turned, surprised to find Trevor leaning through the open doorway behind me. His shirt was soaked in a *V* down the center from what looked to have been a very grueling run.

The class was over, and the ladies were starting to file out. One of the college girls whispered something to her friend as they passed, but Trevor seemed not to notice.

"How'd it go with the kid?" he asked, reminding me that I'd cancelled my appointment with him to meet Jacob at the courthouse.

I grabbed my gym bag off the floor and followed him out, the weight that had temporarily been on hold pressing down on my shoulders once again.

"Not great," I said. "Which has unfortunately been the theme of my day." I didn't really want to get into it, but it was easy to talk to Trevor. When he wasn't around Alec anyway.

Trevor glanced behind us as Jayne locked the door. She'd thrown on her uniform jacket, but still left the shirt underneath open down to her diamond-studded belly button.

"Too bad," he said absently. "I think I'd be doing pretty damn awesome if I just walked out of that room."

I chuckled. "The class was great."

But now all I could think of was finding Alec and laying on the torture until he begged me to finish him. Which I wouldn't. Not until we set a few things straight.

We'd walked down the stairs in silence, but as he opened the front door to lead us outside, I paused. The street was still fairly busy, and the parking lot had good visibility from the street. If I felt uncomfortable, I could always convince Trevor to walk me all the way to my car.

"So how is *Alec*?" Trevor said his name slowly.

"Fine," I said quickly.

"Are you guys going out tonight?"

I glanced around. No Reznik. Not that he would have been following me anyway. Alec had made me paranoid.

"He's working," I said.

"The guy works a hell of a lot." Trevor was scowling, and for some reason this annoyed me. Yes, Alec worked a lot. He had to because he needed the money and refused to rely on his devoted girlfriend for help.

"I'm aware," I snapped.

Trevor stopped, and after a couple steps, I stopped, too. With a sigh, I turned around to face him. We were standing between two rows of cars, the sky purple from the cloud cover and the setting sun.

"Are you sure things are all right with you two?" Trevor asked.

"They're fine." I sighed. "I don't know."

"Hey." Trevor came closer and put his hands on my shoulders. His palms were warm, and as he started to gently rub, I felt some of the tension fall away. Soon his hands were trailing down my arms.

"Are you staying at his apartment still?" Trevor asked. He knew I often walked there after my class at the gym.

I laughed dryly.

"Well that's a really funny story," I said, eyes burning with angry tears. "We actually stayed somewhere else last night, and I got to meet one of his skinny, perfect little ex-bed bunnies. It was basically the best night of my life."

"Where'd you stay?"

I looked up at him. That was an odd question, considering what I'd just said. There was a strange look in his eyes. Almost like anger, but more tempered.

"At a hotel," I said. "Why?"

Trevor's grasp on my shoulders got a little harder. Almost painful.

"Which hotel?"

"Again," I said warily, "why?"

"Maybe I should pay him a little visit."

"Oh, no," I said. "I don't think that would be a good idea."

His nostrils flared as he took another breath. "Just tell me where I can find him."

"Trevor, stop." I wiggled out of his grasp, but his hands just slid down my arms to my wrists. He pulled me closer.

"I appreciate it," I said. "But it's something Alec and I need to work out."

"I know he was in jail."

I took a step back. He let go of my arms.

Trevor glanced up, then met my gaze again. "I know he wasn't working in Seattle. I knew the whole time."

"How did . . ."

"You're Anna Rossi," he said, a red tinge blossoming on his cheeks. "The woman who was taken by Robert Calloway. The news said you were involved with Maxim Stein's bodyman. It didn't take a genius to put it together."

The betrayal scored my insides, and my shoulders drew back in defiance.

"Why didn't you tell me you knew?"

"Because I didn't want to embarrass you. Because . . ."

"Why?" I demanded.

He took two steps forward, and before I could figure out what he was doing, my face was in his hands, and he was kissing me.

There was passion in him. I felt it flowing through his palms, through his chest as it bumped against mine. My body responded in slow motion, trying to process what was happening. My eyes remained open, my hands down at my sides. But my mouth stayed pressed against his.

His lips were different than Alec's. Not as soft. Not as warm. Wrong.

This was wrong.

I shoved him back.

"Get your fucking hands off of her."

The voice came from behind me. I turned, just in time to see Alec reach between us and grab Trevor's sweat-drenched collar in one fist. With the other hand he wheeled back and punched him square in the jaw.

Eighteen

Trevor stumbled backward into the hood of a parked car. He grasped the metal with both hands, his knuckles turning white. Propping himself up on the bumper, he shook his head and blinked rapidly.

"Get up," Alec said, voice as dark as I had ever heard it.

"What are you doing?" Glancing only briefly at Alec, I raced to Trevor's side. I tried to help him stand, but he shook me off.

"Get the fuck up," Alec told him.

"*Alec,*" I hissed. My brain was firing at triple speed where it had been so slow just moments before when Trevor had kissed me. Alec was on parole. Fighting was a violation of parole. If Trevor pressed charges, Alec was going to jail.

He looked past me, fists clenched and ready, eyes nearly black.

Trevor spat blood on the ground, then stood.

"That all you got?" he asked.

"Trevor, no." I got between them, arms raised. "Both of you, stop. This was a misunderstanding. Trevor didn't mean anything."

"Oh, I meant it," said Trevor. Alec lunged, but fell back when I turned and blocked him with my shoulder.

"She's not for you," Alec said.

A few people were gathering at the edge of the parking lot. One of them had on a baby blue gym uniform shirt. Someone was going to call the cops if we didn't clear out soon.

"Alec, you need to go. *Go!*" I shouted. Finally he looked at me, and the broken look in his eyes nearly brought me to my knees. "Please, go," I whispered.

He backed away. One step, then two, holding my gaze, until with a muttered swear, he turned, and stalked away.

I spun back to Trevor.

"Please," I said. "*Please* don't say it was Alec. He'll go back to jail."

"It's where he belongs," said Trevor, clearly disgusted. "He's out of control. You saw him."

"Trevor, please," I begged. My pulse was flying. Behind me, an engine revved, and I looked back just in time to see Alec's Jeep tearing out of the parking lot. Where was he going? Back to the shipping yard? I didn't even know where it was.

"You're kidding, right?" Trevor nursed his jaw, now bright red.

I shook my head, the adrenaline making me tremble.

"Fine," he said finally.

"Thank you."

The manager of the gym was heading out to the parking lot as I dodged around the cars to mine. With shaking hands, I pulled my keys from my purse, cursing as I struggled to find the right one.

"Goddammit!" My voice hitched.

Finally, I found what I needed. I opened the car door and turned on the ignition, but forced myself to take a deep breath before I threw it in reverse. Driving in my current state was a bad idea. I picked up my phone and hit the first number on the speed dial.

One ring, and then it cut straight to Alec's voice mail.

I called again, but this time, it didn't ring at all. He'd turned off his phone.

He thought I was cheating on him. Trevor—stupid, *stupid* Trevor—had just validated the fears he'd voiced last night. Even if Trevor had harbored some ridiculous crush on me, it seemed insane how different he was around Alec. One minute he was a pal, listening, joking, being all around *normal*, but at the first mention of my relationship he turned into a possessive, controlling jerk.

And now Alec wasn't even going to let me explain that this had all been some horrendous mistake.

"Mike," I muttered, when my head was clearer. Maybe he knew where Alec worked.

I took the short drive a few blocks south, and pulled up to the curb in front of the apartment building. Flipping on my hazard lights, I jumped out of the car and ran into the building. Mike was at the front desk, signing in a guest.

"Anna?" He finished quickly, and pulled me off to the side. "You okay? What happened?"

I realized then I probably looked like a wreck. Still in my yoga shorts and an off the shoulder cover-up T-shirt, I was a sweaty, frantic mess. My hair probably looked like I'd just gotten off a roller coaster.

"Do you know where he works?" Embarrassment slashed through me. Alec and I were living together—or at least attempting to—and I had to ask someone else where he worked.

"Who? Alec?"

"Yes!"

Mike frowned. "Is he . . ."

"Where does he work?" I demanded.

"Okay, okay," Mike said. "He mentioned the shipping yards off Causeway. I'm not sure which dock . . ."

"Thanks." I turned to leave, but Mike grabbed my arm.

"Alec and I go way back," he said, siphoning a breath through his teeth. "High school, even a little before. He's seen me through some ugly things."

"Okay," I said, the urgency racing through me.

"But I've seen him through worse," Mike said. "And what he's up against now is nastier than all that. He's a survivor, but how he does it won't be pretty."

"I get it," I said. "I'm a survivor, too."

Mike studied me a moment with his gleaming amber eyes, and then nodded once. I grabbed his hand, and squeezed, then ran back outside.

The docks weren't far, only a few miles, but with the traffic they might as well have been in the next state. The sun had set completely by the time I'd arrived, and it was nearly dark when I finally found his car in one of the employee lots. Its presence confirmed that I was in the right place, but there were at least ten docks that ran up this side of the Bay, all hidden by a maze of metal shipping containers, warehouses, and moving trucks.

There was no way I was going to find him.

Bullshit. I *had* to find him.

I carried my Mace on my key ring, keeping an eye out for any strange people that might be following. Despite the late hour, the docks were fully manned—workers in stained shirts, overalls, and canvas jackets moved boxes and crates by forklift, or carried them by hand.

Everyone I passed looked at me. Some of them whistled. Some of them elbowed their friends and muttered comments I couldn't hear.

Some of them were not so subtle.

I wrapped my cover-up tighter around my shoulders, both to avoid their stares and because of the falling temperature, and walked faster. My legs were bare up to the tops of my thighs. What I would have done for a pair of jeans and a sweatshirt.

"If you're here for an interview, you got the job," called a Hispanic man in his thirties with a goatee. He was wearing a flannel shirt, and removed a pair of gloves as he approached from one of the forklifts.

"I'm looking for someone," I said, cheeks staining.

"I figured that." He frowned. "You better find him and move on. The wolves have already caught the scent." He motioned to a group of men who were ogling from beside one of the shipping containers. One of them grabbed himself, and the others laughed.

"Get back to work!" yelled the man.

I squeezed my Mace tighter.

"Alec Flynn," I said quickly. "He just started this week. Do you know him?"

He shook his head. "Nah. But Dock Four picked up a bunch of new guys a few days ago. Might want to check there."

"Thanks."

"Be careful, chica," he called as I hurried away.

The dock numbers were painted in white across the main walkway, and I jogged past two and three, coming to a stop at four. Bright overhead lights shined down from the roof of the warehouse, but the alleys between the multicolored shipping containers were shadowed, and eerily dark. I looked down each one I passed, finding them all empty.

This was a bad idea. It was stupid to come here. I should have waited for him at the hotel. Or even at his car.

At a turn in the main road, I came to a group of workers, moving large cardboard boxes into the back of a semitruck. My feet slowed, along with my pulse, because my body could sense him even before my eyes did.

Alec was here.

His gray thermal was now ringed with sweat around the collar. The sleeves were rolled up past his elbows, and black stains striped his pants. It took a moment to realize he'd looked this way earlier, in the parking lot at the gym. He must have come on a break.

He worked efficiently, faster than the other men. He didn't chat with them between hauls, but kept his head down and his hands busy. As he turned, I noted the line of sweat down his back that made his shirt dark, and felt a sharp throb in my belly. It was so strong it made my breath catch.

It was at that point that one of them noticed me.

"Hey mama," called a man wearing a black back brace outside his drenched shirt. "Come on over into the light."

He began to walk toward me, another man just behind him.

Nerves trembled through me. Alec looked up at the commotion, and threw his box onto the tailgate of the truck.

"Hold up," he called.

The men stopped. Alec strode over to them, and after a short exchange, they turned back. Alec closed the distance between us, the anger so evident in his movements that I wrapped my arms even tighter across my chest.

"What are you doing here?" he said in a low voice.

"Looking for you."

"You shouldn't have come here. Especially wearing that." He didn't slow, and I hurried to catch up to him.

"We need to talk," I said.

"I'm taking you to your car and you're going straight back to the hotel."

"I'm not going back there."

"Then go to Amy's. And lock the doors. Call the police if anything seems off."

"Alec, *stop*."

I grabbed his forearm, and he finally slowed. But he wouldn't look at me. He looked anywhere *but* at me as I finally pulled him off the main drag into one of the shipping crate alleys. They were stacked fifty feet into the air, a sight which brought on a wave of claustrophobia as he led me deeper into the folds, to a place where wooden crates were pushed up against the walls.

"Trevor's not going to press charges," I said, as he yanked off his gloves and tossed them on one of the boxes.

"Lucky me."

"It *is* lucky." I grit my teeth together. "You could go back to jail for fighting. Is that what you want?"

"Is that what *you* want?"

I stared at him, feeling the dread that had solidified weigh me down. We were unraveling. If we continued this way there would be nothing left.

I turned to leave. I wasn't going to stand here and let him punish me for Trevor when he'd thrown Mandy in my face. This had been a bad idea after all.

"I shouldn't have brought you to that hotel." Alec's voice slapped off the metal.

Taken off guard, I stopped, unwilling to face him for fear of giving in.

"All I could think was that I couldn't let it happen again—no one could hurt you again," he rolled on. "Max spent so much at that place that they comped him a few suites, and before you, yes. I took advantage of it. I knew you'd hate me when you found out and I didn't care, but if you'd done the same to me . . . Christ, the thought of someone else putting their hands on you . . ."

I turned slowly, my eyes drawn to his hands first as they flexed into tight fists. His shoulders were bunched, and I could feel his expectations, like a cold, wet mist on my skin.

"There's nothing going on with Trevor. He's never done that before, and he'll never do it again," I said. "That's the truth. I swear."

He stayed silent, watching. Waiting.

"What do you want from me?" I asked, hating his silence. Hating that I couldn't read his mind right now.

He moved closer, in and out of the shadows, carrying with him an unseen burden he refused to share.

And then he was kissing me. My face was in his hands, and then his hands were in my hair, and his hot, hard body was pressing me against the cold, metal siding of a shipping crate. His kiss hit me with the force of a hurricane, pounding me with his fury, and his fear, and with a need so acute it stole the air from my lungs.

"Did you like that? His mouth on you? His hands on you?"

"No," I gasped, flooded with shame. He didn't give me a chance to explain; he bit my lower lip hard enough to make me yelp in surprise.

"Did you want to fuck him, Anna?"

"*No.*" I tried to shove him back but he was relentless, and soon I matched his rough, unrestrained touches with my own. How could he think I wanted anyone else? Hadn't I shown him he was everything to me?

"He wanted to fuck you. I could see it all over him. He was dying to get inside of you."

He was being cruel, but a dark part of me wanted it. I wanted him to be furious another man had touched me. I needed his possessiveness.

"He can't have you," he said urgently against my mouth. My nails scraped over his scalp. "I won't share you."

This time I succeeded in shoving him back. "I won't share *you.*"

He knew I was referring to Mandy, and whoever else showed up from his past. His gaze narrowed, and he lunged at me again.

His hands were everywhere—over my shoulders, fisting my hair, sliding over my breasts and then squeezing with enough pressure to trigger a craving so dark and demanding, it frightened me.

This was wrong. We were in public, out in the open.

But he was like me. Sometimes he spoke with words, and other times, like this, he needed more.

The thin material of my shorts felt like a thick blanket between us, and as his hands lowered down my back, under the fabric to my ass, I gasped, rocking forward onto his thigh.

His mouth burned a line down my neck, making me moan.

"Mine," he growled, biting me on the shoulder.

His claim made me shudder. Heat poured into my groin, made my breasts swell inside my constricting sports bra.

I clawed back at him, scratching the heated skin beneath his shirt. I pulled him tighter against me, licking the underside of his jaw, tasting the salty sweat.

He spun me around, and placed my hands on the rusty metal. My knees were trembling, but he held my weight, strong arms wrapped around my body.

"No one else touches you," he said.

I shook my head, eyes pinched closed as one hand reached down the loose collar of my shirt, beneath the tank top and my bra, to cup my breast. He pinched my nipple, rolled it between his fingers, and I slammed my hips back against his pelvis. I could feel his erection, long and thick within his pants. The smell of salt in the air combined with a stronger, heady male scent as he wrapped tighter around me.

I wanted him to possess me physically the way he already possessed my soul. I wanted him to know I would give myself to him, because I was bound to him, just as he'd proven in the bedroom of the apartment when I'd been the one who was vulnerable.

His hand plunged down the front of my shorts, finding me hot, wet, and bare. He shuddered as his fingers traced my slit, and then entered me with a roughness that both shocked me and strengthened my desire. I panted as the coarse stubble on his jaw scraped my cheek.

My fingers splayed out on the metal, turning white with the pressure. I ground back into him, and he responded, aligning his body down my spine, showing me just what he wanted to do to me.

I was flying higher. Higher still.

"Do it," I rasped. "If I'm yours, prove it."

He growled in my ear, then in a rush, jerked my shorts down my thighs and freed himself from his pants. His cock brushed against my ass as he bent his knees and lowered, then filled me, first halfway, then out. He adjusted his feet, jerked my hips back, and thrust home.

I gave a hoarse shout as he began to fuck me. Fast and deep. Claiming me. Branding me. And my tender muscles stretched, and then clamped down, sucking him deeper with every stroke. The zipper of his pants bit into the backs of my thighs but I didn't care. I was rocketing higher, about to burst with the sensations pulsing from my cunt.

He reached around me again, over my bare flesh, now sensitized by the cool air. He spread the lips wide, and then grasped my clit with all his fingers, squeezing it in a way that made my knees finally give way.

Voices. Footsteps. They cut in over the crashing in my eardrums.

"Someone back there?"

Alec froze. His hand, previously kneading my breast, clamped down over my mouth.

Two voices were talking. The footsteps were drawing closer.

It was too late.

I couldn't hold back what he'd already started. Bolts shot from my clit across my pelvis. My pussy squeezed his cock. I was coming. Coming. Unable to stop it.

I bit his hand but he couldn't block the sound. He turned my face and kissed me, swallowing my cries of pleasure. He lost himself in it, and soon was fucking me again. One stroke. Two. Two more and his body went rigid, shooting his hot load deep inside, making me his in the most primal way.

He faltered, and then pushed me deeper into the shadows. Hurriedly, he pulled my shorts up, and tucked himself back in. I could still feel him inside of me. The slick fluid, the scoring of my tender walls by his monstrous cock. I was off balance, still flushed and a little dazed, when he grabbed my hand and pushed me in front of him, back the way we'd come.

"This area's restricted!" someone yelled behind us.

As I glanced back, I saw Alec raise his hand to wave, but he didn't turn around. We moved at a clipped pace until I stumbled and caught myself. He wrapped one arm around my waist then, helping me hurry, and he kept it there, all the way until we reached my car.

Nineteen

I returned to the hotel that night after promising Alec that I would. Amy was probably busy getting Paisley ready for bed, and I didn't want to face my own little apartment alone while Reznik was unaccounted for. Alec had agreed to meet me there when his shift was up, sometime near dawn. I'd offered to bring him back a sandwich, but he'd told me no. Part of him was surely worried that I'd gotten him in trouble, but I think the other part, a small part, was embarrassed that I'd seen him carting boxes into a semitruck.

I gave my keys to the valet, a guy about my age with a jagged pink scar running from the corner of his mouth to his ear, as if someone had sliced him straight across the face. Having caught myself staring, I looked away, but he touched my forearm kindly.

"All alone tonight?" he asked, in a way that made me wonder if he was suggesting something.

"Yes," I said, realizing he must have seen me with Alec earlier. "For now." I smiled.

"Will you need the car for anything else this evening?" Despite the scar, he had a handsome face. Hazel eyes and hair the color of nutmeg.

I looked around at the other cars in the drive. BMWs. Limos. Convertibles. And my neon blue Fiesta. A snooty woman carrying a little dog in a handheld carrier walked by, looking at me down her nose.

"Beautiful bag." She motioned to my red pleather purse.

"Thank you," I said graciously. "I got it at Target. On the clearance rack." I leaned closer and whispered, "It was nine bucks."

Her Botox smile stayed perfectly in place, but her eyes rounded with surprise.

It probably would have been funnier if Amy was there to laugh with me.

"I'm good, thanks," I told the valet, peering through the glass walls into the lobby.

Mandy was nowhere to be seen.

The next morning, I woke alone. I checked my phone but there were no texts, no missed calls. Worried, I called Alec, but it went straight to voice mail. Either he hadn't turned it back on after the gym yesterday, or something was wrong.

I called his father's house, but there was no answer. Hurriedly, I got dressed, my mind shifting from a confrontation with Reznik, to wondering if Trevor had reported him to the police, to something as simple as him picking up another shift or meeting with his lawyer. He'd been a mess last night; this case and the recent strain in our relationship were really wearing on him. It would have been nice if it was ending sometime soon, but the trial date hadn't even been set yet.

If it was simple, he should have let me know. That was what people in relationships did, didn't they?

Unless he'd rethought what he'd seen with Trevor and decided to jump ship.

I wasn't due at the salon for several more hours, so I called for my car in valet, and headed for Alec's father's house.

Thomas Flynn lived on the north side of town, in a crummy neighborhood that hadn't seen a cleanup crew or renovation in years. As I rolled down the cracked street, my vigilance increased, and I reminded myself that no one was carjacking a neon blue Ford Fiesta.

At a stop sign, I looked across the intersection to a dingy strip mall, eyes landing on a slightly more furnished restaurant with white curtains over the windows. The sign on the awning said RAW, and though it was closed, there were three cars in the parking lot—all of them just as fancy as the ones at the hotel where we were staying. No sign of Alec's jeep, to my relief.

"What do you want?" I asked out loud, shivers racing down my spine. I contemplated walking inside and asking, but figured Alec would have had me institutionalized if he found out.

A skinny man with stringy gray hair was approaching my car, preparing to wash the windows, so I gave him a "no, thank you" wave and continued on.

A few minutes later I pulled up on the street in front of Thomas's apartment. It needed a paint job in the worst way; the beige on the outer walls was flaking off, showing the old, sky blue color beneath. A few of the windows were blacked out with trash bags, and on the bottom floor, a woman who resembled a bulldog glared at me from her tiny patio.

I parked and headed up the stairs, taking a left at the top. I knocked twice, and was immediately greeted by a dog's low, lazy bark.

"Thomas, it's Anna," I called.

A minute later the door pulled inward, and a bell attached to the wall above rang as I stepped over the threshold. The handsome, older man who greeted me looked a little more ragged than usual, but sober. Nothing a shower and a shave couldn't fix. Sitting at his feet was his trusty Seeing Eye dog, Askem.

"Anna, looking as lovely as ever."

"Ha." I gave him a quick kiss on the cheek, inhaling, just to make sure I hadn't missed the smell of booze. "How are you, Thomas?"

"Better now."

"Always the charmer." He moved fluidly into the kitchen, as if his sight wasn't impaired at all.

"Can I get you something to drink? Maybe a whisky sour? Or a margarita?"

"Nice try," I said.

"Indeed," he agreed. "That helpful son of mine emptied out my stash."

"Poor you," I said. "Speaking of that helpful son, you haven't seen him, have you?"

Thomas paused, his hand on the refrigerator door. "No. He in jail again?" His jaw clenched, in the way Alec's did when he was angry.

"Geeze," I said. "So much for the glass is half full."

He snorted. "My glass is unfortunately, quite empty. Has been for two days."

I recalled the last time I'd seen him, when I'd sorted through his cell phone to call Mac, his sponsor, because in the midst of his weeklong bender he'd tumbled down the last few stairs outside his apartment.

"Good," I said. "I like you better this way."

He smirked in my general direction. "Well, in that case."

I laughed, and shook my head, but the worry gnawing at me did not subside. Alec was still missing. I thought about calling his apartment complex for Mike, but he didn't come in until the afternoon.

Thomas moved into the living room, and sat in the middle of his sagging couch. He patted the seat beside him, and I joined him.

"I'm worried about Alec," I confessed.

Thomas scoffed. "Don't be. He's fine."

"He's not fine," I argued. "He's trying to do too much."

"That's how he is," said his father gruffly. "He's always been that way."

"Not by choice." His dismissiveness irritated me. Alec had been caring for a dependent father since he was a child. He didn't know another way to be.

"He made his bed." Thomas's voice took on a hard edge. "He's the one who has to lie in it. Thought he would have learned that by now."

I stood up, offended on Alec's behalf.

"Wait." Thomas reached for my wrist, and slowly pulled me back down. "My head's killing me. I'm not myself."

"Well whose fault is that?" I asked. "You want to talk about making beds, you're the one who made yours."

"Hell, woman," he said. "You're worse than my sponsor."

His shoulders rounded, and he hunched forward, massaging the back of his neck with a wince.

I sighed. "Lean back."

When Thomas complied, I pressed my thumbs on the pressure points above his eyes, and traced his brows out to his temples. He groaned as the tense muscles in his face began to relax. I pressed lightly on either side of his nose, then followed the lines over his cheekbones, working his jaw with my fingertips. His lips parted with a sigh.

"Drink more water," I said. "It'll help flush the toxins from your system."

He garbled something unintelligible in response.

It was impossible to look at Thomas's face and not see Alec. I was already feeling the urge to keep searching for him.

As if summoned by my thoughts, my cell phone rang. Seeing Alec's name on the caller ID, I quickly answered.

"Thank God," I said. "Where are you?"

There was a lot of background noise, like the sound of a hundred printers hard at work.

"Something came up," he said, and I could feel his exhaustion reach over the line.

"What's something?"

A woman's voice called his name.

"I'll catch up with you later," he said cryptically.

"Who is that?" I asked, turning away from Thomas. My chest was growing tight. What was Alec doing with another woman?

"I'll see you soon," he said.

"Alec?"

He hung up.

"Goddammit," I muttered.

"I know," said Thomas from the couch. "He was supposed to pick up dog food."

"I'm glaring at you right now," I told him.

"I wish I could glare," he said. "I'm blind, you know."

Shaking my head, I gathered my things, and left for work.

Twenty

"He's sort of slim and athletic," Amy told me the following afternoon in the courtyard outside her apartment. Her day date with Jonathan—the guy who'd introduced himself while scoping out her apartment complex—had gone well. Exceptionally well for Amy, who so far was only able to find two things wrong with him: He didn't eat dessert, and he paid for an expensive lunch with cash.

"There's nothing wrong with cash," I told her as we set out the potato salad and condiments on a picnic table that Paisley and her BFF Chloe, a pretty little girl with dark skin and about a zillion intricate braids, had staked out for us. Amy had invited Chloe and her grandmother to our barbeque to take some of the pressure off of her daughter, who still had trouble with new people.

"Not if you're a drug dealer," Amy said. "Or a stripper."

I wiggled my eyebrows.

"He's cute," she said. "But not *that* cute."

We made our way back upstairs to her apartment to get a few more things. Amy had insisted we go ahead with the cookout, despite my telling her that Alec had to work. I actually didn't know if he was working—we hadn't spoken since the phone call I'd taken yesterday at his dad's house—but I wasn't ready to admit that to her.

Not that she didn't already suspect it.

"Amy?" Miss Iris, Chloe's grandmother, called to us from the landing on the third floor. She was holding a phone to her very ample chest to cover the speaker. "You mind if I invite my son? He got off early and was coming to pick up Chloe."

"Um . . ." said Amy. I could hear her swallow.

I glanced at my best friend, surprised to find her speechless. She didn't seem upset, more like her system had hit a glitch.

"That sounds great," I called, elbowing Amy in the ribs.

"Yeah," said Amy. "The more the merrier." She smiled. All teeth.

"Great. I'll be down soon as I finish the macaroni." Miss Iris went back into her apartment, her purple summer dress swaying behind her.

"What was that?" I asked as we retreated into Amy's apartment.

She raced to her bedroom, and by the time I reached her she was standing at the counter in her tiny master bathroom applying mascara and heating up the flatiron.

"Iris's son," she said. "Is *hot.*"

She added blush. Looked down at her T-shirt disgustedly, and then ripped it off, showcasing the rattiest mom bra I'd ever seen. It always made me laugh to think of her wearing that nasty old thing under her sassy clothes at the salon.

"Really?" I said. "You've never mentioned him."

"Way out of my league." She stuck a hairclip between her teeth.

"Doubtful." I glanced out the window to where the girls were now hiding beneath the picnic table. "You're hot."

"Yes," she said. "But he's beyond hot. Hotter than Alec."

"That's impossible." I felt a pang in my chest at the mention of his name. Where was he now? Who had he been with when we'd spoken last? I didn't think he would cheat, but I couldn't think of a good reason why he'd hang up on me while with another woman. Even sleeping without him was hard in that hotel room, especially after how intimate we'd been the last time we'd seen each other.

"Shit!" She dropped the flatiron. "Jonathan is coming."

"You really invited him?" This surprised me. Amy never introduced men she was seeing to her daughter. I'd thought she'd been joking when she'd mentioned this at Rave.

"I thought . . . maybe I'd try something new. He agreed just to come as a friend. No funny stuff in front of Paisley."

I nodded. "Wow."

She shrugged, then looked at herself in the mirror, probably realizing that she'd been thrown into a nervous mess by a man she wasn't currently seeing. Then, with a dry laugh, she unplugged the flatiron, threw her hair back in a ponytail, and pulled on her T-shirt.

"What are you doing?" I asked.

"Jonathan's nice." The defeat in her voice weighed down on me. "I need nice."

"You need romance, too," I said.

She smiled wanly. "I tried romance. It wasn't for me."

There were times I wished that Danny was still around, just so I could kick him in the nuts.

We moved to the kitchen, where she took the burgers from the fridge. I closed my eyes, remembering that she'd told Alec to bring buns.

"I have bread," she said, reading my mind. "Don't worry about it."

I grabbed the half loaf from the countertop, wondering if I should run to the store before we started cooking.

"So how are things with Alec?" she asked, grabbing the ketchup and mustard from the fridge.

There wasn't much use lying. Amy would call me on it in a second anyway.

"Okay, I guess. He's very . . . distracted."

"With the trial?"

I nodded. "With everything."

She studied me a moment, then kicked the fridge door closed with her heel.

"So un-distract him."

"And how do you propose I do that?"

She gave me a wicked smirk.

"I'm sure you'll find a way."

Back outside, the girls were making flower chains with clovers and telling each other stories. Paisley was making a princess crown for Chloe. Chloe was talking about how people during the plague wore flowers in their hair so they couldn't smell the zombies.

"That's nice," I said.

Amy gave me an exasperated look as she poured lighter fluid over the charcoal.

"Need a hand?"

The voice slid over my skin like silk, and despite his recent unexplained absence, my heart leapt. I didn't turn around. I wanted to be mad at him for making me worry, and that was hard when all I could feel was relief that he was here.

His footsteps slowed as he stepped onto the grass from the sidewalk, and I could feel his eyes on my back.

"Oh good, you made it," said Amy, as if the plan had been for him to show up all along. "Yes. Be manly. Make fire. Cook meat."

"Hold on," said Alec. I turned now, and found him just as sexy as ever in jeans and a casual navy shirt, the sleeves rolled up at the elbows. His eyes were narrowed, and he was holding a plastic bag from the supermarket in one hand, which he tossed on the picnic table, as if annoyed.

Resentment straightened my back. He didn't get to be upset with me, not when he was the one who'd disappeared.

"No one told me *she* was coming," he said.

My mouth had just opened to ask him what the hell he was

talking about, when Paisley's friend Chloe jumped to her feet. After straightening her black sleeveless play dress, she cocked her hip out and jutted her chin forward.

"You got *some* nerve, mister." She tapped the toe of one of her sparkly pink shoes that matched her sparkly pink belt.

Baffled, Amy and I watched as Alec engaged in a very intricate high-five handshake with the little girl. By the end, he'd tossed her over his shoulder and she was giggling hysterically.

"How do you two know each other?" I asked.

Alec's gaze met mine for the first time, and it stung to see some of the joy drain from his eyes. Before he could answer, Chloe's legs kicked out, and he tickled her ribs, eliciting a scream right in his ear. Across the table, Paisley had latched herself to Amy's side, and they both were watching Alec with cautious smiles.

"Daddy!" screeched Chloe suddenly.

From the entrance to the courtyard behind Alec, a familiar figure emerged. A man with milk chocolate skin and a killer smile. He was wearing basketball shorts and a T-shirt with the sleeves cut off, which showed the definition in his arms. It looked like he'd just finished working out.

I rose from the bench. "Mike?"

"Oh God," muttered Amy.

"What's this?" Mike asked, grinning. Any tension that had existed between him and Alec dissipated as they shook hands, and exchanged a small nod. *Men.*

"I found this thing running around wild," Alec told him. "Rabid, I think."

"I'll take care of it," Mike said. "Come here, thing." He took the giggling little girl, and planted a noisy kiss on her cheek.

"You're Chloe's dad," I said, trying to catch up. Now that they were together I could see the resemblance. Same nose. Same beautiful brown eyes.

"Chloe's very handsome, very single, dad," he said, glancing at Amy.

My brows shot up.

"Who wants mac and cheese?" called Miss Iris, coming down the open stairway.

"Iris!" The smile returned back to Alec's eyes as he met her at the base of the stairs and took the foil container of pasta. She said something to him that I couldn't hear, then patted his cheek and kissed him right on the mouth. My mind was spinning at this point. I glanced at Amy, who was staring, openmouthed, at Mike.

"Isn't this nice?" said Iris. "So good of you to get everyone together, Amy."

Amy made a noise that sounded like something was caught in her throat.

"Didn't know you'd met my mom." Mike set his daughter down to give me a hug.

"I didn't know she *was* your mom," I said.

He chuckled. "Small world."

"I guess so."

Mike turned to Amy, who was still holding the lighter fluid in one hand, and clutching her daughter against her side with the other.

"Amy, right?" He reached out his hand. "I'm Mike. We haven't met."

She held out the lighter fluid, which he took with a gracious, if somewhat confused, smile.

"Oh boy." I rushed to her side, skirting by Alec, who was still talking to Iris.

"Mike is Alec's friend," I said, inserting myself on the other side of Paisley. "They go way back—as far as you and me."

"Oh." Amy nodded a little too vigorously. I'd never seen her this way with a man before. Even when we were in high school she was always very assertive.

"Amy and I met when we were fourteen," I told Mike. "We work together at the salon now. Amy's a stylist."

"I cut hair," said Amy.

"You have any suggestions for me?" Mike asked, running one hand over his smooth, shaved head.

She laughed, and finally relaxed a little.

"You did a good job with Chloe's mop," said Mike, glancing at his daughter affectionately. "You were all she talked about for a week."

I was impressed; I didn't know Amy had done all those twisty braids. It shouldn't have surprised me though. She was enormously talented when it came to hair.

I glanced from Mike to Amy, and then back. There was a clear connection between them. Mike wasn't hiding the fact that he was checking her out, and Amy was alternating between doing the same, and staring at her feet.

Alec's best friend with my best friend. Both of them with girls the same age. Regardless of what was going on in my relationship, the thought of Mike and Amy together nearly made me giddy.

"Can I borrow you?" Alec was standing close behind me, and as I turned, my pulse kicked up a notch. I blushed, remembering the feel of a shipping crate beneath my flexed hands.

"Sure."

We walked toward a pond in the center of the courtyard. It was a nice day, and a few other families were out. People were laughing, children were playing, all of them oblivious to the uncertainty rolling through me.

"I owe you another apology." He walked a foot away, hands in his pockets. He was tired, I could see that now. He could put on a show in front of the others, but not for me.

I didn't want to be that person to him, the one who made him feel like he couldn't do anything right. But I was mad. It wasn't the first time we'd done something intimate and then he'd gone AWOL.

"I'm sorry," he said, tilting his head to meet my eyes.

"Who was that woman on the phone?" I asked. "I heard her call for you."

He turned to face the pond. "She's with the FBI. They'd asked me not to contact anyone."

The air whooshed from my lungs; I hadn't even been aware I was holding my breath.

"What did they say?"

"Same stuff. More questions about Max. Things I saw. Things he asked me to do. I told them about Reznik, and they're going to keep eyes on him for a while."

"That's good."

He nodded.

"I thought you might have been with her. The woman on the phone."

He reached for my hand now.

"Anna," he said, letting my name linger. There was disappointment in his tone, but I knew it was more for him than it was for me.

He wove our fingers together, and lifted them to his lips.

"You never have to worry about that," he said.

I moved closer, relieved, but I still felt like something was off between us. Maybe it was just my imagination.

"I don't want to feel far away from you," I said. Ever since he'd come back we'd had moments of closeness, but they only seemed to kick us farther apart.

He took my hand and wrapped it around his back, pulling me to him.

"I don't know how to hold on to you," he admitted.

Behind her came a shriek of joy. The girls were chasing Mike around the picnic table while Iris and Amy prepared the food.

I pressed my forehead to his chest, wrapping him tighter in my arms.

"Yes, you do," I said. "You just don't let go."

He kissed the top of my head.

"So," he said. "Mike and Amy, huh?"

I smirked, relieved that he'd taken off some of the pressure.

At that moment, Chloe and Paisley came bounding over the grass toward us. Paisley's expression changed in stages. She was having fun, pure childhood delight in her eyes. Then they landed on Alec, and they turned cautious, and then wary. I'd warned Alec she might be this way, but was sad to see it happen.

"You must be Paisley," he said, crouching down before the two girls.

It helped that Chloe knew Alec. Paisley stood a little behind her, pulling at the end of her grass-stained yellow shirt, but seemed braver with her friend there.

"He's a friend of mine, Paisley," I said.

"He was kissing you," said Chloe. "Are you guys getting married?"

"Yes," said Alec.

I laughed, half wondering if he was serious. Probably not. Of course not. He was just teasing the girls.

"He's kidding," I said when Paisley looked at me with round eyes.

He cupped his hands over his mouth and whispered, "I'm not kidding."

All right. Simmer down, butterflies. But they were beating their wings hard enough they might have been going ballistic.

Paisley stepped forward and smacked Alec on the arm, then ducked behind Chloe again. It surprised me so much, I didn't know what to say.

"Tag, you're it," she said in a tiny voice. Chloe giggled.

Alec rose slowly, a serious expression on his face. Paisley took a step back.

"I'll give you five seconds' head start," Alec said.

With a scream, they bounded off. Alec kissed me on the lips for exactly five seconds—just long enough to steal my breath—and then he chased after them.

Twenty-one

The hamburgers were good, but not as good as Miss Iris's mac and cheese, and not nearly as good as the company. We laughed and played with the girls, polished off a key lime pie that Mike had brought, and let the hours slip away. Watching Alec and Paisley warmed me. He had the same gift that my father did with troubled kids. He probably would have done a good job getting through to Jacob.

Alec made an extra effort to help Amy with anything she needed, and grinned as Miss Iris told funny stories about him and Mike when they were kids. It was obvious they had a soft spot for each other, and that pleased me, too. I was glad he had an adopted mom like I did, even if it wasn't on paper.

Everything appeared to be going well. Until it wasn't.

Amy was clearing the table, hands full of dishes to take upstairs for leftovers, when a gust of wind blew through the courtyard. It caught the underside of one of the plates, causing her to juggle to keep everything upright. Mike, standing in front of her, jumped forward to help, and it must have scared Amy, because she dropped everything.

Which would have been nothing, except for the fact that she blocked her face with her arms, as if she thought Mike was going to hit her.

Paisley was on her feet within seconds. She took one look at Mike, then her mom, and before Amy could lower her hands and laugh about what had happened, she was off like a shot, running up the stairs into their apartment.

"Paisley!" I called after her. But I didn't follow, because Amy's face was white as a ghost.

"Amy?" I'd risen from my seat, and put my hand on her shoulder. She jerked back, as if I'd broken her from some trance, and stared at the ground, where the remnants of our food were strewn across the grass.

"Easy," said Mike, holding his hands up in surrender. "I didn't mean to startle you."

"I can't believe . . ." She dropped to her knees and immediately began to clean up. "So stupid."

I glanced up at Alec, who confirmed my suspicions with a look of pity.

I crouched beside Amy. "Let me help you."

"Where's Paisley?" she asked quietly.

"Upstairs."

"Shit." She rose, and without explanation, walked quickly to the stairs. I nodded at Alec, who I knew would take care of things out here, and followed my friend.

I didn't catch up with her until we were inside. She was in Paisley's room, kneeling on the floor in front of her bed. It took me a moment to realize her daughter was hiding beneath the mattress.

"Pais, honey, come on out. Mommy wants to talk to you."

Amy's voice broke.

"Paisley, *now*!" She started to cry.

Slowly, I approached, feeling too many things at the same time. Sadness, and rage, and anger, because how had I never seen this before? I'd known Amy since we were in high school. I'd come after Danny left. I'd talked to her almost every day of our adult lives, even when I'd lived in different states. I was a social worker, for God's sake, and had grown up in an unstable home. If anyone knew the signs of abuse, it was me.

And then came the hurt, because she'd never told me.

"Give her a second," I said gently, and after a moment, Amy stood, and met me in the hallway.

"Amy, I'm sorry," I said, the tears filling my eyes now, too.

She began to pace nervously, just a few steps back and forth, back and forth. I couldn't hold her in place even if I tried.

"God, that's embarrassing," she said quickly. "That wind came out of nowhere."

"Amy."

"Mike probably thinks I'm a freak."

"Amy."

"I kind of thought maybe it was kismet, you know? Both of us with girls the same age. *Magic Mike* being my favorite movie . . ."

I took a slow breath.

"Good thing Jonathan never showed. That would have been a real shit storm."

I hadn't remembered Jonathan was invited until she'd just mentioned it.

"He didn't call?" I asked.

"He texted. Said he got stuck with some work stuff." She crossed her arms over her chest, and checked the open door to Paisley's room.

"Why didn't you tell me?" I asked, keeping my voice quiet.

"It's not a big deal," she said. "I only went out with him once."

"About Danny." I hated that she was making me say it, but I knew I had to, because she needed me to be strong right now. "He hit you."

Her tears came on with full force.

"Stop," she said, then went back to the doorway of her daughter's room. "Paisley? Come out, honey. Let's go back outside and play."

"Amy." I blocked her way, and didn't let her pass. "I'm your best friend. You can talk to me."

"Not about that," she said after a moment.

"Why?"

"Because I stayed!" she said, this time loud enough that Paisley might have heard. Immediately she lowered her voice. "Because I stayed. And Paisley saw it happen, and I stayed anyway."

My fingers wove together, squeezed until they shook. Amy's self-sabotaged relationships. Her sensitivity to the danger Alec had brought into my life. Paisley's fear of strangers and the way she'd stopped talking after her father had left. She'd known just what to do when her mom had reacted the way she had outside. Run and hide.

My heart was breaking.

"It happened a lot?" I asked, hating myself for every time I'd been in this apartment, talked to her, hugged her, without knowing. Hating myself for asking this stupid question. Once was too much.

"It happened enough." Her face scrunched up as she tried to hold back the sob. "My baby saw him hurt me, and I told her it was okay, and I was okay, and Daddy didn't mean it. I said that to her knowing it was bullshit."

"It's over," I said. "He's gone."

"Because he left," she said, the disgust ripe in her voice. "I didn't kick him out. He left on his own."

Then the strongest woman I'd ever seen fell to her knees, and covered her mouth with her hands, as if trying to hold herself back from saying any more.

It was risky touching her now, when touch had been used against her, but I did it anyway. I hugged her as hard as I could, and I cried with her.

"It's okay now," I said. "We're all okay."

*   *   *

Paisley finally came out, and while she and Amy talked on the bed, I cleaned up the kitchen. Alec and Mike had closed up shop outside, and the last of the leftovers were brought to Iris's house.

After a while, Alec knocked on the door. When I opened it, I stared at him standing in the threshold, and let the gratitude wash over me.

He was not without faults. He'd seen more than his fair share of trouble, and when he screwed up, he screwed up big. He kept too many secrets, carried too much weight, and was as stubborn as a mule. But he would never hurt me. Not like Amy's ex-husband had hurt her.

"How's everything going?" He didn't come inside. I'm not sure he would have unless Amy herself had invited him.

"Okay," I said. "I think I should stay."

He nodded.

Amy emerged from Paisley's room then, her face pale, her eyes red and puffy.

"Go," she said. "We're good here."

I was torn. If Amy needed me now, I wanted to be close.

"Really, you should go." She looked over her shoulder to where her daughter was curled around her favorite teddy bear. "Paisley and I have some stuff we need to talk about."

I hugged her, and went to grab my purse from her bedroom. While I was there, I heard Alec's low voice from the doorway, and paused to listen.

"Thanks for inviting me, Amy."

"Some party, huh?" She laughed dryly.

Awkward silence followed. I started to come out, but stopped when Alec spoke again.

"Amy . . ." He hesitated. "Anna's important to me. I'd do anything for her. And because you're important to her, I'd do anything for you, too. I want you to know that."

My heart did one slow roll in my chest. As I stepped out of the room, I saw the way he looked at my best friend—not like she was fragile, or like he was afraid she would lose it—but like she was made of fucking iron.

I loved him more than ever then.

Amy's shoulders rose with a shudder, then fell, as I returned to the front door.

"Good speech," she said, voice raw from crying. "All that practicing paid off."

He smiled at her, and with a promise from Amy to call me later, we left.

"I heard what you told her," I said when we reached the parking lot. "Thank you." The sunset cast long shadows across the pavement, reminding me how quickly the afternoon had passed.

Alec's Jeep was in the spot next to mine, and he leaned against it.

"It's true," he said.

I stayed a step back. "And what you told the girls outside." *That you want to marry me.* "Was that true?"

He grinned, and crossed his arms over his chest. "What do you think?"

A red alert sounded over my already raw emotions. Before I did something entirely too memorable, like speaking in tongues, I turned away to look back at the apartment.

The guilt, of all things, settled me.

"I should have known something was happening," I said.

"It's not always easy to see."

"If you aren't looking," I insisted. "I should have paid more attention. I will now."

"It's not your fault, you know."

I shook my head. It wasn't, but that didn't mean I hadn't let them down. Amy would never think that, but it was true. And I wouldn't do it again.

"Do you know his name?" Alec asked, not bothering to hide his intent. "Full name would be best."

I faced him, seeing the truth in his set gaze, and feeling thankful for it. But as much as I wanted Danny to pay for what he'd done, I didn't want Alec going to jail for violating his parole. Amy's ex was gone. That was what was important.

"I would give it to you," I said, "but seeing as you've already been in one fight in the last week, that seems a little risky."

It seemed a little risky to bring up Trevor at all, but Alec wasn't fazed. His mouth tilted up.

"Mike and I just want to talk to him."

"Trust me," I said. "You don't want to *talk* to him as badly as I do."

Alec shrugged, as if he'd find the information another way, and maybe it was wrong, but I hoped he succeeded.

I hurt for Amy, but I couldn't pity her. Despite what had happened, she was strong now, and Alec was the one with too much on his plate. Between the FBI, the lawyers, parole, his father, and his work, I wasn't sure how he was still standing.

"Are you working tonight?" I asked, finally facing him again.

He scratched his hands over his jaw, the exhaustion settling on his shoulders once again.

"I'm not on the schedule. But I need to pull together some stuff for my lawyer. Old appointments, credit card receipts. Would help if Ms. Rowe turned up. She kept all that stuff organized. Most of it disappeared when she did." As he faded off, I pictured Maxim Stein's ice queen secretary. Terry Benitez had told me she'd gone missing before Alec had been released from jail. I guess they still hadn't found her. I had a bad feeling about that.

"Have they set the trial date yet?" I asked.

He laughed, as if I'd told a joke.

"Then you can do all that tomorrow," I said.

His brows lifted at my definitive tone.

I thought of what Amy had said, about un-distracting him.

She'd been on to something there. I thought he'd needed me to distract him from everything else, but maybe what he really needed was to focus on one thing.

I came closer, touching his knees.

"Tomorrow I'll help you put everything together for your lawyer."

His eyes locked on mine, and his thigh muscles tensed beneath my hands.

"Did you have something in mind for tonight?" he asked.

Slowly, I pressed myself against him, and kissed him on the lips.

"It just so happens you have a front-row ticket to the ballet."

Twenty-two

An hour later Alec was sitting in an armless, straight-backed wooden chair in the center of our extravagant hotel room. I watched him through the crack in the bathroom door, my smile growing as he fidgeted and tapped his heel against the carpet.

The scene was set. The lights were dimmed nearly to the point of darkness. The iPod dock I used in home visits had been taken from my car and placed near the window. It was currently playing some very smooth contemporary jazz. There was other music ready, though; some hard-hitting techno I pulled out when I needed to clear my mind. It was just like the kind Jayne used in our pole dancing class.

I'd gone heavy on the smoky eye makeup, given my long, raven hair a sexy bedhead tease, and applied my lucky lipstick—*Orgasm*. I was wearing one of the complimentary robes from the hotel, but beneath it was the red lingerie I'd thrown into the duffle bag with the rest of my clothes when we'd torn out of Alec's apartment. I wished I had matching shoes, but the black patent leather pumps I'd worn to work yesterday would have to do.

It didn't really matter. Soon I'd be wearing nothing else.

A rush of nerves raced through my veins as I took a deep breath and switched off the bathroom light. As I stepped into the room, I harnessed my inner stripper, and prayed I would make Jayne proud.

"Let the torture begin," I said under my breath.

I deliberately walked behind Alec toward the iPod player, and when he turned his head, I stopped.

"Did I say you could look at me?" I asked. "Face forward."

He turned his head, chuckling softly. "Yes, ma'am."

I nearly laughed with him, but stopped myself. One of the things that made Jayne so hot was her attitude. I needed to stay in character if I was going to make Alec beg, which I planned on doing.

I rounded the chair, standing in front of him while I swung the end of the robe's belt in a circle. Slowly, I appraised him, trying to appear haughty, but failing because he was so damn sexy, even in pants and a long-sleeved shirt. The more clothes he wore, the more I wanted to rip them off of him.

"Like what you see?" he asked after a moment. In the dark, his eyes reflected what little light there was, and I could feel the power shifting to his corner. I nearly gave in—let him rise, like I knew he wanted. Take me to the bed. Tear off my robe and bury himself inside me.

"Maybe," I said nonchalantly, turning away before he caught me drooling.

I went to the iPod player and scrolled through my songs, taking my time. Making him wait.

"Please tell me you're wearing a tutu under that robe," he said.

I smirked. Hid it. Kept clicking through my songs. If I went much slower the anxiety was going to eat me alive.

"Would you like that?" I asked.

"What I'd like is for you to be flat on your back with your legs spread."

I glanced over my shoulder at him, and caught him staring at my ass. He didn't bother hiding it. I could feel the lust in his gaze.

"You have a dirty mouth," I told him. "You'll pay for that."

As if he couldn't take it anymore, he stood.

"Sit. Down," I snapped.

He dropped back in his seat.

"Better," I purred.

He muttered something I couldn't hear.

"Have you ever been to the ballet?" I found the right song. It started softly, the thump of the bass like the roll of distant thunder.

"No."

"Me neither. I started taking these classes while you were gone." I walked in front of him. Stopped five feet away. "They made me think of you."

"Ballet made you think of me," he said slowly, a skeptical expression on his face.

The bass was strengthening.

I loosened the belt of the robe, it slid off my shoulder, revealing just a hint of red. It was now or never.

"Oh, did I say *ballet*?" I asked innocently. "I meant *pole dancing*."

I shrugged out of the robe and it fell to the floor, pooling around my feet. The adrenaline surged through me like a whip.

His jaw fell slack.

"Fuck," he ground out slowly, fingers spreading on his knees. "You took . . . pole dancing?" His gaze shot to mine.

I ran my hands through my hair. "We did lap dancing, too."

His eyes followed my trailing hands to my breasts, boosted high in the lacy bra.

He shook his head. "Wait . . . who's we?"

"Just me and some other girls," I assured him.

He tilted his head back and groaned.

"Have you ever been to a strip club, Alec?"

He winced. "A long time ago. Mike's bachelor party."

My brow arched. Mike had been married. Interesting.

"And did you like it?"

"Don't remember. Too drunk."

I took a step forward, then another, swinging my hips. I lifted my foot and set it on his thigh, sliding my heel closer and closer to his crotch. His hand gripped my calf a little too tightly, but his eyes dropped beneath my tiny skirt, to the thin strip of damp, red fabric that I'd exposed to him.

"You're going to like this," I told him.

He licked his lips and leaned forward, but I lifted my leg a little higher and kicked him back into the chair.

"Uh-uh." I shook my finger in his face. "You can't touch the dancer."

The bass was climbing steadily. I pitied whoever was in the room next door, but figured they'd rather hear the music than the sounds we were about to make.

"You're killing me," he said.

"Baby, I haven't even gotten started."

I circled around him, running my fingertips over his shoulders, through his hair. When I was behind him I reached around his neck and slid my hands beneath the open collar of his shirt. There I felt the heat on his skin, and the rise of his chest as he took each breath.

"I didn't like this room," I said. "All I could think of when I was here was you touching someone else."

He stiffened. "Anna . . ."

"*Shh.*" I covered his mouth with my hand. "I didn't ask you to speak."

He adjusted his position, but said nothing.

I inhaled, taking a moment to breathe him in. The smell of him was intoxicating, like a drug. I could feel it hit my system, storm through my veins.

"It's in the past," I whispered, tracing the edge of his ear with my tongue. "Now when you think of this place, you're going to think of me, is that clear?" My fingertips found his nipples, and pinched them. He sat a little straighter.

"Yes," he hissed.

"And I'm going to know that's what you're thinking, because you won't be able to take your hands off of me."

He tried to turn, but I shoved him roughly back in place. He let me control him, even though he could have easily done what he wanted with me.

"But not now," I said, rising to walk around to the front of him again. "Now you're going to keep your hands to yourself until I say."

His fingertips skimmed the back of my thigh as I moved by him, and I smacked his hand away.

"If you test me," I warned him, "I won't give you what you need."

I slid my hand down beneath my breasts, over my belly button, and tapped the very top of my slit to show him what I meant. His jaw was working, the muscles in his neck taut.

"This is a dangerous game," he said.

I smiled.

The music was ramping up now, beating hard. I tried to remember Jayne's directions, but it was hard when he was devouring me with his hungry eyes, making lust throb at the apex of my thighs.

The nervousness was gone now. I didn't have to wonder if he'd be into this kind of thing. I could see it on his face that I had him by the balls.

I started to dance. Slow, exaggerated movements, despite the fast beat of the music. My hands felt their way over my breasts, and I squeezed them, watching his face tighten as he saw the pleasure it brought me. I spread my legs and dropped low, the way I'd done in class while holding the pole, only now I rubbed one hand over my damp center, feeling the ache there flare hotter, begging for relief. For a moment I imagined getting myself off in front of Alec. Making him watch me come. The thought of it pushed me even higher.

I touched my legs, arched my back, swung my hips. I turned around and slid the skirt up my thighs, showing him the globes of my ass, left bare by the thong. It was the most daring, erotic thing I'd ever done, and though my heart was pounding, I loved every second of it. Never had I had such power over him as I did right then.

When his heel started beating a hole through the floor, and the knuckles of his fists turned white on his knees, I came closer.

"Do you like what you see?" I asked, using his words from earlier.

"Fuck yes." He thought this was an invitation to touch, but I stepped away before he could reach me.

"Uh-uh." I shook my finger at him.

He groaned, and crossed his arms so tightly over his chest that I could see his biceps flex beneath the shirt. Taking pity on him, I backed onto his lap, keeping my legs on either side so I could maintain my balance.

I reached behind me for his hands and placed them on my hips.

"You can touch me here," I instructed. "Here alone. Understand?"

He gripped me, palms hot, as I laid back against his chest. The bulge beneath his zipper was hard as a rock, straining against his jeans. The rough fabric scored the underside of my thighs as I moved.

"Do you want me?" I asked.

"Yes," he growled. The desire in his voice made me crazy.

"You make me so hot," I murmured, sliding my hand down again. His breath quickened in my hair as I lifted the skirt, and pushed aside my panties, showing him the way I touched myself. My middle finger slid into my slit, found my throbbing clit and massaged.

"Oh." I arched back, my head on his shoulder. His hands gripped my hips even harder as he ground against my ass. I was so close I could come in seconds if I kept this up.

I stopped myself before I went too far. Rising slowly, I turned to face him, this time dropping to kneel between his legs. My nails scratched the denim covering his thighs as I lowered my mouth and bit his cock gently through his pants.

"Jesus Christ," he muttered, jumping in his seat. "That's the sexiest goddamn thing I've ever seen."

I smirked, crawling up into his lap, where I straddled his thighs. He gripped my hips again, and this time as I began to work them, he moved with me.

"Look at me," I said, keeping my eyes trained on his. It was hard to remember to breathe when he was staring at me like that.

"Whatever else happens," I told him, "you come back to me."

His eyes tightened around the corners, and he swallowed. His gaze flicked to my lips, like he was going to kiss me, but I wasn't ready to let him go yet.

He whispered my name, his agreement to what I'd said, and I grabbed the edges of his shirt, jerking it open so that the top button snapped off.

He stilled, and the passion in his dark eyes turned greedy.

I popped the next button, and the next. Each one making me more excited. I was superwoman. From now on I was taking off all his shirts this way.

I rode him hard then, gyrating my pelvis against his, rubbing all the right spots. His hands wandered up my back, into my hair, pulling my body against his while he answered my every movement. Somehow he unlatched the skirt and tossed it to the floor. I reached back and unhooked my bra and rose, letting my sensitive nipples slide up his chest, and then over his open mouth. As his tongue shot out to graze them, I lost control.

The music roared through me. The feel of him burned my fingertips. I couldn't hold off any longer. I ripped his shirt over his head, scratching my nails over his chest. His hands fisted in my hair, and then he kissed me, hungrily, desperately. His tongue plunged into my mouth, and I could feel the vibrations of his groan inside me. The music was loud enough to drown out all other sounds, the lights dark enough to make us the only two people in the world.

But his hand fisted too hard in my hair, and suddenly the desire I'd been feeling was tinged with fear. I cried out, this time in pain, and when my eyes shot open I saw his confusion reflected back to me. Then his body stiffened. He tried to hold on to me, but it was too late.

I was jerked backward off of his lap, straight into the arms of another man.

Twenty-three

It took only a second for my mind to wrap around what was happening, but it was the longest second of my life. A man held me from behind, one arm wrapped around my waist, while the other hand held something sharp and cold to my throat. He wasn't much taller than me, maybe four or five inches. I could feel his belt against my lower back and the buttons of his shirt against my spine.

"That was quite a show," he said appreciatively. He wore gloves. The soft leather stuck to the sweat on my stomach.

I recognized his voice, but couldn't place it.

Alec was standing in front of me a few feet away, shirtless, ripped with muscle. The chair he'd been sitting on was tipped over on its back. He held his open hands up.

"You're a hard man to catch alone," the man said to him. "Between the public spaces and the feds tailing you, you don't make it easy."

The FBI was following Alec? My mind grasped on to the hope that they were close, in the hotel even.

"Let her go," Alec said, over the heavy music. I cursed that music now. If it hadn't been so loud, we would have heard someone break in.

I searched his eyes for recognition, but there was only cold fury. He didn't know this man.

As I struggled, the intruder's hand slid across my belly. All I wore was the lace thong. I might as well have been naked. When he'd grabbed me, I'd covered my breasts, but as he moved I released them in order to try to shove his hands away.

He pinched me hard below the ribs, and I swallowed my shout of pain.

"Let her go," Alec said again, "and I won't kill you."

The man gave an amused laugh. "I guess we found your weakness."

Alec's gaze flicked to mine, and I saw what he needed me to do. Adrenaline pounded through me, overtaking my fright. But before I could try to break free, the man took two quick steps back, dragging me with him. One of my shoes fell off as I scrambled to keep up.

"I could cut her open, Flynn," said the man. "Maybe then you'd get your head on straight."

I turned my head, just a little, and caught a glimpse of a scar running from the corner of his mouth across his cheek.

"I know you," I said. "You work in valet." The buttons scratching my back were part of his beige uniform. I could picture him clearly now, as he'd been yesterday taking my car. How long had he waited here for us? Clearly he knew who Alec was.

He pressed the knife harder to my throat and my breath caught.

"Who are you?" Alec asked, taking a slow step forward.

"That's good enough," said the man. Alec stopped. "You need to listen now, not ask questions."

Alec nodded once, unnaturally calm and still. My eyes darted around the room. The phone was on the nightstand beside the lamp—too far away to grab. The chair was too heavy. I could feel the metal prick my skin, and I jumped.

Alec bared his teeth, as though the knife had cut him, not me. "I'm listening," he said.

"Get the feds to drop the case against Stein. Bobby Calloway took the hit for the woman on the bridge. You do your part and Stein walks. This is the only time we're going to ask."

"And what do you care?" I asked. "You a friend of his?"

"You've got quite a mouth," he said, a smile in his voice. "I used to talk back, too, before someone taught me not to."

I had a grim feeling he was referring to the scar on his face.

"You work for Reznik," Alec said. "Stein is paying Reznik to keep me quiet."

The man didn't disagree. In the back of my mind I remembered Alec saying the FBI was watching Reznik. That must have been why he'd sent this man.

I was trembling now, ready to do what I needed so that Alec could take him down. I only hoped the knife wasn't lodged in my throat when he did.

"He was disappointed you didn't come by to see him at the restaurant." Reznik's messenger nuzzled my ear, and I turned as far away as I could from him. "So what's it going to be, Flynn? Are you going to play along, or do you need a little more encouragement?

With that, his hand snaked up my body and clutched my breast. Even though he was wearing gloves, I felt like I was going to puke.

It was now or never.

Just like Alec and I had practiced, I tucked my chin, shifted my hips, and slipped beneath my captor's arm. Then Alec charged, faster than I would have thought a man of his size could move. I was tossed hard to the side, so hard the wind was knocked out of my lungs as I hit the wall and crumpled to the floor. For a few moments I gasped, seeing stars, but they cleared just as the two bodies crashed into the desk in the corner of the room.

My hand flew to where he'd held the knife. Just a nick. It left a small smear of red on my fingertips.

There was a loud crack, even over the slap of the bass, and the desk broke. Both men rolled across the ground, a tangle of limbs and flying fists. I searched for the knife, but couldn't see it. I backed against the wall; there was no way to help—they were moving too fast, hitting too hard.

Reznik's man shouted in pain; the sound felt like claws raking down my spine.

"Anna?" Alec called. "Talk to me!"

"I'm okay!"

I crawled across the carpet toward the nightstand, jerking the iPod dock cord from the wall as I passed. The sudden silence screamed in my ears as I felt atop the table for the lamp. When my hands were around the base, I stood, and heaved it over my shoulder like a bat. The last light in the room went out, leaving us with only the moonlight streaming through the window as a guide.

I was too late. Alec was hunched over his knees, grasping his side. On the floor before him laid the man with the scar on his face, wearing the beige uniform of all the valets and bellhops in this hotel. His arm was bent backward, like he was a doll who'd had his limb reattached the wrong way. A new wave of nausea climbed up my throat.

"Is he . . ."

"Out." Alec reached toward me. "Don't look at him. Look at me."

The shakes caught up with me then. I trembled so hard I could barely walk. I crumpled into him as he slid back against the foot of the bed.

"Let me see you." He was winded, barely able to speak, and this scared me. Alec was impenetrable. He couldn't be injured.

He touched my neck with one quaking hand, refusing to let go of his side with the other. "Are you all right?"

I nodded.

He pulled the blanket off the bed and tugged it around my shoulders. When I was covered, he pulled me against him.

It wasn't until then that I saw the blood dripping down his side.

"Alec, you're hurt." I peeled his hand back, no longer caring that I was naked beneath this blanket, or that we'd been attacked by men Maxim had paid. Only seeing Alec.

There was a puncture wound on his right side just above his lowest rib. It oozed blood, black in the dim light.

My heart felt like it had stopped beating.

"It's nothing," he said, latching his hand over the wound again. "I'm sorry, Anna. I'm so sorry."

He coughed, and then stopped the sound with a tight groan.

"Alec!" I grabbed him before he fell to the side, and helped to ease him onto the floor. Panic threatened to take control of me, but I pushed it back. Not yet. I wouldn't break yet. Alec needed me.

I glanced to Reznik's man, and found him still unconscious behind us.

"I have to call the FBI," Alec said, voice tight with pain. "Get my phone."

My mind was racing. If the FBI wasn't already here, they'd failed as far as I was concerned.

"I'm going to call 911," I said. "Don't move."

I ran to the nightstand and dialed the numbers. I wasn't connected to emergency services though, I was put through to the building's security. The man that answered already knew my room number and asked what the problem was.

"S-someone broke in," I stammered. "My boyfriend's been stabbed. You have to send someone now." Still holding the phone, I raced back to Alec, who was trying to sit up again.

"Alec, hold still."

His breathing was shallow. Too fast. I pulled the blanket off my shoulders and pushed down on the wound, hoping it would slow the bleeding.

"Find Mike," he said between breaths. "You can trust Mike."

"Shh . . ." I snatched the robe, half under the ruined remains of the desk, and quickly put it on.

"I'm sorry."

"Stop saying that." My voice cracked.

I propped his head on my lap, and kept the pressure on his wound, even as he grimaced in pain.

"You were incredible," he said, siphoning in a quick breath through his teeth. "I fucking love the ballet."

I gave a watery laugh then bit the inside of my cheek. *Don't cry don't cry don't cry.*

"I love you." I pressed my lips against his forehead.

"Sure," he muttered. "You say it now that I'm dying."

The cold prickled my skin.

"Hold on," I said. "Help is coming."

Over his body, I watched the motionless form of the man who'd attacked us, and waited.

Twenty-four

Three hours later I was pacing across the waiting room of the ER. I'd counted the tiles—fourteen from one side to the other—and when I reached the end, I turned around and started over. It was the only thing that kept me from kicking down the door that separated me from Alec.

"Anna."

I looked up as Mike crossed the waiting room to where I was standing. He was wearing blue baggy sweats that clashed with a red, long-sleeved T-shirt. I imagined him reaching for the first pieces of clothing he could find when I'd called and told him what had happened.

Just having him here made me feel infinitely better.

"How's our boy?" he asked.

I stared at the metal doors, blocking us from the patient area.

"I don't know. The doctor said he has a punctured lung and a couple broken ribs. They're not going to operate but . . ." I swallowed. Inhaled. "But he's got a tube in his throat and an IV in his arm and if they don't let me see him in the next five minutes I'm going to start breaking things."

"All right," he said, wrapping me in a hard hug. "Let me see what I can do."

I followed him to the front desk, where a bossy nurse looked down from her high horse just long enough to tell us we'd have to wait for someone to call for us.

She couldn't tell us how long it would be.

She couldn't tell us if he was okay.

She couldn't tell us shit.

"Let's sit down." Mike led us to a row of orange bucket seats. The next row over, a woman laid across the chairs, knees curled up against her stomach, her head in a man's lap.

"Alec's going to be okay," Mike said. "He's a tough son of a bitch."

"He was *stabbed*." My voice broke. I hunched forward, elbows on my knees. "I don't know what's going on. We were back there together, and then two policemen showed up. They took my statement and kicked me out."

I didn't understand why I couldn't stay with Alec. He'd been sedated when I left. Vulnerable. I didn't even trust the doctors to be alone with him at this point. Not after Reznik's man had gotten to us.

Mike placed a warm hand in the center of my back. I was grateful he was here. I didn't want to be alone.

"You're freezing," he said with a frown. He rubbed my arm. I'd been given a set of scrubs when I'd come in, and though they provided more coverage than the blanket, they were still paper-thin. I wasn't even wearing a bra, which was obvious as I looked down.

I crossed my arms over my chest.

He walked back to the front desk, and returned with a thin, pink hospital blanket that he draped over my shoulders.

"This guy that broke in," Mike said. "He hurt you?"

There was an iciness in his voice as he said this, and it occurred to me why Alec had said I could trust Mike. He would serve as my protector while Alec could not.

My fingertips felt my neck, now covered with a Band-Aid. That was nothing compared to the feel of our attacker fondling my nearly naked body.

"Not really."

"How'd he get in?"

"Key card," I answered. "He'd slipped in as a new worker in valet. No one even thought to check up on him." So much for awesome security. "He'd brought wire cutters for the chain."

Mike muttered a curse. "The cops took him?"

"Yeah." He'd roused by the time the paramedics had arrived, but the hotel's security had handcuffed him to the bed frame by then. The manager, a perfectly groomed man with blotchy red cheeks, had been in shock, apologizing to me over and over as I'd stayed with the team that took Alec by stretcher to the ambulance.

"Where's Chloe?" I asked, remembering suddenly that I'd pulled a family man from his home in the middle of the night.

"Took her to my mom's. She barely even woke up."

I nodded. "Thank you for coming."

He put his arm around me, and gave me another squeeze.

A moment later a nurse in pink scrubs opened the security doors and waved to me across the lobby. After vouching for Mike, we were led back through an intricate maze of hallways to a room where one of the two policemen I'd met earlier was standing guard. He must have been fresh out of the academy, with a crisp blue uniform and dark, buzzed hair. I glared at him. He was the one who'd escorted me to the waiting room when I'd refused to leave.

The nurse stopped us both before going inside. "One at a time."

Mike offered for me to go ahead.

"Make it quick," the guard said to me as I passed. I nearly stopped and told him he could kiss my ass, I would take as long as I damn well pleased, but Mike ushered me forward.

The room was sterile, white, without the stock art and bad wallpaper that you found in most hospitals. Emergency services probably didn't keep people long enough to warrant decorations. From behind the half-pulled curtain came a cough, then a raspy sigh.

"Alec?" I rushed to the bedside, finding him pale, baring his teeth in a pained grimace. He was trying to sit up, but was tangled in his IV and heart rate monitor. The tube had been removed from his throat, and been replaced with an oxygen line beneath his nose, which he was in the process of pulling off his face.

"Hey, you need to lie down!" The nurse pushed me aside and blocked him with a firm hand on his upper arm.

He blinked a few times, focusing on me.

"Alec, it's okay. I'm here." I grabbed his hand, held it between both of mine. He wasn't much warmer than I was.

"Anna," he whispered. He pulled me close, and I threw my arms around his neck, careful to avoid the tubes and bandages. His hands fisted in the back of my shirt.

"What are you doing here?" His voice was raw, quiet.

I helped settle him back on the pillow and touched his face.

"I . . . I came with you, remember?" Maybe he was out of it and didn't remember the ambulance ride. I wished I were so lucky. The way he'd fought as they'd intubated him, the blood soaking through the bandages on his side. Those were images I'd never forget.

"They said you'd left."

"No, I'm here. I'm not going anywhere."

His eyes grew wary. With a shake of his head he released me and tried to push up on his elbows. Gently, I pushed him back down. The beep on his heart rate monitor picked up speed.

"It's not safe here," he said. He coughed, then winced.

A chill crept over my skin. I wasn't sure who we could trust anymore.

I glanced over my shoulder as the nurse left the room.

"Who?" I whispered. "The cop? You think he knows Reznik?"

"*Me,*" he said, too loudly, then clutched his side. "You're not safe around *me.*"

He'd pulled his hand away, but I'd come closer and spread my hands over his chest in an attempt to keep him from moving. The gown they'd put him in was untied, and fell open, revealing a thick gauze bandage covering half his chest, a reminder of what had happened.

"Lie back," I said. "Please."

Footsteps crossed the floor. I turned to look, but instead of seeing Mike, I saw a woman in a sharp black suit with shoulder-length auburn hair. Her age was hard to pinpoint—she looked to be in her early thirties, but the confident way she assessed us made me think she might be older. She wasn't beautiful, but she *was* hot. There was a dominatrix-y kind of vibe about her. In her hands was Alec's chart.

"You're going to be fine," she said, speaking to Alec.

Alec's mouth formed a thin line.

"You're his doctor?" I looked for the stethoscope.

The woman's gaze shifted to me. She was all business, not even an ounce of reassurance.

"You're Ms. Rossi," she said. "The masseuse. I've seen you from afar."

"She's with the FBI," Alec said. "This is Agent Jamison."

"You've been watching Alec?" I asked, feeling a spark of resentment flash to something much brighter.

"Obviously not when he's behind closed doors," Jamison answered.

I snorted. "Obviously not."

Jamison gave me a hard look, the kind I'm sure made most people wither. Not me, though. I'd run up against scarier people than her.

"I read the police report," she said to Alec. "Anything you'd like to add?"

"The guy who attacked us was working for Reznik," Alec said. "Max Stein must have paid him to stop me from testifying against him."

Jamison considered this a moment, but didn't look surprised.

"He's getting nervous," she said. "That's good."

"For who?" I asked. "Alec was just stabbed. I was . . ." I threw my hands up. I didn't want to say it again; I'd already told the police.

Jamison's eyes pinched at the corners.

"This is the first attempt since prison?" she asked. I recognized her voice now. She'd been the one saying his name when he'd called me at his father's.

Alec's gaze flicked to me. The cold seeped deeper into my skin.

"What do you mean 'since prison'?" I asked.

She didn't answer, leaving Alec to fill me in.

"Max has connections," he said grimly. "They run deep."

I couldn't believe he hadn't mentioned this before.

"What does *that* mean?" I asked, realizing as I said it what must have happened. "The scar on your back. That wasn't an accident in the metal shop."

Alec avoided my eyes.

"They moved me to isolation," he said through his teeth. "I wasn't permitted any contact with the outside after that."

That's why he hadn't called me or written while he'd been in prison. Not because the FBI was worried about contaminating the case. Because he had already been attacked once, and they were trying to keep it from happening again.

My fear for him—for both of us—deepened.

"Why didn't you tell me?" I asked quietly.

"Probably to avoid that look you're giving him right now," chimed in Jamison, flipping through the chart.

I turned on her, my temper shooting past its boiling point.

"No one asked you," I snapped. "What do you know anyway? He could have died tonight!"

She removed a tube of ChapStick from her pocket and rolled it over her lips.

"I know that if you play with fire, you get burned."

Her intent was clear. She was blaming Alec for what had happened, and me for putting myself at risk by staying with him. If he'd never associated with Maxim Stein, we wouldn't be in danger now.

I stared at her, fingernails digging into my palms. I didn't like her. Didn't like her tone, didn't like her neat little suit. But deep down inside of me, I couldn't say she was wrong.

"Anna," Alec said.

"I'll give you a few minutes," said Jamison. With that, she turned and left the room, taking Alec's chart with her.

I turned back to the man I loved, hating the betrayal I felt when I looked at him. "You told me no more secrets."

"There was no reason for you to know."

"That's not the point." I swallowed to keep my throat from tying in knots. "If I'm going to be with you, I need full disclosure."

He stared at me for one long moment, and in it his emotions and his pain became hidden, as if pulled behind a steel curtain.

"*If,*" he said quietly.

I pressed my thumbs into the corners of my eyebrows.

"If you weren't with me, what happened tonight wouldn't have happened," he said. "A lot of things wouldn't have happened."

"Alec." A pressure, just as heavy as that I'd felt pacing in the waiting room but less sharp, settled on my chest. I didn't like where this was going.

Jamison returned to the room, followed by a doctor in a white lab coat. A nurse came in a second later, her arms filled with supplies—IV bags, bandages, a box of rubber gloves.

"He's safe to transport now?" asked Jamison.

"It's not my preference," said the doctor, an Indian man with a thick black moustache. "But if you must, you must."

He wrote something in the chart, then checked a prescription bottle the nurse handed to him.

"Saddle up, Flynn," said Jamison. "We're out of here."

I gripped Alec's forearm. "Where are we going?"

"You're going home," the agent said to me.

Alec shoved himself up in his bed. The nurse had placed the supplies in a white plastic bag and was pushing a wheelchair up to the bed for Alec. Mike stood in the doorway, kept back by the police officer guarding the door.

"I'm staying with Alec," I said.

"Not possible," said Jamison. The nurse was unhooking Alec from the heart monitor. "He's going into protective custody until the trial."

They were separating us. After we'd both just been attacked together.

The realization suddenly became clear. Alec was the important one. He was going to testify against Maxim Stein in the biggest white-collar case since Bernie Madoff. But me? I was just his girlfriend. The masseuse.

"That wasn't the plan," said Alec.

"The plan's changed," Jamison responded.

"She was supposed to be kept out of all this."

"She was," said Jamison. "You're the one who keeps bringing her back in."

Alec muttered a curse.

"Where are you taking him?" I asked.

"I'm afraid that's classified," said Jamison.

"She needs protection more than I do," Alec argued breathlessly. "They've seen her. They know who she is."

"I've put in a request to have a car stationed outside her residence through the night. I'll press Stein about the attack, but his wall of lawyers is ten feet thick. All we can do is continue to monitor Reznik."

The police officer stepped into the room. I backed into the bed, into Alec, who put a protective hand around my waist.

"Not good enough." Alec was starting to cough with the exertion. The doctor stepped forward to hold his shoulders still.

"Move slowly," he cautioned. "You right lung is at half its normal capacity. The muscle over your rib was severed. Over-exert your body and you'll injure yourself much worse."

"You think *you* can protect her in your state?" Jamison asked evenly. "Maxim Stein wants you, Alec. Not her. With you gone, her risk is all but eliminated."

Alec gripped the side of the hospital bed.

I guess we found your weakness, Reznik's man whispered in the back of my mind.

Alec couldn't actually be considering this. We needed to stay together. I couldn't leave him hurt. And what was I supposed to do if Reznik's men came back, asking questions? Say I didn't know where Alec was? Like they'd believe that.

Alec nodded.

I stared at him in shock.

"Come with me, Ms. Rossi," said the police officer. I took a closer look at him now—he had brown, serious eyes and long black lashes. Honey-colored skin and a square jaw.

He reached for my arm, but I backed away quickly, knocking over the IV stand Alec had just been unhooked from. It fell to the ground with a loud clatter.

"Alec, think about this," I begged. "Look at me."

"What's going on?" Mike had stepped into the room. Relief crossed Alec's face.

"Mike, get her out of here." Alec turned his face away from me as Mike stepped to my side.

"No," I said. "Alec, wait . . ."

"Come on," said Mike gently. "He'll call you when he can."

Alec winced, and the thought crossed my mind that he hadn't planned on calling. That this good-bye was more than temporary.

"No phones," said Jamison. "They'll see each other after the trial."

"We don't even know when that is!" I shouted.

I reached for Alec's forearm, and he drew back too quickly, as though my touch had burned him. I stared at him in shock as he doubled over, gasping, and then fell into the wheelchair.

"Breathe," I said, kneeling before him. "Slow down."

"No more *ifs*," he wheezed as his gaze found mine. "Goodbye, Anna."

"Alec . . ."

"Now, Mike."

Mike pulled me to a stand, and though I struggled, he kept me pinned to his side.

"He's going to hurt himself if he sees you scared," he whispered harshly.

He was right. Defeated, I forced my chin to lift. I tried to clear my thoughts. Alec and I weren't together, but he would be safe in protective custody. And maybe Agent Jamison was right, and I would be better off without him for the time being.

Somehow, believing that just made it harder to walk away.

Twenty-five

We went to the only place I had left—my tiny one-bedroom apartment in South Tampa. The décor was sparse to say the least; most of my things had been taken to Alec's high-rise. I did have some clothes though, and a made bed and a couch. Enough to convince my dad I was living there regularly the last time he'd come to visit.

"Stay here," Mike said as we stepped inside. The air was warm and stagnant. I hadn't bothered to leave the AC on when I was here so infrequently. As he searched the bedroom, bathroom, and closets, I adjusted the thermostat.

Wandering into the kitchenette, I took a look out the window at the patrol car parked on the street. Apparently Jamison had requested surveillance after all.

I wondered if she and Alec would be staying together until the trial. My mind had already started spinning images of a small, dimly lit room with one bed when Mike returned.

"Looks all right." He rubbed his eyes, exhausted. I couldn't blame him, but though my brain was tired, my body was still agitated and twitchy, like I'd just slammed an energy drink.

"Thanks, Mike."

He glanced around the living room. I didn't even have a TV here.

"I'll take the couch."

I shook my head. "Uh-uh. Go home. Get your daughter." I wasn't jumping up and down at the prospect of alone time, but I didn't exactly need the guilt on my conscience either.

He sat on the rose-patterned sofa and toed off his shoes. "My mom's got her until the morning. She doesn't even know I'm gone."

He stretched out, then adjusted one of the pillows behind his head. His eyes closed.

I tried to reason with him. "There's a patrol car twenty yards away."

"Really? I can't see it." He flipped onto his side. He may not have been as big as Alec, but he still looked like a Cabbage Patch Kid on a Barbie-sized couch. One knee was bent to his chest, the other leg hung over the armrest.

"Mike . . ." This was a losing battle. "At least take the bed."

"No, thanks," he snorted. "I'm attached to my nuts. I'd rather your man not rip them off."

At the mention of Alec, my jaw clenched. Part of me was missing without him. At least if I knew where he was, I could picture him there, know he was safe. But now all I could visualize was the thick bandage over his ribs and an FBI officer with the bedside manner of Nurse Ratched. If the knife had been three inches higher, he would be dead now.

If Alec dropped the case, Maxim left him alone.

If we'd never gone to that stupid hotel, Alec wouldn't have said good-bye.

No more *ifs*.

I had to think of something else.

"How long were you married?" I asked.

Mike opened one eye and squinted at me.

"Long enough to know it wasn't for me."

It was too warm for a blanket, but I retrieved one from the linen closet anyway and set it on the floor beside him.

"I get that," I said. Happily ever afters didn't exist. Someone always left. Or died. Or got knifed by a hit man in a hotel room.

He looked surprised. "I thought you and Alec were pretty serious."

I flinched. For better or for worse didn't include a good-bye like the last one he'd given me.

"We get along just great when he's in prison or witness protection."

Mike leaned up on his elbow.

"It's not always this bad."

"That's the thing." My cheeks flamed. "I can handle the bad. I *thrive* when things are bad. It's when they're good that I don't know what the hell I'm doing. It's like the magnets in my brain need recalibrating or something."

He smirked. "I've got jumper cables in my car."

I smacked his arm.

He laid on his back, fingers woven behind his head. "I know someone like that. He went from looking out for his piece of crap dad, to fixing problems for his piece of crap boss. If there's anyone who thrives when things are bad, it's him."

"So we're both dysfunctional. Great."

And now we were both alone, because he'd pushed me away when he needed me most. I got that he wanted to protect me, but it still stung.

The amusement drained from Mike's face.

"What he did back there was probably the hardest thing he's ever had to do."

"I doubt that."

He shook his head. "He's gone his whole life looking for an anchor, and now it's just been cut loose. How do you think that feels?"

I pictured Alec drifting, lost, unable to stop or even slow down. An anchor was steady. Unwavering. I had only fleeting moments of those things. And though I'd told Mike I thrived when things were rough, his words made me question if I was strong enough to weather the storm.

"Good night, Anna."

The conversation was over. Mike had made his point, and if it was possible, I felt even worse than before.

For a while there was only the sound of his breathing.

"Night, Mike."

I went to the bedroom and shut the door behind me. Quickly, I stripped down out of the scrubs, anxious to rid myself of the hospital smell. I looked around the small room, at the nightstand with my old alarm clock and the perfume bottles on my dresser. I hadn't been here since Alec had been back, which felt like a lifetime ago now. It didn't even feel familiar anymore.

Stiffly, I laid in bed and stared at the ceiling, wishing I knew where he was. Wishing I was with him. Wishing all of this was over.

I slept restlessly, and when morning came, I was pulled from my nightmares by a knock at the door. I hadn't been asleep long, and my head was pounding. It took a moment to realize that someone had already answered. Mike.

I sat up, snatched a robe off the back of the bathroom door, and walked out into the living room. There, I found Mike, still wearing the same clothes, talking to an older man in a suit who was standing on the doormat. They both turned to look at me.

"Terry," I said, recognizing my dad's old friend.

"You two know each other?" Mike asked.

Terry gave him a narrowed look. "I should ask you the same."

"Mike, this is Terry Benitez. He's a detective who used to work with my dad. Mike is Alec's best friend."

"Ah." Terry extended a hand, which Mike took a little skeptically.

"Come in," I said, and went to the kitchen to make coffee. It was a useless endeavor, of course. There wasn't enough caffeine in the world to clear my head.

"Heard about last night," said Terry.

"Which means my dad has heard about last night," I added, cringing at my own pithy tone. I didn't want to be rude to Terry. He'd done so much for me.

Terry chuckled. "I made a promise to a friend to keep my eye on you."

"That seems to be a theme these days," I muttered as Mike gave a righteous little snort. He returned to the couch and sat, rubbing his eyes.

"I didn't tell your father," said Terry. "Figured he should hear it from you."

I gave him a small, grateful smile. Yeah, that would be a fun conversation.

"The kid that pulled the knife on you two, his name is Nathanial Chekhov. He's got a sheet about a mile long. Says Alec owed his boss an old gambling debt."

"Well that's bullshit," I said.

Terry nodded. "I guessed as much. He's been connected to someone named Jack Reznik. A real bad character. Had him in county half a dozen times for serious crimes he always manages to weasel his way out of." He glanced out the window. "The FBI came in and snatched up the case before we had a chance to press either of them for more."

And all Agent Jamison planned to do was *monitor* Reznik. Wonderful. Now I felt really safe.

"Alec said he did some work for Maxim Stein," I said.

Terry's brows flattened. "He's done work for a lot of people. Can't link him to any of them." He put a hand on my shoulder. "How're you holding up?"

"Fine," I said. "They took Alec into protective custody." A blanket of numbness descended over me. Funny how quickly my mind had turned to self-preservation. The scar on Nathanial

Chekhov's cheek, the feel of his gloved hand on my stomach, Alec's head on my lap while we waited for the ambulance, they all seemed like an ugly dream now.

The coffeemaker was starting to gurgle, and I reached for the mugs.

He glanced back at Mike. "That why you're here?"

"That's right," said Mike.

Terry looked impressed.

"I've bumped up your escort," he said. "The officer outside will take you wherever you need to go. Follow you if you'd rather. He'll keep an eye on you entering and leaving buildings. Check out spaces where you'll be alone, like your home. His name's Marcos; you met him last night at the hospital. He's a good cop. I've known him since he was a cadet."

I couldn't help the bristle of annoyance, remembering the dark-haired officer who'd told me to make my visit with Alec "quick," but I was grateful, too.

"Thank you," I said.

"I can't promise it'll last forever."

"No," I said. "I understand." A protective detail wasn't standard practice when someone was attacked, especially when the culprit had been taken into custody. This was a gift from a friend, and I had no doubts Terry was calling in some serious favors to make it happen.

The coffeemaker hissed behind me, and I filled the three mugs. "I guess that means you can go home, Mike."

Mike rose and moved into the kitchen for a cup. "Give me some coffee, then we'll talk. If it's good, I might not want to go."

"It's bad," I assured him.

I looked between them—two very different men here for the same reason. I was acutely aware how lucky I was, but hated feeling like a burden.

"Any idea where Alec is?" I asked Terry. "Or how long he'll be there?"

Terry waved off the coffee I offered, and smiled sympathetically.

"None," he said. "My advice, get back to a regular routine. It'll make the time pass faster."

I felt heavy, pulled into the floorboards. Alec hadn't been back long, but already he'd become my routine, even if that routine was highly irregular.

Terry left a few minutes later, and shortly after that I convinced Mike to go, but only after he'd programmed his phone number into my cell and gone out to speak with Marcos, my new best friend. He told me he'd pick up our bag from the hotel before he started his shift, and would bring it by later.

I kissed him on the cheek. "You're all right, you know that?"

He smiled that hundred-watt smile. "Pass that along to your friend Amy for me."

Internally, I cringed at the reminder of what had gone down at the picnic, but Mike didn't seem to be thinking of that. He was still grinning.

"Don't forget to text me when you leave and get to work."

"Yes, sir."

"Teach my daughter that," he said. "She's only seven and she already thinks she's the boss."

"Well, she is," I called after him as he retreated down the steps. I remembered the way they were together. Chloe was a daddy's girl. If she said jump, I was sure Mike asked how high.

As I shut the door, the heaviness descended again.

"Routine," I told myself. I touched my neck, shivering at the feel of the bandage. Slowly, I pulled it free, fingertips brushing the small scab that had formed there.

With two hours to go before I was scheduled at Rave, I decided to check in on Jacob. I found the number in my purse for his foster mother and made the call, but he had already left for school. She promised to deliver the message and told me that he'd been doing well.

"Really?" I asked. "No offense, but he was pretty torn up about his sister last time I saw him."

"I know," she said. "I guess he worked through it. He's been happy as a lark these past couple days."

"Great." I frowned. That didn't sit right.

After that I tried Alec's cell, but it went straight to voice mail. I thought of calling my dad but decided I'd need a lot more caffeine before I even attempted that.

I showered with the door open, the curtain pulled back halfway, and a steak knife next to my shampoo. No one was going to surprise me while I was naked. Not ever again.

Because my car was still at the hotel, Marcos, the officer who'd been guarding Alec's room last night, took me there. It turned out he was a pretty nice guy. A little green. A lot serious. But nice. He followed me to Rave, walked me to the door, and asked that I not leave the building after my shift until he came to get me. I had no doubts he'd be right on time.

I was on my way to the back to drop off my purse and get ready when Derrick waved me over. He was wearing black cargo pants tucked into combat boots today, and a loose white knit sweater that hung off his shoulder. He killed it in that outfit, and already I was trying to replicate it in my mind with items from my closet.

"Anything I should be worried about?" He tilted his chin toward Marcos as he slipped back into the patrol car. There was an appreciative look in his eye—clearly he was admiring the view.

"Oh. He's just a friend," I said.

Derrick hummed the equivalent of "yeah, right" and linked his arm around mine.

"You have a visitor," he said quietly.

My heart skipped a beat. "Alec?"

Derrick's chin jutted out. He stopped in his tracks. "The guy who pulled a gun in the middle of my spa? Uh, *no*. Much as I appreciate him taking out creepy stalker boy, I'm not interested in a repeat performance, thank you very much."

Four months ago, Alec had rescued me when Melvin Herman, who we'd learned had been hired by Bobby to play the role of stalker, had cornered me in the break room. A lot of customers had been freaked out by the whole thing, and Derrick had lost a ton of business. I was lucky he'd kept me on after that.

It took some effort to clear the disappointment from my face. "Who, then?"

"One of your regulars. Looks like the guy from Fight Club. Not Brad Pitt, the one who keeps getting his ass kicked."

Derrick led me into the nail section of the spa, where Trevor was sitting in a pedicure chair looking very uncomfortable. He was still wearing his shoes, which were perched on the outside of the unfilled soaking tub, and he boasted a split lip and the biggest jaw bruise I had ever seen.

"Oh shit," I said under my breath.

"His *condition* was making some of the ladies uncomfortable," whispered Derrick as he walked away.

I marched straight up to Trevor, hiding the cringe when I noticed that his nose was still swollen, and that the dark purple faded to a very ugly yellow at the edges.

"I don't feel sorry for you," I said.

He tried to laugh, but then clutched his head.

"Really," I said. "I don't."

"They had to rebreak my nose in order to reset it," he said, a little nasally.

"Aw, crap." I sat on the low rolling chair where the nail technicians did their work and rested my forehead on the heels of my hands. "Are you kidding me?"

"Yes," he said. "But you did feel bad for a second, didn't you?"

I glared at him.

"What are you doing here?" I said. He didn't even have an appointment for a massage. Not that I would have done it anyway.

He pushed himself out of the huge mechanical massage chair

and stood, reaching out his hand to help me up. I took it be-grudgingly, and let go as soon as I was standing.

"I wanted to say I'm not sorry."

My mouth gaped open.

"You came here to offer a non apology?"

He nodded. "I've wanted to kiss you for a long time, Anna. And for the three seconds before your asshole boyfriend punched me in the face I was really enjoying myself."

I laughed incredulously before I caught myself.

"You're joking, right?"

He shook his head, his grin flattening. "You deserve better than him. He shouldn't even be out of jail."

"You don't know what you're talking about," I said. But for some stupid reason, I couldn't look him in the face anymore. I stared at my toes. "You didn't tell anyone what happened, right?"

There was no denying I felt bad about that one.

"That I almost got mugged outside the gym by five enormous, armed Navy Seals? Fuck yeah. I told everyone."

He took a step closer when I hiccupped a laugh.

"I do know what I'm talking about," he said quietly. "Stay with him, and you're going to get hurt. Really hurt. All the things he's done, and he gets what? A slap on the wrist? People need to pay for what they do."

"You keep saying that. Eye for an eye. I get it." I remembered what he'd said at the deli, before the first time he'd confronted Alec. *"That woman on the news that was driven off the bridge? Someone should make the guy who's responsible jump."*

In my darker moments, I'd wished someone had made Bobby jump, just as he'd forced Charlotte off in her car. Or tied him up and driven him around at gunpoint the way he'd done to me. Last night, staring at the ceiling, I'd even had thoughts of Alec turning that knife on Reznik's man. Thoughts like that were as sticky and black as hot tar.

I may not have agreed with Trevor on this issue, but I under-stood him at least. When I looked up, his green eyes had hard-ened with the same anger I'd seen just glimpses of before.

"What happened to you, Trevor?" I asked quietly.

By some force beyond my control, I reached to touch his arm. He looked down at my hand, the anger rolling into something less certain.

He inhaled slowly, then pulled his arm back. "Stay clear of Alec Flynn. You're not stupid, so stop acting like it."

My shoulders went rigid at his harsh tone.

"Excuse me?"

He turned away. "I've got a lot going on at work over the next few weeks. I'll call to reschedule my appointments."

"Trevor . . ."

"Take care, Anna."

He didn't even look at me. He strode out without another word, leaving me wondering if I was supposed to follow him.

Twenty-six

Four days passed uneventfully. Then four more. Though I knew he couldn't contact me, I checked my cell phone religiously for messages or missed calls, just in case Alec had tried to reach me. I searched my car for notes, or little gifts, like the little license plate he'd left that day, but there was nothing. He was gone, like he'd never come back in the first place.

I did what I was supposed to do. I went to work. I gave massages. I laughed at all of Mike's jokes, and didn't pester Marcos when he gave me a look for crossing a parking lot without waiting for him to hold my hand. I had movie night with Amy and thanked Miss Iris for the chocolate chip cookies she kept sending my way.

But I couldn't sleep. Not without Alec.

I was plagued with nightmares. Of men with scarred faces hiding in my house. Of blood dripping down Alec's chest. Of drowning in a car that was driven off a bridge.

And sometimes I dreamed of Alec making love to me. Slowly. Gently. They were so clear that I could feel the sweet friction of him moving inside me, feel his ragged breaths against my neck. I would often shudder awake, only to find myself alone.

Those were the worst.

It was ten p.m. Sunday night, eight days after Alec was taken from me, that I got a phone call. I didn't recognize the number right away, but the voice was easy enough to distinguish.

"You told me to call if I was going to leave."

I'd been lying back on the couch with my feet on the armrest, scanning through the news on my cellphone with hopes that something new had come up regarding the Maxim Stein trial, but at Jacob's words, I sat up.

"Jacob, what . . ." I closed my eyes, remembering too easily what it was like to be a kid taking off from home alone.

"Where are you going?" I asked.

"To get Sissy."

"Okay." I ran to the bedroom where I'd thrown my purse. Inside was his foster mom's phone number. Hopefully she would know how to contact Jacob's sister's host family.

"We set a secret meeting place. We're going to Georgia."

Shit.

"What's in Georgia?" Keep talking, keep talking. I found the card, and cursed myself for not having another phone to call the police.

"Peaches," he said. "I saw them on a sign once. I like peaches."

I sat on the bed. "You're messing with me."

"Yeah. You didn't really think I was going to tell you where I was going, did you?"

Smart little bastard. "No, I guess not."

"I just wanted to say thanks for the tacos that one day. I know you were assigned to me and everything, but it was cool. I never had breakfast tacos before."

I flinched at the word *assigned*. I'd once said something similar to Alec when I'd learned how we'd first gotten together.

"Stick around, and I'll get you some more tomorrow. We'll bring your sister. Show her what's what in the taco world."

He was quiet. "I got bus tickets."

Double, triple, quadruple shit. "Oh yeah?"

"Yeah. My dad used to send me to get them for him. It's not hard."

No. If you had money, I didn't suppose it was.

In the background I heard the hiss of bus brakes. I stood again.

"Sounds like you're at a bus stop," I said. "Or is that a station?"

Come on, give me something, kid.

"Okay, I've got to go."

"Jacob, listen to me. I've been where you are. I've run away. Nothing gets fixed that way. Things only got better for me when I stayed put." That was how I'd met my father—the only cop on the scene who'd had the patience to sit beside me long enough for me to crack.

Silence.

"Jacob? You still there?"

Silence.

"Tell me where you are and I'll come get you. We'll talk. We'll go get tacos now."

"Bye, Anna."

"Jacob . . ."

Click.

"Fuck!" I stared at the phone for only a few seconds before I dialed his foster mom. On the fourth ring she answered, half asleep, and I quickly explained the situation. I held on while she went to search Jacob's room, but I already knew what she'd say. He was gone.

"I'm calling the police," I said. "You call his sister's home and see if she's still there."

I dialed the number and told them what Jacob had told me. I didn't have enough information—what he'd been wearing, any allergies he may have had—but I could paint enough of a picture for them to put out an AMBER alert. He was last at a bus station or stop, somewhere that still had a pay phone since he hadn't taken anyone's cell, and was trying to connect with his sister.

There was nothing else to do after that but pace.

And I wore a hole through the damn carpet.

It wasn't until three a.m. that I got a call from his foster mother saying Jacob had been found. His sister had gotten scared and stayed in her room. She'd given up the whole story—they were to meet at her elementary school, and then take a bus to Mexico. Jacob had told her she could have tacos any time of day there.

They'd already moved him to the juvenile detention center. "For his own safety."

I thought of him in one of those military-style bunks, surrounded by other frightened boys, completely freaked out by how he'd lost everything in a matter of weeks. He'd probably figured out by now that I'd turned him in. I was sure he hated me for that. The one person he'd trusted enough to call to say goodbye had betrayed him.

Alec's words filled my mind: *"You're not letting him down. You listened to him. That's probably more than anyone else has done."*

I slumped onto the couch and called him, as I'd done a dozen times since we'd parted, just to hear his voice on the message.

"Hi," I said after the beep. I was sure he wouldn't get this, but I continued anyway. "When this is done, come home to me."

I hung up, and clutched my phone to my chest just in case by some miracle he got the message and called me back.

"This is a bad idea," said Marcos, a man of not so many words, the following morning. We were both leaning against my Ford Fiesta facing the courthouse—me with the largest coffee humanly possible, and him with a cigarette.

"Smoking," I said. "That's a bad idea."

"A hundred and fifty ounces of java," he responded. *"That's* a bad idea."

I glanced at him. Had he just made a joke?

"Most people need solid food," he said bluntly. "You should try that."

"I eat."

He took a long drag on the cigarette. "You're wasting away."

"Are you my mother?"

"No," he grunted. "I'm your babysitter."

I rolled my eyes. He was right. I hadn't had the stomach to eat over the last week, but I hardly thought it showed. Maybe a little in my face, but nothing too drastic. I easily could have passed it off as a bout of the stomach flu.

A woman with dyed black hair, tucked tightly in a bun, strode from the parking garage toward a secure side entrance that said NOT FOR PUBLIC ACCESS. She carried a purse the size of a suitcase and was wearing a boxy pantsuit the color of an eggplant.

"Hold this." I shoved the coffee into Marcos's chest.

"Come on," he grumbled as it sloshed up onto the front of his neatly pressed uniform.

I jogged toward the woman, catching her just before she entered the building.

"Ms. Sanchez?"

The woman turned around, surprised to find me there. She glanced back at the door, to the security officer just inside.

"My name is Anna Rossi. I'm a court-appointed advocate for Jacob Rossdale."

"It's 'Your Honor,'" she said curtly. "Yes, I recognize you."

"I'm sorry, Your Honor. Jacob ran away last night—"

She held up her hand. "You can make an appointment. We'll discuss this case then."

"He's a child, not a case," I said, a little too harshly. This seemed to get her attention. Her mouth pursed shut, but she didn't sprint away.

I knew I had moments before I lost her.

"The last time we met, you didn't approve a transfer to a home where Jacob could stay with his sister. Last night, he attempted to run away with her in order to make that happen for himself. Now he's locked in juvie, which is the last place a kid like him belongs, and I'm begging you to reconsider."

My fingers wove together in front of me. To my right, I heard Marcos's telltale sigh.

"The system is in place for a reason," she said.

"The system is broken," I said. "I know. I was a part of it."

She took a step closer, considering me a moment. "I appreciate that. But this is not the place to work out your issues."

"With all due respect," I said. "It's not the place to work out yours, either, ma'am."

She looked taken aback. I prayed I wasn't getting Jacob in further trouble.

"Not everyone fits the model," I said. "This boy will do anything to be with his sister, and the more he gets burned by us, the more he's going to rely on himself to get what he wants. He's vulnerable, Your Honor. If we don't do the right thing now, we won't get another chance." I took a deep breath. "He loves his sister. I wish I had a brother that loved me that much."

She turned away, and my heart sunk.

Then she turned back.

"Jacob Rossdale, you said?"

"Yes."

She nodded. "I'll look into it. And Ms. Rossi?"

I had to contain myself before I broke out cheering. "Yes, ma'am?"

"An appointment next time."

"Of course. Thank you."

As soon as she was inside, I hugged Marcos so hard he started to wheeze.

Twenty-seven

The following evening Amy and I were sitting in the break room at Rave, sharing a roast beef sandwich. She'd picked it up while I stayed in, confined to the premises while Marcos was getting some much-needed rest.

"So it's really going to happen? You believe this judge?" Amy had a habit of tearing her food into pieces, and then eating it with her hands. Today was no exception.

I was still half giddy over the call from Wayne, informing me of the judge's decision to move Jacob. It would have been easier if they'd just given him what he needed in the first place, but better late than never.

"It's really happening. Jacob and his sister are moving into their new place tonight. They're even going to go to the same school."

Amy had taken the whole I'm-volunteering-with-foster-kids thing in stride, and didn't seem even a little bent out of shape that I hadn't told her about Jacob until today. Probably because she'd kept some pretty big secrets of her own.

"Wow," she said. "Go you."

"Go me, indeed." I was still feeling pretty proud of myself

about the whole thing. Later this week I was going to meet with Jacob and see how the new situation was working out, but until then, I was just happy he was safe and out of juvie.

I wished I could have told Alec about it.

My gaze shifted from the newly installed swinging door to the intercom near the sink that rang through to the front counter. It was one of Derrick's recent safety implementations, and though I could now sit comfortably here with Amy, I still had to be in close proximity to the door.

After a moment I realized that Amy was picking more than normal, and eating less.

"I wanted to tell you," she said, staring at her food. "Remember when I called you in Baltimore and told you to move down?"

The air in the room seemed to still. I nodded, giving her my full attention.

"I remember." I could work with her at the salon, she'd said. And there was a studio apartment down the street that was for rent. We'd have fun. It would be like when we were younger.

Something about her voice that day had made me worry, but I'd brushed it off as my own itchy feet. The next day, I'd used her as my excuse for quitting my job and breaking my lease. I'd never asked her what was wrong.

The next week Danny had left.

"I was going to tell you, but Paisley woke up early from her nap. And there was another time before that. He'd broken my cell phone. I told you it had fallen out of my purse and I'd run over it with my car."

"I wish you'd told me," I said. "I wish I'd been there for you."

Amy smiled sadly, face pale. "I'm telling you now. Does that count for something?"

I reached for her hand and gave it a squeeze.

She pushed her food around some more.

"He'd get so pissed off for the stupidest reasons. Then he started blaming me, and when I told him to kiss my ass he'd get all huffy and do something like break my phone. Then buy me a new one, of course."

Power and control, that was what abuse was about. There were people who needed it. Who reached for it when the tension became too much to bear. And then after it was all hugs and kisses and new cell phones.

"Like a honeymoon," I said. Another punch of guilt hit me as I realized Amy had once used this exact terminology when referring to Alec.

She nodded. "And things would be good for a while. Then something would piss him off at work, or I'd forget to pay a bill or something, and he'd spout off again." She rolled her shoulders back. "Paisley was in the living room once when it happened."

It. Part of me wanted to ask what *it* was, but I knew that her talking about this at all was big, and I didn't want to push her.

My fingernails dug into my thighs. "I'm so sorry."

"Not as sorry as I am."

The rage was building in me. A man who hit a woman wasn't a man, he was a monster. I wanted to kill him for hurting my friends.

"Did he ever hit Paisley?" I tried to even out my voice, but wasn't entirely successful.

"His little angel?" Amy laughed sarcastically. "Never."

"But she was hurt."

Amy nodded. "Yes. She was."

She plucked a piece of sandwich off the table and stuck it in her mouth.

"There's a new pizza place near Paisley's school. She keeps calling it sin bust, but I think she means thin crust. We should go there Friday."

"Amy . . ."

She looked up at me, pleading in her eyes, and I knew it was time to put my own needs aside. I leaned back in my chair.

"There are good points to having a boyfriend in witness protection," I said. "Leaves all your date nights open."

She chewed her bottom lip. "I was actually thinking Jonathan might come, too. If you don't mind."

I couldn't help but feel a little disappointed.

"I didn't realize you two were still a thing."

"We had lunch yesterday, and dinner last week. He's great."

"You sound almost as excited as I am about this roast beef sandwich."

She gave me a look. "It's a good sandwich."

"Yeah," I said. "It's *great.*"

She picked up a piece of bread and threw it at me.

"You know, Mike's been asking about you . . ."

She flinched. "What's he saying? 'How's that crazy friend of yours?' "

"More like, 'How's that sexy friend of yours?' "

She blushed. Honest to God, she had it bad for that guy.

"Well," she said. And then she didn't say anything else. Just stared off into space.

The intercom buzzed, and then Derrick's voice came on the line.

"Anna, you back there?"

I rose, and walked to the sink, where the intercom box was attached to the wall. I pressed the red button.

"That depends," I said.

"I need you up front."

"Someone thinks they're the boss of me," I whispered to Amy.

"That's because I am," said Derrick, surprising me. Realizing my mistake, he sighed. "Click the green button to turn off the receiver."

Amy was laughing in the background. Giggling, I let her clean up lunch and made my way to the reception area, where a woman in jeans and a prison-uniform orange T-shirt was looking through the bottles of shampoo. Her back was to me, and her reddish-brown hair was pulled into a tight ponytail.

Derrick nodded in her direction. "Ms. Lannister is looking to set up an appointment, but wanted to meet you first."

This wasn't totally uncommon. Sometimes clients referred friends who stopped by to shake my hand before I had them naked on my table. They were usually the anxious types—definitely in need of massages.

I put on my most comforting smile, and went in for the meet and greet.

"Ms. Lannister, I'm Anna. I'm so glad you stopped . . ."

The words drifted off as Agent Jamison turned to face me. She looked less severe than she had the other night. Pretty even, with her pink cheeks and lip gloss. We were tucked away from the front desk and the waiting area, but I glanced around anyway to make sure no one could hear.

"Where is he?" I asked, a sense of urgency swelling in my chest. "What happened?"

She held out her hand.

"Shake my hand, Anna," she said.

I did.

"He's fine. Don't worry. I'm here because, frankly, he's a pain in the ass."

My inner diva grinned, despite my outer concern. Still, even thinking of him brought back memories of our last time together, when he'd sent me away with Mike.

"What happened?" I asked again.

"His father left some message. Got him all hot and bothered. I don't know. He's refusing to cooperate until he checks in on him."

I pictured Thomas, alone in his apartment. Had Reznik paid him a visit, too?

"What did his father say?"

"I don't know." She kept smiling, but her eyes betrayed her annoyance. "I don't care, to be honest. I just need my source to play ball, and right now he's making it difficult."

"Better do what he says then." *And if I just happen to be at Thomas's house when you guys swing by, well, so be it.*

"Not going to happen," she said. "But as a courtesy, I'm asking you to do it."

I didn't like her telling me what to do, even if I would have done it on my own anyway.

"Does he know you're asking me?"

Her lips tightened. "He's made it very clear anything Anna Rossi–related is off the table."

I wasn't sure what to make of that.

"Why not just call the police if there's a problem?"

She exhaled through her teeth. "I did and they were sent away."

At least Alec's father wasn't in danger. My money was on Thomas drunk dialing him in the middle of a binge, but why he wouldn't just ask someone to contact his sponsor, Mac, didn't make sense.

"I'll do it on one condition."

"Not going to happen," she said.

I narrowed my eyes. "You can't keep him locked up forever."

"Not forever," she said. "Just until the trial. Distance makes the heart grow fonder, think of it that way."

"Then I'm not going to see his dad."

She smiled. "Yes, you are."

Goddammit. She was right.

With that, she gave a polite wave to Derrick, and headed outside.

"She doesn't want to schedule?" he asked with a frown.

It took a moment to harness my death glare.

"Not right now," I said. But my mood lightened as my mind shifted to something she'd mentioned. Alec may not be able to talk to me, but if he'd received a message from his father, he might have access to his voice mail.

"I don't have any more appointments on the book tonight," I said. "Mind if I take off early?"

Twenty-eight

"Alec, it's Anna. It's quarter to six and I'm on my way to your dad's place. I should be there in twenty minutes."

I hung up my cell phone, merging onto the freeway that would take me to the north side of town. Like every other time I'd called the past week, Alec's phone had gone straight to voice mail, but I hadn't thought he might be listening to his messages until Agent Jamison had alluded to it.

My speed climbed. I grinned like a fool. Maybe Alec had done this deliberately—set up a way for us to meet without alerting the FBI. It was a long shot, I realized, but it wasn't entirely out of the question. Marcos was going to be pissed of course when he got to Rave and found I wasn't there. He'd probably sigh, or give me that serious, squinty look of his.

That Marcos. He could be so dramatic.

I probably should have called him, but he was getting his beauty sleep. Though I was fairly certain he was part robot, all the late nights had to be wearing on him.

Quickly, I dialed Thomas's number, but he didn't answer.

This wasn't unusual, but given what Agent Jamison had told me, I was a little concerned.

I exited the freeway, and drove through the familiar slums, rethinking my plan not to alert my escort. It was getting dark, and there were more people loitering on the streets than normal. Most of them stared at me as I passed. One guy in a navy tracksuit nodded for me to turn off into an alley, apparently thinking I was here to score some drugs.

I shivered as I passed Raw, the sushi bar where Reznik spent his time, and though the parking lot was more crowded than the last time I was here, my eyes were immediately drawn to a black SUV, parked at the curb in front of one of the vacant shops a few doors down. They should have put a sign up in the window: "Hey, Reznik, I see you!" But maybe the FBI wasn't trying to be discreet. With the scarred face of the man who'd attacked us at the hotel fresh in my mind, I sped on.

A short while later, I was at the decrepit apartment building, climbing the stairs two at a time. Before I reached the top I could hear Thomas's dog, Askem, barking, and felt my brows pull inward. He didn't usually announce my presence until I knocked.

A little harder than necessary, I beat the side of my fist against the door.

"Thomas? It's Anna."

Askem kept barking.

"Thomas, can you hear me?" I knocked again.

The bark became louder as Askem ran to the door and began to scratch at the wood.

I swallowed the fear clawing its way up my windpipe. This wasn't like Thomas. Even if it took him a little longer to get to the door, he almost always called out.

I pulled my phone from my clutch and called him again. It rang; I could hear it both in my ear and inside the house. I hung up and beat on the door again.

"Thomas!" I called. I tried the handle. Locked.

No wonder Alec had refused to cooperate until someone checked on him. Stupid to think he'd been trying to communicate with me. What an idiot.

I could have called the police and waited, but I had a bad feeling that would take too long. Instead, I squatted to examine the lock—it wasn't a dead bolt, which meant it wouldn't be too difficult to jimmy.

I snagged my wallet from my purse and scanned through the contents. Credit cards were too tough, but a hotel room key, like the one I still had from when I'd stayed with Alec, would be perfect.

"Just like riding a bike," I muttered.

I slid the key between the door and the jamb, remembering how I used to watch my birth mother do this at cheap motels when she'd "forgotten the key." She'd take what she needed, and we'd move on. Even then I knew she was doing something wrong, but that didn't stop me from learning when she'd offered to teach me how.

Maybe I was too hard on her. She'd given me something after all.

I leaned all my weight against the door, and pulled the card as close to the handle as I could without breaking it. One flick of the rusty bronze lever, and the door popped inward.

Had I not been on a mission, I would have patted myself on the back.

The old golden retriever's growl turned into a whine as he came to smell my hand. He began to prance, nails clicking on the linoleum.

The apartment was dark.

"Thomas?" I called.

I went through the kitchen, then peered around the corner into the living room, afraid of what I would find. My keys were gripped tightly in my fist, ready to be used as a weapon should I need one. Askem trotted ahead of me into the hallway.

It was then that I smelled it. The potent, bitter scent of bile that wafted through the air. It grew stronger as I followed the dog, emanating from the bathroom, where a man's shoe was on its side, just beyond the door. I raced forward. The room was dark, but I could still make out Thomas's large form, lying across the floor in a pool of his own vomit.

"Thomas?" I flipped on the lights and knelt beside him, fighting my own gag reflex as I grasped his shoulder. How long had he been like this? Hours? More than a day? I should have asked Jamison when Alec had gotten the message.

I put two fingers on his neck to check his pulse.

He was alive.

"Wake up," I said, trading my worry for something stronger. "Did you hear me, Thomas?" I shook his shoulder, but he didn't move.

I felt around his skull for any lumps or cuts, but found nothing. As I reached his shoulder, he groaned.

"It's Anna," I said. His face scrunched up in pain.

"We need to move," I said. "You threw up."

"Stop yelling already," he said. "I hear you fine."

I leaned back against the wall and contemplated slapping him upside his bound-to-be-sore head. Instead, I pulled my shirt up over my nose and mouth, and helped prop him up against the wall. He moaned like a zombie, clutching his head with one hand, his stomach with the other.

Wetting a towel in the sink, I wiped his pale face, and then did a quick cleanup of the floor. Memories of my birth mother's withdrawal were all too clear. Shaking, fever, hallucinations. If Thomas went that route—if he'd already been that route—we would need to find a hospital fast.

"How long's it been since you had something to drink?" I asked.

"Too long." His cloudy blue eyes were still shut tightly. He was trembling like he had hypothermia, despite the fact that it had to be at least eighty degrees in here.

"It's just after six," I said. "Think about it."

He squinted at me. "Last night. Late."

"Any seizures?" I asked.

A slight shake of his head. "Mac brought pills for DTs."

"What pills?"

"Kitchen counter."

I left him for a moment to find the pills he was talking about. An expired prescription for diazepam, for a Cormac Farrell. The antianxiety medication was sometimes used to treat delirium tremens, a condition brought on by acute alcohol withdrawal. Something I'd been lucky enough to learn about at a very young age. I wasn't sure how I felt about Mac, who had no more of an MD than I did, passing around pills, even if there were only three in the bottle.

I filled up a glass with water, not yet convinced I was going to give him the medication, and returned to the bathroom.

"Where is Mac now?" I asked. If there was ever a time for a sponsor, this was it.

"Gone," he said. "I told him to go."

"And he listened?" I tapped my heel, irritated. There was no way Thomas needed to be left alone now.

"I was persuasive." He'd turned, and was resting his cheek on the cold porcelain on the outside of the shower. "May have tried to hit him. With a bottle."

I shook my head. The man was pitiful.

"Try to hit me with a bottle, and I will take your ass out, do you understand?"

I would take the zombie groan as a *yes*.

"Can you stand?"

He didn't answer, which I took as an *I'd rather not*.

It took every ounce of strength in my body to pull him up, but I finally got him there. Leaning him against the wall, I turned on the shower, and then helped him out of his shirt and shoes. The pants he would have to manage on his own.

"Let's get you cleaned up."

"No sponge bath?" he asked.

I watched him sway, then correct himself. It occurred to me he might still be a little drunk.

"Watch it," I warned.

Thomas showered alone, but I did leave the door open just in case he toppled over. He was a mess, and there was no way I was leaving him here to drink himself to death. But I couldn't exactly stay here either. Marcos would come looking for me sooner or later, and I doubted he was going to take kindly to my visit so near to Reznik's known hangout.

Hoping I had Alec's blessing, I searched through the cabinets, emptying a bottle of Jack Daniel's straight down the drain. There were two beers left in the fridge, and I dumped those as well. The empties clinked against each other as I filled the trash can. I was on my way to search his bedroom when a knock came at the door.

Grabbing my keys, I pulled back the cover over my keychain Mace. I took quiet steps to the door, thinking of Reznik, the man with the scar on his cheek, any number of cronies who could have followed me here.

I glanced through the peephole that came standard in these apartments, and saw the figure of a woman, facing the opposite way. Her dirty blond hair hung mid-back, and in her beige shell and knee-length black skirt she was dressed way too nice for this neighborhood.

I cracked open the door. She turned toward me.

"Yes . . ." I trailed off. Her face was familiar. It took a moment to place where I'd seen her before. At Alec's apartment, soon after he'd come home. She'd said she'd been on the wrong floor and left quickly.

"I recognize you," I said as her cheeks grew rosy.

"I-I'm looking for Alec Flynn," she said.

"He's not here."

She turned to leave, but I lunged through the doorway and snagged her arm.

"Who are you?"

"I need to see Mr. Flynn."

My blood chilled. I gripped the Mace harder, and held tight to her arm even as she tried to jerk away. Quickly, I scanned her body for weapons, but unless she was hiding a knife in the wallet tucked under her arm, she was clean.

"Did Reznik send you?" I asked. Is that why she'd been at Alec's apartment before? Because she'd been looking for him for Reznik?

She looked genuinely confused, but I didn't trust it.

"I don't know what you're talking about."

"How did you find this address?" I realized I sounded paranoid. I didn't care.

She pulled back. My fingers were pressing so hard into her bare skin they were leaving white spots.

"Let me go." There was fear in her voice that wasn't faked, and because of that, I did as she said. Quickly, she fled down the stairs.

"Why do you want to see him?" I called after her.

She didn't answer. I watched her jog awkwardly in her high heels toward the nearest car, a black MINI Coupe, parked under a flickering streetlamp, and speed away.

I only caught the first four numbers of her license plate, but it was better than nothing.

Twenty-nine

After locking the door and texting myself the numbers, I told Thomas to hurry up, and resumed my beer hunt in his bedroom. There, I found a bottle on the nightstand and another in the drawer where he kept his pants. I went to the closet, looking for clean clothes, and found a cardboard box.

The shower was still running, so I pulled back the top. Maybe I was crossing a line here, but the man was a boozehound, and it wouldn't have surprised me to find a case of liquor inside.

Instead I found a baseball. And a pair of baby shoes. And three onesies. I dug a little deeper, finding a stuffed Tigger that was missing an eye, and an MVP Little League trophy. *Alec Flynn* was marked in gold letters across the base.

My heart softened. It couldn't have been easy to raise a child alone, much less with a disease like macular degeneration. But it was obvious from these things that Thomas loved his son. It was a shame that his alcoholism had gotten between them.

I was closing the box when I saw the red women's cardigan, hanging in the very back on a padded hanger. It was an older style, but the same size I wore.

"You can't move things," said a gruff voice from the doorway. Thomas was there, with a towel around his waist. Apart from a fist-sized bruise on his shoulder, he had quite a body, even for a man his age. I jolted up, feeling like I'd been caught with my hand in the cookie jar. I hadn't even heard the shower shut off.

"I know where everything is," he said. "I can't find anything if you move it."

"Like the bottle of vodka in your bottom drawer? Spoiler alert: It's gone now. Along with your stash in the kitchen."

I didn't tell him it didn't matter, because we were leaving anyway. The arrival of the mysterious blond woman had sealed the deal. Thomas was coming back to my apartment where Marcos could keep an eye out for us.

He hesitated. "That's a lot of money."

"So is cirrhosis."

"Nobody asked you to come." He teetered into his bureau, where he felt down the front of the drawers for the one holding his undershirts.

"Ah," I said. "This is the part where you get cranky."

"This is the part where I get a damn headache," he said.

"Which is your own damn fault," I shot back.

He made his way to the bed and felt across the covers, then sat down.

"Get out," he said. There was a cruelty in his tone I'd never heard before, and it thinned my patience.

"What, you going to throw something at me?"

"I might." He lifted his chin, defiant. He bore a strong resemblance to his son just then.

"Try it," I said. "I'd like to see you hit a moving target."

"Go away. I need to rest."

I didn't move.

"*Get out!*" he shouted, then leaned forward and clutched his head.

I waited. Waited. Then slowly sat far enough away that he couldn't take a swing at me.

"It should be him here, not you."

I figured he was referring to Alec.

"Your son's a little busy at the moment. You're stuck with me."

The sound he made in response didn't exactly boost my ego.

"You know, it's possible he needs you now more than you need him," I said.

Thomas was quiet for a while.

"He'll never need me. He's strong."

I scooted a little closer, feeling the regret pouring off of him. I thought of the baby clothes in that box, the trophy from Little League.

"He can't stay strong forever. He'll break."

"Not my son," he said.

Then he leaned forward, head in his hands, and began to weep.

I placed my hand on his shoulders, feeling them tremble. He still smelled like alcohol, but at least the stench of vomit and sweat was gone.

"You're a nice girl," he said. "Don't let him ruin you."

A chill crept over me at his words. "What do you mean?"

"It's what we do. We ruin the good things because deep down we know we don't deserve them. We all have to pay for our sins."

I pulled my hand back into my lap, thinking of Alec's last good-bye, and how he hadn't even attempted to contact me in over a week, and how Agent Jamison had said any discussion of me was off the table.

"And what sin are you paying for?" I asked, trying to focus back on Thomas.

"The oldest sin in the book," he said. "Loving a woman I could never have."

Alec had told me this once, in this very apartment. His mother had been Thomas's nurse, shortly after he'd developed blindness.

She'd been married, and had chosen her family over Thomas, leaving him behind to raise the baby alone.

I glanced at the red sweater in the closet, wondering if that was hers.

"And Alec is your punishment, is that it?"

He shook his head.

"No." His voice was growing weak. "Alec is my redemption. And I've failed him."

For a long while we sat there, each lost in our own thoughts. And when he started to rub his head again, I tapped him on the knee.

"Get dressed," I said. "We're going to get something to eat."

Thomas was hurting by the time I pulled into the parking lot at my apartment. The good news was he didn't put up much of a fight when I told him where we were going, but unfortunately I'd had to pull over twice so that he could puke. While he did, Askem whined from the backseat, where he'd been shedding over every inch of my car.

Alec owed me big-time.

I was leading Thomas toward the stairs when I caught sight of Marcos striding down the sidewalk. He'd finally ditched his uniform, and was wearing jeans and a gray golf shirt, tucked in. He reminded me of my dad with that look. Maybe dressing like a sixty-year-old man was a prerequisite for joining the force.

"Your shift was until eight," he articulated clearly. "We reviewed it this morning."

"Something came up," I said. The second I released Thomas's hand, he grabbed the stairway bannister and sank to the first step, resting his cheek against the cool metal. His trusty Seeing Eye dog curled around his feet.

Marcos eyed them dubiously.

"You could have let me know."

Probably. But you would have gotten in the way.

"I didn't want to wake you up," I lied.

He narrowed one eye. "I wasn't sleeping."

I looked at him, catching, for the first time, a scent of cologne. "Don't you usually crash while I'm at work?"

He fidgeted. Transferred his weight from one foot to the other.

"Marcos." I couldn't help but grin. "Did you have a date?"

His ears turned red. It was positively adorable.

I poked him in the chest. "Is that why you sexed it up with the polo shirt?"

"It wasn't a date," he said roughly, ending the roast. I wondered if he'd just been dumped or something.

"All right, all right," I said. "But you smell *real* nice."

He huffed, fixed his stare over my shoulder. "Who is he?"

"No one," I said.

"That hurts," said a soft voice from behind us. "I've got impeccable hearing, you know."

"He's a friend," I said. "His name's Thomas."

"Father of the great Alec Flynn," came a wry announcement from the stairs.

My head fell.

"You're kidding," Marcos said flatly.

Behind me came a rustling, and when I turned, I found Thomas standing surprisingly straight. Askem edged closer against his leg, and he gripped the dog's collar, likely so he didn't topple over.

"Is there a problem, Anna?"

"Yes," answered Marcos. "There is definitely a problem."

Thomas took a step forward. I blinked at him, blind and hungover, and yet still ready to defend me, and swallowed down the knot in my throat.

"There's no problem." I placed a hand on Thomas's chest, and he put his own hand over mine. It was hard to believe this was the same man who'd been shouting for me to get out of his apartment an hour earlier.

Marcos edged closer. "Your protective detail's off tomorrow, and you pull this now?" His voice hardly wavered, but it was still the most emotion I'd heard him express.

My insides turned ice-cold.

"I didn't know that," I said. Of course it wouldn't go on forever. Terry had been doing this as a favor to my family. The police weren't as invested in protecting me as the FBI was in protecting Alec.

"Benitez pulled all his strings to keep me here, but tomorrow I go back on patrol and you're on your own."

"She's not on her own," said Thomas.

"Right," said Marcos. "I can see that." He turned to leave.

"Marcos," I said.

He paused.

"Can you run a plate for me? Black MINI Coupe. I only have the first four numbers—ICC-1. It might be nothing, but I'd feel better if I knew who it was." I hated asking him now, when it was obvious I wasn't his favorite person.

"Why not?"

"And Marcos?" I waited for him to finish sighing. "Thanks. For everything."

He waved briefly over his shoulder, then walked back to his car. He wouldn't come in. Wouldn't take the couch even if Thomas hadn't been here. This was his job, and he was, as Terry had told me, a good cop.

Watching him walk away, I realized I still hadn't told my dad about the whole situation. Later I would. Maybe.

Right now I had Alec's father to worry about.

Thirty

called in the next day. Between nursing Thomas through his withdrawal and keeping him away from anything remotely resembling alcohol, including a bottle of mouthwash, I was exhausted. He'd finally slept through the early morning hours curled up on the floor outside my bathroom. I'd taken the couch, intent to catch him should he try to make an early morning beer run. Even Askem needed a break, and found a spot on my bed, right on top of my pillows.

Lucky for them both, I was too tired to care.

I woke to the sound of scuffling feet, and a thud against the wall.

"Son of a . . ."

I jumped up, rubbing the sleep from my eyes, and hurried the long, five-step walk to my bedroom. Thomas was standing in front of my dresser, feeling his way to the door. He was wearing my pink plush bathrobe over his T-shirt and jeans. Once the chills had started, I'd reached for the first thing that was handy.

"You're in my apartment." I guided him back to the bed, where he sat down. Even after the shower he reeked like alcohol. He must have been sweating it out.

"I know where I am," he barked.

I was too tired to muster up a snappy response. A glance back at my alarm clock told me that we'd slept through most of the afternoon. It was almost four o'clock.

"Are you hungry?"

"Yes."

"Will you throw up?"

He thought about this a moment. "No."

"My bathrobe looks good on you," I said as he prodded the neck with a confused frown. I helped him toward the couch in the living room. He'd have to eat on my coffee table, I didn't have a dining room here.

"Why the cop detail?" he asked as I took the bread out of the fridge and plugged in the toaster. He was staring straight ahead at the blank wall, which made me think of all the blank walls in his apartment, and how Alec had never seen his drawings or good report cards up on the fridge.

My mom and dad had made certain to do that once I came to live with them. They kept it up well into my teens, and I never stopped them, even when Amy made fun of it. It was nice having someone who cared that much.

"I wasn't sure you'd remember that." My gaze focused across the street, to the empty spot on the curb where Marcos was no longer parked. He'd been there around four a.m. the last time I checked. I wouldn't let it worry me—I would be fine on my own as long as I was careful—but I was sorry to see him gone.

The couch creaked as Thomas leaned back. "It's cloudy, but I remember. I remember you gave him a license plate, too."

I put the bread in the toaster, picturing the blond woman who I'd now run into twice in search of Alec.

"You're in trouble, aren't you?"

"You're trouble enough for both of us," I said.

He pouted, petting the fuzzy lapel of my robe over his chest.

"I may not look like much these days," he said. "But no one's going to hurt you while I'm around. You got my word on that."

Again, I felt a tightness in my chest. Being with Thomas was jarring. One minute he was cursing you out, the next he was in your corner. How Alec had managed it his whole life made me admire him even more.

"Thanks," I said quietly. I buttered the toast and sat beside him on the couch. "Alec's helping the FBI put together a case against his old boss. Not everyone's a big fan. A detective friend put a tail on me just in case anything happened."

"And now the clock's run out."

"Yeah," I said. "The clock's run out."

He didn't pry, and I was grateful. I changed the subject.

"Do you know if Alec ever dated a blond woman? Looks like a professional of some kind?" Maybe she really did work for Reznik, but I couldn't completely dismiss the idea that she knew Alec somehow, that they had history together.

"I'm blind," said Thomas, nibbling on the corner of the toast. "They all have blond hair as far as I'm concerned."

"Mine's black."

His brows furrowed. "That's very concerning."

I elbowed him.

"He never told me about any of the girls he was seeing," Thomas said. "Sometimes he'd say he had to leave to go meet someone, or he'd be late to pick me up for something, but he never got into it and I didn't ask. Figured he'd tell me if she was important."

"So he never brought anyone else to your place?"

Thomas shook his head.

Though touched, this made me feel worse in a different way. If Alec didn't know her personally, had never brought her home to meet his father, how did she know where Thomas lived? She must have gotten his address elsewhere. Possibly from Reznik, or even Stein himself.

Absently, I reached for Thomas's phone and placed it in his hand.

"Call your sponsor," I said.

He grumbled something about a headache, but as I walked away to make coffee I heard him activate the voice recognition feature. Soon he was grunting a response that sounded something like, "I'll be there."

I'd started coffee, but when he hung up and called my name I returned to the living room.

"I have a meeting in an hour," he said. "You should come with me."

I snorted. "If you need a ride, just ask."

He flashed a grin, and his head must have been still hurting, because a wince wiped the expression right off his face.

"You got anything better to do?"

I turned off the coffeemaker. "Not at the moment."

The Circle Club was packed wall-to-wall. It was an open meeting, Thomas informed me, which meant that I could attend even if I wasn't an alcoholic. Askem seemed as comfortable in this setting as he was in his own home, and led his master to the coffee cart, where they were greeted warmly by several people.

A man with a significant paunch and a U.S. Army Veteran ball cap weaved in and out of the crowd by the donut table. He bypassed Thomas without slowing, and wrapped me in a huge bear hug.

"Nice to see you, Anna."

"Mac." I held my breath while he squeezed. "Guess you survived the bottle."

Mac blew out a breath and took off his cap, revealing a half-inch cut on his forehead held together by butterfly bandages.

"I've met my fair share of mean drunks, but he takes the cake. Surprised you got out in one piece."

I scowled. "He was all right. Mostly just sick."

He took off his hat and ran his fingers around the brim. "It was good of you to bring him. I offered to give him a ride, but he said he'd rather keep you close. Must be his new good luck charm."

Or he really had meant what he'd said about keeping me safe.

"Something like that," I said, wondering if it was possible not to love these crazy Flynn men.

At the front of the room, a woman with a shock of white hair wearing a blue denim dress called the meeting to order.

"Sit anywhere you like," Mac said. With that, he approached Thomas, pulled him into a friendly headlock, and then guided him toward the front of the room.

I sat in the second row to the back, picking at my nails while the woman introduced herself and her addiction, then read from the "Big Book," the AA Bible. As she quoted the twelve steps, she was greeted with unwavering support. I could feel it all around her in the room, but somehow it seemed to deflect off of me.

I missed Alec. It was harder now than when he'd been in prison. At least then I knew where he was, and when he was coming back. But here was a place where people accepted one another unconditionally, smiled and hugged and patted one another on the back, and yet all I could feel was the cold cement floor beneath my sandals, and the loneliness weighing down on my chest.

I guess step one was admitting you had a problem.

"First time?" came a low voice from behind me.

I didn't turn around right away. The sound was too familiar, bringing goose bumps to my skin and a hard, painful ache to my heart.

My mind was playing tricks on me. Evil, sadistic tricks.

"Oh, I'm just here for a friend," I said quietly.

"Real pain in the ass, isn't he?"

I turned my head, but his sharp hiss caused me to freeze.

"Keep looking forward," he whispered.

"Alec." I closed my eyes. I wanted to see him, look at his face, hold it in my hands as I kissed him.

I felt my hair move, and then the gentle pull of one small piece as he wound it around his fingers. It sent warm shivers down my neck and back.

"Hey, baby."

"What are you doing here?" I whispered.

His fingers paused. "Hitting a meeting. Same as anyone else."

I glanced slyly over my shoulder, just enough to see a man in slacks and a white button-up shirt, standing by the coffee cart ten feet away. He was watching Alec over the brim of his paper cup. I looked forward.

"You came with a friend?"

"Two," he muttered. The metal foldup chair behind me creaked as he shifted his weight. A moment later I could feel his fingertips graze the skin between the back of my pants and the bottom of my shirt. His touch was warm, electric, and my back straightened in response. A moment later I was leaning back into the cool metal frame, anxious for more.

"FBI?"

"Unfortunately."

His fingertip crossed my spine, inching toward my waist. I shuddered a breath. The agent at the coffee cart couldn't see his hand; someone was blocking his view.

"I've missed you, Anna."

His fingertip climbed beneath the hem of my shirt, just an inch, but enough to trigger a rush of heat through my veins.

I'd longed to hear those words, but they didn't comfort me as I'd hoped.

"What happened to *no more ifs*?" I asked.

"I had to see you."

I rubbed the line between my brows with my thumb.

"How did you know I'd be here?"

"Lucky guess."

"You followed me, you mean."

His hand withdrew, and I kicked myself for being so harsh. I didn't care what had happened at the hospital. I only cared that he was here, now.

"Your police detail ended this morning. The FBI agreed to a GPS on your car."

So I'd been driving around all day being tracked by a bunch of strangers. Great. I didn't know how he'd heard that Marcos had been sent back to his regular patrol, but it didn't surprise me.

"They *agreed* to a GPS."

"I wanted full surveillance, 24/7. We compromised."

"I guess that compromise included a day pass from Safe House Summer Camp."

His fingers returned to my hair, reminding me of the way he grabbed it by the fistful in the seconds before he came.

"They're not holding me prisoner."

I turned, but stopped myself before I could look him in the face.

"Then why haven't you tried to see me before this?" I couldn't hide the hurt from my voice.

It felt like the whole room had gone suddenly still, and in that stillness, everything I'd been trying to hold together started to crack open.

"You left me," I said. Maybe I'd been the one to walk out of the hospital, but he'd been the one to turn me away.

"I had to."

"You left me," I said, quieter this time.

When he spoke, his voice was no more than a rough whisper.

"Two days ago you wore those sexy black boots and a blue skirt that showed your thighs. Every man you passed on your way into the salon couldn't take his eyes off of you. I almost got out of the car and beat some guy half to death just so he would know you're mine."

My body pulsed at his declaration, responding to his possessiveness.

"You've been watching me."

The room wasn't so cold anymore. I could hardly remember what it felt like.

He leaned closer, and this time when he spoke I could feel his breath on my shoulder.

"As often as I can."

Any concern I'd had that his good-bye in the hospital had been permanent was washed away. I leaned back as much as I could, trying to get closer. "Does Agent Jamison know? She said you refused to talk about me."

The room welcomed a new member with a round of applause and a unison "hello."

"When did you see her?"

"She came to the salon. That's how I found out your dad was . . . sick."

Alec didn't say anything for several seconds.

"I refuse to talk about your participation in the investigation," he said. "Your safety . . ." He gave a low groan. "That's a different story."

I chewed on my lower lip, trying to picture him in some safe house trading insights about Maxim Stein for my continued protection.

"I'm turning around," I said. "If the FBI knows I'm here, what do they care if we talk to each other?"

"I'm not taking any more chances," he said. "No one sees us together. No one uses you to get to me."

At the hardness in his voice, I felt myself soften. I reached behind me, placing my knuckles against my lower back. His hand found mine, tracing the lines across my palm. The calluses from his work at the docks were rough and made my smooth skin even more sensitive.

So the FBI knew Alec and I were here together, but Alec didn't want anyone else seeing us. I scanned the room, wondering if anyone on Maxim Stein's payroll had tracked me here looking for Alec.

"You don't have to worry about me," I said.

"Yes," he murmured. "I do."

There was a rustle behind me, and then a man came to sit in the chair beside Alec. I only caught a glimpse of him from the corner of my eye, but could tell that he was wearing black sweatpants and a muscle shirt, and had the bulk to fill it out.

"Time's up," he said.

I looked back, but the people in the room were greeting their neighbors, and the man directly in front of me twisted in his chair to face my direction. He held out his hand, which I shook quickly. When I turned back, Alec was already standing.

He was wearing a hooded sweatshirt, and a blue ball cap covered his rich chocolate hair. It was already growing longer, fringing behind his ears. His eyes found mine, and the depth in them was so striking, I was momentarily frozen, unable to rise. But my gaze was drawn beyond them, to the tight lines around his eyes, the brand of pain, and the prominence of his cheekbones. He'd lost weight since the hospital. His right arm was in a sling, and the hand that emerged was fisted so tightly his knuckles were white.

"Wait." I had a hundred questions—Where was he going? How long until I saw him again?—but the agent who'd sat beside us was already ushering him away.

"Are you okay?" I asked quickly. "Have you seen a doctor?"

He leaned toward me, and this time I felt his lips brush my ear. The brim of his cap nudged the side of my head.

"What you did for my dad, that means something. But let Mac take it from here. No more ties to me until after the trial."

"Wait . . ."

"When this is over, I will come home to you. I promise."

He'd heard my message—the voice mail I'd left the night

Jacob had run away. Knowing he could hear my voice, even if I couldn't hear his, settled me some, but I still wasn't ready to let him go. I stood, and tried to follow him down the row, but was blocked by several people shaking hands in the aisle.

He walked slowly, head down, shoulders hunched, with an FBI agent on each side. They weren't as tall or broad as he was, but it was his size that made him appear even more defeated.

It took everything I had not to chase after him.

Thirty-one

I did try to pawn Thomas off on Mac, but the man was as stubborn as his son and insisted on coming home with me. He moved to the couch despite my arguments, and booby-trapped my front door and windowsills with cups and mugs that were supposed to make a loud noise if someone tried to break in.

Who needed a police escort when I had a blind man and his golden retriever?

Mac came and picked up Thomas in the morning when I went to work. They were going to Mac's restaurant, a burger joint on the other side of the Bay, where Alec had taken me on our first date. There was enough booze there to drown a horse, but I figured Mac would keep his friend on a short leash.

It wasn't easy, but I never told Thomas I'd seen his son. As far as anyone needed to know, Alec was in protective custody. He was safe. And if he got the chance to watch me from afar, I'd make sure he got a good view. One that involved a hip-hugging skirt, an off the shoulder top, and a pair of black stilettos.

I tried to focus on my short time with Alec, not the frustration that I didn't know when I'd see him again. He could hear my voice on his messages, that was positive. And he knew where I was, which meant he might show up for another surprise visit soon.

But he was thin, and hurting, and I seriously doubted the FBI was putting his health before its own needs.

"I guess you probably saw the news."

Amy pulled me from my thoughts. I was sitting in her chair in the salon, twisting a lock of hair around my finger. She was doing something a little concerning with the right side of my head—a twisty rose of hair with a feather she'd pulled from her drawer. Sometimes I wondered if you had to *be* high in order to appreciate her interpretation of high fashion.

"Not this morning," I said. "Why?"

Her hands came to rest on my shoulders. The curling iron was dangerously close to my left eye, but she didn't seem concerned.

"They set a date."

"The new *Bachelorette* couple? Please. Six months, tops."

"Come on, it's at least a year. They have to make it through all the cast reunion interviews." She waved her hand in front of her face. "That's not what I'm talking about. They set a date for Maxim Stein's trial."

"*What?*" I was so loud half of the salon looked my way. Amy pressed me back into my chair.

"Here." She handed me her phone so that I could look up the link to the news.

The story was short, just a couple of paragraphs. After the prosecution had called an emergency meeting with the judge, the trial date had been set. It would start at the beginning of August and was estimated to last two months. Other than a quote from Charlotte MacAfee's brother, who was pleased to begin the proceedings, there was little else.

Two and a half months. I scanned the appointment calendar on Amy's cart. I would see Alec in ten weeks.

I couldn't see Alec for ten weeks.

Had he known last night when he'd seen me at his father's meeting? He couldn't have. He would have told me.

This was all going to be over soon, and then he was coming home to me.

"Wonder what the emergency meeting was about," Amy said cynically. She knew what had happened at the hotel. Alec's lawyer must have informed the judge of the threat.

That didn't mean they'd arrested Reznik though, or put Maxim Stein where he should have been, behind bars.

"You doing all right?" asked Amy.

I wanted to scream *finally*, and *that's too far away*, and find someone who could tell me exactly what to expect once it started. But the sheer force of the date pummeled me. Everything that Alec had been through—that *we* had been through—was about to be laid out for judgment before a jury. He would have to face every demon he'd fought to put behind him, including the man who'd raised him up only to shove him down and attempt to kill him. I was most definitely *not* doing all right.

Ten more weeks without Alec.

"I hope that jury kicks Stein's ass" was all I could say.

Amy squeezed my shoulder. "Me, too."

She returned to curling my hair.

"So what are we doing tonight?"

Any plans I'd had seemed shallow in relation to what I'd just learned, but life went on. There was still a full month to wait before the trial.

"It's a surprise." Tomorrow evening I was going to meet her "friend" Jonathan at the new pizza parlor by Paisley's school, but for tonight, Amy was all mine. Miss Iris was even taking care of Paisley.

Amy squealed excitedly. "Are you taking me to your naughty stripper class?"

I cringed. I hadn't been back to the gym since the last time I had seen Trevor there. He'd been right about putting some distance between us. Even if I did want to talk to him more about the person he loved who'd been hurt, I couldn't while his feelings for me were getting in the way of our friendship.

"Nope," I said.

"Should I bring dollar bills for tips?"

I snorted. "Um . . . no."

"Are we going dancing?"

"I'm not telling you." Honestly, I felt a little bad about hiding it, but she'd never agree to come if I told her.

The lobby door clanged over the Justin Timberlake song piped in through the speakers as someone entered. I glanced back over my shoulder, surprised to see a familiar face. It was almost six, and Marcos must have been off duty. He was wearing the polo shirt again, tucked in to his khaki pants. Maybe his non-date had become an actual date this time.

"I've got to go see someone," I said, raking the feathers out of my hair. Amy made a face, but eventually helped me take down the spiral she'd pinned there.

"You'll pick me up at seven?" she asked.

"Yes. Wear workout clothes."

And there was the second face.

"Please tell me we're not running some hooray-great-cause 5K or something. You know how I detest exercise."

"You'll love it, I promise."

Or you'll kill me, one of the two.

With a reassuring smile, I headed toward the front desk, but paused before I approached. From my view, I could see Marcos, but he couldn't see me. He was talking to Derrick, and the smile on his face was so wide I nearly didn't recognize him.

Derrick said something, and Marcos laughed into his hand. A blush rose up his neck. Derrick fixed his collar, and he didn't shy away, didn't even move.

"Oh," I said out loud.

Marcos wasn't here to see me. Marcos was here to see Derrick.

They both turned at my announcement. Derrick grinned and wiggled his eyebrows. Marcos looked like I'd just told him his grandma had died.

"Anna." Whatever he planned on saying next was lost in a storm of coughing.

"Hey." Trying desperately not to embarrass him, I closed the distance between us and squeezed his biceps. "It's good to see you."

"Rich has something for you," said Derrick.

"Rich?"

"Is my first name," muttered Marcos.

"They give robots first names?" Guess I probably should have known that.

Marcos elbowed me.

"Okay," said Derrick. "I've got some paperwork to do. It was good seeing you Rich." He glanced at me, then back to Marcos. "Um . . . Maybe this is presumptuous, but I have an assistant manager closing up if you wanted to grab a drink later."

Marcos went fire engine red. I was pretty sure his head was about to explode.

"Oh . . . I . . ."

"He'd love to," I answered for him.

"Great." Derrick grinned at him and then walked away.

Marcos's breath left in a huff.

"Looks like you've got a date, big guy." I patted him on the back.

His eyes shot to the floor. I wondered how long he'd been out—or if he even was. If I had to guess, I'd say he was pretty new at this game. I'd have to tell Derrick to go easy on him.

"I ran that plate you mentioned." Marcos retrieved a piece of folded paper from his pocket. "The car is registered to a Jacqueline Frieda. She's clean. No priors. Not even a speeding ticket." He passed me the paper, still unable to meet my gaze.

The driver's license picture was a few years old, and a little fuzzy. The woman in the picture had chin-length hair and was halfway into a smile, making it a typical, terrible license picture, but it was definitely the same person who'd been looking for Alec.

I wished I'd thought to ask him about her when I'd seen him last.

"She's a lawyer," said Marcos. "Not sure if that helps."

What would a lawyer be doing looking for Alec? He already had a lawyer in the Maxim Stein case. Maybe she was working on the defense and was trying to pump him for information. That would explain why she wasn't very forthcoming with what she needed.

I scanned the printout for anything else that might be useful, but he'd already ripped off the corner with her address.

"She causing you trouble?" There was genuine concern in his voice.

"Not really. She's looking for Alec. I was just wondering who she was."

Marcos snagged back the paper. "I could get fired for running his exes, I hope you know that."

I shot him a look. "It's not like that. I'm just . . . paranoid these days."

He softened. "Yeah. All right." Another moment passed before he finally looked at me. "Everything else going okay?"

"They set a date for the trial." I wanted to tell someone who knew how important this was.

"I heard that."

Of course he had. "Does everybody know but me?"

"It made national news," he said. "So, yes."

I shoved him with one hand, and he rocked back on his heels, a hint of a smirk lighting his face.

"You have my number if anything feels off." He reached into his pocket and pulled out a phone. It wasn't fancy, just a small flip-phone. He shoved it my way.

"Got you something."

"Thanks?" It seemed rude to mention I already had one.

He sighed. "It's a burner. We have a few of them floating around the station. Terry and I thought it'd be a good idea for you to carry one in case something comes up."

"Oh." I was touched. "Thanks."

He leaned closer. "Just because I'm assigned somewhere else, doesn't mean I'm not around, all right? I'll keep an eye on you 'til this all gets straightened out."

He had a big brother vibe about him. I liked that.

"You going to camp outside my apartment again?"

"Maybe I'll just run a trace on that phone."

"Stalker."

"Smart-ass."

I hugged him. It took a second for him to hug me back, but when he did, he squeezed me tight.

"You don't need to mention tonight to anyone, all right?" he said quietly.

So he wasn't out. It meant a lot that he trusted me with his secret.

"Who am I going to tell?" I asked as we pulled apart. But as I saw his face I knew he was referring to my friend and his boss, Terry Benitez. I didn't think he would have had a problem, but coming out to a friend and coming out to the police force were two different things.

"My lips are sealed," I said. "I hope you two have fun."

His ears turned pink.

"God, you're in trouble," I said.

Before he could turn serious, I skirted away around a makeup display. My shift was almost up, and I had a date of my own with Amy.

Thirty-two

"What is this?" Amy asked as I pulled into the YMCA parking lot. It was dark out, but the floodlights were on. I parked beneath one in the back; the front spots were all filled, probably for the basketball leagues boasted on the sign out front.

I'd tucked the burner phone Marcos gave me deep in the bottom pocket of my purse. Absently I slid my fingers over the small lump of plastic, comforted by its presence.

"This, my friend, is the YMCA." I started singing her the Village People's song, complete with the arm motions.

"I know it's the YMCA," she said. "I did not leave my six-year-old with a sitter so that I could go to a place where I can take my six-year-old."

I tried to keep my enthusiasm up, knowing that this was going to be a hard sell.

"Give me an hour," I said. "Then we'll go get burgers. I know a guy who has this great place. Sort of a dive, but awesome food." Plus I'd agreed to pick up Thomas from Mac when we got to his restaurant, which I planned on filling Amy in on only after phase one was complete.

She grumbled her consent and I met her outside of the car. We were both in black yoga pants and workout tops—my blue Lycra T-shirt was still a little loose on her, but she looked good in light makeup and a ponytail. Athletic. Like she could kick some ass.

Which is exactly what we were about to do.

Arms linked, we entered the front doors. I hadn't been to this facility, but I'd made sure to get all the details ahead of time. The place smelled like sweat and pool water, and from somewhere to my left came the whir of treadmills.

"Remember I love you," I said. "Don't be mad."

"What . . ."

"Hey ladies." Mike appeared from down the hall to greet us at the front desk. He was holding a clipboard under one arm and was wearing sweatpants and a sleeveless shirt that didn't hide the ripples of muscles in his chest and upper arms. Amy and I both took a moment to appreciate the view before she pinched me hard on the wrist.

"What the fuck is this?" she said between her teeth so only I could hear. Her smile was as wide as physically possible, and more than a little frightening.

Mike pulled me into a hug and kissed me on the cheek. He was warm and strong and made me miss Alec, and I nearly broke down and said that I'd seen him. I didn't though; I didn't want to do anything that put anyone in danger.

"Hi Amy." Mike held out his hand, giving her plenty of room. She stiffly placed her fingers over his, but instead of shaking, he squeezed. His eyes never left hers. He never moved closer.

"I'm glad to see you," he said.

"Both of you," I added. "I'm glad to see *both* of you. I think that's what you meant."

Mike grinned. "Ready to beat me up?"

Amy blinked. "What?"

"Mike does a women's self-defense class every week," I said. "After everything that's happened, I figured I needed a refresher."

She saw right through me, of course. This was for her, and we all knew it. Her fair skin hid nothing and blossomed red, and she shot me a glare that was half fury, half panic.

"An hour," I promised. "For me. Then burgers."

Muttering something about cutting my hair off while I slept, she followed Mike as he turned down the hall and entered a multipurpose room with mirrored walls. We sat beside each other on the blue mats that lined the floor, beside half a dozen other women. Some of them looked comfortable, and joked with Mike as he passed around the sign-in sheet. Others trembled like leaves.

"Welcome to women's self-defense," Mike announced. "If you're in the wrong room you've got twenty seconds to leave before you hurt my feelings."

A couple of the girls laughed. He grinned, his gaze landing on Amy. She focused on retying her shoes. As guilty as I felt for springing this on her, I really hoped she learned something tonight. I didn't want her to be afraid anymore.

"Okay," said Mike. "Twenty seconds is up. From now on, if you leave, expect me to cry." More laughs. He grew serious. "I'm kidding, of course. This is a safe place, ladies, and if you need to step out at any time, go ahead."

He met the gaze of a woman with short gray hair in the front row, who nodded slowly.

"I teach this because it's important to me," Mike continued. "I'm proud to say I've never hit a woman. Never come close to hitting a woman. See, I don't believe in hitting women. My father taught me that, every time he beat my mom."

Amy glanced at me. Miss Iris was Mike's mom. I had no idea she'd been abused.

"Every time he raised his hand to her, it reinforced what I already knew: You don't hurt the people you love. You especially don't hurt the people that I love. My father won't hurt another woman again, but that doesn't mean my mom or I will ever forget what he did to us."

He was looking at Amy again, only this time, she was looking back.

"You all have your reasons for being here. Whatever they are, you're going to leave feeling stronger. I promise."

Amy got up, and walked out.

I jumped to my feet and followed, feeling Mike's eyes on us. He didn't miss a beat though; he opened the class to a discussion of how to avoid becoming a target.

The door squealed on the hinges as I stepped into the hallway. Amy was heading toward the bathroom with her head down, but when she heard me, she spun around. Her shoes squeaked on the scuffed linoleum floor.

"What were you thinking, bringing me here?" she asked. Tears streamed down her cheeks. She might as well have kicked me in the gut. I was the world's worst friend.

"I thought . . ."

She didn't let me finish.

"What makes you think I want to dig into all that stuff, huh? It's behind me. It's in the past."

I took a step closer. "It's not in the past," I said gently. "It's hiding right under the surface. For you, and for Paisley, too."

"Even if that's true, it doesn't mean *you* need to fix it."

She was right.

"I shouldn't have surprised you," I said. "That was wrong and I'm sorry. But I do think you need to do something."

She pressed the heels of her hand to her eyes.

I stepped closer. "One day you're going to meet a guy, the right one, and you guys are going to fight, and I don't want Paisley to run and hide under the bed, or you to be afraid when all you're supposed to be is mad."

She forced a shuddering breath.

"He thinks I'm a victim."

She looked back toward the room, staring at the wall as if she could see Mike behind it.

"He thinks you're a survivor," I said. "Seems like he has a pretty high opinion of survivors."

A long moment passed. I figured we were done here. I'd drive her back to her apartment. She'd tell me she was too tired for dinner. The whole way home I would kick myself for dragging her here when she wasn't ready.

"You've done this before?" she asked tentatively.

"Yes."

"We don't have to talk about stuff, right?"

"Not about anything personal," I said. "Though that would probably be a good idea."

"Don't push it."

I smiled. She groaned. Then sniffled. Then gave me a hug.

"I hate you, you know that, right?"

"I know."

"All right," she said. "Let's do this."

An hour later we'd gone over the definitions of verbal, mental, and physical abuse, talked about body-language cues, and discussed ways to be more aware in our environments. We'd yelled "no" as a group, louder and louder, until Amy's voice rose over my own.

Then Mike had put on a padded suit, and we'd taken turns kicking him, striking him, and pushing him and running away. We'd broken into pairs and pretended to gouge out each other's eyes, then practiced what to do if someone grabbed our wrists or hair. I had volunteered to help Mike demonstrate ways to break out of a rear choke hold, and when I took him to the floor he groaned, and mumbled, "I bet I know where you learned that one."

When it was Amy's turn to wrestle him on the floor, she moved fast—impressively fast—and then escaped to the end of the line where I waited.

I gave her a high five.

"Was that good?" she asked, breathing hard.

"Are you kidding? It was awesome."

"Think Mike was impressed?"

I laughed. "You kicked him in the face. If that doesn't impress him, nothing will."

She looked pleased with herself.

When the class was over, we stayed late to thank him. He put his pads away in a duffle bag and left the room open for the maintenance staff.

"So?" he asked Amy. "How do you feel?"

"Good." She fixed her hair. "Really good, actually."

"You've got some skill," he told her. "You've taken martial arts before, I guess."

"No," said Amy. "Just a careful study of *The Karate Kid.*"

He lifted his arms and right knee, as if to do a crane kick, and she giggled like a teenager.

"So," he said slowly. "I've got to go pick up Chloe. I could give you a ride home if you like." He watched her closely, looking, as I was, for any sign that she was uncomfortable.

Which she was, but in all the right ways.

"Sure." She looked at me. "Is that all right?"

"Of course," I said. "I have to go check on Alec's dad anyway."

"Good luck with that." Mike snorted. "Make sure you text me when you get in."

He was still intent on looking out for me in Alec's absence.

We all walked to my car, and when I got in and shut the door, Mike escorted Amy to his enormous black truck. While he was rounding the front to open the door for her, she gave me a quick wave, and I smiled back. She'd be safe with Mike. And he'd fall in love with her—it was impossible not to. I'd remember this night a few years from now when they were celebrating their first wedding anniversary.

Matchmaking and raising self-esteem. All in a good night's work.

I turned my key in the ignition and pulled forward through the empty spot in front of me toward the exit. Mike had waited for me to turn on my car, but once he saw me moving, he drove away.

I was getting ready to turn onto the main road when I looked over to the passenger side and saw that the window was cracked. Amy hadn't left it open. I specifically remembered her rolling it up before we went inside.

"Keep driving," came a gritty voice from the backseat.

My blood froze. Automatically I reached for the door handle, but a hand, glowing white in the streetlight, had already slid over it to block my escape.

Thirty-three

glanced in the rearview mirror, but I didn't need to see his face to know who had broken into my car.

"Mr. Reznik," I said, trying to control my voice from shaking. "It's a little late for a parole visit, isn't it?"

I watched in the mirror as he stroked his goatee with his middle finger and thumb. It was dark outside, and he'd chosen to leave the sunglasses behind, but his eyes were hidden from view by the shadows.

"I work late hours," he said, inhaling audibly. "It's the best time to catch people breaking the rules."

From below my elbow came a scratching sound, and when I looked down I saw the silver barrel of a gun, glinting off the lights outside. After a moment, he withdrew the weapon, and pressed it into the back of my seat. I could feel the hard knob poking against the middle of my back.

I glanced to the passenger seat where my purse was. Inside was my cell, and the burner phone as well. It seemed stupid keeping them both in the same place now. If I could only reach one of them, I could call the police, call Marcos, or even Mike. He and Amy couldn't be that far away yet.

I had Mace on my keychain and pepper spray in the compartment on the door. I glanced down, but it was missing from its regular place. Reznik must have taken it.

"Whatever you're thinking, I assure you, it's a bad idea."

"Abducting me is a bad idea," I said. "Someone already tried it. It didn't go well for him."

Someone honked behind me. The driver of a silver sedan pulled around, flashed me his middle finger, and sped away. He didn't even look long enough to see the man in the backseat.

"*Drive.*"

I jumped at Reznik's sharp command. An hour ago I'd been yelling "no!" at the top of my lungs, but now I could barely find the air to whisper.

"You know I picked a neon blue car specifically so no one would try to carjack me again?" I asked.

"Ms. Rossi," he said. "You're going to take me to Alec Flynn, or there will be consequences, do you understand?"

I pressed down harder on the brake. I would not move this car. I would not let him control me.

"I don't know where he is," I said, jaw tight.

"Oh I think you do," he said. "He may be hiding from me, but he's not hiding from you."

"I swear," I said. "The FBI has him."

Reznik chuckled. "Drive the car, bitch."

Alec's voice sounded in my head. *If you're already in motion, you can shut it down.*

"Okay," I said slowly. "I'm driving. I'm doing what you want. No need to get hostile."

Cold fingers reached between the seat and the headrest, gripping the back of my neck as if he could snap it by sheer force. I jerked away, but his hands tangled in my hair and held tight.

"You haven't begun to see hostile," he said.

I may not have known exactly what he was planning, but his intent was clear enough to make me shudder.

I moved my foot to the gas, and slowly eased out onto the street. There wasn't much traffic this time of night, but a larger intersection was coming up, and there'd be more people there.

I watched the backlit needle rise. Ten miles per hour. Fifteen. The intersection came into view. It was still at least a mile away.

"Does it bother you that he abandoned you?" Reznik asked. "You could have been killed that night at the hotel."

Slowly, I moved my hand to the cupholder in the center console. I felt around for the kill switch Alec had installed, trying to appear as though I was only adjusting my position. Finally the plastic rose beneath my finger. I had it.

"He didn't abandon me," I said.

"Then where is he?" asked Reznik. "Is he here now, coming to your rescue?" He laughed, and the gun barrel scratched along the coarse fabric on the back of my seat.

"Maybe he is," I said. As much as I longed for it to be true, I hoped tonight was not a night that Alec was watching me. I didn't even want him tracking my car on his GPS. He needed to stay as far away as he could from Reznik.

"I certainly hope so," he said. "He's become a problem for me. At first, I thought we'd just talk. But then he never came to see me. So I had a friend check in on him, and now that friend is behind bars. Another great inconvenience. He's not leaving me many options. The trial is just over two months away now."

We passed another typical Florida strip mall, and like most of the others, it was dark this time of night. Not one car in the parking lot. Not one car passed me on the road. We were getting closer to the intersection though. I had to hold on for another half mile.

"How much is Maxim Stein paying you?" I asked.

Reznik chuckled again. The sound made my stomach turn to water.

"What makes you think he can afford me?"

I wanted to believe he was bluffing, but something told me he was not. But if Maxim Stein wasn't behind Alec dropping the case against Maxim Stein, who was?

We came to the intersection. The light was green. Praying this would work and that Reznik wouldn't shoot me, I flipped the kill switch.

The engine died. The lights in the console went dark.

"What happened?" Reznik demanded.

"I don't know!" I tapped the gas but nothing happened. My car coasted through the intersection; not until we were in the center of it did I slam on the brakes. Cars on either side faced us, their lights blinding me.

"Start the car," he ordered.

"I can't," I said. "My battery must be dead."

"Start the fucking car." The cold metal of the gun pressed against my neck, locking the breath in my lungs.

"I *can't*," I told him again. "Look, okay? I'm trying!" The keys clattered against the console as I turned them.

The lights changed. Two lanes of oncoming traffic crept forward, blaring their horns. The sound scraped my already taut nerves.

"I'm sorry!" I said, though they couldn't hear me. A van pulled close and a man opened his door and leaned out of the driver's seat.

"Hey!" he called, half hidden behind his window. "Everything okay?"

I raised a shaking hand. My heart beat a mile a minute.

"You can't shoot me in front of all these people," I said. "There are witnesses everywhere."

Reznik was still holding my hair and yanked my head back to his ear.

"Listen to me carefully, Ms. Rossi. I'm not afraid to hurt you."

"Ma'am! Are you all right?" The man had gotten out and was

closer now—twenty feet away. He must not have seen Reznik in the backseat. He wasn't proceeding with any sort of caution.

"Some men can't stomach it—the look in a woman's eyes when she's begging you to stop. It doesn't bother me."

His chilly fingers snaked around my neck.

The man from the van was waving now. I could barely see him through the tears swimming in my eyes. Another guy had opened his car door behind me. My eyes shot between the rearview mirror, to the bystanders on the street, to the Mace on my keychain.

"Car must have stalled," I heard someone outside call.

The grip on my hair tightened, and I yelped as a bright flash of pain seared across my scalp.

"If Alec Flynn doesn't agree to drop his testimony, it won't matter where you hide or who's protecting you. I'm going to find you, and I'm going to hurt you. Over and over. Until I tire of it. You tell him that."

I heard my name. It came from far away, a whisper through the crashing in my eardrums.

Reznik opened the car door and stepped out into the intersection.

With the car door open, I heard my name more clearly, but I couldn't place where it was coming from. I scrambled for the Mace with shaking hands, keeping my eyes on the man who'd delivered the message.

He strode to the Good Samaritan from the van, who had stopped short, surprised, if I had to guess, that someone had been lurking in my backseat. I didn't hear what was said, but the man sidestepped so quickly he tripped and fell onto his side.

"Anna!"

My head shot up, toward the voice coming from across the intersection straight ahead. Alec was here. He'd found me. As I stared at him, dodging through the cars wearing jeans and the same baggy hooded sweatshirt I'd seen him in at the meeting, I was flooded with relief.

A second later my heart seemed to stop.

He came to an abrupt halt. I followed his gaze to Reznik, who reached beneath the lapel of the suit jacket he was wearing.

"No!" I shouted. I didn't remember getting out of my car, but I was standing on the street, exposed and unprotected.

"Get back in the car!" Alec was yelling at me, but I could hardly move. "Anna, *move!*"

Before Reznik could draw his weapon, Alec was on him. They rolled across the pavement, a blur of clothing and fists. Alec rose above him, and I watched as his hands closed around the man's throat.

"Stay the fuck away from her," he growled.

Reznik slammed his fist into Alec's side, right in the ribs where he'd been stabbed. With a pained grunt, Alec toppled over as the other man crawled away. He stayed on his hands and knees, one arm wrapped around his midsection.

Reznik clambered to his feet. The metal of the gun glowed an eerie red in reflection of the overhead traffic light as he aimed it at Alec.

Observe your surroundings, Mike had said less than an hour ago. *Anything can be used as a weapon.*

The keys were in my hand, and I hurled them as hard as I could at Reznik. They struck him in the center of the back, and the shot that cracked through the air went high, over Alec's head.

A man yelled something I couldn't make out. Someone behind me was honking their horn. Alec wasn't running away like he should have been. He was gathering himself to attack again.

Horror filled me. I couldn't lose him. Not like this.

But Reznik didn't fire again. Gun in hand, he swung sideways into the still open door of the van. The driver had never shut off the ignition, and as soon as Reznik reached the front seat, the car jerked forward. Tires squealed as he hit the gas, nearly running over the van's owner. Another shot split the night, then two more. I dropped to the ground, searching frantically for Alec. I didn't see him; he must have been around the front of my car.

A woman with auburn hair wearing a button-up shirt and black slacks had opened fire on the van—Agent Jamison. She must have come with Alec. She didn't hit her target; the roar of the van's engine faded into the distance. From the ground, I watched her holster her weapon and reach for a cell phone. The bystanders scrambled. Some of them were throwing their cars into reverse and trying to get away. Nearby came the blare of a horn and the crunch of metal.

Alec was suddenly leaning over me. He dropped to one knee, his face too pale and slick with sweat.

"I told you to get back in the car!" he rasped. "What were you thinking?"

He grabbed me and crushed me against his chest. Though I was trembling, I could feel the hammering of his heart. His arms shook—he wasn't wearing the sling I'd seen before.

"What were *you* thinking?" I cried. "He could have killed you!"

"It's not your job to save me!"

I clung to him, feeling a sudden dose of calm in response to his fear. The ground was hard beneath my knees, sturdy, but my world felt like it had been turned upside down.

"I'm okay," I said. "I'm not hurt."

"I should have been here." He said it again, and again. "I should have been here."

"This is sweet." Agent Jamison loomed over us. "But it's time for us to go. Now."

Thirty-four

"They lost Reznik after he left the restaurant." In the back of a black SUV driven by Agent Jamison, Alec's hands moved hastily over my shoulders, my arms, my face, as if to feel for something broken. To slow him down, I scooted closer, and wrapped my arms around him. He held on as if a strong wind might carry me away.

"Your man has a mean sixth sense, I'll give him that," Jamison snapped from the front of the car. "He knew Reznik was heading your way before your car stalled on the GPS." It may have been a compliment, but she wasn't happy about the situation.

With the black-tinted windows, there wasn't enough light to read Alec's expression, but I could feel his physical pain as if it was my own. Slowly, I eased back. He was reluctant to let me go. I placed a hand on his chest where the wound had been, and he flinched, then held my hand against him.

"She stays with me now, Janelle," he said. "No negotiations. Make it happen."

So apparently Alec and Agent Jamison were on a first-name basis. How sweet.

"Don't push it," she responded. "You're not on my good side right now."

He grunted. "Wasn't aware you had a good side."

I glanced up at the driver, feeling a ridiculous flare of something close to jealousy. Not because I thought Alec would go for her, but because she'd been able to be with him when I'd been kept away.

"What about Reznik?" I asked, still feeling the cold dread in my gut from his last words.

"Local police have been notified," she said. "We have the make and license of the car. He's won't get farther than a few miles."

"You don't sound too concerned," I said. We tumbled into the door as she made a hard left. Alec grunted in pain.

"My job is keeping my source alive, not chasing bad guys."

"They're kind of one in the same, don't you think?"

"What did he say to you?" Alec interrupted.

Agent Jamison—*Janelle*—made a turn down a dark alley between two rows of government housing. I didn't know where she was taking us; this area of town was unfamiliar to me.

I cleared my throat. The words were in my mind, but I couldn't seem to get them out.

"He was looking for me," prompted Alec.

"Yes. He doesn't want you to testify."

"Did he say Stein hired him?" asked Janelle.

"He . . ." I closed my eyes, focused on Reznik's voice. "No. Just that Alec couldn't testify."

"Should've pressed him," muttered Janelle. "Prosecutor would have loved that."

"He had a gun against my neck," I snapped. "I wasn't much in the mood for getting a confession."

"Jesus Christ." Alec rubbed a hand over his forehead.

"What else?" asked Janelle.

It suddenly became difficult to make eye contact with Alec. I looked out the window, watching the broken chain-link fences and tiny weed-infested yards as they whipped by.

"If Alec doesn't shut down the trial, he's going to hurt me."

Alec was staring at me. I could feel his eyes on the back of my head. He didn't reach for me now. He kept to the other side of the car. My teeth were chattering, as if it was freezing outside. I couldn't make myself be still.

"How?" asked Janelle

"He didn't exactly spell it out," I said, my voice hitching. "He said he'd find me and hurt me. He'd take his time."

"What else?" she pressed. "Think."

"Enough," said Alec, with enough finality to make me jump. He touched my cheek. "We'll figure it out later."

The tires rolled over the broken asphalt.

"What about my car?" I asked, desperate for a change of subject. We'd just left it in the middle of the intersection.

"Tenner's going to clean it up. After his nose stops bleeding."

I looked at Alec for explanation.

"He tried to get in my way," he said with a one-shouldered shrug.

"You are by far the biggest pain in the ass I have ever had the pleasure of working with," she grumbled. "My agent tries to stop you from leaving—which is his *only* job, by the way—and you knock him out cold."

Alec fixed his gaze straight ahead, the way his father did when he was processing something.

"I warned him it was coming."

"Well here's a warning for you—you take off like that again, and your next safe house is county lockup. See how much trouble you can cause there."

She couldn't be serious. They couldn't lock Alec up, or me for that matter, when we hadn't broken the law. But her point was clear. We needed to seek cover and wait this out until the trial came, something that would be a lot easier now that we were together.

"How does this work?" I asked, trying to hold on to something concrete while everything around me seemed to be spinning out of orbit. "I guess I need to call my boss and tell him I won't be coming in tomorrow."

"We'll take care of it," said Janelle.

"I should call my dad," I said, head in my hands. "Amy, too." The dark thought occurred to me that Reznik might have seen me with her and Mike. My friends might be in danger. "God. I was supposed to meet your dad."

"We'll take care of it," Janelle repeated.

Alec placed his hand on my knee, a gesture of comfort, but also apology. I squeezed my eyes tightly closed, but Amy's voice from our fight in the salon speared through the jumble of emotions.

What makes you think your trouble isn't just getting started?

The "safe house" was a run-down shotgun house in the slums. It had a patchy front lawn, a detached garage, and a privacy fence that hugged a tiny backyard. The shades were all drawn, and as we entered through the back door, I heard the distinctive buzz of a video camera as it adjusted on our position.

Inside, the house smelled like cleaning products and was sparsely decorated. Two mismatched couches curved around a small TV on a broken bookshelf. A foldout card table in the dining room was surrounded by metal chairs. And a man I recognized from the Circle Club was in the narrow, pea-green kitchen clutching a bloody rag to his nose.

"Is fugging brogen, asshole," he said as we came inside. His eyes narrowed on me, and his thick brows lifted. "Whas she doing here?"

"Anna, this is Agent Tenner," said Alec, placing a protective hand on my lower back.

"She's part of our big, happy family now," added Janelle, tossing her keys on the kitchen counter so hard they slapped into the wall. "Isn't that nice? She isn't even a witness, but we're going to make an exception because Alec thinks she's cute."

I gripped my purse, the only item I'd managed to bring with me from the car, tighter against my side. Alec's hand fisted in my shirt at the base of my spine.

"Good. Maybe she can keep him grounded." Tenner lowered the rag, and I tried to hide the grimace as I saw his swollen, purple nose. Still, I couldn't help but feel a little impressed. He was more muscular than Alec, even if he wasn't quite as tall, and yet I didn't see Alec bearing any bruises.

"Tenner, you're on cleanup duty." Agent Jamison was obviously in charge here. She proceeded to give the man with the broken nose a rundown of the night's events while he shrugged into a jacket and grabbed her keys.

I turned my focus to Alec. He was trying to stand straight, but failing. His shoulders curled forward, and his right arm was bent across his stomach. Gently, I touched his shoulder.

"Let me see." I led him to the couch, where he eased into the squeaking seat. I remembered how he'd run through the cars into the intersection, and the way he'd fallen to the ground to grab me after Reznik had run off. Not even two weeks had passed since he'd been stabbed in the chest.

Slowly, I kneeled on the floor below him and pulled up his shirt, inhaling sharply as I saw the blossom of red the size of my fist that stained his white bandage.

"You need a doctor." I lifted my head. "He needs a doctor," I called.

"He'll fugging live," grumbled Tenner on his way out the door.

Janelle came around the side of the couch, looking down on us warily.

I peeled back the bandage, seeing the damage wasn't as extensive as it looked. Most of the wound had healed, but there was still a large, brown and purple bruise around the scab that had torn open on one side.

"The doc said he's fine. He just needs to rest. Which maybe

he can do now that you're here," said Janelle. There was a hint of regret in her voice, but when I looked up at her, she had turned away. "He's got fresh bandages and painkillers somewhere. Dope him up and he'll be fine."

"What if he's bleeding internally?" I insisted.

"I'm fine," Alec rested his head on the back of the couch and blinked slowly.

"You're not," I argued. My gaze shot up to the woman who'd brought us here. "Does he have a bed here? Or do you make him sleep on the floor?"

Her mouth tightened. She tilted her head. "Down the hall."

I helped Alec up, and he let me without argument. That worried me even more.

The cheesy seashell wallpaper in the hall was bubbled and peeling where it met the worn carpet. The lightbulb overhead winked on and off as we passed beneath it. I wouldn't have been surprised to see a rat run by. Thinking about Alec trying to heal in a place like this made me want to punch Agent Janelle Jamison right in her smart-ass mouth.

"Wait," Alec said as we passed a bedroom. He pushed open the door, to show another man I recognized sitting at a desk surrounded by file boxes and TV monitors.

"Hey," he said. "I'm Matt." He didn't seem surprised that I was there, but as I focused on the grainy black-and-white image on the screen behind him, I saw the back doorsteps, and realized he must have seen us come in.

"Anna," I said. He'd been at the AA meeting as well—the one in the suit I'd seen loitering at the coffee cart.

"I know." He grinned, and I couldn't help smiling back. At least not everyone here was a total dick.

"There's full video surveillance," said Alec in a quiet voice. "Around the house, and out to the street. It's solid. I checked it myself."

I knew why he was telling me this. He wanted me to know I would be safe here.

I nodded.

We continued on to the last bedroom at the end of the hall. It wasn't much larger than the one at my apartment, but it did have its own private bathroom and double bed. There was one small window, but thick red curtains covered it.

"I can't believe you've been staying here," I said. In the quiet stillness of the room I became aware of my pulse, still flying, and the twitchy comedown from my adrenaline rush.

He sat on the bed, pulling me between his knees. His head came to rest against my stomach and I wove my hands through his thick, dark hair. Slowly, my body began to settle.

"It's not so bad," he said. "Sheets are clean at least. I washed them yesterday."

His fingers spread over my waist, warming the ice that Reznik had left inside of me.

"You shouldn't be doing anything," I said.

"Yes, ma'am." His voice was muffled in my thin, long-sleeved cover-up, but I could hear the exhaustion.

"I missed you," I said.

He looked up at me then, dark eyes swimming with emotion. "It's not worth it, is it?"

I held his face in my hands. For a second, I feared that he meant us—that *we* weren't worth it—but his grip only tightened around my waist.

"What isn't worth it?"

"The trial. Testifying. I thought it was the right thing."

"Alec, it *is* the right thing."

Every muscle in his body went rigid. "You've had a knife to your throat and a gun to your neck in the last two weeks. What happens when the trial actually starts?" He turned his face away. "Anna, this is your life we're talking about."

I understood that. I also understood that Maxim was snapping his jaws like a rabid dog backed into a corner. He was running out of options fast. In a matter of months, he would lose everything.

"It's your life, too," I said.

"You don't understand." He gripped his side, the pain bright in his eyes, and he lowered his voice to control it. "You *are* my life. If I lose you none of this was worth it."

His words settled on my skin and slowly sunk in, giving me time to recognize what they meant for both of us. Never had I been necessary to another person, but as I looked at Alec I knew that his need went far beyond the physical.

Mike had told me before that Alec had gone his whole life looking for an anchor, and I was it. I understood that now, better than ever. I could almost feel him grasping for something to hold on to. For me.

I sank into his lap, my touch just as gentle as his was fierce. I stroked his jaw, the tense muscles of his neck. He shivered as I slid my hands beneath the collar of his shirt.

"You won't lose me," I said. "I'm right here."

Slowly, I tilted my head and pressed my lips to his. My eyes drifted closed, and soon there was nothing but the soft warmth of his mouth, and the rough stubble on his jaw, and his fingers rising up my back.

My breath caught as the kiss deepened. He would claim me with that passion. Build a brick wall around us and never let anyone get close enough to hurt me again. I could have let him—I *wanted* to let him—but I didn't. Because what he wanted and what he needed were two different things, and right now when he was raw, and hurting, and afraid, he needed love of a different kind.

I eased back, planting light kisses on his cheek and his brow.

"We're going to get through this," I said, feeling more confident as I said the words aloud. "Maxim Stein is going to pay for what he's done. And one day we're going to look back and this all is just going to be a memory."

He studied me for a moment, pushing back my hair.

"I lied before," he said quietly. "When I said it's not your job to save me."

I ran my fingertips over his jaw, tracing the dark circles of exhaustion beneath his eyes.

"You've been saving me since the day I met you," he said.

Tears welled up in my eyes and trickled down my cheeks. I kissed him again, dampening both our faces with them. Everything ugly, all the chaos and the danger, was left outside. We were here now. Together. That was all that mattered.

I held his hand against my cheek, brought back to reality by the swelling in his knuckles. I pulled his hand down to assess the damage from where he'd hit Reznik, and Tenner before him. There was only one cut, but the bruising had already begun.

Gently, I blew across the back of his hand, smiling when his breathing turned rough. I went to get a washcloth from the bathroom, and when it was damp and cool, I laid it across his skin. An ice pack would have been better, but I wasn't ready to part with him, even for a few minutes.

"Let me fix your bandage," I said.

I helped him out of his shirt, tracing the rise of muscle over his chest. I hadn't been mistaken the last time I'd seen him; he was thinner than before. I was going to take care of that, too, now that I was here.

"Keep touching me like that, and I'm not going to let you play nurse for long."

I smirked, flattening my hands over his pecs, reveling in the way his lips parted, and his eyes rolled back as if I was doing something a thousand times more erotic.

"Lie back," I said. "Nurse Anna's going to take care of you."

He complied, and I reached for the open pack of bandages on the nightstand. Beside them was a full prescription bottle of painkillers.

"Did you just get these refilled?" I asked.

He shook his head. "I don't want them."

"But you're in pain."

"They make me numb."

"And?"

He took the bottle from my hand and placed it back on the nightstand.

"And you don't want to be numb in case I need you," I murmured.

He didn't respond.

I changed his bandage, biting my tongue so as not to complain when I realized he'd been doing this himself the whole time he'd been here. When I was done, I rubbed his temples, and his shoulders, and his arms, imagining him here alone, pacing, staring at the GPS, making himself crazy wondering if he'd made the right decision to leave me alone.

By the time I reached his chest, he was asleep.

Thirty-five

I showered in the tiny stall adjacent to where Alec slept, keeping the door cracked, just in case he stirred. It was getting late, but my mind was running a mile a minute. Jack Reznik. Maxim Stein. Bobby Calloway. Charlotte MacAfee. Their faces kept swimming in front of my vision, even as I squeezed my eyes closed. I'd told Alec moving forward with the trial was worth it because it was. It was the right thing. It was the kind of thing my father would have done.

But then I thought about Jacob, who'd run away from home to protect his sister. Sometimes doing the wrong thing actually got you to the right place.

No. Alec would testify. We were both safe now. The police would catch Reznik, and he would confess that Maxim had paid him to threaten us. And then both of them would be locked up for the rest of their lives.

I just prayed that he wouldn't find other ways to hurt us. Ways that involved the people we cared about, like the two friends I had left the YMCA with earlier tonight. Mike had his daughter to worry about, and nothing could happen to Amy or Paisley. Not after her ex, and not because of me.

Alec was still passed out on the bed when I came out. Seconds, maybe minutes passed while I watched him sleep. The tight lines of worry on his face had softened, making him look younger, less burdened. His chest rose and fell evenly, and even half covered by the gauze bandage, his body was perfection. An impossible combination of smooth skin and hard muscle. A living, breathing statue.

The cheap towel was rough against my sensitive skin as I tightened it around my body. More than anything, I wanted to take it off and lie down beside him. Touch him slowly, make him warm. Heal him, and heal the hurt inside of me as well.

But he needed to rest. And I needed to eat.

I found a pair of his sweatpants and a T-shirt in the small closet, and even though they were huge and I looked ridiculous, I made my way out into the living room.

Tenner was sitting on the couch with his hand in a box of cereal watching a basketball game on TV. He must have gotten back when I was in the shower. Though he'd gotten rid of the rag, his face didn't look much better than before. His nose may not have been broken, but he was going to have a couple of nice black eyes come the morning.

"Did they catch him?" I asked, rushing to the couch.

"Who? Reznik?" He took another handful of cereal. Crunch. Crunch. Crunch.

"Yes, Reznik," I said. "Did the police catch him?"

"Nope."

I rocked back on my heels. I'd already been on edge, and now I couldn't keep my frustration from boiling over.

"Why are you such a jerk?" I asked. "It's no wonder Alec punched you."

He stopped mid-bite.

"Your boy back there may have just compromised the entire trial, you know that, right? I snagged the video feed of the intersection, but any asshole with a smartphone could be uploading a video right now of key witness Alec Flynn attacking some poor chump in the middle of the street. It won't exactly make him look trustworthy in court."

"But Alec didn't attack him," I said. "Reznik had a gun. He was going to shoot him."

"Matter of perspective," Tenner retorted. "I watched the traffic footage. Looks like Alec charges, unprovoked. Reznik draws in attempt to defend himself then flees in a minivan. Which he dumped, by the way, five miles down the road from where you parted ways."

I swallowed, feeling the heat that had risen in my cheeks drain away. I couldn't help but feel responsible for what had happened, and now Reznik was on the loose, and probably righteously pissed off. He could be planning his revenge right now.

"I'm monitoring the Web," said Matt from one of the foldout chairs in front of the card table. He was staring at a laptop, a handheld monitor with a video feed right beside him. "Nothing's surfaced yet. We might get lucky."

"But that's all part of the job," continued Tenner. "What *really* makes me a jerk is that I'm sick and fucking tired of dry cereal and cold pizza." He tossed the box on the couch.

I made my way to Matt's side, staring at the images of outside that flipped by on his monitor. No Reznik. Not that I'd expected him just to be standing out on the front lawn like some horror movie or something. I picked at my fingernails.

"I could cook." It wasn't going to make anything better, but maybe it would serve as a small thank-you for allowing me to stay here.

The first two cabinets I opened were empty. "What kinds of things do you have?"

Matt jumped up to help me search.

"There's a pizza from last night in the fridge. And there's . . . um . . ." He opened the double doors to the nearly bare pantry. "Pancake mix? I don't think we have any milk though."

I took a slow breath.

"It would be a real shame if that guy you're trying to keep from getting stabbed again dies of starvation."

"What about me?" called Tenner. "Does anyone care if *I* die of starvation?"

Matt rubbed the back of his neck, looking sheepish. "We got Chinese one night."

I blinked at him.

Tenner twisted on the couch to face me. "If you seriously can cook, I'll go pick up anything you want."

"Yes," I said evenly. "I seriously can cook."

Five minutes later he was out the door with a shopping list.

While he was gone, I sorted through the kitchen, pulling out mixing bowls, pots, and three measuring cups—all the same size. It wasn't much, but it would work. Matt stayed close by, helping me search for various supplies. With his flat freckled cheeks and broad forehead, he wasn't the most attractive guy I'd ever seen, but his personality made him instantly likable.

"So how'd you end up in the FBI?" I asked.

He searched for some dish soap under the sink, and began washing the dusty dishes I'd set aside to use.

"I ask myself that every day," he said, making me laugh. "It's not a very exciting story. I got a degree in accounting, then another in finance. Learned quickly my chosen track wasn't the best way to meet women, so I applied for a job with the FBI. Figured I could be a secret agent."

"And?" I asked. "Does working for the FBI impress the ladies?"

"I don't know," he said with a short laugh. "Are you impressed?"

I smiled. "Absolutely."

"What about you? Is wit . . ." He looked up, and I sensed he was smiling even though I couldn't see his face. "Is *non*-witness protection everything you dreamed it would be?"

"Everything and more." I found a towel and began drying the

dishes he put on the counter. My voice lowered. "I heard that Alec had made some kind of deal to keep me out of the trial."

"Really?" he asked flatly. "Is that what he and Janelle are always arguing about?"

I wondered just how often I'd been brought up in conversation. The thought of people talking about me when I wasn't around threw me straight back into high school.

"Where is Ms. Jamison tonight?" I asked, noticing that she hadn't popped out of some hidden corner yet. It took some effort to minimize the bitterness in my tone.

"Janelle has an apartment near the field office."

It surprised me just how relieved I was to hear she wasn't staying here. I didn't like the idea of another woman living with Alec, even given the circumstances.

"She isn't a big fan of me," I said.

Matt finished and turned off the water. "Don't take it personally. Her focus is Alec. Alec's focus is you. She finds it . . . irritating."

"Sounds like a bad love triangle," I said.

He chuckled. "I don't think you have to worry about him straying. He's holding a hard line. No one digs into your business. You don't get brought into the trial. He's giving the prosecution whatever they need as long as they leave you alone."

I hadn't considered it much before, but the prosecution could have called me as a witness, especially after what Bobby had told me the night I'd been abducted. I could have been put up on the stand in front of a judge and jury, forced to talk about my sessions with Maxim, and my relationship with Alec, and who knows what else.

But I wouldn't be. Because of Alec.

Still, as much as I appreciated the gesture, I would have done it if it had helped him.

"I'll do whatever I need to do," I said.

Matt paused then. "Think about that before you say it to Janelle. Stein has all the attorneys money can buy, and all they're doing right now is looking for ways to make Alec bleed. Their first attack will be pointing out the flaws in his credibility, and no offense, but given what I know of your history, they'll tear you down before you even see it coming."

I shivered, the danger of what was lurking around the corner clawing another layer deeper.

"He's been taking a beating to keep you out of his business," finished Matt. "That's not something to take lightly."

I wouldn't, but I wasn't sure how I felt about being kept out of Alec's business. I should have been grateful; it was a sticky mess, that was for certain. But I didn't like the idea of him shutting me out.

I woke in stages. First, feeling the warmth of a hard, muscular chest spooned down the length of my back. Then with a shimmer of heat from soft fingertips sliding over my belly.

A soft, wet mouth on the side of my neck.

The rustle of crisp sheets.

His solid length, nestled between my thighs.

We were surrounded by darkness so thick there was nothing to do but feel, trapped in that weightless place between sleeping and awake where time was suspended.

I pressed back into him, inviting his hand to fan open and rise to where the flat of my stomach met the swell of my breasts. He lingered there, tracing the curves of my body, his touch no more than a whisper.

My hips rocked back of their own accord, and he responded slowly, bringing a new awareness of the thin cotton of the clothing that separated us. A flame burned deep in my belly—not a spark, but something slower, and stronger, and more insistent.

"I need you," he whispered, his breath tickling my ear.

I reached behind me to his hip, and down his thigh to where the muscles grew rigid beneath my touch. He pressed himself against me again. His tongue drew a rough line over the delicate skin where my pulse fluttered, making me gasp.

"Is this a dream?" I whispered.

His answer was another kiss, this one on the base of my neck, and then the slide of his fingers between my legs. Even over my panties the sensation was intense, and I pressed my thighs together, trapping him there.

"Don't stop," I whimpered, as his hand began to stroke me. "In my dreams you always stop."

He opened my legs, pulling one over his. Callused fingers trailed down my thighs to my center and began that slow, torturous massage again.

"Does this feel like a dream?" he murmured.

My breath grew heavier. My back arched. I reached back again, beneath his boxer briefs, finding his heavy cock. The tip was smooth, and already damp and sticky, and my tongue rubbed against the roof of my mouth, anxious to have him there.

"I need you," he said again.

"Yes," I said, unable to stop myself from pushing back into his hands. I was wet now. Ready. His fingers peeled aside the crotch of my panties, skimming the hidden parts of me.

With a harsh breath, he grabbed the fabric and pulled it down to my thighs. I prepared myself for him to fill me, but the movement had forced him to sit up too far, and he froze with his forehead against the back of my shoulder. A moment later, he'd caught his breath, and moved closer.

"Alec . . ." I couldn't stand the thought of him in pain. Not when I felt so good.

His hand grabbed my hip, and he pressed against my entrance.

"Alec, wait."

He didn't move. I could feel the clashing of needs inside of him. I understood he had to have this—I did, too—but his body objected. For the first time I felt the thick bandage over his side that had been previously covered by the sheet.

"It's okay," he said roughly.

But it wasn't.

I pulled away from him, and he rolled onto his back, defeated. In the crack of moonlight that came in through the blinds, I could see his thick cock, rising up in defiance.

While he watched, I removed the T-shirt I'd been wearing, and my panties, and tossed them on the floor. Naked, I straddled him, using my hand to stroke him from base to head. His eyes found mine, bright with fire in the dark room, and then lowered over my breasts, and my belly, to the juncture of my thighs where I rose, and took him inside of me, inch by glorious inch.

When he was finally as deep as he would go, I shuddered a breath, and leaned forward over his body.

"Let me take care of you," I said.

He whispered my name as I started to move.

It was slow, and quiet. Hushed breaths, and gentle caresses. And when the urgency took control, I gripped his shoulders, and buried my face against his neck, and trembled as wave after wave tumbled through me. He came just as the last one hit, holding my face in his hands until his eyes drifted closed and he was finally spent.

Thirty-six

We ate leftover fajitas at three a.m. on a squeaky bed by the light of the pale yellow bulb over the bathroom sink. He wore lounge pants. I wore his T-shirt. We talked about everything from Jacob running away, to ambushing Amy with Mike's self-defense class. He kept the focus of the conversation on me with his thoughtful questions and comments, and when the focus turned to him he gently steered it back, as if he felt more at home in my life than his. Witness protection aside, it was the best date I'd ever had.

"Hope Tenner wasn't too rough on you while I was sleeping," Alec said, pushing aside the empty plate. I was pleased to see he'd worked up an appetite.

"Are you kidding?" I teased. "He's a pushover. I fed him and he practically kissed my feet." After three servings apiece, both agents had even offered to do the dishes.

"He better not be kissing any part of you, or else I'll break more than just his nose."

After what had happened with Trevor outside the gym, we both knew he was more than capable.

With a growl, he pinched the ticklish spot on the top of my hips, and I stifled a giggle as I fell back onto the bed. Rather than climbing over me, he grabbed beneath my calves and pulled me closer, so that my thighs straddled his waist.

Smoothly, he lifted my leg so that my ankle rested on his shoulder, and planted a slow kiss on the sensitive place just on the inside of my knee. I bit my lip to hold back the gasp, but the soft tease of his tongue made my toes curl.

"I've missed your legs," he said, studying the inside of my right thigh. I gasped as his fingers glided down my hamstring.

"Just my legs?"

"Is there anything else?"

I kicked him in the shoulder and he laugh-winced, and grabbed his injured side.

"Sorry!" I pushed myself up. "Let me kiss it better."

His grip in my hair grew tighter while he watched as I licked the skin just beyond his bandage.

"Jesus." His voice had become husky. "I missed that sexy mouth, too."

I made my way up to his neck. "You should see some of the other things my sexy mouth can do."

His hands felt their way down my back, then scooped beneath my butt and lifted me onto his lap. We were facing each other, our bodies closely aligned. The thin T-shirt seemed suddenly coarse as his chest pressed it against my hardened nipples.

"This is your favorite, isn't it?" he asked, circling his hips to show me what he meant. The motion caused my clit to rub against his erection, and I squeezed his shoulders and blinked, trying to focus on his question.

"You like being close," he said. "No space between us. You like how it feels."

He was right. I loved how it felt, how deep he could be, how tightly he could hold me. I loved the feel of his hard pecs rubbing against my breasts, and my arms around his neck.

I loved that he knew I loved it.

"What's your favorite position?" I asked. Not so subtly, I rubbed myself against his hard shaft, feeling the tension between us rise.

"All of them," he answered, teeth scraping my jaw.

"Cheater."

His chest rumbled with a low laugh.

"I like this." We were moving together now, a slow prelude of what was to come. "I like watching your eyes when the pleasure takes you. I like feeling your back arch beneath my hands, and having you against the wall, bearing your full weight on my cock. How you submit when you know you can't get away."

The images his words conjured stoked the fire, and I bit my lip to hold back the moan.

He shifted, moving slowly over me. His dark, silky hair fell forward, so much more like the old him than the Alec who had returned from prison weeks ago. I looked for any sign of pain in his eyes, but it was absent. "I love being over you, watching your eyelids get heavy when I kiss you. When you claw my back and dig your heels into my ass. And I like holding you here." He lifted my knees and pressed them against my chest, and then ground his sheathed cock against my wet panties. "When you fight how good it feels but it takes you anyway."

He moved down my body slowly, until his mouth was between my thighs. Pushing my bent legs up, he opened them so I was spread before him. On display. I trembled, a wave of self-consciousness battering the heat in my veins as he admired me hungrily. One finger brushed over the fabric, dampening it with my juices as he pushed it just a little inside. I gasped, the muscles in my legs flexing.

"Always so ready," he murmured. "So perfect." Then, he opened his mouth, and gently bit at my swollen lips. The sensation was so sharp and exquisite I bowed back, fisting the sheets.

"Oh God," I said. "Oh my God."

"I love your sweet little cunt, Anna," he murmured. He nuzzled my pussy and then kissed me, openmouthed. Never in my life had I hated underwear so much.

I nearly begged him to finish, but he wasn't done.

With more power than I'd expected, he flipped me over onto my belly, and, sliding a hand beneath me, hoisted my hips up to meet his.

One hand trailed lightly, lovingly, down my back, into my hair, and he pulled it—not hard, but enough to tell me who was in control. The agents were nearby, just down the hall, but I couldn't stop the moan as my fingers splayed over the pillow.

"I love this," he said. "Driving deep inside you, and when you push back and fuck yourself on my dick." He was tugging me back to him, and each time his cock scored my slit, battering my senses with a new jolt of pleasure.

"I love your ass." His open palm came down with a shock, and he soothed the heated skin with a soft caress. "Spanking you. Fucking you with my fingers."

He stilled, and his thumb drew a line down between my buttocks, over my underwear, to a place that made me buck hard against him. I shivered, uncertainty clouding my desire. He was huge, and I'd never done that before.

"Just your fingers?" I asked.

The pressure increased, heightening the need, but also my apprehension.

"I'm not built for more," he said, relieving me of my worries. He sat, and laid back on the pillows, then turned me so that I was riding him again.

"And I love you here," he said. "When you take what you want. Touch yourself and close your eyes and bite your sexy little lip. I could come just watching you."

"Alec, I . . ." I was flushed and aching. My thoughts were scrambling.

He twisted his hand in my shirt and pulled me down to him.

"What do you need, right now?"

But he had to know. I was rubbing myself against him like I had no pride, no self-control. His jaw clenched, and his eyes were deep and intense. His knuckles skimmed the sides of my heavy breasts. I longed for him to knead them, cup them and take the aching peaks in his mouth.

"I . . ."

"You know what I like," he said. "Tell me what you want."

"I need to come," I admitted, cheeks flaring. I tried to turn away, but he grabbed my face in the palm of his hands.

"How?"

"I don't know." But the change was already taking me. A dark, wild need began coursing through my veins. It made me move. Sweat. Speak. "Your mouth. Your fingers. Then your cock."

For a moment there was only his harsh breathing.

"Good girl," he said. Then he reached beneath my thighs and pulled me up. I scrambled over his chest, until my knees were on both sides of his head, and my pussy was hovering over his mouth.

I made the mistake of looking down; I could have kept some dignity if I hadn't. But he was looking up at me with such savage hunger, I was lost to everything but my own lust.

I grabbed the bed frame and dipped down. My thighs trembled as the last of my inhibitions went up in smoke. He held me in place, even as the rasp of his tongue ignited my senses. He licked me, kissed me, nipped at me, until the bands within me snapped and sent me careening over the edge.

Only then did he use his fingers.

One, then two. Twisting. Rubbing. Three fingers, fucking me hard while his mouth softened and sucked my clit.

I nearly fell, but he held on until I came again, and until that orgasm melted into another.

Then he pulled me down over his body, directed his cock into me, and held me against his chest while he destroyed us both.

*   *   *

The next time I woke it was to a loud banging against the cardboard-thin bedroom door. I jumped up, doused in adrenaline as the memories of Reznik flew back to the front of my mind. My gaze shot around the room, to the clothing strewn on the floor and the empty dinner plates on the bathroom counter, finally resting on the man sitting on the edge of the bed, reaching his hand toward me.

"It's all right," Alec said quietly.

He was as perfect as he'd always been, and the sight of him stole my breath in a different way. The low light of the room darkened his skin, and made the cuts of his body more defined. Even the wound, still somehow covered after our night together, made him appear more savage and dangerous. My gaze lowered down his naked chest, to his growing erection, and I snatched my—or his—shirt off the floor and pulled it over my head. His flawlessness reminded me what a train wreck I must have looked like. My hair was a bird's nest, and I needed to brush my teeth. I would have killed for a little eyeliner.

"Beautiful," Alec murmured, sensing my insecurities. "Come here."

I did as he asked, sliding into his lap as the beating on the door continued. He kissed my collarbone, oblivious to the urgency right outside.

"In the kitchen in five," came Janelle's crisp, no-nonsense voice. The banging ceased, and her footsteps could be heard retreating down the hall.

"I can do a lot with five minutes," whispered Alec. He walked two fingers up my thigh, beneath the hem of my shirt, but I swatted him away.

"Sounds like we're in trouble," I said with a smirk.

"She always sounds like that."

But though his arms were safe, and the dark, heady scent of him was still on my skin, our stolen time was up. Reality was waiting just beyond that door.

"Alec?"

"*Hmm?*" He nuzzled his face against my chest.

"How rough has it been trying to keep me clear of the trial?"

He stilled, just for a moment, before wrapping me up even tighter in his strong arms.

"You don't have to worry about that."

I tilted his chin up, forcing him to meet my gaze.

"Do you love me?"

He brushed my hair behind my ears, a fierceness in his eyes. "More than you know."

The gentleness in his touch made me feel light, and his confession chipped away at my fear.

"It's new to me," I said. "Feeling like I deserve it—like I deserve you. It's such a big feeling, sometimes I don't know what to do with it."

I wished I had better words, but he nodded in understanding. My fingers drew a slow line over his collarbone, then up the cords of his neck.

"It scares you," he said.

I nodded. "Before I'd just move on. I'd find a new town, and a new job, and a new apartment. New people that didn't know me. It felt safer that way—not really knowing anyone. But now, with you, the one thing that feels safest is the one thing that scares me the most. And I'm not even thinking about running."

His lips parted, stormy eyes reflecting my own vulnerability.

"Anna," he whispered.

"I'm not running," I said again. "But I'm waiting for you to realize the same thing I have. You deserve this, too. And you don't have to shelter me, because I'm standing right beside you."

His Adam's apple bobbed. I kissed him as he struggled against my words, as they rooted in his head and heart. And then I stood up, got dressed, and made my way to the kitchen, leaving him staring after me.

The two male agents looked like they'd been on an all-night bender. Matt rubbed his eyes with the back of his hand and blinked, while Tenner rested his forehead on the card table.

"Somebody get me some coffee," he moaned.

"What happened to Mr. Nice Guy?" I asked. "Is it time to feed you again?"

"What *happened*?" He sat up. There was a red mark on his forehead from the table, and his eyes resembled a raccoon's. "What happened is you two kept me up all night fucking like bunnies."

I chewed the inside of my cheek.

"It wasn't *all* night," I said.

Alec came into the room, still looking a little shell-shocked. One glance at the agents and his arms came around my waist. I leaned back, loving the feel of him, even if his body language was shouting "mine" loud and clear.

"He's counting the time he put in afterward jacking off," said Matt.

Tenner glared at him. "Speak for yourself, fuckwad. Least you get a room with a door. I just have the couch."

"Aw, come on," said Matt, who glanced around us to the sofa, as if expecting to see a bottle of lotion and a wad of tissues.

"If it bothers you so much, maybe you should separate them." Janelle swept in from the room with the video monitors, carrying an armful of file folders. She was dressed differently today, in light-washed jeans and a soft blue T-shirt. Her hair was down, and her makeup was even less severe than usual, making her pretty, even sort of striking. She didn't glance our way, even when Alec said good morning.

I remembered the way she'd looked at him last night when I'd been examining his wound on the couch, and how icy she always was toward me. I wondered if she had any idea how she felt about him.

Gently, I pulled away, watching as he inhaled slowly, and sighed. He knew, even if she didn't.

I wasn't sure how I felt about all that.

"So what's on the agenda?" I asked, feeling the weight of the sudden silence. "Swimming at the lake and then crafts in the lodge?"

Matt chuckled.

Janelle's cold stare locked on mine. "Is this funny to you?"

My temperature rose. She was smaller than I was, but she'd called me out, and I had nothing to respond with because I knew I was here on her good graces alone.

"Janelle." Alec edged closer to me.

"Is it funny to *you*, Alec?" she asked. "Because yesterday you didn't seem so comfortable about the situation."

"That was before last night," mumbled Tenner.

"It was a stupid joke," I said. "I understand the seriousness of the situation."

"Do you?" She leaned forward over the desk. "Three times now, Alec's life has been threatened. Twice, trying to save your ass. That puts a burden of responsibility on you that I'm not sure you fully appreciate."

My fists clenched. She had no idea what burdens I woke up with every morning.

"Did he tell you about prison?" she asked.

"Janelle," cautioned Alec.

"He was nearly dead when the guards found him. Left to bleed out on the workroom floor. How many times did they try before they got to you, Alec?"

"That's enough," Alec barked. We both jumped at the sound.

"If this doesn't work," she said, "if Stein walks free, or if Alec's testimony has too many holes, I can't help him. Witness protection ends as soon as the court cuts him loose. He's either going back to prison, or he'll be back on the streets, and what do you think Stein will do to him then?"

A red curtain dropped over my vision. Something inside of me snapped. I swept her file folders to the floor and lunged at her, the table nearly grinding against the floor as it pushed away. I'd succeeded in grabbing the neck of her shirt and jerking her close before the guys tried to separate us.

"Bitch at me all you want to," I said. "But never, ever accuse me of taking his life for granted."

She stared back her challenge, not even a flicker of fear in her green eyes.

"Let go," Alec prompted, easing my knuckles open. "Anna, let her go."

"Or don't," offered Tenner.

"You should listen to Alec," said Janelle. "For once."

I backed off and leaned against the counter, still fuming that she'd gotten under my skin, but now more fearful than ever for what this trial had done, and would do, to Alec. I pictured him bleeding out on the floor in prison, as she'd said. Pictured how it had nearly happened again at the hotel after Reznik's man had shown up. How could I not have known how bad it had been for him? Why hadn't he told me?

The thought of him dying scared me more than Reznik or Stein ever could.

As I looked at Janelle I felt nothing but contempt. But I needed to keep my mouth closed if I wanted to stay here, and more importantly, if I wanted Alec protected. I would do whatever she said to keep him safe.

"How about some coffee?" asked Matt.

I didn't answer. I gripped the countertop behind me so hard my fingernails began to throb.

Alec stayed a foot away, arms crossed. Was he doing that for her sake, or mine? Either way, I wasn't a fan of the distance.

"You need to meet with your lawyer," said Janelle, squatting to pick up her folders off the floor. "Jack Reznik's still missing, and Maxim Stein's claiming he has no idea what provoked him to use his name."

The information seemed to make the air even thinner and more fragile, and through it cut a memory, spurred by her reminder.

"Do you know a woman named Jacqueline Frieda?" I asked Alec, still unable to look straight at Janelle. "She's a lawyer, I think."

"How do you know her?" asked Janelle pointedly. She placed the folders back on the table.

From Alec's confused frown, I guessed he hadn't heard of her.

"She's been looking for Alec. I've run into her twice now, but she won't tell me what she wants. Marcos—the police officer on my protective detail—he looked up her plates for me." I pictured my serious guard. Even if he wasn't technically tailing me anymore, I wondered if he had noticed I'd disappeared.

"She's on Stein's legal team," said Janelle. "What does she want with you? She shouldn't be talking to you without going through your lawyer. That's a serious breach of ethics."

"I don't know," said Alec. "I've never met her."

Janelle considered this a moment, staring behind us, into the kitchen.

"I'll arrange a meeting," she said. "Something secure. See what she wants." She looked back between us, her face showing a hint of color for the first time. "Until then, try not to distract my agents."

With that, she stalked out the door without looking back.

Thirty-seven

The meeting was arranged for eight o'clock that night, at a McDonald's in a town thirty minutes away. These were her conditions when Janelle insisted we discuss whatever had originally brought her to Alec's door.

Thirty minutes after the scheduled time, I moved onto the third fingernail I'd chewed down to the nub. Matt had stayed behind at the safe house, but Tenner was smoking outside the entrance, and Janelle was sitting in the booth behind ours, pretending to read the paper. To my left was a play place, shiny with spilled orange drink and littered with wrappers and discarded Happy Meal toys, and I couldn't help but stare at it.

I hadn't been to a place like this, more or less *waited* at a place like this, since my birth mother had died.

Alec had been sitting across from me, but as I moved onto the fourth fingernail, he slid into the booth beside me. Taking my hands, he clasped them both within his and kissed my knuckles.

"It wasn't my first choice for location," he said.

It was an open invitation, and I didn't want to talk about it.

"She chose these clothes on purpose." I smoothed down the

large long-sleeved T-shirt and cargo pants Janelle had picked up at a secondhand store for me to wear until it was deemed safe enough that someone could make a supply run to my apartment. They were all the wrong sizes. I looked like a child playing dress up.

"Maybe you should take them off."

I elbowed him halfheartedly, my gaze fixed on a twisting ladder and climbing wall beyond the glass partition.

"Why didn't you tell me how bad it was in prison?" I asked.

He shifted.

"Same reason you didn't tell me how hard Bobby hit you."

I looked at him, then down at our clasped hands. Okay. I got that.

"I broke my arm in a place like this once," he said. "I thought it'd be a good idea to jump from the top of the slide. Turns out it wasn't."

"Oops."

"Yeah. One of the rare times my dad took me somewhere." He looked wistful, lost in the memory.

"What'd he do about it?"

Alec's mouth tilted up at the corner. "He said it didn't *look* broken."

Oh, Thomas. Some people thought they were so funny.

I pictured Alec's father, sitting at the restaurant on the water with Mac. How long had he waited before realizing I wasn't coming? Did the other agents contact him, like they said they would? They never had when Alec had been taken to the safe house. I'd had to tell him myself.

And then there was Amy, and Mike, and Derrick at work. What would they think when I simply disappeared? I wished I had a way to contact them, but my new best friend Janelle was holding my cell phone hostage in her black leather purse.

I did have the burner phone Marcos had given me though. I'd tucked it into one of the lower pockets of the cargo pants. It was on silent; I didn't want it somehow ringing and alerting Janelle that I was holding on to safe house contraband. But holding on to it made me feel safer.

"What if Jacqueline's working for Reznik?" I asked. "Or if Maxim's got her doing something less-than-legal on the side?" I couldn't shake the feeling that this could be the worst kind of setup. That we'd agreed to a private meet with some kind of femme fatale.

"Then she won't get far," said Alec. Janelle was armed, though the weapon was concealed. If this lawyer threatened to harm us, she would jump in.

That didn't make me feel better.

My gaze turned to the door as a woman in workout clothes entered. Her blond hair was back in a ponytail, tucked beneath a ball cap pulled low over her eyes. Even though this was the first time I hadn't seen her in business attire, I recognized her immediately.

"There," I said to Alec. He started to stand, but she was already hurrying toward our table.

"Jacqueline." Alec's expression was flat and impossible to read. "We weren't sure you were going to make it."

"How did you know where to find me?" she demanded, keeping her voice low. "And who was that woman that called my office? Do you have any idea the trouble I could be in for talking to you?"

Her concern seemed genuine, and any speculation that she was working for Reznik vanished. "I got your license plate number the last time we met. A friend of mine helped me locate you."

"The woman who called you is part of my security team." Alec had been directed by Janelle to say this. "You can trust her."

Jacqueline laughed cynically. Her eyes darted around the room.

"You're one of Maxim Stein's lawyers," I prompted.

"I'm involved in his bankruptcy case," she said.

"Bankruptcy?" I'd thought the man was made of solid gold bullion.

Her scowl etched deeper. She began to twist a paper napkin left on the table.

"All revenue effectively stopped once the charges were raised against him. He's filing personal bankruptcy to pay for his legal fees. Another firm is starting to look at what they can pull from his company's assets. It'll all be public tomorrow morning anyway." She waved her hand, little bits of napkin floating through the air.

Alec had told me before that legal fees were killing his savings—he was a couple months away from living in a cardboard box. It seemed this trial was sucking both sides dry.

"Why did you want to see me?" asked Alec.

At his pointed question, she stiffened. She looked at his face for the first time, her eyes rounding just slightly.

"You're getting screwed," she said.

"How's that?" he asked.

She sighed.

"You really need to look back over the Articles of Incorporation in Force's founding documents. Point your lawyer in that direction. And if you're feeling really generous, leave my name out of it."

Her vagueness was beginning to rub me the wrong way.

"What are the Articles of Incorporation?" I asked.

"They're the legal papers that define the rules of the company." Alec was scowling. "They were put into place before I worked for Max. Why would I need to look at them?"

Jacqueline hesitated.

"I could be disbarred for this," she said. "Sued. If this gets out . . ." Her face was getting paler by the moment.

I tried a gentler approach. "You already did the hard part. Just tell us why."

She glanced at Tenner outside, who was probably on his fifteenth cigarette by now.

"We've been reviewing the Articles as part of the bankruptcy assessment," she said. "In them is an addendum that says that if any shareholder is convicted of fraud, those shares are forfeited to the company. Do you understand what that means?"

I glanced at Alec, who seemed to absorb this information slowly. He suddenly leaned forward.

"Max was the primary shareholder," he said. "He opened some of them up to Bobby when he announced that his nephew was next in line to take over the company. That's when he let me buy in."

I even bought shares in it knowing full well Max would never give me any voting power.

"Wait," I said, piecing this all together. "Max and Bobby are about to be convicted of fraud. Holy shit."

"Yes," said Jacqueline. "Holy shit."

Alec stared at her. "My shares don't even make up 2 percent of the company."

"Doesn't matter," she said. "If their shares cease to exist, your 2 percent becomes 100 percent."

Alec shoved back in his seat. "How is that possible? I would have known about this. *He* would have known about this."

"I would bet Stein does know," she muttered. "But like you said, that document was written before you came on. No one references it on a day-to-day basis. It's not crucial to the corporate espionage charges the prosecution is raising against him."

I wasn't much for blind trust, but the doubt was already bubbling into something far lighter in my chest.

"You're saying Alec has the potential to own Force," I said. "The whole worldwide, elite aviation company."

She gave a jerky shrug. "Not that it'll be worth much when this is over anyway, but yes. Stein and Calloway have to be convicted of fraud of course, which will be harder with the secretary still missing. Her testimony, considering it matched yours, would have sealed the deal."

"Ms. Rowe," I said, feeling that well of dread inside me every time I thought of her. For all we knew she was trapped in a car at the bottom of the Bay.

Jacqueline nodded. "Since Calloway pled guilty to running that woman off the road—what was her name?"

"Charlotte MacAfee," said Alec stoically.

"Right. Since Calloway's saying he acted alone, the brother's accusations that Stein masterminded the whole thing is at a standstill. Now, Stein's just preparing to fight you, Mr. Flynn. And he's spending a pretty penny to do it."

Which meant that he was scared as hell.

Which is why he'd hired Reznik to eliminate the opposition.

I thought back to the newspaper articles I'd read about Charlotte MacAfee's brother. He'd wanted justice for his sister's murder. Maybe Alec's testimony would give him some of it.

Or maybe I could give it to him. Because despite Alec's efforts to keep me clear of all this, Bobby had told me that Max had ordered my death. Maybe that was enough to lock him away forever.

"Why tell me all this?" asked Alec. "Why go to all this risk?"

"It's going to be public at some point," Jacqueline said. "You'll want your lawyer to be prepared for that. They'll try to say you fabricated your testimony just so you could get Stein out of the way."

I put my hand on Alec's thigh, steadying the bounce of his heel. The thought of him being accused of lying had been a reality before, but now it seemed a hundred times more real. This trial had the potential to push him to the very edge.

"And," said Jacqueline, looking down into her lap. "And I have a cousin who's very close. We were raised as sisters. A few years ago she met Bobby Calloway at a bar. I don't know much of what happened, but I can tell you it didn't end well."

Alec's jaw had begun working back and forth.

"You found her, Mr. Flynn. She'd been severely beaten. I don't expect you to remember." Her voice had gone tight.

"I remember," said Alec. "I took her to the hospital. She accused me of doing it."

"After Calloway's lawyer threatened her," she said emphatically. "She dropped those charges after she told me what really happened. She . . ." Jacqueline cleared her throat. "She owes you a great debt of gratitude. As do I."

Alec had told me about this once, shortly before Bobby had shown me just what kind of violence he was capable of. I didn't know what to say. It appeared Alec didn't, either.

Jacqueline rose. "I appreciate what you did. We both do." She squeezed her keys, looking from Alec to me. "Good luck."

A minute later, she was gone.

Thirty-eight

"Did she just say you're a billionaire, or did I misunderstand?" I finally asked.

Alec was still staring at the door where she'd left. I waved a hand in front of his face, but he didn't even blink. In the next booth, Janelle rose.

"She said you have to win, that's what she said. And even then there might be nothing left." With that, Miss Mary Sunshine hurried outside to talk to Tenner.

Alec was still silently staring off into space.

"Are you okay?"

"Yeah." He scowled. "It can't be true. Maybe Max paid her to come here."

"Why would he do that?"

"I don't know." Alec scratched a hand over his skull. "It can't be true."

The way he said it, all wary and *undeserving* made me want to crawl up into his lap and hold him. Because we were still in public, I settled on pulling his hand onto my thigh and resting my chin on his shoulder.

"Why not?"

"Because miracles don't fucking happen to people like me."

He might as well have kicked me in the stomach.

I pulled away.

"Hold on," he said. "I didn't mean . . ."

"That I wasn't your miracle?" I crossed my arms and raised the wall. "Don't worry, I didn't think I was."

But he was mine. He'd saved me, changed me, made me want to take on the world rather than run from it. It was a shame something as simple as love didn't stack up against the almighty dollar bill.

He stared at me, brows knitting together.

I wanted him to take it back, say this great prospect was nothing without me by his side, but even if he wanted to, he couldn't, because right then Janelle returned to the table. She was holding her cell phone, a scowl tightening her features. At the sight of it, I gripped the side of my leg, making sure the burner phone was still there.

"Matt says someone's been trying to reach you on your cell. They've called four times in a row." She scrolled down the text message and rattled off a familiar number.

"It's my friend, Amy Elgin," I said. "Did you tell her I was with you?"

Janelle's raised brow told me they hadn't.

I shook my head, hating that Amy was worrying about me. She'd likely already called my dad. The cops. The National Guard.

"Then she's going to keep calling until the phone's dead," I told her. "And then she'll start hanging my picture on street corners and doing interviews with the local news."

"Good God," said Janelle. "I don't have time for this shit."

She pressed a few buttons, and held the phone up to her ear.

"Hello? Who's this?" Her frown deepened. "I need to speak with your mother, please."

It took a moment for my brain to switch gears to the six-year-old daughter of my best friend. Without thinking, I stood, leaning close to listen in.

"What do you mean . . . Sure," Janelle said tightly. She handed me the phone. "You've got two minutes."

I lifted the phone to my ear, listening as a small voice said my name. "Anna?"

"Paisley? What's going on?"

She had my number—it was taped to the wall over their house phone for emergency purposes. She'd never called me before without Amy speaking first.

I checked the time on the clock behind the registers—it was late for her. She usually went to bed around eight, but it was already nine thirty.

"Mommy left and didn't come back."

A cold chill crept up my spine. It wasn't Miss Iris's night to babysit; Amy should have been there. She never left Paisley alone.

"When did she leave?"

"At the beginning of *The Little Mermaid*."

Alec came to stand beside me, watching me closely. His mouth formed a thin, serious line.

"Where are you in the movie?" I'd seen it at least a dozen times with them. I knew all the parts. If she could tell me what song they were at, I'd know how long Amy had been gone. It was possible that she'd just run out to her car, or stepped next door to get something from a neighbor.

"Ariel just got her voice back."

Ariel the mermaid didn't break the curse that had stolen her voice until nearly the end of the movie. Amy had been gone an hour, give or take.

Where the hell was she?

"Did your mommy say where she was going?"

"Uh-uh." Paisley's voice was higher now. She was getting scared. "Jonathan came and got her and they left."

The world stopped—all except the fry baskets in the background that hissed as they hit the oil.

Tonight was the night we were all supposed to go get pizza; I remembered that now. I was supposed to meet him for the first time. I had forgotten about it with everything that had happened

"Paisley, is there anyone else at home with you right now?"

My voice was low, unfamiliar. My hands began to shake. Alec gripped my elbows, already gathering himself to fight. We didn't even know what the danger was yet.

"No."

"What the hell are you . . ." Janelle tried to take the phone, but Alec stopped her with one hard look.

"Okay, I want you to stay there," I said. "I'm on my way."

The phone made a shushing noise against her cheek. "Can I have popcorn?"

"Sure," I said. "Hold on to the phone. Don't hang up, all right?"

When I heard the sound of the pantry door opening and the crinkle of plastic wrap, I covered the receiver.

"Amy's gone," I said. "A guy she's been seeing came to get her over an hour ago. Paisley's there alone now." I was already jogging toward the exit. Janelle was saying something behind us, but I couldn't focus on it.

Alec cut in front of me just before we reached the door and placed himself between Tenner and me.

"Keys." He held out his hand.

Tenner smashed his cigarette into the ashtray. "Nice try, asshole."

The muggy night air outside felt thick, too heavy for Alec to move as fast as he did. Before I could blink, he had Tenner shoved up against the glass wall of the building, hands fisted in his collar. The agent bared his teeth, glaring at Alec through narrowed eyes. One hand gripped Alec's wrist, the other reached behind his back, presumably for his weapon.

"It's still popping," said Paisley, the microwave whirring in the background. "But I'm gonna take it out before it burns."

"G-good idea," I stammered.

"Remember last time you tried to stop me?" asked Alec. Broken ribs or not, he was just as dangerous as ever. The only evidence of his pain was the single bead of sweat that formed at his temple. A surge of affection rose up inside of me. He was supporting me without question, without explanation.

And he was fantastic.

"This isn't our problem," said Janelle. "I'm sorry about your friend's luck, but this isn't . . . "

I rounded on her, covering the speaker of the phone with my hand. "Reznik took me from the YMCA. I was there with Amy," I said quickly. "He's seen her. This isn't a coincidence."

She muttered something under her breath.

"Then what if it's a setup?" she asked harshly. "Think, Alec. What does Stein want with some friend of Anna's? He wants you. This is about *you*."

"Keys," said Alec again. "*Please*. There, I asked nicely."

I shivered at the threat in his tone.

"Are you coming yet?" asked the small voice on the line.

"I'm on my way, Paisley," I told her. "Hey Pais, I've got an idea. What if you take that popcorn to your bedroom?"

"I'm not allowed to eat in my room."

I swallowed a deep breath. It took everything I had to say the next part.

"I know," I said. "But I'll tell your mommy it's okay. I want you to go in there and shut the door real tight, okay? And then I want you to hide under the bed."

She didn't say anything for a moment. "Anna, where's Mommy?"

I forced myself to breathe.

"It'll be like hide-and-seek," I said.

But it wasn't, of course. Because that was where Paisley had learned to go when her father hit her mother.

"Janelle, this might be the last chance to catch Reznik before he disappears for good," Alec said.

She checked her watch, then stared out over the parking lot, scowling.

I covered the receiver. "If he's playing us, it worked. I can't leave my best friend's daughter alone." I stared straight into her eyes. "He'll be there."

Janelle glanced at Tenner, and after a long moment, nodded.

"Agent Tenner will drive," she said. "Both of you will stay in the car while we clear the area. Is that understood?"

I nodded, just so we could hurry this up. Tenner smacked away Alec's loosened grip and spat on the ground.

We raced to the black Lincoln Navigator. Alec and I took the backseat, while Janelle sat in the front with Tenner. While Alec shot off the directions, I made Paisley tell me about what she'd done at school today.

Janelle snatched a phone from Tenner's pocket. He looked excited for about a quarter of a second until he realized what she was doing.

"Hey," he complained. She punched in a number.

"Matt, change of plans. I need you to run a woman named . . ." Janelle reached behind the seat to snap her fingers in my face.

"Amy Elgin," I said. Janelle continued spouting orders to her other agent, still stationed back at the safe house. I caught only snippets of it between listening to the rustle of Paisley's cheek against the phone, but "possibly abducted" and "hold off on calling it in" brought on a new wave of nausea.

"What was she wearing? What does Jonathan look like?" Janelle asked.

"Pais, do you remember what Mommy was wearing?"

She thought about this for a moment. "Her gray pants."

I pictured Amy in her gray sweatpants. She wouldn't have

been caught dead going on a date in them, which further confirmed my suspicions that she'd been surprised.

"Gray sweatpants," I said loudly enough for Janelle to hear me. "What else? What color was her T-shirt?"

"I don't remember," said Paisley.

"Can you tell me what Jonathan looks like?"

Paisley crunched a mouthful of popcorn. "He's all right looking. That's what Mommy says."

Not exactly the response she'd had to Mike.

"What color is his hair?"

"Yellow," she said.

"Yellow," I repeated for Janelle's benefit. "And is he tall, or short, or skinny, or fat?"

"He's sort of tall. Sort of skinny."

"Do you remember Alec?" When she said yes, I asked, "Is he as tall as Alec?"

"No. Shorter. And skinnier."

"Shorter and skinnier," I said, watching Janelle make a note on a pad of scratch paper.

"Am I in trouble?" Paisley whispered.

"What?" I asked. "No way. You're in the opposite of trouble."

"I need that phone," Alec told Janelle when she hung up.

There was a short discussion about this before Janelle finally passed it back. Quickly, Alec punched in the numbers.

"Mike, it's me," he said a moment later. "Where are you?"

"Is Mommy in trouble?" Paisley asked.

I swallowed. "No, she's all right. Are you under the bed, sweetie?"

Alec put one hand on my knee and gave it a reassuring squeeze. "Amy's missing. Paisley's at the apartment alone. We're on our way, but . . . Yeah. Chloe's with your mom?"

"But if Mommy's not in trouble, why am I hiding?"

Alec's voice cut through. "We don't know where she is. Some

guy picked her up." He paused, looked at me. "No, doesn't sound like it was her ex."

I shook my head. It had been a few years, but Paisley would have recognized her father. Jonathan—whoever he was—was someone else. I glanced at the window, watching the docks whip by through the tinted windows as we climbed onto the interstate. How long had Jonathan planned this? Did he work for Stein? Reznik? Had he played Amy to get to Alec and I, or was this some kind of cosmic misunderstanding?

The dark fear in my belly told me it wasn't.

After a few more short words, Alec hung up the phone.

"Mike's on his way. If he gets there first, he's going to take Paisley upstairs to his mom's."

I mouthed a thank-you, and he nodded.

"Paisley, remember Chloe's daddy? He's going to babysit you for a while if he gets there before us. Is that okay?"

"Uh-huh."

"You don't come to the door unless it's Mike or me, okay?"

"Okay."

I wrapped my hand around Alec's wrist.

"Hang on, Paisley, we'll be there soon."

Thirty-nine

Every minute seemed to take ten, and by the time we'd reached Amy's apartment complex my stomach was in knots and my scalp was damp with sweat. Paisley had stayed on the phone with me the entire time, though she hadn't said much. I listened to the steady crunch of the popcorn, picturing her curled in a ball beneath her mattress, the way she'd been the day of the picnic.

The complex was painted neutral colors—beige and white and brown—and every two-story building looked the same. If I hadn't been here a hundred times, I would have been utterly lost. Muffling the receiver, I directed Tenner around the carports, over the twisty drive of speed bump after speed bump, until the glowing Christmas lights wrapped around Amy's second-story porch came into view.

She never took them down, despite what the neighbors said.

"There," I pointed. "Two forty-four B."

I unbuckled my seat belt.

"Not until the area's been cleared," Janelle reiterated harshly.

I shoved back in my seat. The floodlights overhead made yellow circles on the ground, and Tenner drove between them, until he was three buildings past Amy's, and parked on the street in the dark.

"How do you want to play this?" Tenner asked Janelle after putting the car in park. She took her cell phone back from Alec and stuck it in her pocket.

"Ladies first," she said. "I'll clear the perimeter. You keep an eye on these two." She tilted her head back to us.

Tenner nodded, and in that moment, I was in awe of her authority. She looked so cool and dangerous, like she wasn't afraid of anything. I almost envied her.

"Maybe Tenner and I should go," Alec offered.

"That's sweet." She removed a gun from the shoulder harness within her black jacket. It was sleek and silver in the floodlights, as lethal as she was. "I guess chivalry isn't dead after all."

Tenner snorted, checking the ammunition in his own weapon.

"The kid's name?" Janelle asked.

"Paisley," I said. Mike still hadn't arrived, so we would get to her first.

She opened the car door and walked across the road into the grass outside the nearest building. I tracked her position as long as I could before she was consumed by shadows.

"It's going to be all right," Alec said, breaking the tense silence in the car.

"It's got to be all right," I whispered through clenched teeth, holding the phone to my shoulder. "Paisley needs her mom."

His gaze locked on mine, deep with understanding. We both knew what it was like to grow up without a mother, or at least a good one. It couldn't be that way for Paisley. I wouldn't let it happen.

"It's going to be all right," Alec repeated, the conviction clear in his tone.

"Someone's knocking," Paisley said.

I could hear it in the background. I stiffened, gripping Alec's forearm. Janelle couldn't have gotten there yet.

"Don't answer," I told her. "Just wait."

Another knock. And then a muffled male's voice.

"It's Chloe's daddy," she said. The phone rustled against her cheek again as she got out from under the bed. "I see him through the peephole."

"Is he alone?" I asked.

Headlights appeared from the opposite direction. They jumped up and down as the car—a utility van—went over a speed bump.

"Get down," said Tenner. He relocked the doors.

I ducked in my seat, Alec's hard body stretching over mine.

"Should I open the door?" asked Paisley.

The van's engine revved.

"What the fuck . . ."

Tenner didn't finish. There was a crash, and the car rocked. The sound of crunching metal filled my ears. The utility van must have hit us. The driver hadn't been going fast enough to hurt Alec and I, but the airbag had deployed, thrusting Tenner back against his seat.

The next few moments happened so fast I could barely keep up.

The driver's door was ripped open and Tenner was dragged from his seat, out of view. A cry tore from my throat when I heard the grunt of pain and the dull thud of something solid coming down against his body. Through the window, I watched in horror as a shadowed figure raised what looked to be a crowbar.

"Move, move, move," Alec chanted, pushing me the opposite direction, toward the door. But when another man strode around the back, Alec shoved me down to the carpeted floor, pinning me beneath him with one knee. The rough upholstery raked my cheek as I fought him and tried to push up.

Before he could get to the door, he froze.

"Be very still," he whispered.

A tap came against the window, metal on glass, and then the door was yanked open. I tried to look up, but my hair covered my face. Still, I could hear Alec slide slowly out of the backseat.

"Let's go," said a gritty, familiar voice.

Reznik.

Terror shot down my spine.

"Both of you," he said. "Hurry, or I put a bullet in her head."

"You don't need . . ." Alec started.

"A bullet," said Reznik calmly. "In her head."

My breath came in hard rasps. I couldn't hear anything on the other side of the car now. Was Tenner still alive? Was he coming with us?

I tried to grab the cell phone that had fallen on the floor of the car beside me, but it was snatched away before my fingers could wrap around it.

I was dragged out of the car by the hair, pinned against the door while my wrists were cuffed, and then hustled into the sliding door of the utility van behind Alec. Reznik jumped in after us while the driver returned to the front seat and exchanged his crowbar for a gun in the front of his belt.

"Nice to see you two again," he said as he tucked the keys to our cuffs in his hip pocket.

"Fuck you," Alec said.

Reznik backhanded him with the barrel of his gun. I screamed, then stifled it in my shoulder. Chaotic thoughts whipped through my head as the driver backed away from the Navigator, and sped down the road, tires squealing. Paisley. Amy. Janelle. Stein—he'd caught us for real this time. We didn't have a kill switch in this car, or a weapon stored under the seat. We were at the mercy of two armed men, going God knows where.

"Ouch," said Alec flatly, spitting blood on Reznik's boots. He leaned back on his cuffed arms against the wall of the nearly empty van. His legs stretched out before him like our captor was no more dangerous than a Girl Scout.

I didn't take my eyes off Reznik, even to see if they'd left Tenner outside on the ground. He crouched, and smoothed my hands over my hip pockets to check for weapons. Keeping the gun trained on Alec, he leaned closer, and slid a hand down my spine, taking longer than necessary to check both back pockets as I shifted away from his touch.

He started to feel down my legs, but I kicked him, square in the shin. He grit his teeth.

"Do I need to frisk you, too?" he asked Alec.

Alec smiled, a cold, daunting look in his eyes. "Only if you really want to."

Reznik didn't, and instead returned to sit on a box across from us, as if daring Alec to try something.

"Where are we going?" I asked in a low voice. Alec's arm brushed against mine, my only comfort in this chilly space.

We hit another bump, everyone jostling. The barrel of the gun swung in a wide arc across my chest and I yelped.

"To meet our mutual friend," Reznik answered.

Stein. Finally we would come face-to-face with him. A tidal wave of rage rose hard and fast inside of me. He'd hurt the people I cared about. He might still have Amy. I wanted to tear him limb from limb.

"In that case," I said. "Mind if I borrow your crowbar?"

Reznik laughed.

"She's got fire, Alec." His free hand stroked his beard. "She'll fight when I hold her down. That's very exciting for me."

"You're a sick son of a bitch," I said.

Fear clawed in my belly, but I tightened my abdominals to trap it there. I wouldn't let him screw with my mind. If he'd wanted me dead he would have already done it.

Alec continued to stare down Reznik across the compartment.

"Is that how you get women?" asked Alec nonchalantly. "I wondered."

Reznik's grin faded.

"You're all talk, Alec. Always have been. That's why I never invited you to work for me. You don't have the balls to follow through when things get dirty."

"What can I say?" he said. "I like being able to sleep at night."

A low hum came from across the van as the lights from the road slashed across his face then went dark. "That's why you're here, isn't it, rat? Why your woman has to look over her shoulder. Why your friends are slowly bleeding out. Because you've always played it so clean."

Alec's jaw tightened, just for a fraction of a second.

"We all have our demons," he said.

"Yes," said Reznik. "At least we agree on that."

Don't listen to him. Amy wasn't bleeding out. She was okay. She had to be okay. Because if she was hurt, it was my fault. I'd brought her into this because I couldn't give up Alec. Not even after she'd warned me.

The van slowed as we came to a stoplight. The windows were blacked out, but I could see through the front windshield that we were about to get on the freeway.

My shoulders were starting to ache, and my fingers prickled, smashed behind my hips.

"Let her go," Alec said.

"No, I don't think so."

My gaze flicked to Alec. I wasn't leaving this car without him.

The van pulled forward, then picked up speed. We were on the interstate now, but I'd lost my bearings. I didn't know which way we were going.

"Drop her off here," Alec said. "Let's you and me settle this alone. Man to man."

Reznik lowered his gun. "As much as I would enjoy that, Alec, I have my orders, and I need my paycheck. Especially after this recent bind Ms. Rossi has put me in with the police."

"What's the price?" asked Alec. "Your usual? Or could Stein not afford that now that he's drowning in legal fees?"

"More than you make working at the docks," said Reznik.

"We're getting close," called the driver.

My heart rate kicked up another notch as the van tilted up an incline.

"Not another goddamn bridge," I said.

The tires whirred beneath us, slowing their rotation.

"Last chance, Reznik." The tension was clear in Alec's voice now. It should have frightened me, but instead I felt a strange kind of calm, as if he had transferred his strength to me.

The older man placed one hand on the handle of the sliding door.

"Here's where we get out."

We stopped, and he opened the door. At his urging, I climbed out, nearly slipping as a gust of wind ripped past. The driver righted me with a rough hand on my upper arm. He was younger than I would have expected. Maybe not even eighteen. His dark hair was buzzed, and he had full lips, but his eyes were vacant.

"Max," muttered Alec as we were led to the walking lane, where a man and a woman stood in the shadow of one of the supporting beams.

But it wasn't Maxim Stein that stepped out into the light. It was a younger man, lanky, with golden hair. A man who didn't belong here now, on this cold bridge with my best friend beside him.

"Trevor?"

Forty

Trevor Marshall looked different than the last time I'd seen him. Not just because the bruise on his jaw from Alec's right hook was fading, or because he was wearing a black jacket and slacks, a change from the casual clothes I'd grown accustomed to seeing him in. His posture was too rigid, and the muscles of his face and neck were too tight, as if he'd been in pain a long time.

"Hi, Anna," he said, voice raised over the wind. The suspender cables clanged against their anchors on the deck like a giant metallic wind chime.

"What is this?" Alec asked, edging in front of me. His fingers brushed my thigh, but his arms were still trapped behind him by the cuffs.

I glanced behind us to not just one, but two utility vans marked with a giant paint can and the words METALCOAT PAINT. Trevor must have come in the other one. They were spotlighted by the overheads posted on the beams above, the only vehicles in sight on this eerily empty bridge.

A muffled scream came from a shadowed barrier on the edge.

"Amy?" I launched myself forward but collided with Alec's back as he blocked my way.

"You bastard!" I shouted around him at Trevor. "What did you do to her?"

Trevor ignored me now, refocusing his hate-filled gaze on the man attempting to protect me.

"Alec Flynn." He stepped onto the street, the soles of his shoes crackling over the asphalt, until he stood an arm's length away. Angry red marks were now visible on his cheek—four parallel lines that were clawed all the way down to his neck.

A second before he swung it was obvious what he was going to do, but though Alec jerked back, he had nowhere to go because I was standing too close behind him. Trevor's fist cracked against his jaw, and the reverberation that went through his body shoved me a step back.

"What are you doing?" I demanded, my voice shrill.

"You don't deserve her, you stupid bastard," Trevor said.

Slowly, Alec righted himself, and for the second time that night spit blood on the ground. He took a step closer to Trevor, and lifted his chin, giving him the chance to strike again.

"Tell me something I don't know."

"Stop it," I said, fearing for a moment that all this was about me. I looked around again, but no one was coming. No one could see us, arms bound. See Trevor with his bloodied fist, or the two men standing quietly beside the open van, guns in their folded hands. We were all alone.

"The bridge is closed," said Trevor. "No one's coming. Except maybe the painters." He motioned to the utility van behind me.

My stomach sank. Vaguely, I remembered reading something about this—the Sunshine Skyway bridge being closed for renovations.

"Where's Stein?" Alec asked.

"At home, I suppose," Trevor said.

I couldn't tell if he was being honest—if Stein was actually behind this or if he was acting alone.

Trevor held his hands out to his sides. "You know what's crazy about this part of the bridge?"

No one answered.

Trevor's arms lowered. "It's the only place not covered by a video feed." He pointed in the direction we'd come. "That way is covered." He pointed the other direction. "That way is covered. Pretty much every inch of this bridge is covered, except for a width of fourteen feet where we're standing right now."

Trevor shoved his hands in his pockets and rocked back on his heels.

"Do you know how I know that?"

Amy cried out again, and it took everything I had not to fall to my knees and beg for him to free her.

"Because there's a one-point-eight-second blackout on the security footage that doesn't show Robert Calloway hitting my sister's car. But he did, of course. And that caused her to swerve"—he was motioning with his hands, moving them back and forth like a swimming fish—"and eventually crash through the barrier and free-fall four hundred and thirty feet into the water below." He stared at the new concrete on the barrier twenty yards away.

I didn't have to close my eyes to see the woman's face as it was in my dreams. Trapped beside me in the seat of the car, red hair floating in the water as the car dragged us farther and farther under.

"You're Charlotte's brother," said Alec.

My head was spinning. Stein wasn't here. Trevor wasn't Trevor, nor was he Amy's date, Jonathan. He was someone else. Charlotte's brother.

"She broke her neck on impact with the water," Trevor continued, so quietly I barely heard him. "But it's hard to say if she survived that and drowned. I can't imagine anything worse than not being able to fight for your life while your lungs are filling with liquid. Actually feeling yourself die. Can you imagine that, Alec?"

"Trevor . . ." I swallowed, starting to tremble so hard my knees were knocking. "Let Amy go. Let us go. We'll straighten this out."

"Yes," said Trevor, dazed now. "Yes, we will."

He strode back to edge of the bridge. Terrified, I watched as he untied Amy. Now that she was in the light I could see the gag across her mouth, and the glistening tear streaks that ran down her cheeks.

I tried to shoulder past Alec again, but he twisted into me, taking me to the ground. The impact radiated through my hip as I fell hard on my side.

"Stay down," he commanded.

"He's going to push her over." I scrambled to my knees. "He's going to . . ."

Trevor dragged Amy over by the wrists, bound in front of her. She thrashed against him, eyes bright and wild.

I climbed to my feet. The relief was only temporary; he hadn't thrown her over, but he still hadn't made his plans clear.

"Please, Trevor," I begged. "She has nothing to do with your sister."

"You should stop calling me that." Pain slashed across his face. "My name's not Trevor. It's William. William MacAfee. I'm sorry I lied to you. I know how much you hate that."

He didn't know the meaning of hate. It cut through the horror like a knife.

"Let's talk, William," said Alec, steering the focus back on him. "You obviously went through a lot of trouble to get us here. Why don't you let the ladies go, and we'll hash this out?"

Trevor—*William*—jerked. He was strung too tightly, not at all the hardened criminal Reznik was.

"If I wanted to talk, I would have scheduled an appointment with our lawyers. No, I don't want to talk. I'm done talking."

"Then what do you want?" I asked.

The man I'd once thought of as a friend tilted his head to Alec. "I want justice."

Amy tried to shake free, but he seemed completely unfazed. His grip held fast while she wriggled like a fish on a line.

Alec stepped forward reactively, and we both stilled at the harsh metal slide of the gun behind us.

"I wouldn't," said Reznik.

"She talked about you," William said, still glaring at Alec. "She said you were going to help her. But you weren't, were you? You knew the plan was to ruin her, *kill* her, all along. That's why you weren't there the night she died."

No. Alec wasn't with Charlotte the night she died because he was with me. Making love *to me*.

Alec's shoulders fell, as if William had just increased the load he carried tenfold.

"I tried to help her," he said.

William MacAfee shook his head hard, as if refusing to believe what was said.

"You *didn't* try." His voice was loud enough to make me jump. "You may not have pulled the trigger, but you killed my sister, and now you're about to walk free. No consequences. No punishment. It makes me *sick*."

"There are consequences," Alec murmured.

I stared at Amy, who was trembling so hard I could see it. She stared at me, pleading and terrified. Not for her own life, I knew, but for her daughter's.

"Yes," said William. "There are consequences."

Eye for an eye, he had once told me. *That woman on the news that was driven off the bridge? Someone should make the guy who's responsible jump.*

I knew then what he intended to do.

The driver grabbed Amy and hauled her to the van. My black hair whipped across my face as I turned to watch him toss her into the back and slam the door shut.

"What are you doing with her?"

"She'll be fine," William answered. "We have a deal. If she keeps her mouth shut, her daughter will be safe."

A wave of hopelessness descended over me. Paisley wasn't safe for long with Mike. And what did Amy have to defend them? A thin apartment door with a dead bolt? A single visit to a women's self-defense course?

This was my fault.

My fault.

I'd let this happen to my friends because I was careless. Because I loved Alec. And because I still loved him, the guilt fogged my senses, so thick I could barely breathe.

The van's engine revved, and then the driver made a turn in the middle of the street. Slowly, it disappeared down the steep incline in the direction we'd come. While I watched it, I thought about running out beyond the fourteen-foot window that William had mentioned, but it would only waste precious time.

Before I could think of another option, Reznik kicked Alec behind the knees, and he hit the ground at William's feet.

He didn't beg. He didn't cower. He strained against his cuffs, hands white and wrists red.

"Your sister was a good woman who tried to do the right thing," he said calmly. "And your project—the Green Fusion project—it was brilliant. If I'd been in charge I would have paid any price you asked to be a part of it."

"Shut up," said Trevor.

"Let Anna go."

Reznik raised the gun to the back of his head.

"No!" I raced toward him, and found myself on my knees as

well. I leaned into his body, feeling his labored breaths. His muscles flexed so hard, I thought he might be able to break through the cuffs.

"Wait. William, think about this." The words jumbled out. "You need Alec to win the trial, that's the only way Maxim Stein stays behind bars."

Jacqueline Frieda had told us Charlotte's brother's case was at a standstill. Surely he had to know that Alec was his best shot at beating the man responsible.

From the determined look on his face, William didn't care.

There was nothing familiar left about him. This wasn't the guy I'd met at the gym, who'd joked about my dance classes and come to the salon for massages to help his marathon running. This was a desperate, sick man who'd carefully planned every meeting with me, and every meeting with my best friend, just to get closer to Alec.

How had I been so blind?

The gun cocked.

"Anna, close your eyes," Alec said quietly. "You're going to be all right, baby. Just close your eyes."

Forty-one

"It hurts already, doesn't it?" William asked. I glared up at him, hating that he could possibly feel anything remotely close to what I felt right then. But he'd lost his sister, and there was no hiding how deep a hole she'd left.

"It never stops," William said. "You'll understand in time."

He reached beneath my arm and hauled me to my feet.

"*No,*" I shouted, just as Mike had taught me. I hoped someone could hear me. Anyone.

I kicked. I bit. I threw myself into him, and then away, trying to throw him off balance.

"Anna!" shouted Alec. "Anna, listen to me. No more fighting."

William elbowed me in the throat, effectively shutting my windpipe. My mouth opened, but nothing came in. Not for what seemed like minutes.

With a roar, Alec rose, charging toward us. There was a shot, and the gravel at my feet sprayed across my legs. If I'd had the breath, I would have screamed, but as it was only a tight groan slipped out.

It was a warning, one that stopped Alec in his tracks, shoulders heaving. His head dropped, and that scared me more than anything else had on this awful night.

He was giving up.

"I'll shoot him if you don't stop," William hissed.

"You'll shoot him anyway," I said.

"No." He shook his head. "You were right. I need him for the trial. I've lost, I understand that now. I don't even have the money to keep it going after I pay Mr. Reznik. Alec's testimony is the only thing that will keep Maxim Stein in jail."

I tossed my hair back, but the wind blew it forward again.

"Testify, don't testify. You have a hard time making up your mind."

Trevor laughed at this, then his expression turned grave.

"He had the choice to keep his mouth shut and serve time for what he did. He chose the easy way out."

I stared at Alec, teeth bared in a tight grimace. His arms were still bound behind him, and the wind billowed beneath his shirt to show a strip of skin above his pants. The barrel of Reznik's gun was still pressed between his shoulder blades, but he hardly seemed to notice.

It didn't exactly look like the easy way out.

"Let her go," Alec repeated.

William dragged me over to the edge. My side smashed against the concrete as I tore my eyes away from Alec's to look out over the black water beyond. It seemed to catapult toward me, destroying my sense of depth. Dragging me down.

Four hundred and thirty feet, William had said.

My arms were bound. I couldn't even hold on to this cold stone ledge.

I turned back at the sound of a scuffle on the pavement. Alec must have tried to escape again; he was now lying on his back on the ground, bleeding from a gash at the top of his forehead. Reznik was yelling something I couldn't make out over the drumming pulse in my ears. His knee was digging into Alec's broken ribs, but there was nothing Alec could do with his arms stuck behind him.

"He needs to watch," said William. "If he doesn't, this was all for nothing. There was no point in dragging him away from the FBI."

My world slowed.

Alec would live, but I would die. That would be his punishment. As if Charlotte's death wasn't enough. As if losing everything he'd worked for—his job, his self-respect—wasn't enough. William MacAfee would make him suffer this as well.

I thought of all the times William could have taken me. We'd been alone at the salon, at the gym, in parking lots and out in town. But it wasn't enough that Alec just hear about what happened to me. No, Alec needed to *experience* it, firsthand.

William turned toward me and I was filled with a strange sense of calm.

"If it's any consolation," he said, unable to meet my eyes, "I did like you, Anna. I wanted you to leave him. I asked you to, remember? At the salon?"

He wanted to believe this. I saw it in his rapidly blinking eyes. But he struggled.

"You'll regret this," I said. "You think it will make it right, but it won't."

"You're probably right."

An idea sparked in my mind. I lifted my gaze to Reznik, my hate for what they'd done to Amy, Paisley, all of us, blending with my fear and my shame. He scratched his goatee, as if he was ready for this to be over.

"I will pay you twice whatever William MacAfee's paying you if you stop this. Let us all walk free."

He smiled.

"A little late in the game for that, isn't it, Ms. Rossi?"

I leaned forward, away from the cold ledge.

"I don't know how much he's paying you, but I promise you, I can get more."

William scoffed. "She's a masseuse. She barely makes enough to cover rent on a tiny apartment."

Reznik's hand lowered. "How's that?"

"Alec," I said. "He's about to be worth over a billion dollars."

Alec jerked. "She's right."

"If he told you that, he lied. He's worth nothing."

"Not yet," I said. "But a lawyer contacted him. He's a shareholder, and if he wins the trial and Maxim Stein is convicted of fraud, Alec will own Force Enterprises."

Which would probably be worth nothing at that point, but I wasn't about to say that.

"He's going to win," I assured him.

Reznik considered this, or at least he seemed to. A second later his face went blank again, and he started to laugh.

William gave a shaky sigh.

"It won't hurt," he said, grabbing me around the waist and hoisting me up. My fingers clawed the ledge. My heels hooked around concrete lip. In the struggle, I leaned back, and nearly toppled over.

The fear froze me.

Close your eyes. Alec's words echoed in my head.

I looked at him one last time. At his beautiful face. I could still feel the scruff on his jaw against my cheeks and his lips brushing mine. I could still feel the way his strong body held firm, and then finally yielded when we came together. He was inside of me, and I would hold him there until I took my last breath.

I closed my eyes.

The shot echoed through my body, but though I braced for the pain it never came. William's grip on me loosened, and then slid away.

He fell to the ground, a bright rose of blood blossoming in

the center of his chest. His green eyes turned up, desperation turning to panic, while behind him, Reznik lowered his gun.

I could hear nothing but the rushing in my ears. See nothing but William—Trevor—grabbing at his chest as if he could scrape the bullet away with his fingers.

I crumbled to the ground.

Before I could sense if he was still breathing, two more shots came.

I screamed. Ten feet away, standing over Alec, Reznik toppled forward, landing facedown on the asphalt.

"Tampa PD!" boomed a male voice. "Hands where I can see them!"

Though the voice sounded vaguely familiar, I couldn't focus on it. My gaze was pinned to Alec, now rising back to his knees. Though his eyes raced over my body, he didn't move in my direction, nor did I go to him. I couldn't. It felt like I was watching him through a wall of glass.

"Anna? You all right?"

From around the remaining van, a young, dark-haired man in jeans and a black polo appeared. My breath came in one hard whoosh when I recognized Marcos behind the barrel of his still raised gun.

"Yes." There was hardly any volume to my voice now.

"Are you injured?" he called, making his way first to Reznik. There didn't appear to be any other cops with him, and he wasn't in uniform. My head must have still been a little fuzzy; this didn't make sense.

"I'm . . . I'm okay." The back of my head pressed against the concrete barrier behind me. Three feet away, William groaned, his chest rising and falling with fast, shallow breaths.

Marcos knelt down to check Reznik's pulse, giving Alec a quick nod. "Emergency services are on their way."

"Is he . . ."

"No. He's gone." He moved closer, eyes flashing over me quickly as he pressed his fingers to William's pulse. "This one's still kicking though."

It shouldn't have comforted me, but it did. As awful as this night had been, I didn't want William dead, especially because of something I'd done.

"How did you know we were here?"

Marcos wadded up the front of William's shirt, and pressed it against the wound.

"The burner phone."

I felt it against my thigh, tucked in the lower side pocket of the cargo pants. I'd completely forgotten about it once Agent Tenner had been dragged from the car.

"I told you I'd check in on you," he said. "Thought it was a little strange you went to hang out on a closed bridge so late at night." He paused, and turned his head, then looked back to William, below him. "Hear that, man? That's lady luck heading your way. Which is a lot more than you fucking deserve."

Did Marcos just swear? I had clearly been transported to some alternate reality. None of this made any sense.

I heard what he had then—sirens blaring from the shoreline. When I looked down the ramp I saw the flashing blue lights. I was surprised at how close they were; the wind must have blocked the sound.

"Amy," I said, chest clutching. "She was in the van with one of Reznik's men."

"She's in my car," he said. "The driver's in custody."

His words renewed my strength, and in a surge I pushed myself back up the wall. My arms were complete pins and needles now, but I preferred that to the complete numbness of my hands.

"How long you been like that?" Marcos asked, nodding to my arms.

"Too long. I think Reznik has the keys. Front pocket."

He grabbed Trevor's hand and pressed it over the wad of fabric on his chest. "Hold this. I'll be right back."

Before Trevor could muster an answer, Marcos sprinted to where Reznik lay. He found the keys without trouble and hurried back. In moments, my arms were free, but they felt as heavy as lead. I stood before Alec, rubbing my wrists and trying to flex my hands from the perma-claws they'd become while Marcos worked on the lock.

He kept staring at me with that same, guarded look I couldn't read. I told myself it was the stress. He'd nearly seen me die right before his eyes. He probably assumed he was responsible.

It was more than that, though. I felt it all the way to my bones.

The cop cars flew up the bridge. One after another, followed by an ambulance. They reminded me, like they always did, of my father.

I couldn't help but wonder what he'd think if he saw me here right now.

When Alec's hands were free, Marcos returned to William to continue providing first aid. Chaos roared around us—shouting policemen, wailing sirens, medics checking us both. But we never moved closer.

"I have to see Amy," I said when he finally opened his mouth to speak.

I didn't look back. I walked down the bridge, dodging past anyone in my way. Two more police cars were at the bottom with their lights flashing, parked beside the gray utility van. A woman with blond hair sat in the open passenger side of one, while an officer stood beside her, just outside.

I ran then, as fast as my legs could take me, until I reached Amy. I tackled her in the front seat, bruising us both in a dozen places from the impact.

"I'm sorry," I sobbed. "I'm so sorry. Where's Paisley? Does Mike have her?"

"Yes," she answered quietly. "He took his mom and the girls to his house. I just spoke with her. She's okay."

I backed away, holding her hands in mine.

"Are you?"

She smiled wanly. "Talk about bad taste in men, huh?"

"*Amy.*"

"I was doing a pretty good job kicking his ass before he gagged me." Whatever humor was in her voice deflated. "He came into my house. He saw my little girl."

I collapsed outside the car, and pressed my forehead against her knees. I thought of the scratches on the side of William's face, and what she must have been through tonight.

"It's over now," I said.

It had to be. It was one thing to threaten me. It was another thing entirely to hurt the people I loved most.

She stood, and pulled me up, and we hugged for a long time, until she finally stepped back.

I followed her gaze to where Alec stood, hands shoved deep in his pockets.

"I'm going to get Paisley," she said.

"Wait," I told her.

I walked to Alec, growing colder and colder with each step. By the time I reached him I was trembling. He must have seen it, there was no way not to.

"Are you okay?" He didn't reach for me. Didn't try to hold me. If he had, maybe things would have been different.

I nodded. "You?"

He stared at me.

"Amy? Paisley?"

"They're fine."

Silence. Infinite silence. Black hole in space silence.

"I'd follow you anywhere," I said. "Willingly. Blindly, if I had to. But they didn't sign up for this."

He nodded.

My heart betrayed me. It ached so hard I could barely keep on my feet. I loved him like I had never loved anyone. Like I would never love anyone again. But something had been broken tonight that couldn't be fixed. I couldn't keep being the object people used to hurt Alec. Even if I could stand the pain, I couldn't handle how much it hurt him.

But more than that, I had promised myself I would never let Amy and Paisley be victimized again, and here I was, leading them straight into danger.

"I can't do this anymore." My voice was steady, but my insides were rattling. I wrapped my arms around my chest.

His eyes, once filled with such tenderness, went dark.

He didn't even fight.

He didn't fight for me.

He didn't fight for us.

"I know."

Those were the last words he said to me.

Epilogue

Two weeks passed. Enough time for the dust to settle from the night on the bridge and for me to start to pick up the pieces of my life. Reznik was dead. The guy I'd once known as Trevor had been moved to a secure facility for medical treatment. Amy and Paisley had started therapy—a referral Marcos had given them after what had happened. So far they seemed to like it.

Without the imminent threat posed by William MacAfee, I had no reason not to go back to work. Derrick begrudgingly took me back yet again, making more than one comment about how high maintenance an employee I was. I made up for it working overtime, every day, until my hands were so sore I could barely make fists.

It was better than going back to my apartment alone.

I didn't see Thomas, but I thought of him often. Mike called to check on me every few days. He told me that Alec wasn't being held in witness protection anymore, but that the FBI was still running him ragged in preparation for the trial.

He didn't mention his name again.

And in every free moment I did what I could for Amy. I cooked, cleaned, even got their groceries so that they could focus on what they needed to: each other.

But I thought of Alec constantly. I dreamed of him every night. When my mom had died, I woke up for months having forgotten that she was gone. Life went back to normal; I felt okay. And then reality would come crashing down, just as hard as it had that first day without her. It was sort of like that with Alec.

Except life didn't go back to normal. I didn't stop wondering where he was or if he was safe or what he was eating for lunch. The memories of his mouth on my neck, and his hand on my stomach, and his knees behind mine when we slept didn't fade away. In my worst moments I grieved for him, in my best, I yearned for him. But I never sought him out, nor did he come to me.

And then one night I came home from work, and all the things I'd brought to his apartment were stacked outside my door. The pictures I'd hung on the walls, the pots and pans, placed neatly in boxes. Even the goddamn spice rack.

That was when I really knew it was over.

"Best tacos ever," Jacob announced as he pushed back his empty plate. It was our second meeting since his new foster placement with his sister, and he'd made a special request for the Taco Bus.

"Agreed," I told him, though I'd hardly touched mine.

"So how's everything going?" He looked smug, even with the salsa smeared across his cheek. He'd put on some much-needed weight, even in the last two weeks, and his eyes weren't as untrusting as they'd been before.

I chuckled. "You *my* advocate now?"

"How are your grades?" he continued, doing his best adult voice impression. "Are you eating your vegetables? How do you like your new house?"

I laughed harder. This was the real Jacob; the kid who acted like a kid. He was a goofball when he wasn't worried about protecting his sister.

"My grades are excellent," I told him. "I eat only broccoli and Brussels sprouts, and my apartment is . . ."

Lonely.

"Great," I lied.

"You're gross," he said, making a face. "Lucia made us Brussels sprouts one night. They're like alien heads."

"That's why I love them."

Now it was his turn to laugh.

"Serious question," I said. "Are you happy now with your sister?"

He nodded, his face turning serious. "It's my job to take care of her."

Trevor—because I preferred to think of him as Trevor, not as William MacAfee—flashed across my mind. Jacob had already gone to extremes to protect his sister. I hoped he never felt the pull to do something as drastic as Trevor had.

"You kind of manipulated us to get what you wanted, do you know what that means?"

Jacob stared down at his lap.

"Yeah."

"You could have gotten hurt, you know. *She* could have gotten hurt."

He chewed on the corner of his lip.

"But we weren't, and now we live in the same house."

It was hard to reason with that.

He looked up at me, brown eyes bright with curiosity.

"Who takes care of you?"

I shifted in my seat.

"I take care of myself."

"Yeah, but isn't there somebody else? I've got Sissy. Who's got you?"

Now it was my turn to look away. I wasn't seeing Trevor any-more, but a man who could level me with his eyes and make me feel safe even as the world as I knew it was crumbling to pieces.

But he was gone now.

"You don't need to worry about me."

"But someone does, I bet," he said.

His statement hung between us, without an answer.

"Can I have more tacos?" he finally asked.

My fingers slowly unclamped from the hem of my shirt, hid-den beneath the table.

"Of course you can," I said.